I0691774

The Lady and The Psaltery

Jacqueline de Sarigny

All rights reserved. No part of this publication may be reproduced, distributed, or transmitted in any form or by any means, including photocopying, recording, or other electronic or mechanical methods, without the prior written permission of the publisher, Marble Book Publishers, except in the case of brief quotations emb odied in critical reviews and certain other noncommercial uses permitted by copyright law. For permission requests, write to Marble Book Publishers, addressed "Attention:

"Permissions Coordinator," via our company contact page.
https://www.llpresley.com/contact

Paperback: 978-1-957191-15-7

Hardback: 978-1-957191-16-4

Any references to historical events, real people, or real places are used fictitiously. Names, characters, and places are products of the author's imagination.

Table Of Contents

CHAPTER 1

I shake the rain off my umbrella and teetering on one leg like a drunken marsh bird, take off my slushy boots on the doorstep, open the front door and pick up the scattered bills. The smell of Rothmans is so strong that - for a moment – it feels as if Franco is back in my bedroom, sprawled naked on the bed among his print-outs, propped up on all available pillows, his black curly hair still wet from the shower.

I even seem to hear the familiar angry beep from his laptop whenever he types faster than it can follow. Franco isn't there, of course; he removed his last pair of socks from my dresser two weeks ago, leaving me nothing of himself except that smell of stale tobacco. And some interesting - oh, all right, pretty potent - memories.

Franco was - and still is, for all I know - a hunk. Now, this may be very beneficial to a women's ego when the said hunk is 17 years her junior and pursues her relentlessly until her better judgment tells her it's time to give in. Franco is no gigolo, either. He could well afford to pay his share of household expenses, and did for the 10 months we lived together. Of course, there was a minimal price to pay on my part in terms of idle self-questioning: What does he see in me? Do I remind him of his mother? Is he acting out his Oedipus Complex?

Indeed, Franco was not after my fortune what fortune? He cares little for money, which seemed strange at times because money is his element. He dives, swims, and splashes in it all day long, tossing bonds and shares, juggling with trends and indexes like a playful seal; and always emerges from it glistening and pristine, without a single drop of greed on his gorgeous body.

Anyway, throwing Franco out of my apartment and my life had brought my morale to an all-time low.

Now, don't get me wrong; I am usually pretty optimistic by nature, but quite a few things had gone awry lately and the spring of my optimism had sprung back one time too many and just lay there uncoiled and useless....

It was November. My birthday was coming up - hardly worth celebrating; birthdays should stop at the age of consent. My Toronto publisher had just gone bust; I had lost my agent and no other publisher appeared remotely interested in my third novel. My daughter Christine was staying on in the South of France for another year and I probably couldn't afford a plane ticket to join her and escape the end of Montreal's endless winter.

Oh, I still had a lot to be thankful for. I still looked O.K. and hadn't given up on the joys of writing. Or men. It was just that... Well, one gets tired of fighting for every morsel when the world seems full of hungry dogs. First thing was to get Franco out of my system. It should not be that hard because, outside of our lust for each other, we had very little in common. I knew his curious interest in me would flag rather sooner than later, and never attempted to include him in any plans beyond the next day. I thought I was keeping a firm grip on my emotions.

* * *

When my husband, Michael, died, my capacity to love a man - heart, body, and soul - died with him. On that day all my emotions went as flat as the line on the monitor by his hospital bed and had remained so for nine years. He had been my lover and my best friend; the only time I cry nowadays is when I hear Rod Stewart singing that mushy song on the radio. He was also my husband and Christine's father; a Leo, fierce pride tempered with humor. I guess he had learned all there was to learn here and now, and he let death remove him to more interesting pastures. Leaving me behind to fend for myself. The sod.

So, I wasn't deeply involved with Franco. He turned me on, period, even if his love-making bore a strong resemblance to skeet shooting. Dark-haired, blue-eyed Northern Italian can be

2

the most beautiful men on earth and Franco is a prime specimen of the breed. He was most generous with all his assets and had an endearing way of offering his manhood with as much flourish as if it was a Cartier diamond necklace.

Trouble is, he tended to offer it to too many women, including my best friend. And literary agent.

The infidelities I did not know about - only guessed - I was prepared to disregard. Franco was very discreet and sensitive in his way. He had nothing to prove by flaunting his conquests and inflicting pain. Nancy was something else; she could not resist gloating in her smarmy way, giving me a hint here and a clue there until no doubt remained and I sent them both to hell.

I suppose I was better off without them, but on that November day, I was not prepared to swear to that.

In the long run, I would probably miss Nancy more than Franco. As a literary agent, she was skillful and effective, even though she could torture me in the name of Grammar and Punctuation with all the self-righteous cruelty of a Grand Inquisitor.

Giving her marching orders to Nancy had left me with the dubious choice of going it alone or finding another 20 percenter - preferably one who had not been trained by Torquemada - to flog my upscale trash to North American publishers. A good lover may be hard to find, but try to get a literary agent! The least of them is snootier than the Duke and Duchess of Germanites rolled into one.

I was just beginning to make a name for myself and had no best-seller to my credit; finding another agent willing to take me on as a client would require more letters than I cared to write to more specimens of that snobbish breed than I cared to meet, in more American cities than I cared to visit.

As for Nancy, I wished her luck with my boy toy; I just could not understand what he saw in her. In a way, she needed his attention more than I did. I mean, Nancy may be young well, younger than I am by 15 years - but she is no beauty by any stretch of the imagination and hers is a fragile buck-teethed ego.

Franco's multiple daily assiduities may fool her for a while, and she may even get to love his aura of stale tobacco, his benighted laptop, and his bloody financial printouts, but she will end up putting two and two together eventually. She is too young for indulgence; she will never tolerate his sleeping around. And it will hurt. Serve her right, the little rat.

* * *

I hung up my wet Burberry before checking the answering machine.

"Hi, Sweety! Irene, here. I'm back. Let's do lunch tomorrow. Do give me a buzz when you get home; I'm off to Montserrat next Friday. Bye."

Montserrat? Do they need Irene in Montserrat? Haven't they had enough problems already? Her message cheered me up, though; lunch with Irene was the kind of picker-upper not to be turned down in the present circumstances. She had breezed through the trauma of the Big Five-O birthday quite a few years before and the continuing saga of her erotic adventures was always good for a few laughs. Her two wealthy husbands having left her well able to travel, she had tried love on the five continents and had lately taken to collecting French Horns as she calls them - in other words, horny French guys, and spending part of the year in France for that purpose.

She finds Montreal men too cowed by Feminists and not macho enough for her taste. She also says I am "too picky." There is some truth in that, but I am not alone; the men who attract me all seem to have stables of "picky" women at their beck and call. I suppose that if you only go for winners you have to put up with their prizes....

4

* * *

It was pouring so much coming out of the subway that my only thought had been to escape bitter sleet and wind into the warmth of my apartment; I had dashed by the video store without stopping to rent a movie. Great. Another evening of falling back on dismal cable offerings. Or forgoing TV altogether for a good read or a stint at my keyboard. Yuk. Working on that new novel felt like running in quicksand.

Now, I never turn on my television before 8 p.m. Why did I do so on that bleak Monday afternoon in November?

It was only 5:30 p.m. and already dark. I guess I did feel lonely without Franco... Or else, destiny was unfolding. In ways, I have yet to fathom.

I flicked the remote a few times and ended up on PBS. And stopped flicking. Entranced.

A shiver running down my spine, I sat down on the floor in front of the set. A group of musicians in medieval attire was playing my favorite ballad! A medieval love song I had heard once on the radio and hunted for through record stores all over the States, Canada, and France until I found it on a CD.

in Nice and treasured it ever since. It had been written by a trouvère for his lady in 1188.

I felt so faint all of a sudden, I wondered if it had anything to do with my skipping lunch. It was the music. Those wonderful, lilting medieval sounds always enthralled me.

Oh, My God. I must tape this. Rummaging through a drawerful of truncated movies, I grabbed a blank cassette, expelled "Die Entführung" from the VCR and inserted it quickly, praying I wouldn't push the wrong button, record another channel and end up with a wrestling bout between The Hooded Dragon and

The Masher, or some such visual delight, as I had on more than one occasion.

I settled to watch, listen, and surrender to the familiar magic. They were a group of six musicians, three men, and three girls - not the ones who had cut my record - wearing colorful costumes and playing on these bizarre period instruments I had learned to identify: timbrel, bombulum, rote, lute, rebec, organistrum, and psaltery. Psaltery....

The camera zoomed in on the psaltery player and I stopped breathing altogether.

At first, I felt the kind of eerie surprise one might experience meeting one's next-door neighbor on a lonely trek in Nepal or Patagonia. Then surprise turned to a kind of subtle elation, as if I had at last found something I had been seeking unawares for a very long time. All these alien feelings crowded my whole being, pushing and shoving one another until I felt thoroughly confused. But there was a disturbing element; a man playing a psaltery?

A psaltery is a woman's instrument! No self- respecting knight - not even a lowly minstrel would be caught dead playing a psaltery! And the man was a knight; he wore a scarlet tunic and a green mantle - colors reserved for knighthood. My thoughts took me by surprise; I could no more understand my strange reaction than control it. Closing my eyes for a moment, I took a few deep breaths to calm down. When I opened them again, the psaltery player was again on the screen, in a close-up, and my heart stood still.

Long pale hair fell to his wide shoulders whether blond or white, it was hard to tell - he was not a young man but there was something ageless about his strong lean face. His very clear blue eyes never looked at the camera but seemed to draw inspiration from a far-away horizon.

The man played very well indeed, drew from his wonderful instrument these mellifluous sounds and harmonies that neither lute nor harp can produce. Yet, I felt... incensed. His playing aroused anger as well as delight. I couldn't help humming the melody, the waves, and twists of it; the words were coming back and I mouthed them with the singer, resenting the time the camera spent on him instead of on the psaltery player.

Alas, Love, what a hard parting....

He was the best looking of the three men and he wore his elegant attire with a kind of aristocratic nonchalance. But - I caught myself thinking - he would much rather have been wearing his hunting habit, and couldn't wait for the performance to end so he could jump on a horse and take off through the woods.... He still blinks on the high notes, too!

I sat there dumbfounded. What on earth could prompt me to have such thoughts about a perfect stranger? It was as if I knew this man intimately without ever having met him.

My face burning, I leaned against the sofa, unable to move from the floor. I couldn't believe what had come over me....

Still listening to the music and staring at the screen, I racked my brain to recall when and where I had ever seen him before. He had not been part of the few concerts featuring ancient music I had attended or watched on television; I would have remembered his face. Besides, the feeling seemed to go much deeper than a casual acquaintance; this man had been part of my life at some point... I realized I was trembling from head to foot. Can break up with an unfaithful lover do that to you? I tried to be thoroughly objective and admit any hurt caused by Franco's departure. This weird feeling had nothing to do with Franco. Definitely not.

I kept on staring at the screen. The man's blondish-white hair would have covered his lean cheeks, had he not pushed it back behind his ears. He looked 30 or 50, depending on the angle of the shot. On two occasions during the thirty minutes or so that the concert lasted, I came close to remembering who he was and where I had met him and why he fascinated me so. But the evanescent impressions disappeared like mirages, leaving me as frustrated as a thirsty traveler in the Sahara. The more I played and rewound the tape the more my memory seemed to go blank.

Time was abolished in a kind of dream; I spent hours glued to that television screen, munching apples and chunks of Swiss cheese. Until I became thoroughly annoyed with myself, decided I had had enough, and turned off the VCR after carefully writing down the credits.

The group's name was Le Fin'Amor and the players were either French or English; except for the psaltery player who had a German name, Kurt Meissen.

And all I remembered from four years of school German was "Ich Liebe Dich." Not such a bad beginning, at that.

I turned off the TV set and looked at my watch.

It was two a.m. A little late to call Irene about that lunch tomorrow.

CHAPTER 2

It was not until the middle of December that Irene and I managed to get together. Three days a week, I work as an editor for a small struggling travel magazine, and the Christmas rush at the office had provided a ready excuse to postpone our lunch. I did not feel like facing Irene just yet because I knew I would end up telling her about my weird experience and my even weirder behavior, and I needed time to come to terms with them before confiding in anyone.

I was well on my way to a full-fledged obsession over the long-haired musician.

An intense curiosity urged me to learn more about him, to get to know him, to find out whether there actually was a connection between us or if I was simply losing it.

The morning after that fateful evening, I was late for work and uncommonly restless; I got through the day by devising ways to reach the performers of Le Fin'Amor. Though I seldom use the office telephone for personal calls, I figured this warranted an exception; I had to get through to Vermont ETV during business hours.

I did and lied to a kindly lady about being interested in bringing medieval musicians to Canada. She graciously supplied me with the name of their agent in London they were a British group after all, even though two of the performers were French.

I had to wait till the next morning to call the U.K. from my apartment. At the London agency, a frosty female inquired about my business and appeared to doubt the existence of such a thing as "A personal matter." She reluctantly informed me that Le Fin'Amor was touring somewhere in Europe but blankly refused to tell me where.

As for giving me Herr Meissen's phone number, it was out of the question. All mail addressed to the performers had to be directed to the agency that would forward it to their clients. And that was that.

Besides confirming my blanket opinion of agents, this friendly exchange pushed me even further along the path of deception. Increasing compulsion was prodding me; I had to reach the German minstrel!

Writing to a strange man to tell him he was part of your life at some point, only you don't remember when, where, or how, is rather a daunting challenge to anyone who has no wish to be thought totally off her head. I finally settled on a ploy involving - I am ashamed to say - the magazine I work for.

On office stationery, I wrote Herr Meissen and his five co-performers professional letters explaining that many of our readers traveling to Europe were interested in medieval music concerts, and that, as I was writing an article on the subject, I would greatly appreciate an interview in either English or French - or even German - at their convenience.

The more I thought about it, the better I liked the idea. Aside from any peculiar personal involvement. It was worth approaching my muddle-headed boss about. Outside of golf courses, he doesn't pretend to know anything about Europe, let alone European culture, and would probably mumble something about effete tastes and give me the go-ahead. And then I waited.

By the time I met Irene for lunch, I had already started going to the office on my days off to check my mail. So far, none of the musicians had seen fit to answer my query. They were all as ill-mannered as their snarky agent. My minstrel included.

* * *

When Irene walked into the restaurant, quite a few heads turned. She was her usual polished self. Everything about her - from her creamy smooth cheeks to the crisp tailoring of her purple coat - whispered "Money" with a capital M. Irene is the type of woman about whom people say "She looks so young!" Thereby implying they know she is not.

I knew, and still found it hard to believe she could have been my mother; which would have been more fun, but one must not speak ill of the dead. Irene was disarmingly philosophical about her age, anyway.

"There comes a time, my dear Sandra...." My name is Alexandra, but my friends call me Sandra. "There comes a time when looking even twenty years younger than one's birth certificate is no longer enough... I know my days as a sex object are numbered, but to hell with it! I haven't breathed my last and I'll go down fighting."

And she was still in fighting trim. We kissed on both cheeks and she settled down in her armchair with a contented sigh and a sharp look at my face.

"My dear Sandra, what's wrong with you?

You look positively grim!"

"Gee, thanks, Irene. And meee-ew to you too. Never mind me, tell me about you, I could do with some mindless entertainment."

She laughed and started to rummage in her shiny black purse devoid of any vulgar designer initials. Retrieving a large envelope, she reverently extracted from it a 5 by 7 photo, which she scrutinized with soulful eyes before handing it to me.

"Here, feast your eyes on this one."

"Oh, oh! Not young, but extremely good looking! Harrison Ford ten years from now... Very distinguished. Not your usual type. Tell me more."

She snatched back the handsome man's picture, for fear I might drool over it no doubt. "Well, this time it's the real thing." With a coy look, she added, "I'm not sure I should tell you about it...." She was replacing the photo in the envelope, smoothing its edges and slipping it back into her purse. "You might spoil everything with your usual cynicism. And you always interrupt."

"I won't. I promise. Do tell me, I'm dying to hear."

And she was, of course dying to tell. "You remember how depressed I was when I left for France. All my hopes for some sort of permanent relationship were crushed within a month. First that distinguished widowed American politician I'd helped elect, safely ensconced in Washington and availing himself freely of the local bimbos...." "Oh, yes. And that seductive divorced restaurateur who up and sells his restaurant and moves to Vancouver - after you had gained ten pounds eating lunch and dinner there every single day for two months! A

proper run of bad luck!"

"Indeed. And don't forget the cute single tennis pro, who turned out to prefer male players for indoor games."

I nodded in sympathy. "Yes. Wasted wooing at its worst." The waiter was hovering by our table, loath to interrupt the exchange or, more likely by the look of him, hoping to hear the name of the tennis pro. He took our orders for Pamplemousses Marie-Louise and spritzers and reluctantly departed.

"But you know what," Irene continued, "Paris always grants my sex life a stay of execution." Her laugh reminded me - and men seated at neighboring tables - of a cooing dove. "First I narrowly escape three accidents in the taxi taking me from Roissy to the Ritz because, instead of watching out for his crazy fellow drivers, the chauffeur keeps winking at me in his rear-vision mirror, pursing his lips and blowing me kisses."

"The nerve! What was he like?"

"Oh, too young. Good looking in a beefy sort of way. Not my type, but...."

I know what she meant. We were long past being sticklers for "our" types. Beggars can't be choosers.

She went on, the shadow of a smile on her full lips. "Anyway, as you can guess, he is not the man in the picture. I kept my cool with the taxi driver and sent him on his way with a good tip for making my day."

I was appalled. "You gave him a good tip for harassing you!"

"I don't call that harassment. Harassment is when the guy is a drip and you wouldn't give him the time of day. This boy was cute, lusty. That deserved a tip."

"You are such a reactionary, Irene! You have the mentality of a strike-breaker!"

She shrugged off her violet coat, revealing the understated elegance of a simple black dress. Tight enough to show off her firm assets. "I'd rather be that than a ball-breaker. Since when have you been on strike, anyway? I would say our common situation is more akin to a lockout at times."

"Very funny. To proceed, I'm all ears."

"Well, the next morning I went to the Louvre. I try to do a few rooms every time I'm in Paris. I mean, there's more to life than sex.... Anyway, I was having a look around with a bunch of tourists, until it became fairly obvious that this Frenchman, a real dreamboat...."

"For God's sake, Irene, these corny expressions date you so!"

"Sandra, do you want to hear about my latest French Horn, or don't you?"

"Of course, I want to hear about him. Hearing is about the only sense of mine that gets titillated these days. Go on."

"Thank you. So, this tall, elegant, silver haired man was following me around the exhibits. At the Egyptian Collection, he gives me a steady look; at the Mona Lisa, he smiles...."

"Mimetism. You know, imitating your environment. He was influenced by the Mona Lisa."

Irene swallowed a sharp retort and continued, unsmiling. "At the Venus de Milo, he starts whispering in my ear that he finds me far more attractive than the Venus. No! Don't say it, Sandra! I know that particular statue is obese and has no arms, but still...

Then he follows me to the exit, asks for my name and my phone number, which I don't know by heart - my hotel number, I mean, not my name. But I remain aloof until he hands me a beautifully embossed card and begs me to call him between seven and nine p.m. Or rather, he says it the French way, you know, nineteen hours, twenty hours... It always sounds like doomsday to me and I find it most confusing."

"So, you called at the wrong time?"

"No." She says, eyes downcast, "I didn't call at all."

"You got cold...feet? That's not like you at all, Irene."

She laughed. "No. His bloody card must have fallen out of my coat pocket in the taxi that took me back to the hotel. I couldn't find it anywhere."

"Then how come you have his photo?"

Her eyes sparkle, she exclaimed triumphantly, "He had followed my taxi in his car! He did not call my room that evening; but the next morning, when I came down at eight, he was waiting for me in the lobby. After that... Oh, Sandra, he is so wonderful!

We have something to say to each other. For once, I find a man my age who is not decrepit, or a curmudgeon, or going through his bimbo stage! And is he ever fit! I mean buns of steel and the rest to match. This is serious, Sandra.

I am in love!"

"Why are you here, then? Shouldn't you have stayed on in Paris?"

"Well... He is traveling in Germany for business at the moment. He is involved in television programming."

I pricked up my ears but refrained from interrupting the flow of her gushing reverie. I learned that the man had a title and a crumbling castle to go with it somewhere in Aquitaine. "His family has lived in it for nine hundred years!" Enthused Irene. She informed me he was a widower with three grown-up sons. Sons caused fewer problems to fathers' girlfriends than daughters, according to Irene, who had no kids of her own but was an expert on stepchildren.

"He is in the process of easing out of a... relationship; he is so considerate; he does not want to inflict pain on the poor girl by a sudden break-up."

Another one of those, I thought. We know the type: He is in your life, but you're hardly in his... Anyway, Irene could take it; she had dealt with enough rascally rogues in her days. The man looked and sounded interesting, and Irene would rather share a gourmet meal with other women than dine on her very own bowl of unsalted oatmeal. I used to think her attitude made a lot of sense - until I was confronted with the option of sharing my love with my best friend. And rejected it.

15

We went on talking about The Marvel through the crab salads. Over espressos, Irene finally asked me what I had been up to since Franco's exit and I ended up telling her everything. For all her self-involvement - or perhaps because of it - she is shrewd and unstinting with her advice. I had found many times that I could do worse than follow it.

Anyway, the hardest part of my tale was trying to describe the feelings the musician inspired in me; overwhelming curiosity mixed with surprise, awe, and excitement. Incipient joy?

She kept silent throughout the somewhat shamefaced confession of my attempts to contact the man. When I stopped on a self- deprecating giggle, she said matter-of-factly, "Maybe you did not meet that musician in this life, Sandra, but in a previous one."

Oh, no! I had forgotten about her esoteric phase; her rantings about Astral Bodies, Chakras, and Reincarnation. For quite a while, she had not mentioned any of the weirdoes who had sponged off her for two years, so I had assumed she was through with the New Age.

With a frown, she added, "You know, I never told you, but the first time we met - when I brought you the manuscript of my story to translate into French - I had a very similar feeling about you; I just knew we had been friends in the past... And that was long before I got involved with the Omega Group. They opened my eyes and it all began to make

sense, I mean, reincarnation and all that. I still believe we met in a previous life."

I made a good attempt at laughing off my surprise. "Look, Irene, I sort of presume that part of us may survive death, and, at times, I even get the feeling Michael is hovering around me, protecting me... But this American-style reincarnation bit is too pat and convenient."

"Well, that's just it, don't you see?" She drained her cup of coffee. "It makes so much more sense! One life is hardly long enough for us to make mistakes, let alone learn from them."

The fey waiter was placing the small bill tray near her crushed napkins; I tried to snatch it from her, but she would have none of it.

"Stop that, Sandra! And listen to me. You may end up learning something by contacting that musician, but somehow, I doubt it. He may have no recollection of you whatsoever, even after meeting you face to face. I know a better way...." She paused for effect and it worked. "Well? What is it?"

"Have yourself hypnotized. You know, regressed... To that particular life. Sometimes it can be done, and I know someone who does it. I've never tried it myself; my life is fascinating enough, thank you very much, without having to dredge up past excitement. Besides the fact that, quite frankly, the whole thing scares me."

"Oh, great! And you want me to go through with it? As a guinea pig? Thanks a lot."

"I'm only trying to help. Here let me give you her name, phone, and fax number... E-Mail address even; it seems witches have gone techno." Resting her 18-carat gold Cartier spectacles on the tip of her nose, she leafed through her little black marocain book, scribbled the info on the back of a crumpled envelope, and insisted I take it.

She drove me back home through the blowing December snow in her black Mercedes convertible - with the top up, thank God referring for the umpteenth time to her encounter with Trudeau on the Trans-Canada highway many years before, and her vain attempt to engage him in a tag race. "Of course, his car was ancient, but, like him, it still had what it takes."

* * *

Back home, I honestly tried to make a dent in the long list of North American agents I was proposing to approach, in the hope that one of them would take me on as a client and find a publisher for the novel I had completed three months ago. The work in question - an adventure tale set in the Orient - sat on my desk, neatly packed in a box, waiting for some member of the uppity breed to give a positive answer to my query letter and deign to read it.

Going through the mailing list was a mechanical task; a simple matter of merging the text of a standard letter with the names and addresses of the agents. It seems I was incapable of getting it right and had to spend hours poring through the Mastering Word Perfect 5.1 manual to correct my innumerable mistakes. My concentration was deserting me; I kept thinking of Irene's words. About our having been friends long ago. In another life.

I had to admit I had developed an instant liking for her the first time we had met eight years before; truly, it had felt as if I had known her all my life. As for Michael - my dead husband - it was also true that I seemed to feel his presence at times.

But that was just wishful thinking.

* * *

The next day, the next week, the next month brought no answer to any of my letters to the musicians. My obsession did not let up. I would watch the video I had taped again and again every night and remain as clueless and curious as ever.

We were now in the middle of winter and had reached that January peak when snow is still tolerated - but only just - for the magic beauty it confers to the town. The Christmas holidays were over. Nine-to-fivers were back at work, their kids back in school, leaving us weekdays skiers the run of the slopes. But neither work nor writing, tennis nor ski, could take my mind off my obsession. I was seriously considering a visit to a psychiatrist. Instead, I decided it was time to call London again and pry more information from the tight lips of that charming female at the Performing Artists Agency.

* * *

She sounded far more pleasant than the first time. Told me she had forwarded my letters to the musicians and that one of them – the singer with the alto voice - had sent it back to her with his regrets; he was off to Australia for a series of solo gigs and was leaving the group for a few months. She said that, for a start, she would mail me a copy of their spring and summer engagements in France, England, and Germany, and assured me I would be able to interview the remaining members of the group if I was prepared to travel to Europe and arrange to meet them after one of their concerts.

"I'm certain you'll find them all most helpful for your magazine article, Ms. Pearson... That is, the three who can talk to you."

"What do you mean? One of the four left refuses to be interviewed?"

"Oh, no. It's not that at all, I'm sorry, I thought you knew. You see Herr Meissen; the psaltery player suffers from paralysis of the vocal cords. He is mute."

CHAPTER 3

The London agent eventually wrote back to inform me that three of the minstrels would gladly grant me interviews during their French tour in April and May.

Herr Meissen had not bothered to reply. She also supplied their spring and summer schedule as well a short bio of each performer. I skipped over the first four

resumés to read about the psaltery player; he was Herr Doktor Meissen, an associate professor of Medieval Studies at the University of Tübingen. How could a mute give lecture? Perhaps he could still hum....

At any rate, it was one more clue, which I decided to act upon immediately.

I wrote back to each of them expressing my gratitude and proposing three dates and locations in France where we could meet in April. As for Herr Doktor Meissen, I included him in my thanks even though he had not seen fit to answer my first query. Without mentioning his infirmity, I offered to submit to him a set of written questions he could answer in writing at his leisure while reiterating my wish for a brief interview.

I sent a duplicate of this letter care of his department at the University of Tübingen with the proper address in German. And, on an impulse, even called that department. A very articulate secretary informed me that Herr Professor Meissen was on leave of absence for an indefinite period. Yes, she would make sure his mail was forwarded to him.

By then, we were in the grip of February and longing for relief from freezing rain, snowstorms, icy sidewalks, and the numbing arctic cold of our dazzling blue skies. This crazy quest had at least taken my mind off Franco.

To be quite honest, I still missed him, but with a kind of affectionate concern, as if more gentle feelings, no longer pre-empted by physical attraction, were coming to the fore. I wished him well but lost no sleep over him. The same could not be said of my Minnesinger. Booking my flight to Nice for the end of March buoyed me up considerably. I would spend some time with Christine, even if she had to bone up for her exams in International Law. Then, I would borrow her car to follow the musicians like a true groupie, and attend several of their performances in different towns before meeting them for the interview.

I set to work on my article in earnest, helped by the fact that some of their performances would take place in churches and cathedrals, about which I could add some tit-bits of history of interest to the readers.

My boss had approved the idea, with his usual vagueness.

"Yeah, yeah, sounds okay to me. Go ahead, so long as you don't ask me to help." Heaven forbids.

Provided his March golf junket to Myrtle Beach improved his game and his mood, he would probably cover a week's worth of travel expenses - rooms in two stars hotels and meals in truckers' greasy spoons.

He is not a bad man, just a very lazy one, who milks his business dry. His inefficiency keeps the office in a state of endemic crisis over unpaid bills, chaotic accounting, mislaid color separations, and contradictory instructions to printers. At times, I think he has a weak spot for me; I like him well enough but he is short, bald and twenty pounds overweight. As Irene puts it, I am too picky.

* * *

I was still plagued by a strange restlessness. A kind of impatience that haunted me in the small hours of the night with feelings of guilt; as if I had failed to do everything in my power to get to the truth.

Meanwhile, Irene kept calling me to find out if I had been to see her witch and urging me to do so. When I told her about the musician's infirmity, she was appalled.

"This is ridiculous! God knows it's hard enough to communicate with a man who can talk; what are you hoping to achieve with one who can't? Come on, Sandra, don't be a woosy skeptic! Give Daphne a try! And stop calling her a witch she is - or was - a shrink. Yes, a trained psychologist of some sort. I'm pretty sure she can help you, go and see her!

What have you got to lose? Oh... O.K... A

hundred dollars. So, what, I'll gladly pay for it, if that's what's keeping you from making an appointment. No! no! Please! Don't get huffy with me, you know I'm tactless... Look, I'm off to join my Lord next week... No, Sandra, I didn't say my Lord and Master. Not yet, anyway. I'm willing to do anything he wants...except obey."

She extracted from me a promise to seriously consider consulting her witch and, in return, assured me we would fly down too. Nice for a few days in April when I was there - with or without the Seigneur. Meanwhile, I could always leave a message for her at the Ritz.

* * *

Two weeks later, on a day I wasn't going to the office, I got up early. While enjoying one of the only reliable pleasures of life - fragrant coffee, whole wheat toast, cheese, and bitter orange marmalade - I glanced idly at the minstrels' schedule. They would be performing in Geneva the next day – March 2nd.

Showered and dressed, I sat down at my keyboard to begin work on a translation that would help pay for my forthcoming trip. I had more or less given up on my new novel until I could find a publisher for the previous one, and spent my time away from the office translating various documents for private clients who paid well.

But my brain refused to get into gear. One look at my watch told me it was the best time to call Geneva.

So, I gave in and phoned the Grand Théâtre on Place Neuve, asking the name of the hotel where the medieval musicians would be staying. It took quite a bit of shuffling around of personnel - and many ticking minutes of silence that would be reflected on my phone bill - before I got an answer. The Ambassador. Four Star. Not bad for jugglers; so, they traveled in style.

I looked at the hotel number scribbled on my agenda. What good would that do? I could hardly phone a man who couldn't talk, Could I?

I did. Call the hotel, I mean, and asked for his room number - To hear him breathe on the phone? He was out, thank God. I was turning into a grotesque stalker!

* * *

What can I say? Irene had already left by the time I called Dr. Daphne Blake for an appointment, but her name worked wonders; a few poor souls got bumped off in my favor and the witch insisted on seeing me the very next day.

* * *

The house was a stolid Greystone on a quite tree-lined Westmount Street. Posh, but not ostentatious.

Dr. Daphne Blake opened her door and welcomed me into a large entrance hall with a grey marble floor under fine rugs. At first glance, she looked the part. Frizzy hair as rusty as steel wool long forgotten by the sink; carmine lipstick snaking into innumerable fine wrinkles around a shapeless mouth; amorphous body swathed in a profusion of nondescript garments of clashing patterns and colors. Out of which emerged fluttering bony hands with long red talons for nails. Where was the black cat?

Yet, the kohl-ringed black eyes which seemed to bore through me were bright with humor and warmth. And sanity. They seem to deliver a wordless denial of her masquerade - a kind of warning that Dr. Daphne Blake refused to be taken seriously - while probing your face with unabashed professional curiosity.

"Ms. Pearson." She extended her claw. "I'm Daphne. May I call you Sandra?" But, her hand still in mine, she paused, closed her eyes, and nodded her fuzzy head as if to acknowledge a message from above.

I squirmed a little and pulled my hand from her clutches. She opened her eyes and smiled.

A smile that lit her wrinkled face most amazingly.

"Don't be embarrassed. Something prompted you to find out more about yourself. That is good. I'll do my best to help you, and we'll see how it goes... But there's no guarantee I'll succeed, you understand?"

I nodded, still unconvinced she was a likely catalyst for enlightenment, and followed her into a spacious living room, its unexpected elegance in total contrast with every facet of her persona. French furniture, mostly Louis XVI fruitwood inlaid pieces with sober lines; square armchairs upholstered in pastel brocade; tasteful flower arrangements in Limoges bowls. Nothing I could afford.

The kind of refined decor one would tend to associate with pre-revolutionary aristocrats rather than with a contemporary crone with extra-sensory pretentions. While admiring the subtle touches - miniatures on ivory, tapestry bell-pulls - my eyes kept returning to Daphne who acknowledged my surprise with an indulgent grin.

"Some believe we tend to feel most at ease in surroundings which remind us of our last enjoyable life. Even though mine ended rather abruptly on the guillotine, it was, all in all, I think, quite a pleasant one."

Oh, boy! I thought. Must I listen to this nonsense? My taste runs to stark rooms, dark oak, and stained glass; what am I to think of that, then?

Motioning me to an exquisite chaise-longue she sat herself down ponderously on a dainty armchair. "Make yourself comfortable, my dear. Relax...and enjoy. Let's just think of this as getting to know and trust each other; without trust, we cannot proceed further than conscious thought."

At a hundred dollars a shot, her acquaintance did not come cheap.

I let myself lean back against the down-filled pillows and stretched my stockinged legs on the chaise, feeling quite an at ease. My eccentric hostess was observing me closely. A delicate fragrance pervaded the room, bringing to mind my wedding bouquet of jasmine, many years before.

Dr. Blake pointed to the largest fresh flower arrangement, a wonderful medley of roses, delphinium, and a white flower I couldn't identify.

"Hosta. White Hosta. Hard to find at this time of the year. I'm very fond of the scent myself."

She had been watching me and needed no mind-reading skills to surmise I would notice the unusual fragrance. Still. Anyway, I liked her; there was something down to earth about her, a kind of benign indifference that said, 'If you don't believe I have a gift, it's your loss, not mine.'

She waited in silence for me to come forth with some explanation of my presence in her old-world living room. I found myself telling her about that November evening.

She did not interrupt but nodded all the while as if this type of experience was nothing out of the ordinary. When I fell silent, she gave me a reassuring smile and said, "I see. Now, Sandra, your friend Irene has told me little about you, apart from mentioning

that you were a writer with considerable literary talent. I would like to know more; Would you mind telling me about your life?" "No, I don't mind. Stop me if you get bored; nothing is exciting about it, you know."

"Let me be the judge of that." I could detect a subtle shift in her tone as if a note of professional authority had crept into the attentive empathy of her welcome.

"As you wish. I was born in Vancouver. My father was a mining engineer who had served in the Canadian forces during World War II and brought himself back a war bride from France. After the war, he took a job with the federal government and traveled constantly.

He was a handsome man. A jolly man who enjoyed life, especially away from my mother, I believe. She was a rather dull, poor woman; very French middle-class and incapable of shedding a single one of her set ideas. She came from the South of France and hated the rainy winters of Vancouver; she refused to learn English and complained the food was inedible. Life for her - and with her

- was a real drag. Which may have been a blessing in disguise for my brother and me; just to be contrary, we both decided that life was a real treat to be relished to the last morsel."

"What brought you from Vancouver to

Montreal?"

"When I was twelve, my father decided to move the family to Montreal in the hope my mother would adapt better and enjoy the French environment. Enjoy? The word wasn't part of her vocabulary. I mean, we had a nice house and a pleasant life, we traveled back to France every summer, but for her, there was always a good reason to mope."

"She had no sense of humor?"

I opened my mouth to agree but paused to give the matter some thought.

"Well... She did. But always at her own expense. I don't think she liked herself very much. I wonder why...."

"I see. And do you like yourself, Sandra?" "Let's say I can live with myself... Anyway, coming back to my family. After four years in Montreal, my father gave up. On the day, he took us aside, my brother and, told us he was moving back - alone - to Vancouver and said

we would be welcome to come and live with him any time we wanted. My brother was twenty at the time and he went the following year, soon after graduating. He is still there now, a pilot with Air Canada. And so is my father, for that matter - getting on in years but still jolly - with his second wife he calls his 'Chirping Bird.'"

"What about you, weren't you tempted to join them."

"Of course, but I couldn't very well desert my mother, could I? Not that she was any less miserable than before; but by that time, I had learned not to let her pessimism get me down. I stayed on in Montreal and started writing in earnest, went on to McGill University to study languages, and fell in love with a friend's brother.

He was a man about town years older than I was, with an M.B.A. and a prestigious banking job; yet quite intelligent. And very sexy. We got married. Even though we eventually discovered other common interests, sex remained the staple on our menu. I think a sensual bond is like a lottery ticket; it may not win you anything, but without it, you don't stand a chance. In Michael's case, I won what the French call the Gros Lot, the top prize. I adored him. He called me Sandy. We lived well, but he was a workaholic who got his first - and last - heart attack at fifty. Leaving me Christine, our daughter, who has been a joy to this day. End of story."

"Why? Why would it be the end? You are a very attractive and youthful woman, Sandra. Do you consider your life ended with your husband's death? Are you now content to live vicariously through the characters in your novels?"

"Of course not. Writing has helped me to deal with grief and put things in perspective, but I haven't quite given up on men." I told her about Franco, and his fling with Nancy, my literary agent. "I got so angry! Not so much over Franco's unfaithfulness, I mean, I knew what he was about; but I think there was an element of spite in Nancy's betrayal of our friendship which I found quite hurtful."

We remained on the subject of my life for a while. Dr. Blake had certainly developed a good listening technique. While encouraging a frank appraisal of one's share of responsibility in most of life's bad turns, she was prompt to absolve guilt.

"Guilt is worse than useless; it drains your life energy. You know you should not have sent your mother alone on that cruise, and you feel sorry for what happened. Well and good. She knows it too, by now. So, stop reproaching yourself for her death...or your husband's heart attack, for that matter; it wasn't your fault that he lost half his money in the crash of 1987.

I would rather you told me what you think you have learned in this lifetime." "That's not an easy question to answer. Let me see... I would say, to stand on my own two feet and accept responsibility for my actions. Also, to be thankful for all the opportunities I have been granted to enjoy life."

Even though I had been doing most of the talking, it did not feel like a session with a shrink. Daphne radiated such genuine sympathy I enjoyed basking in the glow; it felt like the warmth of a wood stove after a day in the snow.

Still, I had come for a purpose and it had to be addressed. I repeated the account of my strange experience in front of the television, emphasizing the intensity of my reaction to the medieval musician.

"Why did I get the feeling this man had been part of my life when I know perfectly well that it is not so? Am I going insane?"

Her smile was rebuttal enough. She shifted her position slightly; she had moved hardly at all during the hour or so I had spent with her. Yet, she was far from passive; now a keen awareness lit up her dark eyes.

"Two parts of your mind conflict and my task is to reconcile them. Now, I do not pretend to be successful every time, but I daresay I get better results since I strayed from the straight and narrow path of professional orthodoxy. I practiced clinical psychotherapy for many years, growing more and more certain all the time there was more to the human psyche than Freud let on."

She permitted herself a small laugh and freed a bony hand from the folds of her robes. "Alas, poor Yorick... Never mind. Have no fear, I won't bore you with the details of my conversion. Suffice to say that, in my desire to help my patients, I began to probe deeper and deeper into their past with startling results. For them and me."

"But what makes you so sure I'm not making the whole thing up? To compensate for the loss of Franco, perhaps? After all, I write fiction, and - even if I say so myself - I am endowed with an over-fertile imagination; it could be playing tricks on me... Sprouting weird stories...."

She dismissed the possibility with a moue that turned her mouth into a crimson aster.

"I won't deny many writers use their own past life experiences in their work. And why not? It's as legitimate as their present ones. But I believe they mostly do so unawares. In any case, I would not hazard an explanation of your case at this stage. Memory is very strange; you may indeed have met this man or someone similar - when you were a small child, though you have forgotten the encounter."

As she went on talking, explaining the hypnosis technique she would use, what it could and could not achieve, I sensed a subtle change in her manner; she became quite brisk. more focused.

"I will not be putting you to sleep, Sandra. And I will not tamper with your willpower, either. I'll merely guide you into a state of mind - call it a trance, if you wish - that happens to favor imagination... and remembrance. You will feel drowsy and relaxed, but you will remain very conscious of your present surroundings, and you will remember everything you experience because your attention will be entirely focused. Before we start, though, I have one more question about your fascination with medieval music.

Did you ever write a novel or a story about the Middle Ages?"

"No. Not really. Some notes, yes. I did jot down a few ideas, but I must admit I've always had a predilection for that period." She looked at me so intently I found it unsettling; a small shiver of apprehension ran down my spine. This woman was far from flaky.

"And now, do you think there is a story to be told?"

"Yes. Definitely. This partly explains my curiosity, I suppose. But not entirely. What is foremost on my mind is the deep concern I feel for this musician, as if I owed him something...."

"I see. We may not be able to find out if you do, but we will try." From the folds of her gowns, she extracted a small writing pad and a fountain pen, which she placed on the small fruitwood table by her side. "First, you have to learn how to reach the right level of concentration."

She had me relax every part of my body, from my toes to my forehead. Then she told me to clench and unclench my fist repeatedly, raise and lower my arms again and again, while I concentrated my attention on the picture hanging on the opposite wall - a pleasant garden abloom with flowers. Her voice was very soothing and I felt more and more comfortable.

"Now, Sandra, you are going to have a funny thought; you will imagine your right arm has a will of its own and wants to extend straight in front of you even though you are trying to prevent it from doing so. All right... Now, can you stop your arm from extending?"

Well...no. I couldn't stop my arm from extending. And the strange part was I found the weird experience profoundly amusing; if I hadn't felt so drowsy, I would have giggled. "Good." Said Daphne. "You can stop it if you so wish, you know, but you don't want to. You are now using your imagination instead of your willpower. We can proceed."

31

Jacqueline de Sarigny

As she did, I felt myself slipping deeper and deeper into a state of relaxed well-being. "Now, Sandra, close your eyes and concentrate on your hand. Are you aware of the fact it is alive? Are you conscious of the blood coursing through your veins and arteries?"

"I am."

"Let your hand rest loosely by your side now, and forget it exists. I want you to concentrate in the same way on every part of your body and tell me if there is a part that feels uncomfortable." She remained silent while I did my best to follow her instructions.

"My whole face feels tight, I think."

"Good. Let us work on that. First, we slowly release the last of the tension...."

Repeating her instruction over and over again, she had me relax my forehead, my cheeks, my jaw, my tongue even until all tightness had disappeared. I felt so limp I was hardly aware I had a body.

Surrendering myself to a kind of well-being I had not experienced since Michael's death.

CHAPTER 4

Well, my first hypnotic session felt very pleasant; only I fell asleep almost immediately -which wasn't intended - and Daphne had to wake me up.

My second hypnosis felt great too, but it did precious little to enhance my memory of a supposed past life.

Daphne did guide me back to childhood and made me re-discover long-forgotten places and faces. In answer to her questions. I found myself back in nursery school and remembered the names of my playmates; little May with the runny nose and pesky Johnny who peed on my sandcastle.

Beyond the first year of life, she drew a blank. Literally. All I could come up with was a black screen in front of my eyes; or, more accurately a closed curtain - dark and opaque - behind which, I knew things were happening I could not see.

After an hour or so, Daphne sensed a growing frustration and cut short the session after telling me I would feel wonderfully rested and alert when I came out of it. And I did. Despite the rather disappointing results, I did not regret meeting Daphne; she seemed the kind of woman I admire: bright, openminded, and honest. While I braced myself to get up from the downy comfort of her chaise, she was busy putting the final touch to the notes she had been taking during the session. She stopped, raised her head, and smiled.

"You responded very well, which is hardly surprising, as you are intelligent and unplagued by irrational fears. You understood right away that hypnosis doesn't affect your self-control, and you remain free to accept or reject my suggestions. We just need more time to establish a deeper trust." She stood up as I did and followed me to the entrance hall to retrieve my coat and boots from a closet cleverly hidden behind a mirror.

As we shook hands, she added, "First sessions do not always bring results. I wouldn't be disappointed, if I were you, Sandra. But I'm not you, and you have to decide for yourself whether you want to continue with this or not. Without making any promise, I can tell you there is a good chance of getting better results next time; you went pretty deep today, which is a good sign. There is a blockage at birth, but it may be overcome in another session. For one thing, you will probably experience an even deeper trance - and much faster - next time. Anyway, it's up to you. If you can live with this fixation over your minstrel, fine and good. If you can't, come back and we'll try again."

Though I had no wish to commit myself for a third costly visit, that business of the closed stage curtain had increased my curiosity. Something was going on behind that dark barrier... So, my mind refused to reveal its secrets, did it? Well, we would see about that.

I made another appointment with Dr. Daphne Blake for the following week.

* * *

I had not mentioned any of this to my daughter Christine over our frequent telephone calls. She knew about the end of Franco's reign, of course, and I think she was both sad and relieved on my behalf; she is very protective and had worried I would invest too much emotion in a relationship that gave every sign of being short lived. Christine and I are very close; she is a remarkably well balanced young woman who can be relied upon to find a positive facet to any situation. I was looking forward to hearing her comments on my weird fixation. As soon as I could bring myself to tell her about it. As soon as I had regained some sanity.

* * *

Meanwhile, literary agents were not falling over themselves to get me as a client. In fact, not one of them had even bothered to use the S.A.S.E - the sacrosanct Self-Addressed Stamped-Envelope - I had provided, to tell me they did not need another hack, thank you very much.

The office was quiet and efficient minus its head; we got through the layout for most of the summer issues of The Travel Bu before our golfing wiz returned and had a chance to mess things up.

Still, I was far from rational during that week; my days were spent thinking of the minstrel, my evenings under the same compulsion to watch the tape, and my nights were filled with vivid dreams. Even though I would invariably forget in the morning what the dreams were about, they left me with the impression the drawn drapes had opened just enough to reveal part of the mystery.

In a way, Daphne had quieted my concern over my sanity, made me believe that a logical explanation could be found for my obsession; but, for some reason I couldn't pinpoint, she had also increased my fear of what I might eventually find out.

I did believe the curtain would part and I would know the truth. I was no longer sure I wanted to.

* * *

I forced myself to keep the appointment, and told her my obsession gave no sign of abating on its own. She considered me thoughtfully for a moment.

"You don't strike me as an obsessive- compulsive type, Sandra. I've read your two novels; I liked them very much and found them eminently sane. Now we have more or less eliminated the possibility you met this man when you were a child, we could try a path of Jungian symbolism with attending enigmas...." She dismissed this alternative with an impish smile. "May I assume

- since you are here - that you are willing to consider the possibility you may have met him in a former life?"

I nodded dumbly and let her go on. "Very well, then. We'll try and find out. You are an excellent subject. This time, I'll record the session; a very deep trance may induce amnesia in some subjects. If this proves to be the case, you will still be able to know what was said."

She set up the small tape-recorder and went through the same relaxation ritual as before, but this time it took very little prompting to make me glide effortlessly into the weightless comfort of the trance. As she began to go back in time from the present to my infancy, I answered her questions readily. She had me re-live my own breach-birth, which must have been pretty traumatic for my mother and, later, made me consider her chronic depression under a new light.

I floated through all this with a good deal of indifference, as if I was observing someone else's life. At the same time, in a strange phenomenon of dissociation, I was both the observer and the observed. Some visions of my infancy were extremely clear; others faded as soon as they came into view. Then Daphne started taking me back further in time.

* * *

At first, nothing happened, or rather the same blackness as before engulfed me. I was so relaxed, I didn't even mind; just let myself be led on.

Daphne prodded on, "You are going back to the year you first met the psaltery player. Where are you and what are you doing?" Then a pinpoint of light became visible in the darkness. As she spoke, it seemed to grow brighter and brighter, became a whirling spiral swallowing the night. And me.

* * *

Why is the scene so vivid when everything in it is grey?

Not quite everything, the helmsman and four oarsmen wear red and blue doublets already darkening with sweat. But the clouds are as leaden as their reflection in the deceptively still waters of the wide river which hides its strong current under playful eddies. The land is flat, hardly rising over the dried reeds which line both banks; its dim horizon part of the greyish sky.

My Lady Adela is dozing on pillows under the silk awnings of the pavilion, in the stern of the boat - gathering strength for what is to come, no doubt - while I sit at her feet on a narrow stool. She opens her eyes now and again to gaze at all this greyness, and brings a scented cloth to her nose to ward off the acrid smell of her crew. With a desultory wave of her ring-laden hand, she commands me.

"Play, Alix. Play."

I pluck a few chords on my five-string harp until she closes her eyes again.

She has discarded her grey cloak edged with silver, freed her white neck from wimple and barbette. Does the thought of her lover kindle her soft flesh thus, that she no longer feels the cold dampness which makes me shiver? I both envy and pity her.

She lifts her head, open her eyes to look at me and says in a gentle voice, "Do not pine for fair Walther of the Golden Voice, child. Such longing will bring you naught but torment. Though he may have enthralled your heart, he pays no heed to you; for which you ought to thank the Lord, for beautiful Walther is known to be fickle and soon wearied by his conquests.

He has caused many a maiden to rue the day he set eyes on her. You would do well to cast his image from your memory." I blush but do not answer. My Lady Adela may try to remind me that Sir Walther von Altdorf, the high-born German knight whose songs surpass those of any minstrel, will never love me; but she cannot prevail on me to desist loving him.

I pity her, for she is a dull creature who has neither lofty aspirations nor the will to fulfill them, whereas I, but a maiden still, seethe with them. Aye, she is dull, but guileless - for which I am grateful as I am her constant companion - and her mind is as bland as the scenery.

* * *

When I become aware of Daphne once more, I reluctantly open my eyes. Her face appears somewhat blurred compared to the vividness of my vision; she is leaning forward on her chair, intent on my every word. My mouth is dry and my voice sounds alien to me. "This is too incredible! I want to go back!" "As Alix are you aware of your present identity, I mean, aware of the fact that you live now, as Sandra, at the very end of the XXth century?"

I shake my head slowly, annoyed by her interruption, anxious to let the vision unfold as it should, and close my eyes again. Her soothing voice lulls me back into the past.

* * *

There is no wind; the grey sail stays furled, of no help to the men who have been propelling the craft since dawn three hours ago. Smoke from invisible hamlets feeds the ashen clouds. I know where we are going, yet am not sure we will ever get there; it is as if we have entered a realm where no one ever reaches a destination.

Yet, we will, in an hour or so. We will disembark on the slimy wooden pier, at the foot of the looming town walls and hold up our skirts as we pick our way on the muddy path to the postern, followed by our red and blue varlets carrying their long oars over their shoulders as if they were made of straw. Travelling by land would be faster, but my Lady Adela enjoys neither horse nor litter. So, we have come to town this way once a month for a year now, on market days. To make purchases from cloth merchants and silversmiths, and pay a visit to the Lady Matilde, her bosom friend. Or so my Lady tells her Lord.

Her lover is no lord. Not even a knight, but a mere Venetian commoner, who once owned a ship and ferried pilgrims to the Holy Land, or so he says. Perhaps it is true, as he wears silk robes and a velvet cloak and lives in a goodly house with five clean servants. Not that we ever go there, for the lovers meet in Lady Matilde's chamber while she repairs to her cellar and busies herself with her preserves and wines.

The man is short, and dark; lively as quicksilver. Yeast to my Lady's doughiness. He keeps her enthralled with tales of wondrous lands which she faithfully repeats to me on the long way back to the castle after every tryst, dulling the sharp edges and hues of the stories with her monotone voice and colorless mind. I would rather learn more about his amorous feats, but she keeps silent about his talents. Me thinks she derives more pleasure from his tales than from his sinewy body.

Imagining their dalliance brings to my mind the thought of Walther. Walther, the handsome German knight with the golden voice who visited us for Michaelmas with Bertrand de Born, a troubadour of great fame and a friend of Sir Eudes, and departed but two days ago.

His image shines in my memory as brightly as the stained-glass windows of our chapel, bringing fire to my cheeks. Indeed, his face is as the Archangel Gabriel's and his eyes bluer than the azure on Sir Eudes' shield. Though a noble knight, he plays the lute most pleasingly and sings virelays, tensons, and estampies, in German, French, and even in the southern tongue, which he is now learning. Alas, beautiful Walther paid me no heed, and only had eyes for Adela and her wanton friends, Branwin, Marguerite and Beatrix. Would I was a married lady to receive his homage and pledge my faith to him... But, alas, no seigneur has asked for my hand; I am poor and own no land in my own right. Sir Eudes will decide on my fate, whether it be marriage or convent.

Where I in my Lady's exalted position, I would choose Walther as my lover and would not wager my fate and fortune - nay, my life even - for a few hours of pleasuring with such a common man as her Venetian. I would favor a lover powerful enough to protect me from my Lord's ire. As Old Queen Alienor who cuckolded one king with another and found herself all the better for it.

But my Lady's wit is feeble and the Venetian's glib tongue has made her forget caution as well as duty to her Lord. Her rashness gives me cause to fear; my own position being most precarious. I am but a ward of her Lord, Sir Eudes, who welcomed me into his house at my mother's death, in memory of my father, who had fought the Infidels by his side and who had died saving his life. Sir Eudes is a powerful baron.

He has shown himself kind and generous to me, his ward; treated me better, in fact, than his own daughter, who was married off to an old enemy when she was barely ten in order to secure a few feudless years for Eudes while he helped King Richard re-conquer Aquitaine from King Philip of France. She is fifteen now and abets her husband in his open revolt against her father.

For all his generosity, Sir Eudes is a forbidding man, whose fits of rage can make a whole castle tremble.

* * *

The image fades. I am still shivering with dread at the thought of running afoul of my lady's husband, but loath to open my eyes. Daphne notices my agitation and gets up quickly; she places a soothing hand on my forehead and murmurs, "There, there. Calm down. Would you like us to stop now? We have unlocked the way to the visions and they will come back to you. You are still deep in a trance but you can wake up if you wish." No!

I do not wish it! I don't want to return to the present! These people are now part of me as I am part of them. Eerie feeling. But stranger still, I take it all for granted, as if it was the most natural thing in the world to discover one's hidden past....

"No! no! Please, Daphne! Please let me go back! I am Alix and I want to know what happens to me!"

I am aware of her hesitation. "Very well, then.

What happens?"

* * *

We are walking up a steep and narrow cobbled lane, my Lady and I.

The horsemen are lagging behind, dodging night soil thrown at them from the jutting upper stories of tall stone houses by giggling serving girls. They are handsome strapping fellows who set me dreaming whenever my eyes rest too long on them. The girls tarry at their windows and exchange bawdy gibes, which the horsemen enjoy with great guffaws and lewd gestures.

Her skirts still caught in her belt, my Lady walks straight on, eyes lowered, careful not to tread in the muck and soil her soft grey slippers. She hardly bothers to nod when greeted. Women stop on their way to stare at her rich attire, comment in hushed tones over her diaphanous grey veil, the lacing of her tunic, the silver cord fastening of her cloak. Men watch her pass and strip her of it all, for she is comely and her hips are rounded and pleasing to their eyes.

She is Sir Eudes's third wife. Espoused for her dowry four years before I came to live with them, which was three years ago to this day. She has brought him vast domains which will again fatten great herds of cattle as soon as French and Anglo-Norman warriors see fit to stop ravaging the land.

She has given her husband two children he dotes on and who will no doubt have to take up arms one day against their two brutish half-brothers from Eudes' first marriage.

Their married half-sister - from Eudes' second marriage - bears them no ill-will. For now.

I love Adela's son, little Robert, and his sister Eloise dearly; I fear they will be no match for their cunning and war-hardened siblings. But then again, one hardly knows who will survive these troubled times. Did not mighty King Richard himself succumb to a mere flesh wound just a few months past....

* * *

Again, my visions are interrupted by the brief consciousness of my present existence and its modern surroundings. I close my eyes tightly lest opening them give Daphne a chance to ask questions.

* * *

We reach the draper's shop. Walking backwards, the man himself draws us into its welcoming darkness. I breathe in deeply, relishing the spicy fragrance of soft silks and stiff brocades from faraway Oriental lands. I even enjoy the wintry smells of fine woolen cloths from Flanders; they ward us so well from the chill that oozes from the thick stone walls of the keep.

Life comes to my Lady's eyes as her white hand caresses a bolt of green velvet the draper has just placed on the wooden counter for her inspection.

The man is holding his breath in quite comical fashion, darting nervous glances at his shelves, mostly bare of goods if not of dust; wishing, no doubt, that some miracle would enable him to replenish them. But war is taking its toll, and ships bearing cloth from the Orient are few and far between.

Even when they reach port, bands of roaming soldiers and looters kill their crews and seize their goods. The draper must now rely on local weavers who produce nothing that my Lady Adela might covet.

"Is that all you can show me, draper? You said last time that a ship from Genoa was due in Aigues-Mortes with patterned brocade of a new design. Well?" Her vague eyes stare at the man, devoid of anger, more disquieting to him than the shrill testiness of the other great ladies who patronize his shop.

He bows and stares at the muddy floor. "My Lady must be lenient, the ship, alas, has not arrived. Perhaps next month. Perhaps...." What is there to say? She knows as well as I do the draper cannot be blamed for the turmoil in Aquitaine. In the end, she settles for the bolt of velvet and what is left of his brocades. I dare not inquire if she will have a new bliaut made for me; she is generous enough but mulish at times and it would be ill-advised to ask.

As we leave the shop empty-handed - for the oarsmen will carry the parcels to the boat and make our way further up the lane to Dame Matilde's house, I cannot help wonder why my Lady, whose head is filled with chivalric romances and who can recite by heart the 31 Laws of Courtly Love, has given her troth to the Venitian. Not that I expect her to love Sir Eudes, her husband. As Countess Marie of Champagne so rightly decrees, courtly love cannot exist between spouses, for lovers grant everything freely whereas married people are always compelled to submit to each other by duty.

No, let her take a lover, to be sure, but a worthy one who will do proper homage to her beauty and swear to serve her till death, as Tristan swore to Queen Isolde. How could the Venitian dedicate any feats to her when he lives in idleness and does not even bear arms? We stop by the silversmith. More for the sake of appearances than from any great need, my Lady selects a silver ewer of fine workmanship and four green glass hanaps pleasantly trimmed in vermeil which his apprentices have just finished engraving. The silversmith has yellow skin and thin lips; I do not like the gleam in his eyes when he looks my way.

Dame Matilde is awaiting us in the great room of her house. Big logs forever smolder in the grate without warming the frigid stone floor scattered with rushes that break underfoot. She arises slowly from her chair to kiss her friend on the brow and grant me a faint smile.

She is a very large bony woman who could well have donned coat of mail and helm, and unseated more than one knight in tourneys, had she not been born to wear skirts. She is a widow, old before her time, whose flesh has withered for lack of male attention. I do not think she even envies her friend Adela her dalliance. But who can tell?

She nods twice to my Lady, their silent signal to indicate that the Venitian is already waiting in the upstairs chamber. Why she cannot say so, I do not know, for no servant is about; she has sent them all away on various errands, as if they could be prevented from knowing what's what.

I am now free to go where I please until the lovers are done. I will be back in two hours, when the church bells ring the noon Angelus.

*   *   *

Something suddenly brings me back. Fear? I emerge from the vision with a beating heart as if the images were just a prelude to events I don't really wish to remember.

But where do I go during those two hours? I want to know more. Daphne's voice guides me back to the dream.

"Relax, just let the scenes come back to you. You'll remember it all, trust me. All in good time"

Sure. It's easy for her to say, she doesn't take the plunge, just pushes me off the pier.

* * *

I wander around the crowded and noisy market, in front of the big church where I just said a short prayer to Our Lady, without mentioning by name beautiful cruel Walther who gave me nary a glance the whole time he stayed at the castle.

I am bored with the stalls and the wares they display. Too often have I wound my way between chicken in wicker cages, mounds of pears and apples, squealing piglets and smelly cheeses, without being tempted to purchase anything. But how else will I while away the time? Today is lucky; a merry strolling juggler has gathered a crowd around him to tell of Reynard the Fox and the tricks he plays on all the other animals, even Noble the Lion; how he fools them into doing his bidding. To a maiden who has longed in vain for a fair trouvère with golden locks, the juggler's ribald tales sound more entertaining than all of my Lady's courtly romances.

I push my way through the crowd of listeners, taking advantage of my small size to slip by some great big churls who should be tilling their Lord's fields instead of idling their day in the burg, listening to the irreverent bard. The man plays neither viol nor harp, but holds a mere tambourine in one hand, which he uses most cleverly to punctuate Reynard's frolics. He looks bedraggled and slightly the worse for drink, but he can recite well, and holds his audience enthralled and amused.

I reach into the pouch hanging from my belt and throw a few sols on the torn cloth he stands upon. The villains around me take a step back as if the example I give is little to their liking; they prefer their amusement to be free. I look at them with scorn and... catch sight of the three soldiers.

Black Foulk, Sir Eudes' seneschal, is among them, he of the fiery eyes; as ominous as a raven. I tremble at the sight of the beard, as black as charred wood, whence comes his name; for he obeys no one but Sir Eudes and tales of his cruelty have reached even my ears.

The three of them are leading their horses by the reins, following one of the oarsmen. The man is not carrying his oar; he is talking to them and pointing up, across the market-place toward Dame Matilde's house. Cold dread enfolds me.

I close my eyes and immediately escape into the present.

CHAPTER 5

Daphne is telling me to open my eyes slowly. Then she starts shouting at me: "WIDE AWAKE NOW! WAKE UP!"

I do, more or less against my will. She is hovering over me, panting and grunting like a friendly bear.

"I think you have had more than enough for today, Sandra. Don't make me sorry I took you back that far." She steps back and let herself sink on a chair. "Phew! I knew right away you were a good subject, but I must confess I wasn't expecting anything of the sort. So vivid. You make me feel as if I was there too...."

I was slowly getting my wits back - what was left of them, anyway - and asking myself, what now? There was no way I could stop there, and Daphne knew it. She sighed.

"I guess I'm going to see more of you, and quite frankly the whole thing intrigues me so much we will forget about my fee. Come back the day after to-morrow if you feel up to it. I'll keep the tape for the time being; I have a feeling you remember everything. Meanwhile, go home, have a hot bath and try not to wonder about what you saw."

I nodded, sat up, tried to get off the couch, and decided to remain seated a while longer. Except for the wobbly legs, I felt fine, certainly a lot calmer than I had been before the session. I was now convinced I would soon learn more, and I was prepared to wait. As for not wondering about the whole episode, it was a bit much to ask.

"This is amazing! I can't believe this girl is me, yet I know she is! The sounds, the smells... She is so much more alive than I am!"

"In what way?" Daphne was leaning forward again.

"She is so aware of everything and everyone! With all her senses! Her vitality is extraordinary...

I had forgotten how good it felt to be sixteen, and strong...and pretty! Her emotions... Scorn, fear, love... What can I say? She invests herself completely in them... She adores Adela's children, for instance; she dreads Black Foulk... Her feelings are so intense. She makes me feel inert, apathetic.

Like a vegetable."

"Aren't you exaggerating a little? I am sure there are people in your life for whom you care deeply too."

"So, few." I shrugged. "I seem to keep everyone at arm's length... And I think we all do. For fear of getting hurt perhaps, or because our emotions have been watered down by too much make-believe in our lives... Perhaps we invest so much time and attention on images, icons, and artifices of all kinds that everything becomes blurred and superficial. We are numb. She is not!" "I see." She nodded. "But don't forget she is sixteen. Surely you are not the same now as you were at sixteen in this life. We evolve. You say Alix is afraid of this man Black Foulk...." Daphne caught her breath and I noticed beads of perspiration on her forehead.

"How can you wish to experience fear? Don't we usually try to avoid that kind of

unpleasant feeling at all cost?"

I thought about it for a moment. "If that was the case, Stephen King wouldn't be a billionaire. But that's just it; fiction, TV, movies, newsreels even, have debased fear, and all our other emotions...."

Daphne shook her head. "There are still millions of people suffering on this planet, Sandra, who experience them first hand." "I know! And perhaps they are like Alix... Visceral? Who am I to say? But are we? Yet, we know very well what makes us feel fully alive: The roller-coaster of deep emotions. Only we look for it in substitutes; we turn to vicarious thrills."

"Or to the flush of new love affairs that die before love has a chance to be born." Daphne was watching me with thoughtful eyes. "I think I see what you mean about Alix." "And this girl is not afraid to stand on her own two feet; she is an individual. Unique. Alone. She does not perceive herself in terms of a race, a nation, a language, or even a family. Now we are all drowning in collective thought, sinking under the weight of our multiple labels! I for one am sick and tired of it!"

"How can you tell so much about Alix? After all, you've just met, so to speak." Daphne keeps a straight face but the irony in her eyes betrays her.

"I'm her, Daphne!" I put so much feeling into my exclamation that I startle her. "What I tell you is...is like the tip of an iceberg compared to what I experience! When I relate what's going on, I am both observer and observed; it's very difficult to put into words."

She nodded. "I'm aware of that. Anyway, I think it's good that you like Alix. You like yourself as you were. Perhaps, she will remind you of what you have forgotten, teach you a thing or two. Now, tell me, do you think this German knight, this Walther Alix is in love with, might be your Herr Doktor Meissen?"

"I can't say. All I have is her memory of Walther to go by, and, as far as I can tell, he doesn't look like my mute musician; but there is something...." I hesitated, for fear of sounding ungrateful. "Having to tell you what's going on disturbs my concentration. It sort of distances me from Alix in a way."

"I know." She agreed, rubbing her wrinkled cheek thoughtfully and observing me with great concentration. "I wonder why your recollection started at this particular time and not with your meeting Walther. It's been my experience that memories of this kind do not flow in a steady stream and that one tends to recollect key events, turning points in one's life. So, this might be a defining moment in your life as Alix."

* * *

I watched the medieval music tape only once that evening. Pausing on the handsome face of Herr Doctor Kurt Meissen long enough to get a fair idea of who he might turn out to be. The next day, I brought a bunch of red roses to the office and invited the five other members of staff for a drink after work. Outwardly calm, inwardly jubilant.

* * *

"Now, Sandra, you are going back to the market place. You have just spotted the three soldiers, Black Foulk is among them. Can you tell me more about him?"

I shake my head, annoyed at her interference. She does not insist. "All right. Just tell me what is taking place, then."

* * *

I am back among the jostling churls.

I close my eyes, wishing with all my might that the soldiers be but a dream. When I open them again, they are getting even closer. Without another thought, I push my way back through the crowd of gawkers and I start running, holding my dress up with shaking hands, running... Up the steep narrow lane that will take me to the house faster than the main street. The sharp cobbles hurt my feet as I climb, faster and faster. Hardly breathing. The door is closed as I fall against it, my throat on fire from the run. I lift the big iron ring and use it and my fist to pound on the thick wood until the heavy door opens and I push past scowling Dame Matilde to rush up the steep steps. To the chamber where my Lady is closeted with the Venetian.

"Child! Get thee back here this instant!" She follows me up the stairs panting and groaning. "I forbid you to go in there!"

I cannot go in there, but I can most assuredly yell and cry. "My Lady Adela, for the love of Our Lord please come out! Sir Eudes has sent Black Foulk after you with men at arms!

Please open the door! They will kill us all!"

I hear a cry, shuffling, whispers and muffled words. Still the door remains closed. "Please! Hurry! They will be here any moment!"

Dame Matilde has heard; she adds her voice to mine and gets them to open the door. My Lady is standing by the rumpled bed, in her shift - hastily donned to all appearances. Her face is white with fear, her eyes unblinking, like those of a dead serf I once saw by the wayside. The Venitian is pulling a long dagger from its sheath and looking with wild eyes from door to window, uncertain of the best route of escape. His thin legs are bare under his short tunic, yet his defiant mien saves him from ridicule.

Dame Matilde rushes to Adela, enfolds her in a brief embrace, pushes her swiftly out of the chamber and motions for me to follow them down the narrow passageway leading to other parts of the house.

The soldiers are at the door!

To their loud knocks succeeds the grating noise of its hinges as they open it, for Matilde, in her haste to follow me, had neglected to bar it again. Adela stops, her mouth twisted into a silent cry of terror. Matilde pulls us into a tiny dark closet at the end of the passage and turns the huge key into the door lock. With a finger to her lips, her chest heaving, she points to a large wooden chest against one of the walls.

I pull her long sleeve and whisper to her, "We cannot hide in this coffer! Surely the men will search your house, break the door down and find us!" But she shakes her head vehemently and lifts the heavy lid. Yells and grunts reach us through the door of the small room, to tell us the Venetian is losing ground to the men on the stairs.

Dame Matilde reaches inside the empty chest and seems to lift its bottom to the side revealing a narrow stone stairway leading into musty darkness.

"Follow the steps and the tunnel to the end. They lead to a door in the fullers' court. You'll be safe."

Safe to go where? Matilde doesn't say.

I step into the chest and take my Lady's cold hand, pulling her after me. Before Matilda has time to close both lids, we hear a scream that ends in a gurgle more horrible than anything I have ever heard or wish to hear again. Ever. Then a ghastly thud, outside. They have thrown him out the window.

* * *

A surge of revulsion and fear lifts me up and drops me back on the shore of consciousness like a half-drowned shipwrecked body.

"Oh...no! I cannot...take this!" Dr. Blake remains silent. "You heard me, Daphne! I said I can't take it anymore! I don't care if I never find out what happened next. I just know it's bad, anyway. I don't need this kind of shit; there's enough of it in my present life without going to look for more in previous ones. Do you hear me? I want to go home!"

"As you wish, Sandra, but calm down." Her persuasive voice is most welcome to hear. "Just calm down, dear, breathe slowly. That's it... Very deep breaths. Very good. Now, concentrate on your breathing. Fine. There is nothing to fear. You are now perfectly safe and feeling relaxed and lucid."

"Are they going to kill us too?" My throat feels dry and my hands are shaking. "Perhaps, but somehow I doubt it. This life as Alix would be somewhat incomplete, if you were to die so soon, but one can't say for sure." "What is the point of all this, Daphne? What has it got to do with my present life?"

"I don't know, Sandra; only you can find answers to these questions. They're in there somewhere, but you may no longer wish to look for them...."

"Oh, but I do!" Something moves me to sit up and exclaim. "It's just that...it's very scary. I'm not used to this kind of frightening situation, you understand?" She nods. "I can't stop now. I have to know."

"Very well. Let us try and go back." She doesn't even tone down the satisfaction in her voice. "Remember, Sandra, the past is past, and you can come back to the present any time you wish.

Whatever happened to Alix, when you wake up, you will feel only pleasantly tired and will experience no fear or pain."

I take another deep breath. Here goes.

* * *

The darkness of the stairs is such our eyes do not get accustomed to it. Adela barely stands and would fall without the support of my arm around her waist. I whisper soothing words in her ear, urge her to be valiant. In the musty blackness which entombs us, I cannot tell which way is down.

I touch the dank stones of the wall and, one cautious step at a time, grope our way down the narrow steps, still supporting my Lady. Forever. Or so it seems. Until I feel under my feet the beaten earth of a sloping gallery. We hear squeaks and scuttling sounds. My Lady clings to me with a small cry as scurrying rats brush against the hems of our dresses.

Where are we to go when we reach the fullers' court? My Lady cannot be seen in the burgh clad in her shift, without wimple, tunic or cloak. What am I to do? The thought of the Venetian makes me shiver. I know as clearly as if I had been there that they have slit his throat and thrown him out from the high window onto the cobbled lane.

The passage goes on and on, under lanes and cellars, methinks. The rough stones of the wall tear my hand as I fumble on. The scant air we breathe is full of foul odors that make us want to retch. My Lady's moans grow louder, until I perceive a faint change in the darkness and I pinch her plump side, and tell her to be quiet.

We reach a heavy wooden door barred with iron rods; its warped frame allows meagre light into the tunnel. Adela's numb face is streaked with grime and tears.

"My Lady, you cannot be seen thus. I will remove my tunic for you to wear, at least. I am but a maiden and will not be shamed." I cautiously withdraw the arm which supports her and she falls not. I fast divest myself of my favorite green bliaud wondering how my

mistress will ever lace it over her bounteous flesh. Much effort is needed for her to put on the tunic

She lets me wipe her face as best I can with the underside of her shift and, shaking her head from side to side, continues to moan piteously.

"In the name of the Holy Virgin, my Lady, hold your peace and help me pull the bars that hold the door shut, my hand is bleeding, I need your help."

Without much effort, we pull the two well- oiled rods. My heart is beating wildly. Are we to go back to the boat as if nothing had happened? What sort of lies will suffice to explain our strange attire?

"My Lady, we must tell everyone we were drenched with foul water by some wanton serving girl on our way to Dame Matilde, and were thus forced to discard our clothes. Dame Matilde will have them cleansed for us by her servants." Even though she nods mutely, I fear she has not heard my counsel. I push the door open and step out.

I blink, blinded by the bright morning light. The courtyard is deserted.

Save for Black Folk and the two soldiers.

* * *

Black Folk takes a step toward me and I stand rooted in front of the heavy door. But he pushes me aside, reaches for my Lady and, taking the cloak - her cloak - which he has slung over his shoulder, hands it to her. "Here, my Lady, cover yourself, if it is not your wish to set tongues a-wagging." His face is a mask of indifference. "You are to go back to the castle by boat, the way you came. I shall escort you to the wharf." Catching her fearful glance to the soldiers, he adds, "The men will wait here with my horse and will ride back with me. After I have seen you safely off on the river."

"What... What is to become of me?" Her voice is feeble, on the verge of falling into the void of silence. He glares at her, scorn in his dark eyes, but doesn't reply. He pays me no regard, signals to the men to depart and closes his rough hand on my Lady's arm. I follow them meekly.

I feel villains' eyes on me all the way back to the river; I stare ahead brazenly, as if walking about in one's shift was a new whim of great ladies. Adela stumbles along and would have fallen many a time if Black Folk had not held her arm in his iron grip.

The four oarsmen are already in the boat when we reach the shore, their cheeks a bibulous red, their oars ready to dip into the grey waters to take us back to the castle. To Sir Eudes and his wrath.

Black Folk helps my swooning Lady settle under the awning and jumps back ashore, signaling to the men to depart.

I fill two tumblers of wine from the crystal aiuière which we keep in a chest, with sweetmeats and cakes for the journey. My Lady is wont to frown on my drinking wine, for she fears it will stir unseemly desires in my breast. But she will not scold today; she reclines on her pillows and will not open her eyes. If her ample bosom did not heave like the bellows of Master William the blacksmith, I would think her dead.

I touch her arm and hand her the tumbler which she drains with her eyes closed. I sip my bitter wine, trying to think up some deceit that will preserve me from the convent. Or the dungeon.

But my mind is confused, my wits are abandoning me. I feel a great heaviness settle on my limbs, and can no more lift my arms or my legs than if they were not mine. I sink into a dense torpor before tumbling into the black void of slumber.

* * *

Water is trickling down my face and I do not know whence it comes, whether it be tears or rain. I run my hand over my wet cheeks before opening my eyes. I am lying on bare boards in my damp and cold shift; my head aches sorely and my limbs are so heavy that surely, they will not move. I shiver and open my eyes; one of my Lady's long grey sleeves is slowly dripping water over my face as I lie on the floor alongside her couch. Drip. Drip. Drip.

Water? I sit up, blinded by sudden faintness. And I let out an unearthly shriek which affrights even me.

My Lady is reclining on her pillows wrapped in her cloak. Couch, pillows and cloak are soaked with water. Strands of damp ebon hair snake across her ashen face, over her startled eyes that do not see me. Kneeling, I throw myself against her, embracing her, weeping and praying all at once.

"My Lady! My Lady! Do not leave me! I beseech you! What will become of your wee babes? Oh, Good and Merciful Virgin, do not let her die!" And recoil in horror before the truth.

I become aware that the boat is motionless and that the oarsmen have lifted their oars. The helmsman appears by my side, looking contrite and sorrowful.

"It is God's will, maiden. Our ill-fated Lady leaned over too far to pick a water lily and fell from the boat! Strong eddies swallowed her and carried her afar before we could reach her. We searched and searched the river for hours until we found her close to the shore, caught in a bank of reeds where the current had brought her. It is well that you slept, young mistress."

I read the man's lies on his devious face as plainly as he has spoken them. Yet hold my peace, overcome with grief and remorse at my frivolous disdain of the unfortunate creature who lies dead and drowned by order of her own Lord. For I doubt not that in adding a sleeping draught to our wine, the helmsman was obeying Black Foulk and Sir Eudes' command, and would not have drowned his mistress of his own volition.

What is to become of her children? Dear little Robert and my wee Eloise, whom I call Doulce for her sweetness! What terrible fate awaits me for having abetted her adultery?

Who will protect us from Sir Eudes and Black Foulk? Alas, no knight is my champion; least of all fair Walther who had no eyes for me....

I can but weep in silence by the cold body. I try in vain to close those eyes that seem to reproach me and note that her lips are parted in the shadow of a smile. Perchance my Lady and her Venetian are together in death... I shiver at the thought of Hell. No. The Good Lord is merciful and cannot but forgive their trespasses to those who love. He will not permit the poor benighted soul of my Lady to know everlasting torment! I do not believe such a place as Hell exists anywhere else but on earth; the priests only lie the better to make us obey their commands and keep them well provided with meats and wine.

But suffering is our lot in this life, Sweet Jesus! What is a maiden to do to avert a most undesirable fate? Run away from Sir Eudes' house? Flee in the night through the dense forest where hungry wolves roam at will and renegade soldiers lay in wait for unwary travelers?

Yet, I trust in Providence and refuse to let hope desert me.

I look at the helmsman and feel his small eyes hurt my soul. He turns his back on me and goes back to the helm. The oarsmen obey his command and the boat moves again. I gaze at the low shoreline, unable to tell how far we still are from the castle.

Weeping and lamenting over my Lady's lifeless body, I let my grief drown my fear of the fate that awaits me.

CHAPTER 6

Daphne is breathing heavily, her amber eyes full of concern; she places a trembling hand on my forehead. "We should stop for a while. I've never encountered such vivid memories in a patient...and been so affected by them myself...

I think it might be wiser perhaps not to probe any further." Her voice is strained. I shake my head vehemently, but she insists, "Those were cruel times, Sandra, and God only knows what you might have to live through...again. You are hard to wake up and I can only do so much to shield you from the distress that...." "Please! I have to know. Whatever happens I can't stop just like that and spend the rest of this life wondering what happened in the previous one! You must understand!"

"Oh, I do. I do, indeed." An impish grin lights up her brown eyes. "It's your lives, after all, so I suppose the choice is yours to make. But let's both calm down."

She insists I join her for tea before going home. I follow her to the back of the house and sit at the pine table in her quaint kitchen that smells of cinnamon while she puts an old-fashioned kettle on the stove and reaches for a cookie jar. I feel both extremely weak and quietly elated. As I watch Daphne, I am struck by the lightness of her efficiency; there is about her an aura of strength I had not noticed before.

"So, you're quite sure you want to go on with this?" She inquires while pouring Lapsang Souchong in Royal Doulton cups.

I nod dumbly, feeling a new surge of excitement - and apprehension - at the thought of what might lie in store for Alix. Daphne does not insist, but her obvious concern touches me. Her renouncing her fee has caught me by surprise; I mean, I like her very much and she appears to like me, but I am a patient like any other... Why is she showing such interest in my case?

I wonder how old she is. Her face is a puzzle; the myriad wrinkles and outrageous make-up more like a mask deliberately put on. Her jaw line is firm and the skin of her neck between the folds of her silk scarfs, strangely unblemished. The multiple layers of her robes may add to her bulk but do not disguise her unmistakable vitality.

I drink my tea gratefully and refuse her kind offer to drive me home. I am to come back every second day at 6 p.m. God willing. Is it all a dream?

* * *

It was snowing softly as I waited for the bus to take me home that evening. For the first time in many years, I looked at the big lacy flakes of snow, watched them settle gracefully on the shiny tarmac and disappear, wondering at the significance of their ethereal beauty. I felt so tired, yet whenever I allowed myself to remember the scenes I had just re-lived, bolts of excitement split the numbness of my exhaustion like lightning.

I fell into a dreamless sleep as soon as my head hit the pillow.

* * *

As I wasn't going to the office the next day, I spent the morning and afternoon at the Westmount public library, reading medieval history.

Not that there was much hope of finding anything significant; I didn't even remember the name of the town. A walled burg on the bank of a river, somewhere in Aquitaine.... Good luck.

The year, I had no trouble ascertaining. A few months after Richard Coeur-de-Lion's death meant 1199, as the English king had died in April of that year.

800 years ago. Could it be true? If I had really lived then, why had it taken me so long to be reborn? Surely, I must have been up to some kind of mischief in the mean time? Metaphysical questions were crowding out my hitherto complacent indifference to spiritual matters. I had always believed that whoever had seen fit to grant me life would prove benevolent enough to recognize my puny - and so often unsuccessful - attempts to live up to the three principles which had been the sum total of my religious dogma: Faith, Hope and Charity. A little scant admittedly, and unlikely to provide many spiritual answers to present questions. One could always keep on looking for historical ones.

Names, we had few to go on. There had been a Sir Eudes, but he was Duke of Normandy; somehow, I didn't think that my Sir Eudes mighty baron though he appeared to be wielded that much power. I would have to remember more. A Foulk of Neuilly had preached a crusade at some point - at Soissons in 1202 to be exact - I couldn't find much else about him. From dastardly henchman to preacher? History is full of those.

As for Walther, the handsome knight and minstrel who had captured the heart of Alix my heart - I found a well-known Bavarian minnesinger who bore that name by no means uncommon in Germany at that time.

History books are written by snobs; they tell us everything we don't want to know about the lives of important people; their importance usually reckoned in terms of the number of deaths they caused through wars or assassinations. And precious little is said about the victims.

By the time the lights were turned on in the library, I had at least learned enough about unending medieval warfare. Men in power then showed as little taste for peace as their modern counterparts; their game was war and they were never short of pawns to play it. Alix, her fears and her lust for life, became somehow more understandable; life was precarious at the best of times and had to be lived to the full.

Still reeling from the clamor of battle, plunder and arson, clash of arms and cries of the wounded and tortured, I reluctantly tore myself away from this charming period befogged by pestilence and ignorance, and went home through the icy drizzle. A history of the Crusades snugly tucked under my arm.

* * *

"Now, Sandra, I know you would rather relive the past without telling me what is going on. You don't like me to interrupt your visions; but that's all right. You see a lot more, I am sure, than you can ever tell me. Only, for your own sake, it might be good to have names and precise descriptions. If you can give them.

For instance, what is the name of the castle?"

Daphne is right. I hate it when she interrupts. Which is rather unfair of me? "I'll try. Names do not seem to matter to me. To Alix, I mean. Family names."

"The reason names might be useful is that your visions may not follow a chronological order. Next time, you might suddenly find yourself years later, in a totally different situation. You never know beforehand what might surface. But, so far, we have managed to go back where we left off, so shall we try again, then?" Daphne asked with uncharacteristic diffidence before going through the relaxation routine. "You were in the boat beside your dead lady.

I took a deep breath and nodded. "Yes. We were nearing the castle."

* * *

With dusk, a chill settles on the water. I shiver in my damp shift and lift my face from my praying hands. Crows are flying across the amber sky. We have left the wide river for the Beune, a tributary that will take us to the keep.

The river is getting narrower and the rower's strain against the current to maintain their speed upstream. Both banks are rising into darkling escarpments covered with dense vegetation. I know that, as we round the next bend of the Beune, the castle will loom above us from the highest crag. I also know I should stop trembling from cold, guilt and fear. And wishing Sir Walther of the Golden Voice were here to protect me. Alas, my fair knight had eyes only for the wanton ladies who answer his daring verses....

The sudden thought of Adela's poor babes gives me the strength to rise from my knees. I cover her ashen face with her sodden cloak.

We have reached the curved bank of the small bay at the foot of the fortress. In the flickering light of torches, some men are waiting for us on the granite ledge where we are to disembark. The last rays of the setting sun still play on the odd-shaped fortress looming above us, but the river is plunged in darkness. Black Foulk - for it is he waiting on the shore with his two soldiers - shows no surprise or grief when told of my Lady Adela's untimely death. He pays little attention to me until I insist on staying by my poor drowned mistress until they bring a decent litter to carry her body to her chamber, and a proper escort. He glares at me, but, trembling inside, I defy him boldly and dare him willfully to have me removed by his henchmen. He does nothing of the kind but turns his back on the boat and orders one of his men back the castle to summon bearers and a proper escort.

* * *

Daphne's earlier question about the name of the place hovers briefly in my mind, casting a shadow over my vision like an unwelcome inquisitive bird I manage to shoo away. Does the castle have a name? It must, but I cannot recall it.

* * *

It is a mighty stronghold, where Sir Eudes resides when not engaged in fighting King Philippe's French knights. Built on a hill at a point where the river Beune meanders; a deep moat surrounds it on all sides. Sir Eudes would fain dwell in that gloomy place rather than in one of his pleasant manors - for he has many in his demesnes - because it is the strongest of all and he keeps it well garrisoned with his own men. These are troubled times, when loyalties shift like clouds in the autumn sky.

I know Sir Eudes to be sorely afraid of his enemies' - and his friends'- treachery. He sleeps but little of a night, and trembles in his bed. Or so I once heard my Lady confide to her friend Mathilde. Well, may he now sleep no more, the fiend!

For I doubt not that Sir Eudes wished my poor Lady dead; whether or not he gave the order to Black Foulk to have her drowned. This wicked steward merely did his bidding, he and his soldiers, and the helmsman. Devil incarnate that they are! Sweet Mary, Mother of God, preserve me from the likes of them!

Waiting in the boat for the men and the litter, my thoughts are all of the children and my eyes fill with tears. How to tell them of their loss? They love their mother so much.... I dread more than ever crossing the drawbridge into that dark fortress, where the sun rarely shines and where, winter nights the young squires' teeth chatter from the cold as they sleep on pallets in the great hall.

My Lady would often plead with her Lord to let us repair to one of his goodly manors which she favored for its most pleasing appointments, its bright Solar's and flowery bowers. Minstrels' songs easily bloomed forth in such setting, and their verses to the ladies' beauty did not go unanswered. Sir Eudes would grudgingly allow us a few days in this blessed abode, but never would he join us there.

Alas, poor Adela, she enjoyed her sweet bower but a short time! Her shade, perchance, may haunt it still; though I would rather she haunted the castle, brought her Venetian ghost along with her, and cuckolded her Lord in his own chamber!

Yes, Sir Eudes ordered the death of his wife and her lover. The more thought I give to her hapless end the more I incline to blame him for it, even though dastardly Black Foulk, the soldiers and the helmsman did the deeds. Black Foulk is an ambitious wretch, and his lowly stewardship chafes him sorely for he deems it unworthy of his high birth. Indeed, he claims King Henry of England as his sire, which - to my mind - is no great distinction as that monarch sired enough bastards to people a fair-sized barony - thus sorely trying the forbearance of his Queen, Alienor, who had not been short of lovers in her days.

Be it as it may, King Henry only cared for one of these bastard sons, Geoffrey, who remained faithful when his legitimate sons turned against him; but never did he give any thought - let alone riches and fiefs - to the others. Black Foulk included.

So, whether or not Black Foulk is Henry's son, his birthright comes to naught; he remains a landless knight forced to give homage to Sir Eudes and do his bidding in the hope that one day his liege will endow him with an estate and a manor of his own.

Once, as I asked my Lady about him, she said, "Do not ask questions about this man." And shivered.

But I insisted, "Why, my Lady? Has he not served you well?" She opened her mouth and raised her hand in warning while I added, "Methinks he would be a most handsome knight if he were to rid his face of his ghastly black beard...."

Adela's look cut me short; turning around, I caught sight of Black Foulk standing behind me.

The next morning when he appeared in front of Sir Eudes in the great hall, we all stared; his pale cheeks bore not one single hair. But his fiery eyes dared us to laugh.

Since then, he has let his beard grow again which is not customary for a knight but may perhaps serve him well to make his face more fearsome to his enemies.

* * *

I don't want to wake up now; yet I do. I open my eyes briefly while, in my nostrils the smell of river slime and burning resin calls me back to that dank shore.

Daphne is scribbling on her note pad. Why? She is now recording all our sessions. Who cares? I close my eyes again, eager for the darkness.

Comarque. The name of the castle is Comarque.

* * *

We go up the arduous path in a small procession. Black Foulk leads the way, four squires light the steps of the bearers, and I follow, numb from cold and fear. The rough stones hurt my feet but the balsamic scent of pines is soothing to my breath and my thoughts.

The churls who carry my lady's litter are clumsy and toss it hither and fro like a stag on a pole after the hunt. Anger makes me run up the path and catch up with them.

"Slow your pace, villeins! Show some respect for your dead mistress and bear her gently!"

A hand seizes my arm and roughly turns me around. Black Foulk is standing over me, glowering.

"Bridle your tongue, maiden, lest you lose it!" Yet his eyes hold no anger.

We reach the wall of the first bailey. The draw-bridge is down and the gate is open; only a few of the villagers are about and cross themselves with lowered eyes along the path of the sorrowful procession. We reach the high battlements of the fortress and cross the second draw-bridge to enter the castle.

At the center of the narrow courtyard, in the flickering light of smokey torches, stands Sir Eudes, still in hunting garb and surrounded by a dozen squires.

His face is as the stone saints in the church at Saint-Loup-de-Naud where my mother took me to pray as a child. White and unmoving. The heaving churls put down their litter in front of his feet; he takes one step forward, uncovers the ashen face of his victim, gazes at it but an instant and turns his back on her. Black Foulk at his side, he strides back to the great hall while we all catch our breaths.

Bogo, the Chaplain with the hollow cheeks and flinty eyes tarries by the litter in the company of his young clerks and the fat Almoner. My Lady's funerals will not come to pass without these two quarrelling over the proper rites. They are already arguing in hissing tones about where to take the body, while the tonsured youths - such a waste of young manhood - stare from one to the other with suitably grave miens.

I look around feverishly for the children and their nurse. Merciful God has spared them yet a while the knowledge of their mother's death and their father's felony. But where are they? My heart grows cold at the thought that... No! It cannot be. Sir Eudes has shown great love for Robert and Eloise; even his ire would not lead him to harm them. But their cunning half-brothers resent them sorely....

I hesitate to abandon my Lady's body to the clerics, but as the courtyard empties of squires and men-at-arms, no one pays any attention to me. I run to a small door by the side of the great hall and climb the dark spiral stairs that lead to the children's chamber and mine, calling their names all the while.

They are not in the main solar, where we usually stay during the day. The thick wooden door to their bedchamber is closed. I shiver, and with bated breath lift the heavy iron latch to push it open. In the dim light of candles, I see Helga, the children's nurse sitting on a stool, elbows on knees and chin on palms.

She is watching them as they play on the floor. I catch my breath and call their names softly.

Little Robert is the first to come running into my arms. I kneel down to embrace him, weeping silently, and press him to my heart until he cries out in pain.

"Alix! You hurt! Do not hold me so tightly! Let me go to my mother! Alix, why are you crying? Don't cry! Why are you dressed funny?"

Before I can answer, sweet Eloise encircles my neck with her small arms.

I wipe my tears on my sleeve before looking at their trusting smile in the flickering light of the torches burning in the wall brackets.

The whole shadowy scene suddenly becomes dark, as if the rushlights had burnt themselves out, and I wake up abruptly.

* * *

Before Daphne has time to utter a word, I sit up and hide my face in my hands. "What?" She is up instantly. "What's the matter? Tell me! Why did you wake up so suddenly? What did you see that could startle you so?" "The little girl! Eloise! Oh, Sweet Mary Mother of God! Eloise is... was... my own daughter, Christine!

How can this be? She doesn't look like her, but I know! Eloise is Christine!"

CHAPTER 7

The insistent ring drills through layers of sleep and forces me to open an eye and reach for the phone by my bed.

"Hello! Sandra? Are you awake?"

"Yes, Irene. I am, now." Who else but Irene would wake me up at 6 a.m. on a Sunday morning? Her booming voice magnified by transatlantic distance; she does not wait for me to protest.

"How are you, sweetie, and how is your regression coming along?"

"Don't ask." I half sit up, plump a pillow behind my back and sigh.

"Why? What's wrong? Did you find out why you're nuts about that mute singer, or musician or whatever? What do you think of Daphne? Peculiar enough for you?" She pauses long enough to catch her breath before adding, "And what about your past life? Did you have one?" As I still don't answer, she starts to get seriously worried. "What's the matter, Sandra? Talk to me! Is anything wrong? Is it Christine?"

"Not really, but... Are you sure you want to hear? You're calling long distance and...."

"Don't be silly! 'Course, I want to hear! Before I give you an earful about the marvelous time I'm having here with Olivier." "Well, for a start, I can tell you I got more than I bargained for. I'm not sorry I met Daphne; I mean, I like her very much, but the whole scene has gotten out of hand, sort of..." "What do you mean?" Now she is really paying attention.

"I mean, if you stir things up, the past has a way of taking over. Now I see why forgetting our previous lives is a blessing."

"You are not making much sense, you know." Irene's patient tone is a surprise; love's mellowing effect?

"Perhaps. But, believe me, the whole thing makes very little sense. It's just... mind boggling."

"So, you have found something about the German guy?"

"Yes and no. I found out a lot about myself and, would you believe it, about Christine. My daughter was part of the scene eight hundred years ago. Irene, this is crazy, but the worst of it is, I think it's real and it's taking over my whole life."

"It sounds scary. I'm glad I let you try it first... What does Daphne think of all this?"

"Oh, she takes it all in stride; but to tell you frankly, I haven't seen her for a week. I really needed some time to get my bearings after finding out that Christine had shared my past. Anyway, she does her best to reassure me; says that discovering you already knew people in a previous life is part of the game...

Some game. She calls it Group Karma. According to her and those who study that kind of thing, we are reincarnated with other people until we can work out our differences."

"Ah, you see. Didn't I tell you we could have been friends before? Wonder what our conflict was about... One of these days, I might even let Daphne try her routine on me.

Who knows, Olivier might turn up in my past somewhere; it's as if this man had always been part of my life. I have a strong feeling of déjà-vu about him and he doesn't look one bit like any of my previous French lovers. Have you met me yet in your medieval life?"

Her infectious laugh shames me out of my somber mood.

"Heaven forbids! That particular life is difficult enough as it is, thank you very much. Never mind. I'm so glad to hear you are happy." I'm also glad she called; there are worse ways to start a late winter Sunday than to listen to her cheerful voice.

"More than happy! I can't begin to tell you... Next week, we're off to Périgord for ten days... Wine, foie-gras, love...."

"Périgord?" My voice sounds hollow. The Beune river flows in Périgord.

"Yes. That's where Olivier comes from. He wants to show me his estate, his castle. I told you about it; his family has lived in it for 900 years! I can't wait to get there. Isn't it romantic?"

Romantic? Can love actually reveal a romantic streak in Irene? This passing thought does not side-track my curiosity.

"Which part of Périgord?" I am gripping the phone so tightly that my fingers hurt. Either this is pure coincidence or God has an egregious sense of humor....

"No idea. You know me, outside Paris and the Riviera, I don't travel in France much. That's one of the reasons I'm looking forward to driving down in Olivier's car and stopping in country inns on the way. He is planning for us to go back there in May for an extended vacation."

She goes on cooing about this guy Olivier, who sounds O.K - so far - while I try to put in a word edgewise.

"He sounds like a real prize, Irene. I'm sure you'll have a great time in Périgord. Call me back when you know exactly where you'll be staying; I might drive up and pay you a visit if you're there in early May.

My German minstrel and his medieval group will be performing in Bordeaux during the first week of May, and Bordeaux is not that far from Périgord."

She welcomes the idea with great enthusiasm. We agree to meet in France one way or another, either in Périgord or somewhere else. She hangs up laughing.

* * *

A ray of sunshine is sneaking in through the drawn drapes. I can hear a bird - a cardinal? on the bare lilac tree outside my window. Stretching in my bed, I feel relaxed and, yes, happy, for the first time since my last session with Daphne. She was right about my coming to terms with Christine's role in my past. I'll get used to it. I just wish I could bring myself to tell Christine about it. Without sounding insane.

Daphne has been positive and comforting. "Sandra! You have to accept the fact that you are not alone! This sounds like a truism, I know, but it's not. You are part of a whole; your life is intertwined with other lives. What is so disturbing about sharing other people's destiny? Now, think back about your marriage; was it perfect?"

"Of course, not." I sighed. "We loved each other deeply - too deeply perhaps - but that did not stop us from bickering; we were often at each other's throat without any valid reason... If I had to do it over again...."

Daphne smiled. "My point exactly. It takes more than one lifetime to perfect a relationship. Perhaps, we are given the chance to do so. Who knows?

As I mentioned to you before, some also say we choose the conditions under which we are reborn, as well as our parents... Anyway, apart from the shock of finding your daughter was part of that former life, did you experience any particular emotion?"

"Yes. Gratitude, I think. I am glad to share Christine's life again. All the more so if what you say is true; which would mean she chose me as her mother! That's both touching and flattering.

She is such a wonderful and vital girl! I loved her then and I love her now." "What about the little boy, Robert?"

"What about him?"

"Did he seem familiar to you?"

I had to think over that one to give an honest answer. "Well... Not really familiar, but...there is something about him, now that you mention it."

Identifying Eloise as Christine seemed all the stranger because of the fact there was no physical resemblance between the two. Christine has auburn hair and green eyes, while little Eloise was dark-haired like her mother though her eyes were very blue. Yet the feeling was unshakable; a certitude I did not even attempt to question.

"You may not be immediately conscious of the present identity of people you encounter in that life. It might take some time for you to know them. I think that, in the case of your daughter, you knew at once because you are very close and she is very dear to you. In any case, try not to let the past take over the present; remembrance is not meant to make you lose your grip on present reality, just to help you learn more about yourself".

What counts is here and now. She paused as if to emphasize her point. "Now, we still have to reach our goal: Find out about the relationship you had with that German musician in the past and - most of all - its significance in your present life."

When I told her about Irene's mention of Périgord and expressed my uneasiness at the coincidence, she nodded thoughtfully. "Synchronicity. That's what Carl Jung called meaningful coincidences. Périgord is part of your unconscious, we know that; and perhaps of Irene's as well."

"Yes, but what has her new boyfriend got to do with all this?"

Daphne smiles wryly. "My dear, if we could answer that question, the puzzle of destiny would be partly solved. That man might be part of your cycle of evolution as well, without necessarily being involved in your own past life.

You see, the whole concept of reincarnation also implies that people on earth evolve from cycle to cycle, and that groups of them may decide to pursue that evolution under similar circumstances, by being reincarnated more or less at the same time. On top of that, of course, there's Group Karma, which is of a much more intimate nature."

She fell silent, but I felt loath to question her further. She sighed and added with an obvious effort at cheerfulness, "We can only hope your recollections will continue. They might provide us with some kind of explanation." But she was adamant we should not resume our sessions immediately; according to her, I needed a breather. She told me to call her when I felt perfectly calm and ready to face new revelations.

Over the week, the emotional turmoil caused by the discovery of little Eloise's present identity abated. I resolved to pursue the regression experience without allowing it to encroach too much on my present life.

Easier said than done.

* * *

"You haven't been back to the library?" Daphne inquired, slight disappointment audible in her voice.

"I thought you might be tempted to look up Comarque castle, now that you know the river Beune is in Périgord and find out more about the medieval history of that region."

I shrugged. "I had to work longer hours at the office; leaving for Europe demands some planning, which is no easy task when my boss is around. Besides, you said I should digest everything I have learned so far before going further."

"You're absolutely right, and I shouldn't put pressure on you." She leaned forward in her chair, disturbing the multiple folds of her green robe with resulting whiffs of incense and mothballs.

"I must confess that in your case I let my curiosity gets the better of my judgement; never have I experienced such involvement with a patient's past life. I feel a kind of deep personal concern in your case." She looked genuinely puzzled.

I studied her lined face carefully, still unable to venture a guess about her age, and asked gently, "Do you have memories of a past life, Daphne? Did you ever experience a... regression?"

She nodded. "Oh, yes. When I first came against the phenomenon in some of my patients, I decided to try regression on myself with the help of a trusted colleague."

"And?"

"Well, that's when it all fell into place, really. As I mentioned briefly on your first visit, it turned out I had lived...and died during the French Revolution. At least according to my so-called memories."

"Why so-called? You don't actually believe you have lived before, or that I was Alix in another life?"

She dismissed my interruption with a wave of her bony hand. "What I believe is irrelevant. It's not that simple, Sandra. Try and understand that from a scientific point of view, experiences of this kind are worthless, or at best suspect.

Some neuroscientists do take an interest in them, try to reproduce them in parts by zapping some region of the cerebral cortex, and claim it's all brain chemistry anyway. But for most of the scientific establishment, it's quackery at its worst."

"Are you sure? It seems to me Science has become a lot less dogmatic of late." I objected. "Look at modern physics, it's a lot stranger than anything Poe ever dreamed of in Eureka. Fuzzy logic, simultaneous realities, Black Holes, Dark Matter, Complex Relativity...

These guys come up with the most bizarre theories without batting an eyelid and still take themselves very seriously."

"What may be true in physics does not necessarily apply to psychology or medicine. The medical establishment is rather reactionary in its approach. I'm afraid; it seems bent on debunking any "spiritual" phenomenon.

At any rate, I repeat, what I believe is irrelevant to your own experience. When all is said and done, you have to make up your own mind about it. One has to accept responsibility for one's beliefs, as well as one's actions."

"I grant you that, but, without prying, of course, I would still be interested in learning more about your own...destiny. If you care to tell me, that is."

She seemed to hesitate. "Destiny is a big word which cannot be applied to a single lifetime, and my... memories refer to one life only, as I never attempted to delve further into my soul's past. Still, they helped me understand some traits of my character and deal with them. I was an aristocrat in my previous life, died on the guillotine... But in this life, I got to marry the man who had sent me there. And I made sure he atoned for it." Her sudden smile took me by surprise; it was a flash of unmistakable cruelty.

I did not pursue the matter.

* * *

Helga, the children's nurse, is a large Norman woman with pale bulging eyes and blond plaits as thick as my arms. She stands over us and scowls at me for keeping both children so long in my embrace.

" Demoiselle, why for does our Lady go to her chamber without one look at her wee ones? They be restless all day and Good Saint Christopher, who carried Our Lord on his back across the river, was never so weary as I am from carrying these two and bearing up with their mischief since morn!"

Whenever we are alone, Helga speaks French to me - albeit with a coarse accent - rather than the southern Oc tongue she can scarcely use and comprehend. French is our mother tongue, though she is but a peasant woman and her knowledge of it is as scant as her learning in other matters. I can speak the language of Aquitaine, and some Latin as well, for my father and mother - May God grant them everlasting felicity - had me well taught in reading, writing and music. For all that, at times dumb Helga knows more about the world than I do.

"Their mother is dead, Helga." I whisper.

"Our Lady has drowned in the river." No need to acquaint her of the cause of the tragedy, as yet.

She stares through me with those pale eyes that betray little understanding.

"Dead? Drowned?" She mumbles, sudden fright taking hold of her. "Sweet Mary, Mother of God! What's to become of us?"

The two orphans look from one to the other of us and start to fidget in my arms. I release them with a smile and address them in their own language, "Go and play in your bedchamber, little ones."

With a grateful yelp little Robert runs to the solar where his miniature knights await his hand to storm his toy castle; but four-year old Eloise, firmly planted on her little legs, stands her ground.

"Mummy. I want mummy!"

Helga swoops down and lifts her in her arms, twirls around until Eloise is cooing with glee, and says, "Mummy sick. If mummy see Eloise, Eloise sick too. No good." Then Helga breaks into a funny nonsensical song of her own invention to stem the tears welling up in her limpid blue eyes.

Helga's blandishments prevail and Eloise let herself be carried to her supper and bed without further ado, leaving me alone between these four stark walls where the sputtering torches and greasy candles throw strange shadows.

As I start to reflect on my precarious fate, longing for a particular strong knight to protect me, Helga, still carrying Eloise, steps back into the room, hands me a blue tunic to wear over my soiled shift, and disappear before I can thank her. I put it on without bothering to lace it.

If my father had not indebted himself for the Crusade - to such an extent that his lands and manor were forfeited to his greedy liege, the Bishop of Saint-Loup, to repay the loan - I wouldn't find myself today in such dire straits. Fighting in the Holy Land to reconquer Jerusalem from Saladin brought him little else than a glorious death and - one should hope - a place in Paradise. But my mother had instilled in me a strong distrust for the priests, their promises and their threats. Her last years were spent ranting against the dastardly bishop who had seized our lands, and her hatred extended to all his ilk. She never failed to acquaint me with new examples of their greed, pride and treachery, of which there appeared to have been many.

I hear Helga singing to the children in the next room, a very old pagan song I do not comprehend any more than she does. I have not the heart to go and sit with them; I shall wait until the orphans are bedded to go and kiss them goodnight. I sit on a wooden chair by the stone hearth, where a smoldering log affords little relief from the insidious cold, and listen to the wind whistling in the chimney.

I look around the room as if it were the last, I would see of it; my eyes tarry on the red and yellow silk hangings Sir Eudes brought back from Palestine, a small part of the spoils he wrested from wicked Saracens, and I reflect I have been happy enough in this solar, though it be dark of a day, and in my small bedchamber next to it.

Like the Lord's and Lady's chambers, this part of the dwelling is of more recent construction than the ancient and gloomy great hall; added to it for the comfort and privacy of the castellan and his family. Sir Eudes has decreed that the newly-built white stone keep which towers over the courtyard would now house only the men-at-arms. The castle's garrison remains his first concern. His whole life revolves around fighting, though he be a devout man in his way who always heard Mass before going to battle.

How could he have ordered his wife dispatched in a state of mortal sin? Without giving her a chance to repent her amorous folly and do penance? Though his temper be fierce, I did not hold him for a cruel man....

A gust of wind is beating down the smoke of the wood fire. The acrid smell reminds me of the winters of my childhood, huddling close to the hearth in our own great hall to escape the more insidious cold of Ile-de-France.

I hear voices and footsteps on the stone stairs as a group of heavy-footed men ascend the spiral staircase. Trembling, I rise from my chair and take a pace toward the door.

A young squire appears, holding a lantern. He steps aside to make way for Sir Eudes who walks into the solar, and with a stony face goes and sits in the chair I have just vacated. The look in his eyes terrifies me.

CHAPTER 8

Sir Eudes stares at me with unblinking eyes, as empty of feeling as the eyes of those poor insane wretches who wander the woods about the castle and subsist on what the villagers give them, more out of superstition than Christian charity. His face has turned ashen; he sits motionless and looks more dead than his drowned wife. He remains thus for a long while before addressing me.

"I will not hold you accountable for your Lady's trespasses, Alix." Without giving me time to express proper gratitude, he cuts short my sigh of relief. "In all other respects, you have shown yourself a dutiful ward, but I cannot abide your presence here any longer."

I hold my breath.

We are alone in the cold chamber, facing each other. The squires have withdrawn, but I can hear them whispering at the foot of the spiral stairs. All the familiar sounds of the castle reach us. Unchanged. How is it possible when nothing can ever be the same?

"Keeping you here, Alix," Eudes deigns to explain, "Would remind me daily of... what is past and gone."

It seems to me his eyes are filling with tears, but it might be my own blurring my sight.

Would a murderer cry over his victim? One can never be sure of these things.

Looking through me, he delivers the rest of his sentence. "As you are without a dower and no knight has so far shown any desire to wed you thus, I am sending you to a convent."

My heart appears to stop and I hardly hear the rest of his words.

"You are to leave on the morrow and will therefore gather your belongings to that effect."

I feel so faint it is a wonder I do not lose the use of my senses. I close my eyes and mutely appeal to Sweet Jesus and His benevolent mother not to send any more trials for I can bear only so much in one day.

"I will provide an escort to take you without delay to the Priory of Our-Lady in Espagnac. Mother Clara, the prioress, is kin of mine; a genteel lady who approves my decision and gracefully consents to receive you. Under her guidance, you will join the saintly women she has gathered there in the hope of one day founding a proper convent."

Should I throw myself at his feet and beg for mercy? Tell him his hapless orphans need my care? Something stronger than my anguish holds me back. I shall not abase myself in front of such a cowardly felon, doubly contemptible for having others do his odious bidding instead of avenging himself by his own hand!

I remain standing, hoping to express by mere looks all the loathing I feel for him. He stirs in the chair and stretches his old-fashioned side-laced boots in front of him, crushing the rushes under his heels. In a brusque move, he tears his wool hunting cap from his grizzled hair, drops it on the stone floor and shakes his head as if to chase an importune fly. His dark eyes narrow and become more alert.

"Do not presume to pass judgement over matters you know nothing about, Alix." His voice is soft and holds no threat, but his hands grasp the arms of the chair until I fear they will break for he is a strong and violent man. "Come here, child. Do not fear me." I take a step forward and turn my head aside from the smell of his sweat, which mingles with his sour breath in the most offensive way.

"I mean you no harm, Alix, and it is not my wish to punish you by sending you to Mother Clara." His strangely pleading eyes do not mollify me. "Though you be comely, courteous and well-learned, no knight will wed you without a dower and I can no longer provide you with one. Since King Richard's death, and his brother John's ascension to the throne, peace has been precarious. King John has already offended many barons and now refuses to homage to King Philip Augustus, who is his rightful liege. This will no doubt result in more fighting."

Sir Eudes sighs and rises so abruptly that I hardly have time to step back to let him pass. Seemingly unheeding of my presence, he starts pacing the room, clasping and unclasping his hands behind his broad back. I listen for sounds from the children's room, but all is silent behind the heavy wooden door. "What is a vassal to do?" Sir Eudes mutters, more to himself than to me. "King Richard Lionheart, God rest his soul, was my liege, but his brother John has shown himself treacherous to his own father, his brother and even...his wife. Whoever would do homage to him, would surely live to regret it. Yet King Philip is hardly more to be trusted, and has proven himself false to his friends as well as his enemies. Am I expected to serve a woman, then, since old queen Alienor has taken it into her head to rule again over Aquitaine?"

Listening to Sir Eudes' monologue, I can scarcely believe my ears.

Never has my Lord addressed more than a few words to me, and only in the presence of others. He is a dour and haughty baron, overproud of his lineage like all the Beynacs who hold sway in Périgord; and defter with sword than with words. What prompts him to bare his thoughts so readily in my presence?

I have always felt in awe of Sir Eudes and seldom even raise my eyes to his face to look at him. He is so different from my own sire leastways what I remember of him. Sir Eudes never allows his face to betray any feeling, save rare and violent anger.

He is most abstemious and eats but little, even on feast days, usually discarding most of the food off his trencher into the alms baskets on the table; to the gratification of his almoner who has grown fat deducting more than his share from their contents before he distributes them to the beggars. Sir Eudes never drinks much either, even during Lent when lords and ladies tend to relieve the tedium of six weeks of fish eating by downing floods of ale and wine.

His addressing me thus leaves me both confounded and apprehensive. Perchance, he is unaware of speaking his thoughts aloud and will be angered to find he has a listener. Or am I of no account because he has no intention of letting me live - an embarrassing witness to his crime?

My fears appear unfounded when he suddenly stops and faces me.

"I have to marshal my forces, child, and though I own that your father saved my life, I cannot endow thee at this time. Better you should be safe at the Priory; it is more fitting for a maiden to learn to serve God than to remain here among soldiers and at the mercy of attacking enemies."

"What of your children, my Lord? I cannot accept sanctuary for myself while Eloise and Robert are exposed to the dangers of war."

He allows a fleeting smile to light up his blank eyes. "I shall see to their safety. Robert is six years old; it will soon be time for him to be schooled as a squire in another lord's household. It is my intention to have him and Eloise taken to Hautefort castle, which Constantin de Born has now made impregnable. Sir Constantin has pledged to school Robert well in the knightly arts and keep both children in safety. Constantin de Born?

I dare not interrupt Sir Eudes but wonder mutely about the unending game of shifting alliances and betrayals that our great lords play so readily. Constantin de Born was until recently Sir

Eudes' sworn enemy for having wrested Hautefort castle from his own brother, the troubadour Bertrand de Born. The two brothers are engaged in a merciless feud. Yet Sir Eudes still calls both his friends! Why, 'twas Bertrand himself who brought fair Walther von Altdorf, of the azure eyes, to Comarque castle to enjoy sir Eudes' hospitality but a few days ago! This game of shifting loyalties is more confusing to a maiden's mind than chess. But perchance more entertaining to the players as well. Albeit far more dangerous.

I venture a plea. "Would I be allowed to follow Robert and Eloise to Hautefort rather than repair to a convent."

"Do not defy me, maiden," He scowls and seize my wrist in his strong hand. "And consider yourself fortunate to escape my wrath." He looks down at me and lowers his sallow face as if to take a closer look at my features. Then he releases my arm and turns his back on me.

I feign embarrassment and withdraw a pace with a meek bow he does not see. Yet, truly, I am no longer abashed by his presence or his decrees. Though my heart still aches for poor Adela and her unfortunate babes, my own fate is now a matter of indifference to me.

He goes on pacing the rush-strewn stone floor without giving any more thought to me, and keeps on mumbling about his dilemma. "Yes, perchance, King Philip might prove a more advantageous overlord than King John. Philip's kingdom may be small and surrounded by barons who, though his vassals, wield more power than he does, but he is skilled at sowing discord among them and may one day gain the upper hand. How is one to know?

Eudes' step is heavy and his raw-boned strength all but spent. How enfeebled and irresolute he appears! Where is the fearsome warrior in shining helm and hauberk; or the great lord who sat at the head of the banquet table, his beautiful Adela by his side!

Jacqueline de Sarigny

I watch him with distaste; why should I feel pity for him who had none? If it were not for the children, I would fain go to the nunnery to escape from this coward's abode.

I wonder mutely by what means I might persuade him to let me go to Hautefort with Robert and Eloise.

* * *

"So, tell me Sandra, as Alix, are you looking forward to ending your days as a nun?" Daphne's face creases even more into what I can only describe as a wolfish grin. At times, Dr. Blake's sense of humor gets the better of her.

We are sharing a pot of tea in her cozy kitchen, where I now feel quite at home.

I shrug. "Rightly or wrongly, I get the feeling she will not end her days in a convent. One thing puzzles me, though, and it's the ambivalence of her feelings for Sir Eudes. Perhaps I didn't make that clear to you in relating what I experience.

She had a kind of unconscious reverence for him, as a father figure, a powerful lord and a fearless warrior; but now this admiration has turned to contempt. I think she despises Eudes not so much for having his wife and her lover killed but because he didn't do it with his own hand. It's so strange to me to feel the way she does about murder, yet I understand. Do you see what I mean?"

Daphne nods and pushes back the wide sleeve of her indigo cotton tunic to pour us fresh cups of tea.

"There is so much violence in our world today," She says, "That we are hardly in a position to judge other times and mores. Honor was a powerful motivation in those days." "I suppose."

"Now, correct me if I am wrong, Alix is only sixteen - prompt to judge and condemn - but I still got the impression she felt a little sorry for Eudes."

The smokey fragrance of the tea blunts the edge of immediacy from my recollections of this last session; distances me from Alix. "Perhaps. I wish I could describe to you the thoughts and impressions that go through her mind."

"I don't expect you to; not while you are reliving them."

"First of all, she is in a state of shock. Who wouldn't be. I mean, she has to confront treachery, fear and...."

Daphne leans forward. "Death?"

I am about to reply casually that death is such a commonplace occurrence in her world that she is rarely upset by it, when I feel literally choked by a surge of indignant incredulity.

"I can't believe this! I just can't! This is all bunk and I am dreaming the whole bloody scene!" Startled, Daphne places a soothing hand over mine. "What's wrong, Sandra?" "I just cannot believe I would react as indifferently as Alix does to such horrors as rotting corpses of peasants left hanging in the trees by the enemy, or the moans of wounded soldiers brought back from the battle field to die in the castle! She seems so...inured to it all."

I shake my head, still unwilling to believe I could ever be so callous. Oh, yes? What about my unseemly reaction to the ship purser's explanation of my mother's bizarre death on that fateful Alaska cruise?

With other passengers, she had apparently been watching a female moose and her young calf swimming across a fiord, when suddenly, in less than a second, a killer whale had emerged and disappeared with the young one in its jaws. Causing my mother to suffer a fatal heart attack on the spot. The mournful purser who had the unenviable task of telling me about it had looked properly astounded when I started giggling and just couldn't stop. I felt so ashamed of myself.

I mean, I was the one who had persuaded the poor woman that she would enjoy the calm waters and serene sceneries, and urged her to go. Just to give my husband and me a short reprieve from her constant whining...

I refrain from acquainting Daphne with this disgraceful episode.

"But, Sandra," Daphne objects. "Alix did grieve for Adela. She doesn't sound callous to me."

"It's more the circumstances of Adela's death that shatter her illusions, I suppose." I sighed. "You know, Daphne, all this is so vivid...so real, but there are times when I just can't take it anymore. I get the feeling It's just my imagination playing havoc with my peace of mind. Delusions. That's what it is. Delusions." She doesn't answer immediately; merely looks at me with a thoughtful expression, drumming her finger on the pine kitchen table.

"What are delusions? Is the brain an emitter or a mere transmitter? I cannot explain the phenomena, I am willing to accept them as they occur. Are you, and will you tell me more? Whether you're making it up or not is irrelevant to me."

I nod resignedly. "While Alix is listening to Sir Eudes, she contrasts his pathetic mien with the way he looked at the last banquet in his fine robes of green velvet trimmed with grey fur and gold embroidery; the proud lord, whom everybody admires and respects.

She also recollects the food and her mouth waters at the thought of broiled venison with pepper sauce or pickled figs, her favorite treat. For such a slender girl, she seems to enjoy eating a lot and often thinks of food." "So, what else does she remember of that particular day?"

"Well... She thinks of Adela who looked so confident in her blue silk samite dress, and she shivers, for death is a capricious predator, who often spares old prey to pounce on youth. It's all very fleeting, you understand. The German knight is on her mind all the time.

He is really quite a handsome man; in his early thirties, I would say, tall, broad- shouldered and slim waisted, with a definite eye for the ladies. I get the feeling he pays little more than lip service to the courtly ideal of platonic love."

"Poor Alix! Actually, she doesn't strike me as the platonic type either. Am I wrong?" "Well...." I feel myself blush; something that hasn't happened in eons. "You're probably right. She seems to look forward to the loss of her maidenhead, preferably for the benefit of fair Sir Walther, with less than chaste apprehension."

Daphne joins in my laughter. Then frowns and stands up abruptly to refill the teapot. "Why didn't my recollections start on the day of my meeting this man?" I wonder aloud. "Alix is positively obsessed with him. Just as I am with Herr Meissen."

Daphne pours the boiling water and lifts her head. "Adela's death must be a turning point in Alix's life. You'll probably meet him again at some point."

Our sessions will soon come to an end; I wish they wouldn't, but something is pulling me to France and Kurt Meissen's trail. I am both looking forward to my trip and wishing it did not have to mean the end of my forays into the past.

It now takes very little prompting on Daphne's part to lead me back to a deep hypnotic trance and immediate recollection. Daphne says we have now successfully bypassed my need for self-control and that, if I am willing to practice self-hypnosis, I might even find it possible to achieve regression on my own. She cautions that none of her previous patients has ever succeeded in doing so; but, according to her, I am an exceptional subject. "You can't expect continuity in your recollections, though,

Sandra. In fact, I find it rather unusual that we have managed to go back to the same situation over and over again. Let's try to do it again next time."

At the next session, I find myself in a strange nunnery, where I seem to have been ensconced for a few months. Greatly to my delight.

* * *

Indeed, but for the fact I sorely miss Robert and Eloise, convent life offers few hardships and many a surprise. The least of which is not Mother Clara, the Prioress.

CHAPTER 9

By her very presence, Mother Clara seems to bring warmth to the cold stone cloister occupied by her small community.

The cloister is part of the Augustine Priory of Our Lady founded by Bertrand de Grifeuille. The monks own the large compound, the oak and juniper woods and the rich fields surrounding it, and even the serfs who work them.

Nineteen years have gone by since Mother Clara first persuaded the Augustine Prior to let her use part of the domain to gather there a small number of women bent on seeking salvation through virtuous practices and charitable work.

Mother Clara is very rotund and as bouncy as those apples in a tub of water that peasants try to bite at village fairs. Not that I would wish to bite her, for she has made me welcome in her priory and continues to show me much kindness and attention, though she be already most overburdened with the thousand duties she imposes on herself.

I now believe there is magic in her smile, for by it, even more than by the good example she gives, she has coaxed her little priory into becoming a beehive of good works. We pray and study, tend to the sick and hand out warm fragrant bread to the hungry.

Mother Clara is never still, even in prayers, and considers idleness the handmaiden of sin. No sooner has she allowed herself to sit and partake of some food with her sisters, or to kneel down and join in their singing and prayers, that she is up again, running to some more urgent task.

With one exception: When she sits on the stool in front of her copying lectern, a great calm appears to descend over her; her ebullient spirit tamed at last guides the hand that holds the quill. For three hours every day, except on Sunday, she concedes to herself and her sisters the tranquil bliss of copying and illuminating precious manuscripts.

Not that she remains silent for long. While she works, she may read to the other nuns around the table engrossing passages of the text she is transcribing, or make comments of her own.

When the manuscript is done, she reluctantly passes it on to Sisters Blanche, Marguerite and Bertha who are more skilled than she is -

or so she says - at illuminating the capital letters with designs and drawing pictures to illustrate the text. The wondrous talent of these women leaves me in awe; from the intricacy of the limning to their choice of heavenly colors heightened by gold, their art far exceeds that of the best copying monks, and is most deserving of praise. Though my father counted some beautiful books among his most precious possessions, none was illuminated with such art.

Mother Clara does not impose a rule of silence on the sisters either. If it happens that one of them is copying some instructive manuscript which she wishes to bring to the others' attention, Mother Clara will most gently suggest that she read for the benefit of all the parts she judges most enlightening and that they all share in the ensuing discussion by voicing their opinion. I often speak up.

"We are here to learn about the World." She warned me on my first visit to the copying hall. "What better way to praise the Creator than to study His creation?"

And indeed, the rules she has established for her small community of twelve nuns and six lay sisters are most conducive to study as they entail surprisingly few hours of prayers outside of dawn Mass, Vespers and midnight Matins.

"Prayers can never suffice to thank the Lord God for granting us life, if, by our ignorance, we show contempt for the world He has given us."

The prioress is fond of repeating, while her pudgy finger follows the line of the manuscript she is copying.

"And dedicating one's life to His worship should be a happy calling, not a cruel penance to be endured with gritted teeth and a soured mind. Mortifying the flesh does not bring us closer to our Creator, on the contrary, I believe it to be another form of contempt for his Creation."

So, Mother Clara makes sure the sisters enjoy some creature comforts while they do their share of the joyous learning from dawn to dark. But woe betide the lazy who shirk their tasks, for her eyes see through them, and a look of disapproval from her stings more than a lash.

Still, for all her tireless exertions, she shows herself quite forbearing with us mortals of a weaker cast. During the three months or so I have been here, never has she raised her voice to any of the women - who, mercifully for me, also have a long way to go before attaining her kind of extraordinary virtue - nor imposed on laggards any of the cruel punishment which are the rule in many convents. For that matter, neither has she deprived me of that clement smile which has reconciled me to the monastic life. At least for now. She remains a mystery to me.

She may be old - fifty or so, about Sir Eudes 'age, I do believe - but she is still quite beautiful. Her round face is unlined and lit up by the most brilliant green eyes, forever twinkling with delight in the Lord's creation. She is very neat in her dress and her wimple is always clean.

She was about thirty when she entered monastic life, no doubt even more beautiful then than she is now. Her noble family could well afford to endow her as they have endowed her priory.

What could have induced her to renounce the world? She shows neither fear of men nor distaste for them, and seems to relish her encounters with those who come from the outside, be they visitors or book traders who supply the priory with manuscripts, parchment and paint. She appears to enjoy amiable relations with the Prior of the Augustine monks. Has she ever known a man? I look at her rounded form in the grey wool dress, and repress a giggle. As for the great partiality she demonstrates for the children of the poor, it leads one to believe she would have been a most loving mother had she married and had babes of her own. Is hers a shining example of genuine saintliness?

* * *

"I'm surprised Alix doesn't show herself more devout."

Daphne's raised eyebrows disappeared under her rusty curls.

"I don't agree. She is devout. She prays a lot, to Jesus, the Virgin Mary, various saints. She prays for Adela's soul every night, for the children, and for her own parents. There is no doubt in my mind she sincerely believes in the God of the Church. Only, her own mother's ranting against clerics has fostered in her a strong distrust for the Church itself and those who are supposed to serve it.

It is true that many of them seem to break their vows and even flout the Ten Commandments openly, particularly the ones relating to gluttony, greed and lechery."

Daphne allowed herself a chuckle. "Human nature is not easily denied...."

"Alix is still under her mother's influence, but she is aware of her obvious bias. I mean, the woman had good reasons to hate the Church in the person of the greedy Bishop of Saint Loup who was trying to throw them out of their own castle. There was another motive as well; the Church had excommunicated the mother's lover."

Daphne eyebrows rose again. She put down her teacup to ask, "A lover? While her husband was alive?"

"No. Alix's father had died at the siege of Acre - which, incidentally, happened in 1191; I looked it up - and so had his son. Alix was the only surviving child. Anyway, from what I can gather through the childhood memories that drift through Alix's mind, it seems that, when she was about nine, her mother's lover taught her to play the lute and harp, to ride and to swim.

He even gave her a sling and encouraged her to use it until she could hit a small target at fifty feet. He was a well-known troubadour, by the name of Guilhem de Berguédan. A high nobleman from Catalonia, but a proper rogue with a surfeit of caustic wit and a great lack of scruples. Guilhem was fleeing from his liege's justice after treacherously murdering a friend of his.

He sought refuge with Alix's mother who was a distant cousin of his, and she soon succumbed to his dark good looks and devilish charm. The became lovers."

"Didn't Alix disapprove her mother for taking a lover so soon after her husband's and son's death?"

To answer that question, I have to go over the fleeting memories which I share with Alix when in a trance.

"I don't think so. She didn't resent Guilhem; he may have been a knave, but he showed her respect and was kind to her, taught her to compose music and poetry, and to appreciate music. He kept the acquisitive Bishop at bay.

In fact, she felt quite sad when he was killed by a drunken soldier some years later. All the more so since her mother was so despondent over the rascal's death that she fell ill and died a few months after him."

"I see. Can you tell me more about the Priory?"

"Well... Time seems to acquire a different texture there. Three months feel more like three days. The daily routine has a lot to do with it, I suppose. Up at dawn, chapel and Mass - the chaplain comes over from the Augustine Priory. Then daily tasks: Handing out loaves of bread to the hungry; weaving or embroidering; preparing herbal and other remedies for the sick who come knocking on the door every day.

Did you know that coriander speeds up labor in childbirth? Or that cupping glasses are quite effective against bronchitis? How come I have forgotten all this? I mean not only my life as Alix, but all the things she learned in it?" Daphne's smile lacked its usual warmth. "Only the changes in your soul remain. Some even say you take with you only what you have given... But who knows?" She looked annoyed at her own ignorance. "I don't pretend to have all the answers. I don't even have beliefs, only trust and... doubts." She sighed. "So, Alix is comfortable in the Priory?"

"Yes. She feels safe. As if Mother Clara's sunny disposition could somehow keep any danger at bay. Alix is also eager to learn. Don't get the impression that this woman, I mean Clara, has cut herself off from the world. She writes to quite a few erudite people and receives many answers, which she sometimes read to us in the copying hall. As I mentioned, she also reads from the manuscripts she is transcribing, and some of them express quite unexpected ideas."

"For instance?"

"One day, she read from a text by some churchman called Pier Lombard and he said if God had wanted woman to obey man, he would have fashioned Eve from Adam's foot and not from his rib, which meant He wanted them to live side by side as equals.

Not the kind of metaphor we have been taught to expect from medieval church writing, is it?" "True." Daphne concurred somewhat impatiently. "Anything else?"

"Well, some other day, she was transcribing a Lapidary - that's a text about precious stones written by a bishop called Marbode, and he described all the magical virtues of the stones; say, green jasper will cure fevers and dropsy.

It sounded so...pagan. But Alix was fascinated; she adores jewels of any kind. That's another trait I haven't inherited from her! Jewelry means nothing to me; I never wear any."

I paused. Why did I stop in front of Birk's window and admired their display of diamonds and emeralds then, no later than yesterday? I dismissed the memory with a frown.

Daphne took the teacups to the sink without appearing to notice my sudden uneasiness. I felt bad about not telling her everything, but a kind of wary numbness had taken hold of me; I had to get my own bearings. Was I fated to experience emotions vicariously through Alix for the rest of my days? Was Alix taking over my present life?

And Daphne worried me, too.

There would be time for three more séances before I took off for France. She had asked me twice already to confirm I would be back the day after tomorrow for a long one. Her attitude was puzzling; she seemed to invest a lot of herself in my story and ask many probing questions - too many, I sometimes thought - before, during and after the trance.

I couldn't shake the feeling that her involvement in my strange tale went beyond professional interest and simple curiosity; reached the depth of her own psyche. Though she appeared eager to learn more every time, she was the one who interrupted this last session, just as I was enjoying the company of Mother Clara and the other nuns. And she couldn't even come up with a valid reason for doing so.

Her face looked different too; her features both younger and more animated by her curiosity, but harder in a way. Forbidding when she was not smiling. There were times when she intimidated me. It might be loneliness on her part; though she had other patients, she lived alone and, from what I had been able to determine, had no friends or relatives in Montreal.

Just before starting the session, she insisted on showing me around her house. Upstairs, her bedroom was very XVIII th century. Too formal and too tidy; for all its Rococo gilt and brocade, and the scent of pink jacinth in a Meissen pot, it felt as chillingly empty of human presence as her late husband's stark unoccupied room. Passing a closed door on the landing, she opened it briefly to reveal what looked like a young girl's room with white-painted furniture and flowered chintz. "Alice's room. My daughter. She had Down's syndrome. She was eighteen when she died." Her face didn't betray any emotion, but my heart went out to her. Tears came to my eyes as I reached for her hand. She pressed mine with a reassuring smile, adding, "That's all right. She was a wonderful girl."

When we were back in her drawing-room and I was settled once more on her couch, she leaned forward and asked, "Do you know what a random dot stereogram is, Sandra?" "Let me think... Some kind of squiggly picture with something hidden in it?"

She nodded. "Yes. More or less. It is an image which looks like a meaningless pattern until you look at it in a certain unfocused way until a three-dimensional image is revealed and seems to jump out of the page." She tilted her head, satisfied.

"Well, for me, your case is like a random dot stereogram. I know there is something crucial hidden there, but I just haven't found the proper way to look at it. Or rather to listen to it, for I spend hours listening to your tapes...." She shrugged. "Nothing. I still can't bring out the hidden picture."

When the session was over, I tried to steer her back to these intriguing remarks, before leaving her warm kitchen to go back home.

As a way of finding out more about her, perhaps.

"Daphne, will you tell me what makes you think there is something important you should know about my past life? In what way does it concern you? You tell me so little about yourself."

She dismissed my questions with a wave of her expressive hand.

"When I understand what is going on, I'll tell you. All in good time. Be patient. Some elements are still missing and I have to figure them out before we can reach Anagnorisis." "What's that? It sounds a little ominous."

Her smile was indulgent. "I mean clarification. I want to get a clear picture of your case. And of my personal involvement in it. I am very intrigued...."

"About Alix or about yourself?"

"Both." In spite of her smile, I sensed she didn't find the question amusing. "Now, let's get back to the Priory. What about Sir Eudes and the children?" She keeps on prodding.

"Has Alix heard from them?"

"Oh, yes. Helga, the children and their escort of men-at-arm stopped at the Priory on their way to Hautefort castle, about two weeks after my - I mean Alix's - arrival there. It was a brief and bittersweet reunion that left her both sad and hopeful; she told them she would ask Mother Clara to plead with Sir Eudes, so she might join them in Hautefort."

"Sir Eudes wasn't escorting his children?" I shook my head. "No, but he called on Mother Clara a week later. I... Oh, to hell with this! If I keep saying I, it's because I must be Alix, after all! So, you'll just have to bear with me and my recurring doubts. At any rate, I didn't know about his visit, but Mother Clara mentioned it to me.

He never expressed a wish to see me, but inquired about my welfare and my behavior. When she remarked to me how gaunt and sorrowful, he looked and how much he had aged since his wife's untimely death, I could have sworn her eyes were brimming with tears."

"What about...Black Foulk?"

I recoiled involuntarily and Daphne looked away, as if her own question made her uneasy.

"What about him? There's nothing to... He wasn't there."

For some strange reason, I couldn't bring myself to tell Daphne about Mother Clara's revelation on my first day at the Priory.

I felt a shiver running down my spine as I recalled the words of the Prioress on that day. When I complained about Sir Eudes' miserliness and ingratitude in sending me to a nunnery instead of endowing me, as honor demanded he did in memory of my father who had died saving his life, Mother Clara had looked at me with great sadness.

"My dear child," She had murmured, taking my cold hands in her warm ones. "It may be as well for your sake that he failed to give you a dowery at this time. For if he had, he would have had to keep the promise made a long time ago to his seneschal. You see, Sir Eudes has sworn to give you in marriage to Black Foulk of Sardac."

CHAPTER 10

Throughout the next day, questions kept popping up in my mind, interfering with my office work. I wondered if perhaps I should have been more honest with Daphne and mentioned what Mother Clara had said about Alix being pledged to Black Foulk. Why had I kept this information from her?

What else did the Prioress know about Black Foulk? Was she aware of the part he and Sir Eudes had played in Lady Adela's untimely death? Why did the idea of Alix becoming Black Foulk's wife both repel and excite me? In between routine editorial tasks, I gleaned more information on medieval minstrelsy in books borrowed from various libraries. I already knew quite a bit about troubadours and their instruments, as well as the evolution of their art in the Middle Ages; but I pride myself on the accuracy of any historical details I give our readers.

Needless to say, the real motive for my research was the hope of finding a reference to Fair Walther von Altdorf, while learning enough about the genre to interview the musicians of La Fin'Amor without sounding musically challenged.

Listening to their music on the tape - as I still did every night - I now felt that their rhythm was not quite right; in fact, even the spirit of their music seemed different when I compared it with Alix's memories. They could hardly be blamed for that, of course, as no notation has come down to us about the tempo of the pieces still extant. Lately, I had come to regret my lack of musical training. Too bad there was no time left before my trip to start taking lute, harp or...psaltery lessons.

Passing by my desk, Lynn, my young secretary, pounced on a small book entitled "The Erotic and the Obscene in Medieval Poetry." Opening it at random, she burst out laughing and started regaling the whole office with choice excerpts from the translated works. Even the boss lifted his nose from the current issue of "Golf Digest" to listen and join in the sniggering.

"Master Roger, the bawdy priest of Ghent Gives my Lady Giana her comeuppance Belabouring her nether mouth With his Rod of Dalliance She so relishes the penance

She will go on sinning, no doubt Till his priestly zeal is all spent." She bowed to mixed applause.

"Eh, you're not planning to use that stuff in your paper, are you Sandra?" George inquired with slight embarrassment. "I mean, we're a family periodical."

I snatched the book back from a flushed Lynn still shaking with shamefaced mirth, and shrugged.

"Why not? Don't you like it, George?" As he was still staring in vague alarm, I took pity on him.

"Of course, I'm not going to use it, but one can't pretend to be accurate about troubadours without mentioning their coarser side, which is so often overlooked. Besides, a little spice never hurts readership these days."

"Well, keep it mild, will you. We distribute in Ontario."

The dear man harrumphed a few times for good measure before reaching for his "Golf Illustrated" and his foul cigar.

Glancing at the name of the author of the song, I was only mildly surprised to find it was none other than Alix's musical mentor, rascally Guilhem de Berguédan. Well. Well. Little wonder Alix's mother had pined after his death. The rogue would be proud to know his verses could still elicit a blush on maidenly - or otherwise - cheeks.

I wished I didn't have to wait till the next day to see Daphne. But I felt loath to call her; after all, I was not her only patient and I invaded her life enough as it was, without any monetary compensation. I resolved to bring her back a really nice present from France. Some little rococo trinket. Genuine. She was worth it. Why did I feel sorry for her?

I hadn't quite understood what she meant by her random dot stereogram metaphor, but it brought to mind a picture of a starlit night, as Alix and her contemporaries viewed it. As medieval people looked at the myriads of stars in the sky, they somehow beheld the face of God.

As for Daphne, something obviously bothered her; she wasn't her usual warm and sympathetic self. One thing remained certain: She was just as eager as I was to continue with the sessions. I vowed to forget about my doubts and keep an open mind. Even about the fact that Alix's memory of Fair Walther's face and Herr Meissen's were now fused in my mind. Like two superimposed transparencies.

* * *

At lunch time, Lynn and I decided to treat ourselves to Sushi. As we were tramping along Sherbrooke Street in slushy March snow, we passed Lucas' jewelry store. I didn't stop, but, glancing at their glittering display, I caught sight of my reflection in their window. Only, it was not my reflection, but a young smiling face framed in a mass of blondish curls. I turned around sharply; there was no one around except Lynn whose dark hair has been shorn ever since she saw that G.I. Jane movie.

I felt a wave of fear breaking over me. Was I losing my mind?

Up until now, re-visiting my past with Daphne's help had been a deliberate choice on my part. Also, I trusted Daphne and felt she could always bring me back to the present any time things got too rough. But this was different, an experience I had not sought and I could not control. What would happen next? The experience so unnerved me that I couldn't eat; the few bites I took tasted like tissue paper. Lynn ended up wolfing down most of my sushi plate Back behind my desk and still shaking, I began to have second thoughts about my resolve to go on with the hypnotic regression no matter where it would lead me.

* * *

As soon as I walked through her door the next day, Daphne asked, "Anything the matter?

You look very tense, Sandra. Something is bothering you."

I told her about my strange vision. She remained quite calm.

"Past, present and future are really one, and reality is made up of strands of space-time in a perpetual flux; we cannot pretend to seize it without distorting it. The present only exists because we stop the flow with our mind. I take it that it was Alix's face you saw?"

I hesitated. "I believe so, but I really don't get to see my own face when I am Alix... Or rarely, for she seldom looks at herself in the small polished silver mirror that was a present from her mother."

"Why should you be more upset at seeing Alix's face than you are re-living her life?

Your life. She is part of your memory, because she is you."

"But this is now! Don't you think it's a little hard to take? I already get Sir Walther's and Herr Meissen's faces mixed up, and now I start to hallucinate! This vision came out of the blue, I did nothing to bring it on! I mean, regression is fascinating, and I do want to learn more about Kurt, or Walther, or whatever his name is... And what happened to Alix, of course. But the whole thing is getting too invasive! This...fantasy is driving me insane!"

"Relax, Sandra. Neither of us really believes it is a fantasy any more, and you know very well you are not losing your mind. I think you just can't let yourself go because you don't like the idea of losing control of anything, do you now?"

I took a deep breath and nodded. Daphne was right, of course; there was no point in denying it. Ever since Michael's death I had been restricting my life experience to whatever I could control. Even during my love affair with Franco, I hadn't relaxed my guard. Let's face it, I was afraid to take risks. Well, it was time to let go. To let things, happen whatever the consequences. And to hell with caution! Daphne was watching me with a smile of approval, as if she knew what was going through my mind.

"It's up to you, Sandra. Either we stop, or you accept the experience with an open mind and... trust. Trust in what?" She shrugged and one of her shawls slipped off her shoulders. "I don't know, just trust. So? What is it going to be?"

"What do you think?" I laughed. "Alix wouldn't have been afraid, would she? So why should I? I'll do my best to stop being a control freak, and start enjoying both my lives."

She nodded confidently, as if she had known all along, I would never give up the quest for my lost love.

* * *

She was very patient, but no matter how gently she urged me to let go of what she called my "Defense mechanisms," I couldn't reach the usual state of total relaxation.

"Don't deny your fear and anger, Sandra. Experience them. Feel the fear, feel the anger in your muscles. Pay attention to every part of your body and tell me what you feel. Let us start with the top of your head. Listen only to the sound of my voice. Nothing else matters now...."

We went through the routine she had used in the first sessions and subsequently dispensed with, as it got easier for me to slip into a trance and a warm feeling of comfort.

She went on repeating her soothing instructions over and over again until she succeeded once more in guiding me back to the past.

To the next significant event in Alix's life.

* * *

In the faint breeze, peach trees in bloom let a gentle shower of petals rain on me and settle on the pale green folds of my new tunic. I lift my eyes to look at the pink tracery of blossoms against the vernal blue sky. Their delicate fragrance fills the air of the walled orchard, silent but for the chirping of a red robin, the murmur of water in the fountain, and the high notes from the good sisters' hymn singing in the chapel.

Would that the joy of springtime rid my soul of the odd melancholy that plagues it today... Not even heavenly songs echoing in the chapel can draw me from the stone bench where I choose to sit in morose solitude. Eighteen months have elapsed since Mother Clara bid me welcome, and we are now in the year 1201 of the Incarnation of our Lord. Life at the Priory has been sweet indeed; but the passing of time causes me no small disquiet. I am now past my seventeenth year, and my chances of ever leaving the convent dwindle with every passing month.

Despite my repeated pleas to Mother Clara, I shall not be allowed to join Eloise and Robert at Hautefort Castle.

"Sir Eudes wants you under my care, Alix." Mother Clara reminds me gently. "You are making fair progress with your copying, though you tend to use gold ink a little lavishly. As for my sisters and I, we most relish the fine music you provide for us on your lute. Do you not enjoy our company? Feel free to speak your mind, child."

"I am most grateful for your kindness, dear Reverend Mother, and I do indeed appreciate the good fortune of being part of such a godly and literate congregation, but the thought of the little orphans deprived of their mother's love rests heavy on my mind."

Mother Clara frowns and looks away. "Sir Eudes has not forgotten you, my child. Be patient."

Patience, I did not inherit, and it is not easily acquired. The company of holy women and clerics, be they virtuous and wise - and some of the monks' behavior raises doubts on that score - has not dulled my eagerness for life.

I have made friends with two sisters at the Priory. Sister Marguerite is rather plain of face and serious in her demeanor, but so deft with a brush and paints that she can illuminate books with a radiance such as must await the righteous in Paradise.

She is teaching me her art and, finding me an earnest and obedient pupil, never stints her praise. While Marguerite has been a nun for twenty years or so, Isabelle, who is but fifteen and quite comely, joined us but seven months ago, and is no more a novice in spirit than I am. She appears to harbor no particular talent save a mirthful disposition, being prone to long peals of laughter that others never fail to echo in a chorus. Mother Clara's mirth sounds like the cooing of a dove.

Blithe Isabelle and I have become fast friends, but alas she may not stay on at the Priory much longer. Only yesterday a raggedy squire came to the Priory to convey to Mother Clara the wishes of her impoverished family.

Isabelle is to be affianced to a rich widowed baron prepared to take her without a marriage portion.

I failed to rejoice at the news; I shall miss her sorely and I envy not her fate. Who wishes to share the bed of some doddering old baron? Not I. Yet... However pleasant a course the days follow at the Priory, I do not relish the thought of ending them between its high walls.

For the nonce, Isabelle has lost none of her jollity. If one is to believe the portrait, she painted for us of her betrothed, laughing all the while at her own description, there is a price to be paid for leaving the Priory and becoming the Lady of the castle.

"Sir Guy is so old that moss grows on his head. He is so ugly that beggars turn away from him rather than receive his alms.

Methinks his late wife died of fright upon seeing his face on the pillow of a morning!" In truth, I would fain remain here than trade place with her, even if I am little inclined to the contemplative life.

I should be thankful to the Lord God for being granted retreat within these high walls which keep the troubled world at bay. In this peaceful haven, we are indeed spared famine and pestilence, pillaging soldiers and cruel renegades, thieving lollards and wandering friars.

All around Espagnac, feuding barons still think nothing of burning their neighbor's crops and dispatching their serfs, even at the risk of losing a few of their own through retaliation.

But a surfeit of peace is as cloying as too many helpings of rose pudding. The tedium fails to douse the fire coursing through my veins at the thought of strong-limbed knights in general and Sir Walther in particular. Alas, this fire burns for naught; even if Heaven granted me the joy of meeting him again, he would find me no more to his taste than Sister Branwin who is nearing eighty!

Would I have the beauty of Queen Iseult whom Tristan loved more than his own life for her blue eyes and golden hair, fine and straight as spun silk. My own hair is unruly, neither blond nor dark; my eyes, neither blue nor green!

The singing ends. The soothing sounds of water remain. The robin keeps chirping as it picks up straws and twigs to build its nest.

But an unwelcome din is heard in the distance and soon grows louder; a troop of horsemen is approaching the Priory. From the heavy thud of hoofs, clanking chainmail and neighing horses, these are armed men mounted on powerful steeds.

I rise from the stone bench; should I stay in the garden or go inside?

As they reach our compound and ride along its walls to the main gate, their rough voices reach me over the orchard wall, together with a strong smell of the stable. They are a large band, by the noise they make. One of the men is barking orders to the others and causes me to shiver. Black Foulk. I cannot mistake this harsh voice. I fall back on my seat, trembling. Why is he coming to the priory? Is he escorting Sir Eudes? And to what purpose? I will stay in the orchard. And pray.

I lift my face to the sky, hardly daring to mention what I wish to be spared, and my eyes tarry on the beauty of the peach blossoms; I look at them as if for the first time, and the words of the prayer die on my lips. Superfluous. For suddenly time seems to come to a halt, as acceptance of whatever fate the Good Lord has decreed for me fills my heart with a great peace.

* * *

"Alix? Where are you, Alix? Are you hiding from me?" Isabelle's voice puts an end to my peaceful reverie. She is only pretending to look for me; her impish nature thrives on such childish games.

"You can see me as well as I see you, Isabelle. Come and sit by me. I heard all those false notes you sang in the choir a while ago!" "What if I did? Not everyone is gifted with as beautiful a voice as yours, Alix." Her comely face framed by her novice's white wimple which I do not have to wear - reflects great puzzlement.

"How could you tell it was me?"

"I could not, of course. I am just teasing you, as punishment for interrupting my devotions!" "Devotions indeed!" She rails. "To a fair minstrel, no doubt! For being a cruel tease about my singing, you will not partake of these almond cakes I purloined from Sister Branwin in the bakery. I shall eat them both with great relish in front of your greedy eyes!"

From behind her back, she brings out a lefthand dripping with honey from the freshly baked pastries, the aroma of which would assuredly move Saint Antony himself to gluttony, and for the nonce interrupts my resolve to become as abstemious as Mother Clara.

I reach out for a cake, but Isabelle is too swift. Lifting her grey tunic with her free hand, she dashes away between fruit trees, trampling Sister Anne's daffodils under her dainty feet, and counting upon my pursuing her till we both laugh so much we have to stop. As I am about to catch her, Sister Marguerite appears at the gate.

Isabelle stops, falls silent, and swiftly hands me one of the cakes. We both compose ourselves, keeping our left hands out of sight behind our backs.

"Isabelle, you are to go and help Sister Anne with medicinal herbs. Alix is to stay here, in the orchard and await the coming of Sir Eudes. He is paying Mother Clara a visit and has expressed the wish to meet with his ward."

Isabelle and I exchange abashed smiles, and both decide in the same instant to extend our left hands and offer Sister Marguerite our honey pastries - no mean sacrifice on my part. Sister Marguerite shakes her head with a lenient smile. "Do eat them quickly! And, Alix, do go to the fountain and wash off the honey from your fingers before greeting your guardian."

While they depart, I dispatch the pastry in three bites and walk to the stone basin of crystalline water. The water is icy cold and quietens my senses as its murmur soothes my mind. From the round basin, the spring flows into a stone runnel which ends inside the Priory. I am reminded of Brave Tristan and Iseult the Fair, who used such a runnel to exchange signals and arrange their love trysts without King Mark being any the wiser for it....

I shake my hands and turn around, Sir Eudes is standing by the portal. His face seems but a mask of bones and dark shadows; his eyes shine as January ice. He walks towards me, and, extending his hands, takes mine, surprised at finding them wet.

"God keep you in health, Maiden." He forces a smile on his stern mien.

"God grant you his mercy, Lord." I give him the mere shadow of a curtsy.

He frowns and opens his mouth to rebuke me, no doubt, but changes his mind and merely releases my hands. "I rejoice to find you thus, child, growing in knowledge and likewise... in beauty. Mother Clara tells me your wish is still to join my children in Hautefort Castle; I cannot grant it yet for I have other concerns about you."

Turning his back on me, he starts pacing, as is his wont, crushing Sister Anna's remaining daffodils with feet far less dainty than Isabelle's; for under the azure and gold tunic that bears his coat of arms, he wears full iron mail and heavy boots. At his belt are hung a sword, and a dagger with a sapphire in its guard. Master Marbode in his Lapidary avers that sapphire protects from poverty. Which, methinks, is of little benefit to paupers who cannot afford to own one in the first place.... I wait patiently for Sir Eudes to resume his talk.

"Do not think I will ever renege on the promise made to your dying father in Acre, child. I shall give you a proper marriage portion and find you a suitable match."

Halting suddenly, he turns to face me, seeking my eyes. "But I must forthwith apprise you of another promise...." He pauses, as if reluctant to say more, sighs deeply and adds, "I once pledged you in marriage to a man I have now come to despise. For good reasons. Breaking such a pledge causes me great qualms, but I cannot bring myself to deliver you to the likes of... Foulk de Sardac."

Sir Eudes watches my face closely. I show no surprise, yet his words bring me such elation I ought to fall on my knees to thank him with fitting reverence. My sigh of relief a measure of the fear Black Foulk inspires in me.

Taking heed of my agitation, Sir Eudes bends his thin face closer to mine the better to look into my eyes.

"Listen to me, child and do not be over prompt to judge. Black Foulk had always served me well and I thought his high birth - albeit illegitimate - worthy of your own lineage. But, upon learning of the dishonor my Lady had wrought upon me, I took it very ill and gave way to inordinate and prideful anger. Failing to set a guard upon my tongue, I uttered rash threatening words in front of Black Foulk, who took it upon himself to make them come true. With the direst consequences for a hapless sinner!" Pausing for a moment, Eudes hangs his head.

"I have not ceased to rue my sinful wrath and his cruel officiousness to this day and for the rest of my life will endeavor to atone for a death that weighs heavily on my conscience. I will not make you another victim of this tragedy by giving you to Black Foulk!" I cannot but marvel at such a confession, which I dare not interrupt.

"Black Foulk is a devious man, skilled at dissembling. He will not leave my service and rid me of his presence without what he considers his due. I have to find means to address his greed without prejudice to you, child. Have no fear, I will not betray your trust! Never will any harm come to you by my doing!" He frowns and appears to hesitate.

"Surely your wish is not to marry

Black Foulk, is it?"

"In truth, Lord, it is not! I fear and despise the man with all my heart!"

"Then, upon my faith, you will not be given to him!" The fire of deep emotion bathes his eyes in silent tears as the sun melts ice. His vow carries such fervor that it moves me to take his hand and bring it to my lips. Withdrawing his hand from mine, he takes my arms in a gentle grasp and, bringing me close to his armored chest, buries his tears in my curls.

CHAPTER 11

We have been riding through the dark forest since the break of dawn. Ribbons of mist tarry on the path, like banners abandoned by sprites at the sound of our cavalcade. Dense thickets on both sides of the rutted path are dark forbidding walls between which we make our way and whence perils might issue at any moment. No bird sings here. Pity the lone traveler, for who can tell what such darkness might harbor?

But we are well guarded by a strong retinue of eager young squires, men-at-arms skilled with swift bows and arrows, and fully armed knights in iron mail with terrible maces hanging from their saddles, we need not fear. Or so says my Lord.

The path is narrow and merely allows two young squires to ride on each side of me. I do not see their faces in the feeble early light which guides our progress. They are courteous and show fitting respect for their Lady by speaking only in answer to my questions. A most proper and advantageous discretion, as silence gives me freedom to delve on the strange circumstances that have brought me here.

I have yet to rejoice in what most would consider my good fortune, but, from time to time, the thought of my freedom fills my chest with a fleeting surge of elation. For am I not freer than I have ever been? Yet Mother Clara's words of caution still ring in my ears.

"Take heed, Alix, you may find the constraints of matrimony lighter than those we impose on ourselves here, but do not be deceived; your Lord will own you to do as he pleases. Is this the path you choose for yourself?" The thought of Sir Walther had made me nod; I would never see him again, if I stayed on at the Priory.

For the nonce, my lord's presence by my side is rare and, far from weighing heavily on my life, makes it lighter by the care he takes for my comfort and safety.

Gladness comes to us never quite complete in this life and we must accept its imperfections, for imperfection is our lot. I shall always remember the Priory with fondness and shed tears at the thought of Mother Clara and all the good women - even vinegary Sister Anne - who made me welcome among them and taught me so much. Leaving them was the price to pay for being reunited with the children, and I was willing to pay it. Albeit not without some regret.

* * *

After his visit to the Priory and his strange confession to me in the orchard, three months went by before we heard again from Sir Eudes.

The sweet breath of summer was upon us and I had recovered my good spirits. Isabelle had left in April to be married, promising she would pay us a visit as soon as she could secure permission from her greybeard. And she had come back in early June, in a horse drawn painted carriage such as we had never seen before, with a retinue of young liveried squires whom she appeared to treat with great familiarity.

Her fine veil was held by a circlet of gold to match her ornate belt buckle, and her tunic and shift were of the softest silk in the rarest shades of blue, and gave off the most delicate scent of flowers. She was her customary cheerful and generous self, having brought presents for all of us, even the lay sisters. For me she had a buckle of finely wrought silver.

I shall treasure it always and a tiny glass vial of the very scent she wore. "Oh, Alix, do not thank me so! You must be weary of the smell of incense by now!" When I inquired about her lord husband, she laughed most heartily.

"I shall be the death of him yet! The man does strain so to take what is his! But all his exertions come to naught. Surely, he cannot survive many more such attempts! Me thinks I shall take my maidenhead with me to my next marriage bed. Unless one of these comely yonder squires prevail upon me to follow another course of action...."

We had a most pleasant visit and swore to remain faithful friends till our dying day. Immediately after Isabelle's departure, Mother Clara had me called to her presence. Holding a letter which had been sealed with red wax, she looked thoughtful.

"Sit yourself down on this stool, child, I have much to tell you." Following my example, she settled herself on a carved wooden chair and sighed. I glanced quickly around the white- washed room where I set foot for the first time.

The walls were bare, save for a large crucifix bearing our martyred Lord, placed above a thin pad on the stone floor, where she no doubt knelt for her devotions. The only light in the cell was provided by a narrow window set very high in one wall, and by the flickering light of a thick waxen candle in a small recess.

To my surprise, there were no rushes or straw on the stone floor, but brightly-hued tapestries of the most intricate and beautiful design, such as Sir Eudes had hanging on the walls of his own solar. Catching my eyes upon them, Mother Clara said, "They came from the Holy Land; Sir Eudes brought them back and made me a present of them. These Infidels are as skilled with colored wool as our glaziers are with stained glass. I find it more fitting to walk on pagan art than to adorn my walls with it." She closed her eyes briefly before addressing me again, giving me time to notice the thin pallet that served as her bed.

"Now, Alix, you are past seventeen and well into your marriageable years. Watching you closely since you came to us, I have reached the conclusion that you are little inclined to the religious life and long to be free of its fettles, however light we try to make them. Forcing you to remain here against your desire would be detrimental to your soul, for you would end up resenting God through those who choose to serve Him here. So, you might deem it wise to consider the offer I am instructed to make, however odd you may find it."

Her intriguing words lifted a heavy weight from my mind; the thought of ending my days at the Priory had somehow defiled the pleasure of living there. I leaned forward with the intention of falling on my knees to thank the Prioress with proper deference, but she held up her hand.

"Stay, child, and hear me out. This cannot be decided on a whim. Now, this letter is from Sir Eudes. In it he informs me that, having ceded to Foulk de Sardac the rich fief of Rimeuil, he considers himself released from his pledge to his seneschal whom he has dismissed forthwith from his service. Knowing full well your desire to be reunited with his younger children, he therefore asks you to consider becoming his wife."

Mother Clara paused, but not long enough to let me gather my scattered wits about me. "His wife? Sir Eudes' lady? But...he is...old! Why, he could be my grandsire! He has buried three wives already! Am I then to be the fourth?"

Mother Clara's eyes sparkled with benevolent mirth; she reached for my hand. "There, there, child. Do not speak thus. Life can indeed surprise us." The smile died on her beautiful face, and suddenly pensive, she added.

"Let me tell you more about Sir Eudes, child. If you are to decide your own fate, you must do so in full cognizance of the truth. What I am about to tell you, I have never confided in anyone, bar my confessor; but I have come to love you as a daughter and I feel you are owed the truth."

She paused and absentmindedly smoothing the folds of her habit with a white hand, she looked at the bare wall as if what she was about to say was inscribed on it.

"I have known Sir Eudes all my life for our families, though unrelated, were closely allied and never reneged on this alliance through many troubled years. Now, as Eudes and I were entering our seventeenth year...." She paused again, seemingly in the throes of a deep emotion. Taking a deep breath, she resumed her narrative with a trembling voice. "Love grew between us until we could no longer deny its commands. We became lovers."

I stared at her, hardly able to believe she would thus confide in me. But she pursued her thoughts with more confidence.

"Disregarding Eudes' wishes, his family saw fit to affiance him to Philippine de Belcastel. He married her and sired two sons, Romée and Hugh, whom you know well enough for their fractious ways. Their villainous conduct might well be Eudes' punishment for betraying his marriage vows by keeping me as his mistress...

Be it as it may, Philippine died in childbirth but a few years later. God rest her soul. Eudes was still a young man. Yet he remained unmarried, though far from celibate, for five years." A fleeting smile seemed to play on Mother Clara's pink lips.

"I was still enamored of Eudes and had turned down all offers of marriage from other lords in the hope he would one day make me his wife and lady... Alas, I had a much younger sister of great beauty whose name was Astruge. She was but eighteen at the time. Eudes married her on my thirtieth birthday."

She fell silent. Sharing the grief, she must have felt, I dared not move for fear of interrupting her sad reverie.

With a shrug of her plump shoulders, she dismissed her melancholy thoughts.

"It is in the nature of man to seek in women what they themselves lack: Meekness, innocence, kindness... Astruge was endowed with such qualities, which men appear to prize above all others; whereas I had always been bold and never willingly submitted to Eude's vassalage, however much I valued his love. Now, I never begrudged them both their ill-fated love, but it was then I decided to retire from the world and devote the rest of my life to study and prayer."

Her smile held such warmth I felt comforted by it and hoped she would tell me more.

"Astruge bore him a daughter before being carried away by a fever in the Holy Land where she had followed Eudes in the last Crusade. Their daughter, Beatrice, has never forgiven her father for securing a truce with his enemies at her expense; even though she despises her husband, she abets him in his fight against Eudes."

"But, Dear Reverend Mother, how can you find it in your heart to forgive Sir Eudes for the grief he caused you? And advise me to consider his offer of marriage, after...after Lady Adela's...death?"

Mother Clara rose suddenly, as if she meant to put an end to our talk, but when I half-rose from the stool, she gestured for me to remain seated while she went to a wooden chest and lifted its heavy lid to retrieve a rolled parchment.

"I know all there is to know about lady Adela's death, child. I have here a letter Sir Eudes wrote on the very day she died and in which he confesses to the threats he proffered in anger. He brought this to me himself and swore on my Holy Relics of Sainte Eulalie that he had never ordered his wife's death." "And you give credence to this oath?"

Sitting herself heavily on the chair, she raised her finely arched eyebrows. "Did you not believe him, then, when he honored you with a similar confession in the orchard, three months ago?"

I blushed and stammered, "Aye. I... did. Yes, indeed. He appeared raked by remorse for having caused her death by his wrathful words. But, I...."

"You still hold him to account. And you always will." She sighed.

"I do not blame you, Alix. T'is true Eudes married Adela for her lands and felt no great passion for her, but she was nonetheless dear to him and the mother of his children." As an aside, and more to herself than to me, Mother Clara mused, "I suppose he found her dumb passivity restful." Repressing a small laugh, she crossed herself.

"May God accept her benighted soul in his paradise, for me thinks her sins are fully atoned for by her death, and also by her very marriage to Eudes, whose fits of anger always struck fear in her heart...as if she had foreseen that one of them would be the cause of her demise.

Eudes now endures great anguish. And, if truth be told, I still bear him great love, though I have long renounced his own and the carnal joys it brought me...."

Was it the memory of these joys which made her eyes sparkle so?

"Do not grieve for me, Alix; it is not my wish to encumber you with guilt by telling you, my story. You will come to understand that the flame of love burns with many different hues. Give ear only to your own inclination."

The day was waning and Mother Clara's cell would soon be in darkness. Rising again from her chair, she went to fetch the candle still burning on an iron tripod and set it on the floor between us. Its flickering light cast strange shadows on her face, and I was struck by the serene cast of her features. Our eyes met. The smell of hot bee's wax will remain forever linked in my memory with the look of silent empathy we exchanged.

It took me many days to give Eudes an answer.

I sought counsel in prayer, but in the end, I knew the decision to be mine, and mine only. As Mother Clara had advised, I resolved never to blame anyone for the choice I made.

I was either to devote my life to contemplative pursuits or to enter into marriage with a man who inspired in me little esteem and many reservations.

In what way was Eudes better than that wretch Black Foulk, whom I had rejected for the scorn and dread he inspired?

As the son of a king, Black Foulk considered himself entitled to homage, fiefs, riches, and thought nothing of using any means - fair and foul - to acquire them. As for Eudes, who had everything bequeathed to him, he used the very same means to keep what was his.

Yet the world condemned Black Foulk and held Sir Eudes in great esteem.... At times, the ways of the world confound my feeble discernment. In the end, I chose to pledge my troth to Sir Eudes.

I can hardly believe it was but five days ago that I became his lady.

We were married in the Priory chapel, standing before the stone altar where the gold reliquary of Ste. Eulalie glittered in the candlelight, in the presence of Mother Clara and a retinue of mail-clad knights whose steps resounded between bare walls and stone pillars.

Hours before daybreak, for Eudes had decreed we would start forthwith on our long journey to Paris as he could defer his homage to King Philip no longer.

The jocund chaplain of the Priory read through the rites most expeditiously, darting fearful glances at Sir Eudes' impatient scowl all the while. The rain fell so heavy on the slate roof that it drowned the rumble of distant thunder.

Standing by my lord in the dank chapel, I shivered in my woolen travelling cloak - from cold, hunger and lack of sleep. The smell of damp wool and the fumes of incense filled my nostrils and made me feel faint. My own rising breath blurred my eyes and I came to doubt it was not all a dream.

A sense of foreboding took hold of me, that would linger all day long.

Mother Clara stood close to me, watching her former lover without any sign of enmity. Rendering good for evil; would that I be granted such fortitude. The knights murmured among themselves and shuffled their iron feet impatiently while the priest hied and fairly choked on his Latin.

The day was not entirely bereft of enjoyment. I was given three reasons to rejoice. The first was the most beautiful ring of gold adorned with a glowing ruby of the purest red, which Sir Eudes presented to me when the solemnities were concluded. I thanked him courteously and refrained from laughter remembering that - Master Marbode dixit ruby keeps the hair from falling out and averts strangulation. I am to receive many more jewels when we reach Paris. So, I should at least be safe enough.

The second was Eudes' promise to take me to Hautefort to join Robert and Eloise upon our return from King Philip's court.

And the third was the vow my lord and husband had taken on the eve of our marriage; as atonement for Adela's death, he would refrain from consummating our union for a whole year.

* * *

"Why on earth did you wake me up, Daphne? I was having a wonderful time riding through that forest and reminiscing about my wedding day...and my postponed wedding night!" I sat up, thoroughly aggravated. At times I found the woman hard to understand.

"Well, you wouldn't answer my question. And anyway, there's no harm done; you'll probably go back to the same sequence." She stood up and took a few steps between gilt chairs, to stretch her legs perhaps. I glanced at my watch. 9 p.m. already! No wonder Daphne looked peaked; she had been a captive audience for two and a half hours. All sense of time was lost when I was entranced. "Sorry I was so abrupt, Daphne, but discounting saddle soreness, the journey was most enjoyable; what with all these different castles on the way, where lords and ladies bade us welcome with our whole mesnie.

Their notion of hospitality was far wider than ours, methinks..." I excused myself with a sheepish laugh. "Sorry, I mean, I think it was very generous of these people to welcome and feed a whole troupe in this manner."

Daphne shrugged. "Pride. Vanity. Noblesse obli es or simply a form of insurance; their generous welcome was extended only to their peers who might eventually return the favor. Her disparaging remarks did nothing to deflate my enthusiasm. I clung to Alix's pleasant memories of the feasts that had greeted them everywhere on their way. Most of these manors, larger and better appointed than Comarque, put up their guests in warm Solar's decorated with fine Saracen hangings and rich furnishings. Alix had spent the lonely nights of the journey in all kinds of splendor, while her lord slept on a pallet in the Great Hall with squires and knights. With no one finding anything untoward in the arrangement.

As if she could read my thoughts, Daphne asks, "Is it not strange that Eudes would stay away from his new wife's bed for a whole year?"

"No... Not in those days. Not on the part of a very devout man. And look at what goes on even now among religious fanatics." I laugh though it's far from funny.

"It seems these people are always looking for new ways to make themselves - and others - miserable in the name of their religion. Well, it was no better then, I can assure you! Some fasted, others flogged themselves and yet others remained celibate whatever their degree of love for their spouse."

"Daphne keeps on probing. "Do you think Eudes is actually in love with Alix? And what does Alix think of her strange marriage?" I have to think back a while before answering her double question.

"Is Eudes in love with Alix? Hard to say. He is very courteous and attentive to my needs, I mean Alix's needs, and appears to enjoy our conversations as much as I do; but then I'm a good audience. There is, at times, a peculiar gleam in his eyes which leads me to think the year of abstinence will seem longer to him than to Alix. But I may be mistaken."

"What about you?" She leans forward as if the answer really mattered to her, while I search my thoughts to recapture Alix's state of mind. "Oh, there's no doubt Alix is relieved not to yield her maidenhead to such an old man; she would rather bestow it on Fair Walther; but in a way she admires Eudes for not claiming it." "How come?" Daphne's eyebrow disappears under the red fringe of her curls.

"Oh, it's a little difficult to explain...." All this probing is getting a little tedious. I would rather be telling her about the wonderful food; the mouthwatering fare enjoyed in castles' great halls while serfs starve outside the walls.

"You see, Alix has read Chrestien de Troyes' stories and the Lais of Marie de France, and this is the kind of sacrifice a knight might do in one of these tales of courtly love, like the romance of Tristan and Iseult, of which she is very fond. At one point of the story, Tristan tells Iseult of the White Hands that he has made a vow to abstain from embracing and kissing her for a year. The fact that it is a lie is only incidental to the spirit of the myth. Or the spirit of the time."

"I see." I get the feeling she doesn't, but who cares. She murmurs as if to herself, "Zeitgeist." And nods.

"On the whole, I think Alix is quite happy with the arrangement." I conclude. "She is now a married Lady who enjoys being welcomed by barons or castellans and their ladies in sumptuous abodes, and entertained lavishly. It certainly beats gloomy Comarque, and even the pleasant routine of Mother Clara's convent!

You wouldn't believe the food they serve at these banquets! A dozen or more dishes, so appetizing you just had to taste them all. Sweet and sour venison, Civey of Hare, spiced pasties...."

Daphne is rubbing her chin and giving me the kind of clinical look, she probably reserves for her most fruit cakey cases.

"And the subtlety! Do you know what a subtlety is, Daphne?" She is shaking her head slowly, without taking her eyes off my face.

"Well, it's a kind of very elaborate sugary show piece, what the French would call a pièce montée, that they paraded around the table. Did you know they used to change the white cloth on the trestle tables between every course; they don't even do that at the Ritz nowadays! Most of our hosts had minstrels announcing the meal, as well as good entertainment during its courses, and dancing to follow. I love the dancing beats!"

She nods. Still considering me thoughtfully, she resumes her place on her favorite chair near the couch. I guess it was her frosty manner that brought me back fully to the present.

"Look, Daphne, I know how silly all this must sound to you, but I wish you could share the experience...and the wine. It's...oh, never mind. What was the question I wouldn't answer?"

She rubs her mouth a few times before answering.

"Why would Black Foulk renounce Alix so readily? From what you have told me of the man, it does not make sense." The question leaves me puzzled.

"To tell you frankly, I don't know. I don't think about him. All I have been told is that Black Foulk was well satisfied with Rimeuil, a rich fief which included a fortified castle and all surrounding lands, livestock and serfs. And that Eudes who is not one to part gladly with a valuable piece of property - had long hesitated before deciding to give it to his former seneschal."

"But Black Foulk wanted you as well, did he not? Didn't you ever get the feeling he was lusting after you? Wanted to make you his own?"

It is such a strange remark coming from Daphne that it leaves me speechless. She goes on before I can answer. "The likes of him would never forgive Eudes for going back on his promise and taking you from him. Never." She is breathing heavily, two red spots on her wrinkled cheeks, a wild look in her eyes. "Oh, Dear God. Here I go again... Forgive the ranting speculations of an old shrink. Go home, Sandra, dear. We both need a rest.

We'll feel better tomorrow."

CHAPTER 12

To reach the small kingdom of France, we have travelled for many days across the lands of many a powerful lord. These men may call King Philip their overlord, but their domains are not part of France and they obey no one but their own whim.

As we near King Philip's capital memories of my childhood under these gentle skies crowd my mind. The scenery has changed little; undulating fields, verdant trees now tinged with the golds and russets of autumn. The bountiful crops are already garnered, villeins are now plowing the rich loam behind their oxen or slaughtering the beasts to be preserved for winter. Fragrant wood smoke drifts over the hamlets as pigs are smoked for winter feasts.

Everything is as I remember it, but for the gloom that pervades the whole kingdom. Aye, it is felt even here, in these mellow domains. Indeed, life has been joyless all over France since the Lord Pope excommunicated the king and placed the whole kingdom under an interdict.

Churches remain closed to all but the priests; their portals barred with iron; their crosses and statues draped in mourning cloths. Bells are silent. All festivities, marriages and even burials have come to a halt. Why, had the Priory been in France instead of Périgord, I would not be Eudes' wife today... But only the king's domains are stricken by the interdict. Mass can no longer be heard by lay persons, as we found out upon entering Philip's domains. Even though our first night in the kingdom was spent as honored guests in a rich monastery, we were barred from entering the chapel.

My lord and husband was most aggrieved. His piety waxes more extreme by the day; he has so far demanded that we stop for lengthy devotions in every church and chapel on the way as part of his inordinate penance.

I confess I do not share his dismay at finding us thus deprived of such tedious worship. All the more so since the monks' hospitality, though most generous in the way of food - for they do themselves proud - includes little in the way of entertainment. If we do not dance any estampie - a lively step I most enjoy after a feast - at least we are spared long sessions in dank chapels.

Eudes now appears to seek in my company the solace he can no longer find in front of altars. Indeed, he rides mostly by my side, holding back his steed to match the slow gait of my white palfrey.

I do not resent my lord's presence for his manners are most courteous and his discourse often entertaining and always instructive for a maiden eager to learn about the world. I sometimes wonder how I could ever have been in awe of him.

His limbs may be as strong as ever but, at times, pride deserts his eyes, to be replaced by a pitiful sorrow that makes me want to comfort him like a child. I do not, but I show him due respect and he readily answers my questions about his travels and the battles he has waged, the state of the realm and what awaits us at King Philip's court. In his replies, he finds occasions to vent his scorn for the man to whom he is about to pay homage. "Philip's obdurate arrogance will be his undoing! He rules over a small domain and has powerful enemies. Why defy the Lord Pope so foolishly, incur the wrath of his barons, nay, of his whole kingdom, for the sake of a woman?" "For a woman, my lord?"

I feign ignorance even though Mother Clara had once commented on the king's marital woes and used his marriages as examples of man's overbearing fickleness. After losing his first wife, Isabella, whom he had nearly repudiated because she was too fat, King Philip had married Ingeborg of Denmark and, taking an instant dislike to her because she was too tall, found himself unable to consummate the marriage.

As Ingeborg refused to be cast aside and return meekly to Denmark, Philip had her locked up in a convent, persuaded some bishops to annul his marriage to her, and wed the daughter of the Duke of Bohemia, Agnes of Meran, who brought no dowry, but instant reassurance as to the state of his manhood. "Yes, a mere woman! Philip is so besotted with Agnes, his unlawful queen, that he swears he would rather lose half his domains than part with her! He will lose all of them, if he persists!

The Lord Pope is adamant, Philip must send Agnes away and take back Ingeborg, his lawful consort, before the interdict can be lifted. Philip may well moan and groan and envy Saladin who, as he says, had no Pope over him; but his stubbornness has alienated not only the Church but the very people he cares most about, the burghers of Paris."

"Why should he care more about burghers than about his noble lieges?"

"Why indeed! He had six of those upstart merchants on the Council of Regency when he left for the Holy Land! A dangerous concession to low-born vermin!"

The old prideful fire burns bright in my lord's eyes and his lips curls disdainfully.

"Philip inherited little land from his father, King Louis, and even though he has proved himself astute enough to enlarge his domains, he feels most secure in Paris, which has always been his favorite place of residence. He has lavished care and gold on that city, surrounded it with a stout wall, paved many of its streets in stone because he found their stench offensive and built himself a castle outside the walls in case his good burghers ever become unruly."

Eudes' derision turns into outright laughter - a rare occurrence that lends a strange gentleness to his craggy face. "I recall my lord Lionheart's words at the siege of Acre. Upon learning Philip was abandoning the siege before the town had fallen, and returning to France because of sickness, Richard said 'Let him go, he cannot survive away from Paris'" "But my Lord, you cannot hold King Philip's return to France against him! He was beset by sickness and has been ailing ever since he came back from the Holy Land!"

My parents had taught me to admire and respect King Philip as a man who had the good of the kingdom at heart and never took his responsibilities lightly. I had only seen him once, when I was seven and my father was departing with him for the Holy Land; he had looked down from his horse and smiled at me, leaving me the memory of a bright-eyed young man with sparse red hair and plain raiment's.

In spite of Mother Clara's disapproval of his uxorious habits, the remembrance of King Philip remains dear to me, and his unusual - nay, unheard-of attachment for his present queen does not tarnish his image in my mind; perhaps Countess Marie of Champagne was wrong after all, and love can indeed flower between husband and wife....

"He was brave enough in battle..." Eudes concedes with a frown. "But never sought to perform feats of valor to match bold King Richard's." Eudes falls silent, turning his attention to memories of those glorious days with such a rapt expression that I feel the need to spoil his sycophantic recollections of that reckless sodomite, Richard the Lionheart. "But my Lord Eudes," I ask innocently, "Is not King Richard a thousand times more deserving of the Lord Pope's wrath than poor King Philip? Is it not true that Richard was known to indulge in a repulsive vice whose name would soil my soul were I to say it, whereas King Philip merely shows great devotion to his lady queen?"

Eudes' mouth falls open. He turns his chain mailed head to stare at me as if I had grown horns and a tail. "How dare you! You... Do not let your tongue run away with you thus, Maiden!" Swallowing his hasty words, he bridles his mounting anger as firmly as he reins in his horse, and, breathing heavily, adds in quieter tones.

"Lady Alix, if you wish to please me as your lord, you will refrain from such sacrilegious talk! You are young and foolish, and appear to have profited little by Mother Clara's instructions. Do not ever presume to censure the Lord Pope! If he has seen fit to excommunicate King Philip and place his kingdom under an interdict, know then that it is God's will!"

His words fail to persuade. In fact, they bring to mind Mother Clara's reply to the inane, ignorant and haughty young prelate who once visited the Priory and tried to lord it over us. With the sweetest of her heavenly smile, she had looked him in the eye and said, "Know, my lord bishop, that we were not born submissive to our inferiors." The foolish bishop had departed on the hour.

I ask God's forgiveness for entertaining such sinful thoughts about the Lord Pope, and turn to Eudes with a contrite smile.

But, spurring his horse, my lord and husband chooses to deprive me of his company, and disappears in a cloud of dust toward the head of our column. Leaving me in the care of my four young squires who had fallen back, respectful of our privacy, and gladly surround me again with their smiles.

The misty blue sky of this windless October day is gentle to the eye, and the slow pace of my docile mare favor's dreaming and reveries. The sights and smells of this mellow earth caress my senses and I breathe its bracing air with relish as elation fills my heart at the thought of Paris, now so near, and the royal court. I am curious to see King Philip again, but my heart goes out to his hapless queen, for I fear his love for her - great as it may be - will not stand for long in the way of his kingly zeal. Queen Agnes comes from Bavaria. And so does fair Walther von Altdorf.

* * *

I opened my eyes and for a moment failed to recognize the strange woman leaning over me.

As I gathered my wits about me, Daphne settled back in her chair with a sigh and said, "Ah, you are back in the present... And you can't accuse me of waking you up this time! What brought you back, anyway?"

"I don't know. I was thinking of the royal court and meeting the king and queen... And somehow it was all so incongruous that it woke me up."

"What do you mean by incongruous?"

"Well... Don't you think that actually meeting Philip Augustus who reigned 800 years ago is preposterous? All the people I have encountered so far have been unknown to me, except my daughter Christine, of course, who was little Eloise; but Philip! King Philip Augustus! He was a great king; we learned about him in school, you know, and he has always fascinated me. Now I know why. Do you realize I am about to meet him in person! I find that pretty incredible." I sit up, recall one of Eudes disparaging comments about my king and start laughing quietly.

Daphne's eyebrows withdraw behind her flaming red bangs. "What's so funny?"

"He wasn't really called Augustus by anyone but his own chaplain; but he liked the title so much, he wanted everyone else to use it too. His enemies didn't, of course. And he had quite a few."

"He sounds rather insecure to me." Daphne remarked with a slight moue.

"Oh, but don't you see? He had every reason to be, what with his small kingdom of France caught between the Anglo-Normans and the Teutons of the Holy Roman Empire, he had no choice but to use every means in his power - fair or foul - to preserve his domains! Don't you understand?"

"I do. I do." Daphne raised a placating hand. "No need to get offended. I also understand Alix is a staunch supporter of her monarch, which is rather surprising in view of the fact that she does not appear to take kindly to his kind of machismo."

"Wrong. Alix's attitude reflects the views of women in her days. Vastly different from ours. We have all been fed romantic drivel about love and men. Medieval women were realists; they knew men for the polygamous bastards they have always been, and were not averse to enjoying this particular male proclivity whenever the occasion presented itself.

They might pay lip service to the rules of courtly love but they were not fooled, and made the most of reality. And without any whining, either, about their rights and privileges; what they wanted, they took, using their own devices, whether men liked it or not!"

"You mean women were stronger than now?" "I think everybody was stronger because life was so much harsher. Women relied more on their own strength. They were individuals, not members of a bloody downtrodden minority!" How could I sound so nostalgic about a time when pertinence and leprosy were rampant, maiming and torture commonplace, warring and massacres wholesale? But perhaps the sum total of per capita suffering may be even greater in our own century.

"Let's have a little break, Sandra; then we can try to take you back. Unless you are tired and would rather call it a day."

"No. I do want to go back. After all, we only have one more session and I still don't know if I can succeed on my own. I have yet to try...."

* * *

Upon reaching the vicinity of the Abbey of Saint-Germain-des-Prés on a fine morning, we find ourselves in the midst of a tumultuous and noisy throng of gawking students, drunken clerics and tattered lollards, all jabbering in Latin. They slow our progress almost to a halt and give off a most offensive smell that would surely make me gag, held I not a little vial of scent under my nose.

Still, being thus surrounded and loudly praised by such a bold crowd of young men is far from unpleasing. My dutiful squires keep them at a safe distance and I feign not to comprehend their bawdy Latin verses, avoid their brazen eyes and modestly wrap my green velvet cloak over my tightly-laced silk bliaud. I confess I am not unduly sorry thus to ascertain that my present attire is becoming in the eyes of men. Even without the future enhancement of an emerald clasp.

Riding through the multitude of scholars along the massive arches of the Abbey, I marvel at such a gathering of men intent on the pursuit of knowledge; but I envy them not, for men are easily distracted from their studies by many nefarious pursuits, whereas women show far greater singleness of purpose and steadfastness in learning.

Mother Clara once told us there was no scholar who did not study or teach in Paris and that no scholar ever felt a foreigner there. She professes great admiration for that departed master, Pierre Abélard. To my mind, the man was too infatuated with himself and not undeserving of the sad loss of his manhood for having sacrificed the love of good Heloise to his overweening ambition. I suppose one could learn many things from attending one of these famous schools where revered masters impart knowledge through Trivium and Quadrivium, but I am content to learn from books. Whenever I can find some. Sir Eudes has yet to hear how much I value book learning.

My Lord is eager to reach the city and urges us on through these fields of learning without giving any heed to the pleasant scenery. T's pity, for the splendid monasteries of Saint Víctor and Saint-Germains-des-Prés, and Sainte-Geneviève which is built on a hill each one of them a prestigious school - stand amid verdant fields dotted with orchards and make a full fair sight to behold.

Eudes let us not tarry in this Latin Quarter, as some call it, and we soon reach the banks of a narrow arm of the River Seine whence Paris can be seen in all the magnificence of its new walls and multitudinous houses.

Espying this wondrous sight, I rein in my horse and bid him remain still while I admire the towering white stone ramparts embracing myriads of tall abodes and rich churches. In the distance, on the Island of the City, rise the towers of Bishop Sully's new cathedral, which will surely extend Our Lady's protection over the whole town.

Paris is indeed a fair and rich city, said to be full of many prosperous Gilds of merchants who have grown rich selling cloth of wool and silk, spicery from faraway lands and all manner of wares; as well as goldsmiths and silversmiths most skilled in their art.

My lord and husband join me before we cross the wooden bridge to the south gate, the closest to the St. Augustin quarter where we are to reside. Taking umbrage of my overt admiration for this fair city, he snorts, "Bah, this town is but a miserable burg, in no way to be compared with the splendors of Constantinople! Constantinople is the most magnificent city in the whole world! Shame it is that it remains in the hands of wily Greek heretics!"

He has already described to me the glories of the Byzantine city and made me wish to see them with my own eyes; but, for the nonce, Paris will suffice.

We reach a wooden bridge which spans this arm of the river Seine. Under its arches pass a great number of barges of all kinds, laden with mounds of fishes, whole carcasses of beef and many other victuals. Unheeding of the throng of horsemen, clerics and burghers on foot who attempt to cross the bridge from either end, the knights of our retinue boldly make their way across the wooden planks, and roughly push everyone aside. Including four serfs who stand in our way as they drag an enormous barrel on a trolley; I fear the barrel will roll off their cart and crush the unfortunates' feet, but my lord's orders are to make haste, and they must be obeyed. Through the rounded south gate flanked by white stone towers, we enter the city proper. The awe it inspired from afar soon fades into distaste at the foul odor of its streets. Once inside its walls, the whole town seems but a warren of narrow lanes between inordinately high abodes.

As we ride along one of the wider streets bordered by goodly houses, I peer into these grim alleys and wonder how the people who scurry along them can bear to live thus, like ants in a hill. Far from being paved the streets of Paris are so awash in slime and nightsoil that I fear to be spattered by horses' hooves and bid my squires slow their pace. The stench is indeed worse than the smell of unwashed scholars.

At last, we come to a wide square, paved with grey stones, around which a tempting array of shops promise numerous delights to well moneyed patrons. Drapers and mercers, booksellers and goldsmiths vie with one another to attract the elegant ladies who stroll about, followed by their retinue of maids and liveried men-at-arms.

Would I be free to join them, but today my lord's wishes take precedence over mine? Bidding me to dismount in front a half-timbered house of goodly proportions, Eudes informs me that it belongs to the Count of Flanders; we are to stay there as his guests in his absence. He gives orders to the Count's servants to show me to my bedchamber on the upper floor and bows most courteously.

In the large room is a wide bed overhung with a tapestry canopy and red velvet drapes, as well as a high-back chair and several carved chests. A pleasant view of the square is to be had through a glazed window, the like of which I have never seen before for we have no such luxury at Comarque.

I marvel as I touch the panes of clear glass, gingerly lest they should break, but they appear to be solid enough even though one can see through them most amazingly as if they were not there at all. Indeed, there are

many wonders in this world! I am full pleased to be staying here and will prevail upon Eudes to stay longer than the five days he intends to remain in Paris.

But Eudes hardly gives me time to call my maids before sending word we are to go forthwith to the palace.

The Count's servants are well-taught and soon a dozen of them bring in the largest wooden tub I have ever seen. While my maids go looking for Eudes' Master of the Wardrobe to bring back fit attire for the royal occasion, the servants come in a procession to fill it with enough warm water to bathe a castleful, pouring into it as well a full pitcher of some spirit redolent of Jasmin.

Even the fragrant warm waters of the bath fail to soothe my agitation; obscure yearnings make my flesh burn while thoughts of fair Walther fill my mind, until, snatching the drying cloth from my maids' hands, I emerge

from the tub and start rubbing my feverish body till it hurts.

The two girls help me don my new embroidered white chemise with long ruched undersleeves, and over it, a softly pleated overdress of the most exquisite aquamarine shade, cinched at the waist by a double gold belt and trimmed at the hem with a wide band of gold embroidery. My curls are tamed into long plaits under a white veil held by a circlet of the same work.

Elaine, a sweet girl of 14, hardly more than a child, holds her hands together as she looks at me, and exclaims repeatedly, "Oh, my lady! Oh, my lady!" Till she shames me out of my delighted complacency.

"These clothes are indeed beautiful, Elaine,

but neither they nor their wearer are deserving of such admiration! I thank you both for your help, now go and inform my lord Eudes that I am ready to meet our king."

* * *

Eudes rides by the side of the litter he has thoughtfully provided for me. It is considerate of him, for the days of travelling on horseback have left me sorely tender in some places, and the king's palace is a fair way from our abode in Saint-Augustin.

The castle King Philip has built for himself on the right bank of the River Seine, stands outside the walls that gird the city. To reach it we have to cross two more bridges and the Island of the City where the cathedral towers rise. I would gladly stroll there for its streets - duly paved to spare the king's sensitive nose - are bordered with fair palaces, many of them surrounded by walled gardens, where, through open gates, one catches sight of wondrous climbing roses and shady arbors. At last, we find ourselves at the main gate of the resplendent royal castle. Its numerous buildings of pale stone - many of them yet unfinished - surround a massive round keep where the treasury of the realm is kept. The whole palace still exudes the smell of freshly hewn stone and shines like a fairy castle under the pale northern sunshine.

Cleanly dressed squires lead us along courtyards so clean and well swept I hardly have to lift my gown. We pass through vast richly decorated rooms thronged with courtiers and visitors. My lord's step has regained its assurance; he strides boldly by my side in his beautiful green velvet robes trimmed with precious grey fur.

I try to keep my eyes trained on the back of our fare young guide, but cannot resist glancing sideways at the courtiers who line our passage; haughty barons puffed up with the king's favor, scowling battle-scarred knights in thread-bare cloaks, high ladies in fur-trimmed sleeves and hearty-living clerics in sumptuous raiment murmur among themselves as their eyes follow us along the way. The air is redolent of strange spicy scents, as if these richly attired men and women had bathed in them.

The drone of their voices grows fainter as we approach the throne room. I feel hunger gnawing at my inside, for we have not eaten since we broke fast at dawn. Or perhaps it is trepidation that makes me feel faint. Will I bring honor to my lord and to the memory of my brave father by my demeanor, words and deeds?

We enter the vast room. At the far end of it, on a raised dais, sits a balding man in dull brownish robes, who leans forward in his carved chair the better to peer at us. The king. Even though he is known for his parsimony and his abhorrence of wasteful display the drabness of his attire comes as a surprise amid the sumptuary excesses of his court. How tired he looks! I lose my fear and boldly return his stare. Then I look around at the few men who surround him, and gasp.

For, on the king's left, amid some Hospitallers garbed in their black tunics crossed with red, stands Walther von Altdorf, his azure eyes blazing, deep in conversation with...Black Foulk. They watch our approach with murmured comments, nods, and sniggers. I try to close my eyes, but their shared laughter still rings in my ears as we reach the throne. Faintness overcomes me.

CHAPTER 13

The king is looking at me.

My lord and husband holds my arm in a tight grip; his new-found gentleness all but forgotten. Just as well, for I stumble over the hem of my gown and would have fallen onto the king's lap had Eudes not pulled me up sharply.

King Philip opens his mouth in surprise, revealing some gaps among his white teeth. Still, an impish light flicker in his pale eyes and illuminates his sad face as he pretends to ward me off playfully with extended hands. "Why, Sir Eudes, I will not have your fair lady kneel before me! I should be the one paying homage to such beauty!" I can hear Eudes exhale as he lets go of my arm. The courtier's sycophantic laughter greets the king's words. Eudes squirms and I strain my ears to catch the sound of Walther's voice. Rising from his throne, King Philip reaches out for my hands and bows most graciously, his eyes firmly on mine. He is not very tall but strong-limbed, and he stands very straight, secure in his quiet strength. What a fair knight he must have been before his red hair deserted his brow and that strange ailment from Palestine made his flesh soft and sallow. Now great weariness suffuses his handsome features. Only his eyes remain fully alive, lighting up his face with intelligence.

King Philip is a charmer women must find hard to resist even now; yet he remains loyal to his beloved Agnes in spite of the Lord Pope's vindictiveness. My heart goes out to him. Queen Agnes is nowhere to be seen. Trouvères call her "La Fleur des Dames" -the Flower of Ladies. Was she the one who brought Walther von Altdorf to court? Releasing my hands, the king sits down again with a faint smile. "Do not let my jest embarrass you, Lady Alix. This court is honored by your presence." I do not reply for Eudes has admonished me in the strongest terms to bridle my tongue at court.

With a wave of his hand, King Philip vaguely motions me toward a group of women standing some way to the right of the throne. "Our ladies are most eager to bid you welcome, do join them while I confer with your lord."

With a mere blink of his small eyes, Eudes bids me obey. I curtsy to Philip and move aside with measured steps and churning thoughts to join the group of court ladies. There are seven or eight of them and they interrupt their assessment of my apparel to greet me with various degrees of effusiveness. Their cheeks are rouged like strumpets'.

Being in the presence of the king himself in his own throne room does little to hush their chatter and they soon enclose me in a wall of babble. But then, no one in this vast blue and gold great hall appears to be cowed by the royal presence; men and women carry on with their private conversation while Philip, his reddish eyebrows knitted in a frown, leans forward in his massive chair and listens to Eudes' prepared address.

Safe amid the women, I risk a glance across the room toward the black-garbed Hospitallers. Black Foulk is no longer among them. Walther still is, and he is looking straight at me. The smile on his lips sets my cheeks afire and turns my blood to ice.

Without leaving me time to gather my wits, the rogue crosses the room with bold steps and bows to the group of court ladies. They part ranks and admit him in their midst with little cries of delight, leaving me thus defenseless against a warrior who - if one is to judge by the ladies' miens - has already carried off more than one Virtue among them. I briefly recall Mother Clara's veiled reference to Philip's court as a place much given over to gluttony and venery.

Sir Walther is standing in front of me, more handsome even than in my most vivid dreams; his fair hair a halo of gold around the bronze of his strong face. The ladies look on with parted lips and misted eyes. Some of them are young and fair, with boldness to match his own; yet, I am the one he came to greet... My mouth is so dry I cannot swallow. God forbid he should know how I feel! Bending down slightly - the better to will me to meet his eyes again - he exclaims, barely loud enough for his admirers to hear, "My Lady Alix has kept her promise!"

Curiosity gets the better of me, I look up and meet the full onslaught of his look without flinching. "Promise? Which promise would that be, my lord? I never...."

"When I first saw you at Comarque castle, my lady," He murmurs, "You gave promise of great beauty and you have kept that promise!" His smooth hand rests on my arm for a second and bending his head until his fresh breath caresses my cheek, he whispers in the language of the troubadours - not without a faint German accent, "Na Alix al bel cors avenens*"("*Lady Alix of the beautiful body.") Promises remain empty of meaning until they are shared. And so, it goes for Beauty. Remember that it is meant to be transmuted into the delights of love... And only by those who know how to sing its praises."

Stricken with dumbness, I glower at him, for lack of a fitting rebuke to his impudence; but he straightens up with a last admiring glance and turns on his heels as if there was no need to say more.

Bowing to the youngest of the court ladies - a pale maiden with flaxen hair whose blue velvet bodice hangs flat on her meagre chest he gives her his full attention and keeps her enthralled in it. When he draws her back a few paces away from the group, her tense court smile dissolves forthwith into overt bliss.

They stand under a tall window against the blue and gold wall, and she looks up at him with such adoring eyes I feel truly sorry for her as I curse her. Not for the first time, my guardian angel whispers in my ear that worshipping this man will bring me nothing but grief. But love is deaf as well as blind.... The other women surround me again with curious eyes and probing tongues; how well do I know Sir Walther von Altdorf? I elude most of their questions but listen eagerly to their comments while I keep my eyes on him and try to still my wildly beating heart.

It seems Fair Walther is known as much for inflicting the Deadly Joy and the Happy Pain as for composing and singing melodious songs about them. For, contrary to most Trouvères or Minnesingers he does sing his own verses. Not a small part of his seductiveness, as I can vouch from memory.

"Sir Walther is too brazen for his own good." Whispers a plump woman with black hair on her upper lip.

"Courting Douce d'Entrevènes is more than foolhardy; she is affianced to Romée de Villeneuve, an overbearing man known for his vile temper and who can work himself into a rage if a man so much as looks at his bride-to-be! Romée knows nothing of courtly love and will not brook such unseemly familiarity. Besides, Douce is but a maiden; Sir Walther could at least wait until she is wed. He may live to regret his temerity...." It is hard to tell if the woman is fretting over Walther's fate at the hands of the jealous lord or welcomes the thought of such comeuppance.

"She seems very young," I venture, "To hold her own in a joust of wits with such a seasoned knight...."

The woman, whose name is Iselda, shrugs plump shoulders encased in purple silk. "Douce is not witless by any means, just besotted with Sir Walther. She will not give ear to reason." Iselda smiles with rueful indulgence. "She will not see him for what he is, a man, and he will break her heart for not living up to her illusions."

Her words remind me of my dying mother. I can still see her eyes burning with the last flares of life in her gaunt face. Holding on to the sheet as if to life itself, she had whispered in my ear, "Always accept life as it is, Alix, and never let your illusions spoil it for you."

I take a strong liking to Iselda.

She remains by my side, seemingly pleased with my company. I listen with one ear as she describes life at court where the Papal Interdict has not put an end to amorous pursuits. As for her, she declares herself a mere observer of these courtly intrigues.

"Ah the game of Love!" She sighs. "It is played for too high a stake! Our poor Queen is dying of it! T'would be better for her had she not felt for the king the kind of love minstrels sing about. I, for one, am content to serve my dear lord and husband and enjoy his esteem rather than seek abroad some ungodly passion!

The said lord must esteem her lot; she has, so she tells me, already borne him five children. Well, I shall be spared this...marital bliss yet a while. But the thought of little Robert and wee Eloise brings warmth to my heart.

Rash Sir Walther is still blithely courting the piteous maiden when my own husband comes over to reclaim me from the ladies. Eudes grants them each in turn a perfunctory bow and drags me away with a scowl. Courtiers are drifting out of the hall to allow squires to set up trestles for the king's board.

Something is troubling Eudes for he looks sorely vexed, and I dare not ask if we have been invited to stay and partake of the midday meal. As he seems in too great a hurry to be out of the throne room, I walk as slowly as I can to give Sir Walther a chance to notice our departure and perhaps rush forward to delay it. But the knave does not turn his head even though I am almost sure he has seen us depart. What is there to say?

Whoever is foolish enough to sigh for his kind cannot hope thereby to change the nature of the man. I cannot say, like Guiguemar in one of my favorite poems, "I die for your love; my heart is in agony from it." For it is the privilege of a knight thus to declare his passion. Women must wait. And I hate waiting.

Eudes seeks a stone bench for me to sit, and stands by my side aloof from the other courtiers. Some of them throw us covert glances and nod as they exchange cryptic remarks. Without parting his teeth, Eudes mumbles something about the limits of his forbearance.

"Pray speak louder, my lord, for I cannot hear you."

He sits down brusquely and hisses his grievance in tones made hoarse by anger. "Black Foulk de Sardac will be a guest at the banquet! A curse upon him! Through deceit and bribery, the wretch has made many allies at court and has been engaged in weaving malevolent tales about me. Am I then to share salt with him at the king's board? What is one to do? Philip himself bade me stay. As well he should!"

"As King Philip's honored guest, you will surely be seated near the head of the table, my lord," I point out with a smile. "While your former seneschal can only be assigned a place at the lower end of the board, with menial knights and sundry squires. I would not forsake the chance to hold the king's ear, while his mood be mellowed with food and wine, because of Black Foulk's presence.

Whatever favor he may enjoy now, he will lose forthwith, for his is a felon's heart and sooner or later he is bound to obey his true nature and harm his new-found friends as he...."

My words die on my lips. Strutting into the courtyard, not ten paces from us, Black Foulk stops suddenly in his tracks and fixes his dark gaze upon me. His countenance a puzzling blend of hostility and pleading.

* * *

Night is falling as we leave the great hall; my lord sated with honor's, food and wine, I uncommonly hungry for not having swallowed a single bite of food. While Eudes' mood has mellowed considerably, I find myself in a state of great confusion. In part from having partaken too freely of the sweet golden wine squires kept pouring in my cup, but mostly from the nearness of my beloved who sat but two places away on my right, between Lady Iselda and a safe dowager of sour mien.

What has come over me?

Banquets had always brought me much enjoyment. Not only the wonderful aromas of the plentiful fare but the glee, the laughter and sallies of the guests wearing their finery; the music and songs of minstrels... And this feast was by far the most sumptuous I had ever attended.

Never had I seen such a host of young squires bringing in a profusion of elaborate courses and changing the white cloths on the tables between each of them. Never so many richly attired lords and ladies sharing bread in such a magnificent hall, with much laughter and clever repartees. On account of the Interdict, no churchman was present which may explain the lack of restraint. Even the servant who spilled wine on a lady's lap was sent away with cheers and no more punishment than a box on his ear. As for the king himself, even though his mien was sober, he would smile faintly from time to time as some naughty retort reached his ears.

At the start of the banquet, as squires carried around the hall a particularly clever Subtlety a dressed peacock in a field of flowers made of colored almond paste - its progress around the table was followed by all the guests who craned their necks for a better view. All but Sir Walther.

As I happened to glance in his direction, I caught his eyes on my face and had to lower mine forthwith, such was the audacity of his gaze. Throughout the banquet, though I dared not look at him again, I felt his eyes upon me.

I became so tongue-tied and bereft of any wit that the king's cousin with whom I was sharing a plate, as custom demands, must have found me dull company indeed. But then again, he was so busy wolfing down my share of the delicacies that he hardly found time to address me. To talk of nothing but horses and swords.

At last, the unending succession of redolent dishes came to an end. Spatchcocked birds, dressed pikes in galantines, sides of deer. I would have relished them all in other times, but could not bring myself to taste the pieces on the plate, which pleased the king's cousin no end as he has quite a strong appetite.

Though melodious music was heard throughout the banquet from a group of minstrels hidden in a gallery, the king had decreed there would be no dancing while his ailing queen kept to her chamber.

Having talked much and eaten little King Philip rose from his chair as soon as the sweetmeats were brought in, and bidding his guests remain yet a while to enjoy his hospitality, departed with his suite; but the courtiers knew better and all hastened to leave the table. Just when a dish of pickled figs was being presented that might have coaxed me out of my self-inflicted fast.

As Eudes tarried in conversation with a fat lord in a fur-trimmed cloak, Sir Walther appeared suddenly by my side. I stood very still and tried to keep my eyes on my husband, noticing for the first time the coarse grain of his skin on the nape of his neck. Walther's silence took me by surprise; whereas I had expected another impertinent remark, he contented himself with remaining thus close to me without uttering a word.

After a while, I could stand it no longer and glanced up at his face. It was lit by the fire in his eyes; such an ungodly fire that my cheeks burnt from the shame of it.

"Lady Alix, won't you show some pity" he said, half in jest it seemed and half in earnest. "On a poor knight smitten by your beauty? For whither can I flee Now that I have seen thee?"

Lady Iselda was standing under the gallery, eating candied almonds and observing the departing courtiers with her big round eyes. I blindly rushed to her side through the crowd of courtiers, leaving my lusty minnesinger laughing most indecorously.

* * *

That night, alone in my cold wide bed, I regretted my silly flight and berated myself for my lack of wits. Why, I should have kept my composure and racked my memory for an apt reply to his wanton verses. What was the point of memorizing so many of Chretien de Troyes' and Marie de France's romances if I remained so shamefully tongue-tied? Resolved to keep a cooler head next time I found myself face to face with the handsome rogue, I tried to fall asleep but slept hardly at all, torn between excitement, apprehension and hope that Sir Eudes - who declared himself satisfied with the king's welcome might wish to prolong our stay in Paris.

* * *

"Well, well." Daphne chuckles in a most annoying way. "Your minstrel doesn't believe in long courtships!"

"How many times do I have to tell you he is not a minstrel! Minstrels are just lowly performers of the poets' songs. Walther is a Minnesinger, or a Trouvères if you prefer, as well as a noble knight related to the German Emperor!"

"And a womanizer to boot. Don't the other courtiers resent his predatory ways with their women?

"Oh, I don't know." I hesitated, searching

Alix's memory for the court lady's comments.

"I think men make allowances for fearless warriors. Walther has proved himself and his bravery is well known." As I said this, I recalled his face, conscious that a long thin scar I had not noticed in Comarque now tautened his left cheek. "Some husbands are really incredibly tolerant and even derive pride from the praises their wives receive from famous trouvères. It's very hard to explain... Their way of thinking is so different from ours."

My head a swim with conflicting notions of time and space, I found it harder and harder after every session to tear myself away from the past and get back fully to the present. I was beginning to feel totally swallowed by Alix; it was now a struggle to abandon her persona and her passion for Sir Walther which was so much more potent than my obsession with Herr Doktor Meissen, his modern incarnation.

I now came out of my trances oblivious of my own life, eager to go back to the past and to re-live the exhilaration of Alix's passion. Why had I become so sedate in this present life that losing Michael, and even Franco, had left me if not indifferent at least far too apathetic? Had I lost the capacity to suffer as well as enjoy? How could I have changed that much from one life to the next? How tepid were my emotions now compared to the burning flames that consumed me then! Why had I made peace and security my goals in this life? Had my existence then been so rife with turmoil and anguish I now wished for nothing better than this kind of dull status quo?

Some of the emotions that racked me must have shown on my face; Daphne leaned over and placed a soothing hand on my arm.

"I know it's our last session for quite a while," she said softly. "But you look so upset I think we should call it a day. You never know, you might be able to induce a trance on your own and carry on with your probing by spontaneous regression and self-induced trance. So, what do you say? Shall we go out and have dinner in a local restaurant? Drink to the good old days of the early XIII th Century?"

Still caught in my mystery, I didn't reply immediately.

With a wry smile, Daphne rose from her chair and took a few steps across the Aubusson rug, her face suddenly drawn in pain. It occurred to me that she must be suffering from some kind of ailment, arthritis perhaps, and I suddenly felt a rush of concern for her. "Look, Daphne, if it's all right with you, I would like to try to get back just once more today... Do you understand? I really must know what happened between these two before I approach Kurt Meissen. I believe something is going to develop soon." Still pacing back and forth, she nodded and soon resumed her seat with a sigh.

"Very well. Let's go back, then, but forward in time."

* * *

We are still in Paris, but only till tomorrow. It is morning and once again Eudes has risen before dawn and departed on one more mysterious errand to the palace or elsewhere, leaving me alone - and free - to dispose of the hours till the mid-day meal as I see fit.

Eudes has just informed me yesterday that he is contemplating taking up the cross again. In his quest for God's forgiveness - whereof he has great need - he is prepared to join the gathering host of knights already assembled around the young Count of Champagne and the Count of Blois.

In order to find out more about the holy enterprise, Eudes plans to attend a gathering at Compiègne. I will therefore be sent back to Comarque on my own, with a strong escort, while he tarries with the crusaders and makes the appropriate arrangements to join them. This proposed parting leaves me less distraught than my lord perhaps expected. My first concern is to ask about his children. Will he allow them back in Comarque or must we stay apart much longer?

"I shall send word to Hautefort that they are to return to Comarque under proper escort, if that is your wish, Alix." He allows most grudgingly.

"I shall not tarry in Compiègne beyond a month and will return to Comarque myself in time for us to get ready for the long journey." "For us, my lord? Am I then to accompany you?"

"Most certainly. And so will Robert and Eloise. Many barons' families will follow the host. It is most fitting that you should share in the blessings that will be bestowed on us by the grace of Our Lord Jesus Christ."

There might be other advantages to undertaking the journey....

* * *

A pale sun is trying to shine through the grey Paris sky. I tarry in my bed, enjoying the faint lavender smell of the clean sheets and embroidered pillows and relishing the thought of my morning freedom. Shall I purchase that red cloth from Tyre that the wily merchant set aside for me yesterday? Would such bright hue flatter my complexion?

Eudes has been most generous and handed me a bougette heavy with gold coins to spend on my attire. Perhaps I should visit other cloth merchants before deciding. Memories of Lady Adela on her last day suddenly intrude on my thoughts, clouding my pleasure, and bring me back to the musty shop where she looked through bolts of cloth on that fateful morning, unaware she would never live to wear any garment made from them.

Life is cruel. And short. All the more reason to relish what it offers us. Whatever the cost. Before I even have time to call for my maids, young Elaine knocks on the low door and rushes into the room to hand me a roll of parchment tied with a gold cord.

"T'is for you, my lady, a groom left it with the porter and said to deliver it to you most promptly."

I thank her, untie the cord and unroll the small sheet. Its musky fragrance seems somehow familiar, though I cannot identify it. As Elaine gives no sign of leaving and hovers by the bed, curiosity written all over her round face, I scold her and tell her to be gone.

Is it too late to reveal the longing?

I kept hidden from you when we were near? Am I to suffer then for remaining?

Silently in your thrall for all these years?

If I am never to be forgiven And forever deprived of your sweet beauty Then all I wish is to die unshriven For Heaven is no match for your pity.

In vain do I scan every part of the parchment for a name. The poem is unsigned. Not only do I know who sent it but I do not intend to leave it unanswered. I have found out where the rogue is staying. I call Elaine and tell her to bring my writing case.

CHAPTER 14

Driving my daughter's car through the back roads of Provence and Périgord helped to restore my sense of balance. It was a part of south-western France I didn't know and discovered with much pleasure. The small Renault handled well and the scenery was a delight of verdant hills dotted with red poppies and picturesque villages huddled around stone spires or towering castles.

I have always liked driving; I find it akin to meditation. Besides giving one a feeling of alertness and control, the road empties one's mind of thoughts and fills it with impressions. I had been in France for a week - living in the present - and things were beginning to look more normal.

My daughter Christine had skipped a lecture on international tax laws to come and pick me up at nice airport. She was waiting in the front row of a crowd when I emerged from passport control. As soon as she caught sight of me, she sneaked under the restraining fence and rushed to hug and kiss me. We held on to each other in mute rejoicing.

She is a tall girl, and very affectionate. I thought she was looking great; but I probably wasn't. Holding my shoulders at arm length, she gave my face a long hard look.

"Mum! What's wrong with you? You look so... so...tired! Are you sick or something?"

"No. No. Don't worry. A little jet-lagged perhaps; it's always worse flying east. I'll be all right. I have had a lot on my mind lately." As I said this, I felt tears filling my eyes; silent tears that ran down my cheeks and that I couldn't hold back. I felt really silly. "What is it?" Christine was staring at me, thoroughly upset. "Mum, tell me! Is it...Franco? Do you miss him that much?" She put a protective arm around my shoulders "Absolutely not." I dismissed poor Franco with a laugh, wiping my wet face with a crumpled, but real, hankie; I hate tissues. "Look, we can't talk here. Let me get my bag. Wait for me at the custom exit and I'll tell you all about it in the car. I promise." Taking her arm, I led her back to the fence where law- abiding welcomers were still waiting patiently for my fellow passengers to walk by.

* * *

During the long sleepless hours of the flight from Montreal to Nice, I had decided to tell Christine the whole crazy story. I trusted her judgement, and after all she was in it too as little Eloise.

Strangely enough, it was the crowded environment of the plane - the plight of travelers on a budget - that brought back a sense of normalcy and allowed me to put things in better perspective. Though I felt quietly upbeat I still found it hard to make sense of my last visit to Daphne.

* * *

On the day of my departure, just as I had finished packing everything including my laptop, Daphne called. She sounded a little blurry, and I wondered for the first time if she was not perhaps a secret drinker. At 8 a.m.? She began to plead with me to come back to her house "just for an hour or so," arguing there was lots of time for me to catch the limousine to the airport, wasn't there?

While I was still eager to find out what had happened in the past, I felt that Alix, my Alter Ego had been getting far too invasive lately;

to the point where I was losing a grip on myself. I badly needed to step back even for a short while before meeting Herr Meissen. I told Daphne as much, but she insisted rather forcefully, implying it was the least I could do, until I relented and took a bus to her house.

When she opened her door, I froze.

She looked so startlingly unlike her usual persona that I just stood there speechless for a few seconds until she told me to come in. Instead of her shapeless robes, she wore a well-cut and rather severe grey tweed pant suit that made her look pounds thinner. Her face was scrubbed of all make up and her hair severely pulled back.

"Why, Daphne!" I could not refrain from exclaiming. "You look...so...elegant! Are you going somewhere?"

She grinned without answering and ushered me into the black and white entrance hall. She was not wearing the strong incense-like scent that had become associated with her in my mind.

At first, she would not tell me why she wanted us to have another session. But I prodded her so much that she finally relented. "It would seem I have become much too involved in your story for my own good, Alix... I mean Sandra." She paused with a wry smile.

"I had a dream last night. A very vivid one. I already knew I was not without some psychic abilities, which I do not like to delve into for reasons of my own, but this was very strong. And very strange indeed. I found myself in your world, everything was exactly as you describe it to me.

It was as if I was both witness and participant to the scenes. It wasn't an ordinary dream, either. I have never experienced anything like it. Ever." Her usual composure seemed to have deserted her.

"I see. Welcome to the club!" My awkward laughter failed to hide my uneasiness. I did not like what she was telling me for two reasons. First, she seemed shaken by her experience. Weakened by it. For me, it was a letdown; I now realized how much I had been relying on her strength and unshakeable sanity throughout the weird experience. Also, we now had to face the possibility that this phenomenon was contagious...

Was Daphne going to be engulfed by it too? Absurd. But also, quite funny.

"So. Did you like what you saw, Daphne?" I teased. "Was I in your dream, or were you in mine?"

"Well... both, I suppose. You were there. And so was...Black Foulk. Following you everywhere."

"Black Foulk?" I repressed a shiver.

"Following me?"

"He meant you no harm. In fact, there was so much hopeless love in his heart that I woke up in tears."

I - or Alix - dismissed that likelihood with derisive laughter. "Come on, Daphne, Black Foulk is a ruthless knave capable of any vile deed that will serve his ambition!"

"That may well be so...." She was shaking her head. "But you told me yourself that these people thought and behaved differently from us. Perhaps you are misjudging the man. He may have ordered Lady Adela to be drowned from a sense of duty to his lord; after all, Adela had dishonored Eudes by her infidelity."

I could hardly believe my ears. "You are not serious, are you?" I stared at Daphne with open mouth. "You are actually defending the villain? That viper!" I admit I derived some satisfaction from deliberately baiting Daphne. "You are condoning murder!"

"No. I'm not." She appeared to be taking me seriously. "Don't get upset with me... fair and fiery friend!"

156

As she uttered these strange words puzzlement clouded her eyes. She sat down on her dainty bergère as if overcome by a sudden weakness. She sighed and, as if dismissing her dream with a shrug of her shoulders, touched my arm lightly. I waited for her to go on but she remained silent and closed her eyes.

"So?" Somewhat embarrassed, I asked soberly, "Am I supposed to fall in love with Black Foulk now? Is that what you would like me to do? The man is evil. He gives me the creeps and I doubt that Alix ever kindled any passion in his heart, if he has one.

Oh, he would have married her readily enough if Eudes had kept his promise and endowed her accordingly, but love has little to do with this kind of marriage." Daphne was still shaking her head, but she let me conclude.

"Now, to tell you frankly, Daphne, I don't really feel like travelling back in time, today. I need a break from Alix; she is taking over my whole life and I must say it would be nice to be myself - I mean Sandra - for a while." Daphne looked so disappointed that I finally relented. "O.K. If you insist, let's have one more go."

* * *

Reaching the proper trance state proved very difficult at first. Either the changes in Daphne's appearance - and manner, for there was a diffidence in her that had not been there before - interfered with our routine, or I was at long last rebelling against the past's intrusion into my present life.

For over an hour, Daphne tried in vain to put me under. I was getting restless; I like to be at the airport at least two hours before departure and time was running out. I was about to get up from her couch when I suddenly felt myself slipping away once more.

* * *

The brief letter delivered to Sir Walther by Elaine, my maid - not without much blandishment on my part for she greatly fears Sir Eudes' wrath - has remained unanswered.

As I stand among the faithful craning their necks around the square in front of Our Lady's cathedral, I know not if he will do my bidding and present himself to receive a token of my forgiveness. My fingers seek unbidden the small roll of vellum I have read so many times since yesterday.

As Eudes forbids my strolling through Paris streets without a proper escort two of the four squires he has assigned to my protection stand silently twenty paces away. So does fearful Elaine. They likely wonder why I spend so long contemplating the portaled facade of the towering church.

Part of my mind is awed by the magnificence of the cathedral, forty years in the making, by the heavenly beauty of it. I stand fascinated by the intricate lace of its stone work and the sheer height of its white towers. I watch stone-masons hoisting statues above its portals, and listen to echoes of wonderful polyphonic singing from behind its closed doors; but all my senses are focused on Walther. Will he appear?

As I observe the crowd of quarry-men, carpenters and burgers who come and go around the church, I have but one wish: catching sight of his fair countenance.

Not quite true, I also wish my squires would move away. Alas, having experienced Eudes' wrath, they have no wish to provoke it again. They take their duties very much to heart and will not let me out of their sight.

This morning, when I expressed the wish to visit the nearly completed cathedral, one of them the older one of the two, he must be all of eighteen. Like me - voiced his surprise. "But, My Lady, the doors of the cathedral are closed by order of the new bishop. Though he be the king's cousin, Bishop Sully has taken the Lord Pope's side and forbidden entry into his church."

"I still wish to see it. We shall have to be content with admiring the outside of it, then." Many people are doing so. Some even genuflecting, praying and crossing themselves until I feel thoroughly ashamed of my own purpose and close my eyes to beg Our Lady's forgiveness.

As I open them, Sir Walther is making his way in great strides through the throng of workmen pulling cartloads of white stone. I feel a weakness come over me and take a deep breath. Alas the choking stone dust fills my throat and starts me coughing in a most undignified fashion.

Elaine rushes forward and finds no better remedy than pummeling my back with her fists. I dismiss her with a wave of my hand and wipe my teary eyes on the long blue sleeve of my second-best gown. Walther is gazing down at me with a smile that could be considered mischievous.

"Fair Lady, granting me leave thus to express my devotion is a most unexpected honor. Rest assured I shall show myself worthy of your grace and virtue, and serve you faithfully for the rest of my life." He reaches for my hands and bows so low over them I fear he will kiss them. He may or may not be speaking in jest. How does one tell spurious words from genuine oaths? True or false, his pledge of devotion makes me tremble with elation.

"You are forgiven, Sir Walther, and...." "Forgiven, my lady?" His eyebrows raised in surprise, he straightens himself to his full height, keeping hold of my hands. "Pray tell me why I am in need of forgiveness! In what way did I ever give you offense? Do describe my transgression so that I may forthwith atone for it!"

"But...you are the one who asked for forgiveness for...for...." How can I say "for not telling me you loved me"? Not in so many words. Not to his impish smile. More than ever at a loss for words, I disengage my hands, retrieve his letter from my sleeve and hand it to him, with my best attempt at a noble tilt of the head, "Your words touched my heart, Sir Walther, and made me wish to set yours at peace."

Taking the vellum from my hands, Sir Walther unrolls it slowly and reads the lines; his grin hardens into a frown.

"Forsooth, my lady, you misjudge me greatly. Never would I write such lame verse." Glancing up from the poem to my reddening face, he tempers this astounding announcement with a warm smile, "These lines are unworthy of your beauty, Lady Alix, but...they do express some of the devotion which fills my heart when I see you. I too feel regrets for my silence in Comarque." This time I will surely faint, and no one is here to grasp my arm; I take hold of myself somehow.

"But...if you did not write these lines, Sir Walther, who did?"

"Surely, you do not lack for admirers, Lady Alix. I do not know them all, but is it in any way surprising that you should count a bad poet among them?" He hands me back the roll of parchment but still holds on to it and seems to hesitate, "T'is true I know a knight who has long been sorely smitten with love for you, but I doubt he would choose this way to break his long silence, for he is prone to deeds rather than words...."

I have no wish - or need - to ask for his name. Why should I let Black Foulk's shadow cast gloom on this moment of utter felicity?

As we each hold one end of the rolled letter, our hands touch again and the gold cordlet that ties the parchment appears to link them the way lovers bind their hands in many romances to symbolize their fealty to each other. Our eyes meet and the notion of Paradise becomes clear to me.

* * *

I had started telling Christine the whole story on the way from the airport to her one-room apartment, but had to stop as it took

160

her mind off the road and she was no longer paying life-saving attention to the antics of Nice drivers.

Once home, she had sat me down in her small kitchen while she made us coffee and wouldn't allow me to move before I had concluded my narration. In the end, she just nodded silently, a cryptic look in her eyes. I held my breath. Did she think I was losing my mind?

"Mum, I believe you. And do you know why I do?" I shook my head, flooded with relief. "You say I was little Eloise and Daphne told you we choose our own parents, right?" I nodded dumbly. "Well, I believe you because that's exactly what I would have done given the chance, I mean, chose you as my mother." "Oh, my baby!" I reached for her hand and squeezed it, too moved to say I couldn't have wished for a better daughter. She knew that, anyway.

The next morning, she crept out of her bed in the one room we shared and went out as silently as possible so I could catch up on my missed sleep. She must have dashed out to the bakery before walking up the hill to the Faculté de Droit because I found freshly baked croissants on the kitchen table, together with Swiss cheese and marmalade. So, I decided to cook her a proper lunch, as much to surprise her as for the fun of going shopping to the outdoor market.

We both relished the asparagus sauce mousseline and quails flambées au cognac. Between two mouthfuls of baba-au-rhum, Christine shook her head and remarked, "You know, Mum, there's something different about you. For one thing, you look much younger than you did in Montreal. And I have never seen you enjoy your food so much!

How can you stay so slim eating the way you do?"

Swallowing a sip of rosé de Provence, she added with a laugh, "And you are wearing jewelry. You've always hated jewelry." "What jewelry?"

"Well, your gold bracelet and the turquoise necklace Dad gave you. You never wore them before."

"Oh, that. Did you know turquoise protects wayfarers?"

"No. I didn't. It suits you, anyway. You look great, Mum. You really do."

"Thank you, love, so do you. I wish you wouldn't have to work so hard."

"Oh, I don't mind. It's interesting work." She shrugged. "It might get me that job in Paris, if they go ahead and open their Paris office."

"They" being her Montreal employers, Boison Tellier Hubbard, Attorneys-at-Law, who were branching out in Europe.

I stood up to clear the table, bent down, gave her cheek a quick buss and touched her thick mane of auburn hair. "Your hair has grown. I'll do it for you the way I used to, if you like."

"Oh, Mum!" She took my hand and we both laughed to hide our emotion.

* * *

There was no way she could spare the time to come along to Périgord; she was cramming for an exam in International Tax Agreements and spent all her spare time at the Law Library. As she wouldn't be needing her car, I decided to leave earlier than planned.

I had never been to Périgord and the idea of staying in small auberges de campagne and sampling the local cuisine really appealed to me.

Christine was right, ever since Alix had entered my life, food had become quite important to me. While I had always paid attention to my diet, food had never been the source of sensual satisfaction it had now become. I read recipes voraciously and actually cooked for myself every day; splurged on gourmet meals I could ill afford in Montreal chichi restaurants, and started to salivate at the mention of dishes I had never sampled. So far so good, I had not put on an ounce of fat. Curiouser and curiouser. Anyway, I decided to drive by Comarque to get a feel of the place before going on to Bordeaux to meet the musicians. And perhaps Irene, if she made good her promise to drive down with or without her French lover.

I had planned to attend the Sunday matinée concert that La Fin'Amor, Herr Meissen's medieval ensemble, were giving at the Grand Theatre in Bordeaux. The other musicians had all agreed to a group interview after the show.

I still didn't know if Kurt Meissen would agree to be interviewed; but I couldn't wait to come face to face with the mute psaltery player, and find out if the passion he had once inspired in me had survived the centuries.

To reach Comarque I had to get off the main road at a village called Les Eysies and take a smaller Departmental Route, that ran along the right bank of the Beune River. As Sarlat was the last town I would cross before reaching Les Eysies, I decided to secure a room in that medieval burgh and change into jeans and sneakers before I went exploring. According to my guide, access to the ruins of the castle was somewhat difficult.

I drove into Sarlat around eleven. If I skipped lunch - not a mean sacrifice - there would be enough daylight hours to drive there and back. Even though Comarque was no more than twenty kilometers from Sarlat as the crow flies, I wasn't a bird and, taking into account the twisting roads, reckoned it would take close to two hours to reach the castle. Distances in France can appear deceptively short to North Americans used to driving miles on straight roads unencumbered by crawling overladen trucks.

I had never set foot in Sarlat, yet it seemed vaguely familiar. I drove right into the old part of town and found a parking spot on a small square called Place de la Liberté. In a side street, I located the B & B recommended by the guide.

The building was certainly interesting; high facade of creamy ochre stones; ground floor very medieval; upper stories obviously added by successive generations of occupants. I was shown to one of those pleasant rooms of dark wood and Toile de Jou only to be found in French country inns. From the mullioned window, I could see part of the square on one side, and on the other a high round tower that stood by itself.

I stared at the tower, the void feeling of déjà vu fill my chest, and instinctively stepped back from the window. Come on, what's the matter with you? I berated myself. Isn't that what you came here for?

I changed quickly. On the way out, I asked the lady at the desk if the tower was all that remained of a castle.

"Oh, no. That's the Lantern of the Dead and it stands on its own. Historians say it was built in 1147 to commemorate Saint Bernard's visit to the town; but nobody knows its exact purpose."

I thanked her as I handed her my key. That tower stirred something in me. Had Alix seen it? It was possible; she may have visited Sarlat, a prosperous medieval market town. With one last look at the tower, I got into my car and drove off.

The drive did take close to two hours. I nearly got lost twice on dirt lanes before reaching the right turn onto road 48 as the guide recommended. I counted kilometers, more to keep my mind occupied than from any real need for the path that led to the ruins was supposed to start across the road from another and more recent small castle that was clearly visible. I spotted it quickly enough, parked my car on the grassy side and locked the doors.

The path appeared to go down sharply toward the river through dense woods of oaks and junipers that partly hid the ruins from view. But no tree could hide the towering keep. My mind a blank, I stared at it for a long while before setting out on the path.

Well, here goes, I thought as I entered the woods, vaguely wondering if I should look for a stick or something to wield in case of untoward encounters with wild boars.

The terrain soon levelled off into a soggy litter of last fall's leaves, with a few clearings where tall grasses hid the seeping water. Over the muddiest parts, attempts had been made to throw logs and planks. I still managed to get both feet soaked.

Upon reaching a kind of glade, I lifted my eyes from the soggy path. There stood Comarque, right in front of me. Transfixed, I stared at the sight for a full minute before I realized the castle was in fact on the other side of the Beune and there was no way to cross the narrow river. So much for the guide's instructions! Comarque.

The looming fortress was holding me spellbound.

Perched on a rocky outcrop, it still commanded the valley from the great height of its giant keep, all sharp angles and creamy white stone streaked with the black of ages.

The deep moats now empty of water showed their vertical walls, like man-made cliffs cut deep into the stony hill. Part of the chapel which had been built on a ledge had fallen into the ditch. Of the outer bailey outside the moat, of the villagers' houses, of the lord's dwelling even, only a few crumbling walls remained. I could see no trace of the communal oven or the stables.

Besieged by trees and vegetation, Comarque withstood their onslaught, as proud and undaunted as ever. Even though parts of the castle had obviously been altered through the ages, the huge keep seemed exactly as I remembered it. Both defiant and sinister.

I shivered. It felt so uncanny I had to sit on a log before my legs gave way. I could not take my eyes of the sight. Overcome by a strong yearning to both remember and forget.

For a few minutes my thoughts were a blank. Nothing but timid bird chirpings marred the silence of the woods; the pungent smell of decaying leaves filled my nostrils. Suddenly, a host of recollections seemed to leap through the gap of time and take my mind by storm as I sat shivering uncontrollably and gasping for breath.

Without actually re-living them as I had during my Daphne-induced trances, I began to remember events that had taken place at Comarque as if they had happened in the recent past of my present life.

Rooted on the spot, I let vivid memories take over my mind.

* * *

We have been back in dismal Comarque for several months, the children and I. As for Eudes, preparations for his pilgrimage to the Holy Land mercifully keep him away most of the time.

He did return for Christmas but hardly remained more than a few days before setting off again.

Eudes appears to be full of rancor and scorn for his fellow pilgrims, both for their vainglorious preoccupation with ostentatious pageantry, and their lack of eagerness to depart. According to him, dissent and quarrels already mar the gathering of knights. He does not even approve of their choice of a leader, the Marquis de Montferrat, whom he dismisses as a scholar and poet, even though he has shown himself a valiant warrior on more than one occasion.

Of all the knights who have taken the Cross, many are those who have done so because of the Lord Pope's promise to deliver them of all their sins if they serve in the host for one year. Others have been attracted by the prospect of riches to be gained in Palestine.

Eudes will be gone a while this time, as he is on his way to Venice; sent there to secure ships for the Holy host which already numbers five thousand knights and twenty- thousand-foot soldiers. The Great Old Doge, Dandolo, has many ships and galleys at his command that can transport the pilgrims to the Holy Land; Eudes and his party are to negotiate the cost of this service.

I was not grieved to see Eudes go; for one thing, he has partaken little of the Christmas feast I have gone to great trouble to prepare for his return. Worst still, he hardly acknowledged the presence of his two young children, Robert and Eloise.

It was as if he deemed himself unworthy, in his state of sinfulness, of the joy they have always brought to his heart.

I feel so sad for them. And for Eudes.

For he is not a bad man, and the penances he is imposing on himself for Adela's death go beyond the bounds of reason. Needless to say, his vow to remain celibate for the first year of our marriage meets with my full approval, and I raise no objection either to his squandering most of his wealth on a large contingent of slothful knights who enjoy filling their bellies at his expense. Both penances seem to me fair steps on the path of atonement; but me thinks there is no call for him to deny himself the solace of his children's love, and cause them sore grief at the same time.

I try to make it up to them, for they are my joy, especially little Eloise who is growing up sweet and gentle. Many a pleasant hour is spent reading to her and teaching her to form letters on a tablet.

Robert has grown apace too, but his masters at Hautefort castle have taught him but too well to become a man. All his days there have been spent learning how to kill and maim.

Not quite eight years of age, little Robert is already contemptuous of women's ways, shuns the company of his sister, and tries to imitate the ponderous step of knights in armor.

I am not fooled; when he calls for his mother on cold winter nights, and Helga sleeps on undisturbed, I am the one who rushes to hold his hand and coax him back to sleep. I love him dearly. I think he loves me too, but a strange light comes to his eyes at times when he looks at me. I am not his mother.

Poor ill-fated Adela! Her sad memory still haunts me. At times, when reading alone by the light of a flickering candle, wrapped in my wool mantle for Comarque is as cold as a tomb, it seems to me she is back at my side, warming her hands in front of the smoldering fire. As baffled by death as she was by life.

* * *

Life at Comarque is rather dull. No feast or dance relieve the tedium when the Lord is away. Winter days follow one another, filled with the duties I am now bound to perform as Lady of the castle.

The new steward, or seneschal, is but an elderly knight, bereft of his left arm, still bedazzled by his new estate as successor to Foulk of Sardac, whom he used to hold in great awe.

His name is Gilbert; I like him well enough and value his judgement. He rules serfs and servants with quiet tongue and rare but harsh chastisement. He has grown weary of battles and appears to enjoy the humdrum of his position as much as the fine robes and laden purses that go with it.

Sir Gilbert has taken over from Bogo, the wily chaplain, all accounts of the household and demesnes, lands and fiefs. Upon learning I could write and knew how to add, he very willingly showed me how to list revenues, acreage and livestock for each manor and calculate the rents and profits. I have made it a habit to check how many oxen, calves, sheep and fouls - not to mention beer and wine, and bushels of grain - are consumed every week by the household; and how much of it is given out to the poor by the almoner. Sir Gilbert also plays a fair game of chess.

As for the chaplain, Bogo, he is the bane of my life. Upon Eudes' return, I intend to beseech him to send Bogo and his gaggle of young sycophants to another of his strongholds, where the vile cleric can exert his nefarious influence on another garrison.

It is my misfortune to start my days at sunrise with mass in Bogo's domain, a dank chapel built under the great hall that smells of mold, incense and unwashed clerics. Emerging from the mist of half-remembered dreams of my brief encounter with Fair Walther, I wake up with the drone of his mumbled Latin and long-drawn rituals while his smooth-cheeked attendants fawn all over him.

More than once have I caught myself wishing for the whole choir - which is actually built on a ledge high above the moat - to collapse and disappear into its dark waters with Bogo and his helpers.

What makes me despise him so? For one thing I suspect him of having betrayed the secret of Holy confession by warning Black Foulk, or even Eudes himself, of Adela's infidelity. Moreover, he overtly disapproves of Eudes 'marriage and has been spying on me ever since I refused to let him hear my own confessions. He once had the audacity to remark to his familiars in my presence, "Could it be that My Lady Alix has been enticed by practitioners of that hateful heresy that is gaining adepts around the town of

Albi. Let her beware, for the Lord will surely punish such aberration...."

I held my piece but decided to avoid Bogo as much as possible. Which is somewhat difficult. The keep is so large that our courtyard is narrow and, crossing it one cannot help meeting every member of the household at least once a day.

Before going back to my chambers of a morning, I usually pay a visit to the sleeping children and share a few laughs with Helga while she plaits my hair as a concession to my married estate. I hate wimples and refuse to wear one; they are too confining and remind me of Adela.

I glance at my face in the small mirror that hangs from my belt and rejoice that there is as yet no need for skin whiteners and rouge on my cheeks. While the wee one's sleep on, Helga and I break our fast with some bread and honey, washed down with wine or ale. The forenoon is spent over the accounts and various duties and chores, such as supervising laundresses as they soak and scrub household linens with ashes and soda; or berating the cooks for not properly scouring the giant soup pots, or not using enough salt in the brine curing solution.

I do not dislike these menial tasks; relish the smell of lavender buds sprinkled on clean linen or the mouthwatering aroma of peppery sauces that lingers in the kitchens, where we never run short of spices.

I enjoy leisure time on my own too, for I can play the lute to my heart's content. I keep playing the three songs I know of my beloved. Over and over again. Also, a beautiful ballad written by Conon de Bethune, because its verses speak to my heart.

"Alas, Love, what a hard parting...."

The thought of Fair Walther is never away from my mind and keeps me cheerful through the dull winter days.

When we parted in front of Our Lady's cathedral, he solemnly promised to visit me in Comarque before I leave to accompany my husband on his pilgrimage. Will he keep his promise, he who seems to have broken so many?

I am both resigned and hopeful. In spite of his alleged fickleness, I have reasons to hope for the look we exchanged told me our fates were linked forever. Eyes reflect the soul and therefore do not lie. When our hands touched, he trembled as much as I did. Would a deceiver let himself be moved in such a way? Kindred of Eudes who accompanied him on his Christmas stay at Comarque mentioned between two belches that Walther von Altdorf and Foulk de Sardac were taking up the Cross and joining the gathering host.

Whether Eudes heard him or not, he refrained from any comment. I composed my face and asked the man what could compel those two to depart for Palestine; he did not know and went on filling his mouth with juicy capon and describing the colors on the enameled shield and banners he would use for the expedition, without paying any more attention to me.

I was too busy to question him again, having to keep watch over the service of the banquet, making sure courses followed one another in the right order and guests' trenchers were properly heaped up.

The minstrels and jugglers were late and caused me no small concern before they finally tumbled into the hall having obviously tarried by the wine cask longer than desirable. My last fear fortunately unfounded - was that unmannerly servants would start quarrelling among themselves as was their wont, and bring shame on us all.

So, the guests departed without giving any other news of Sir Walther.

However, little I learn of my beloved, my love sustains itself. I seem to burn inside with a joyful passion that feeds on the memory of our brief encounter and requires nothing more to keep me in a state of elation. Part of my mind judges this blind devotion for what it is: the acme of foolishness. Yet, I know my soul is right to love him without conditions or demands, for it is the only true way to love.

* * *

On the morning of the Feast of Kings, the 6th day of January of the year of Our Lord 1202, Sir Walther stands at the castle gate alone but for his squire and two horsemen in iron. Asking for shelter.

What dare I say of this blessed day?

This morning, when Sir Gilbert greeted Him in the lower courtyard, Elaine happened to be there. She ran all the way to my solar to tell me of Fair Walther's arrival.

Brimming with elation, I tried to compose my face and find the right words to welcome my visitor without revealing my excitement. Would Sir Gilbert first take him to the small but richly adorned room we reserve for highborn visitors?

Would he make sure Walther was provided with the best linen and silk robes, as well as a bath if he so desired? I dared not go and inquire for fear of revealing the state of my emotions.

I waited. Asking Elaine over and over again to describe my beloved in every detail. At last approaching steps were heard on the stairs. Preceded by two squires, Sir Gilbert was leading Walther into my solar. He was still in his travelling attire; rich leather garments trimmed in fur of some kind.

Bowing very low, he begged my forgiveness for presenting himself thus in front of me and expressed the wish to remain a while at Comarque, hereby to await Eudes 'return as well as the arrival of his own knights and men-at-arms. For, said he most humbly, he has taken the vow to join my lord and help him fight the Infidels in the Holy Land. Even Bogo, who had followed the little procession up the stairs and, much to my annoyance now stood surveying my solar with flinty eyes, could not voice disapproval of such a pious wish. With compressed lips, he turned his back on us and shuffled back down the stairs.

I dared not look at Walther, but his eyes compelled to do so. The look we exchanged while I mouthed words of welcome held such depth of meaning that the words died on my lips and I could only gaze at him for an unseemly long time before bidding him stay in our mesnie as long as he wished and handing him to Sir Gilbert's care. I watched them depart, holding on to my chair to remain standing.

As soon as they were gone, I hastily sent for the cooks and gave orders to set up trestles in the great hall for a midday meal worthy of such a visitor.

A feast it was. In every way. Walther was seated on my right and sharing my trencher!

Sharing every delicious morsel! How could I enjoy the food so much, feeling him so near, when I had been unable to swallow a single bite at King Philip's court? Love is indeed quite contrary and defies reason.

* * *

Now it is evening and I am waiting for him to join us again in the great hall.

Though I have ordered many good wax candles to be used, the hall is sparsely lit and I sit in its darkest corner on my carved chair, idly plucking the strings of my lute. Waiting.

Steps make me look up and rise from my seat. Walther is here and he has brought me a gift. With a bow he presents it to me. Wrapped in scarlet silk cloth. As I carefully lift every fold of precious fabric, they reveal a psaltery. I look up to Walther's smiling eyes with mute gratitude.

A psaltery!

A rare and precious instrument I have long admired and coveted, as much for the fact it is played only by beautiful highborn ladies as for its mellifluous sounds.

"It was brought back from the Holy Land." Says Walther, moving closer. "Some call it psaltery, others Dolce Mello, which is most appropriate as it means Sweet Honey."

The boldness of his eyes and the nearness of him make me tremble. He murmurs in my ear, "If you will allow me, My Lady, I shall teach you to play it." I look around the hall in a state of great confusion.

Elaine is quietly embroidering in a far corner. Sir Gilbert has retired for the night and Bogo is mercifully absent. As for Walther's squires, they are warming themselves in front of the roaring fire at the other end of the great hall, quaffing much ale in the company of our more bibulous knights.

The great hall is dark and they are paying scant attention to us.

As I sit on my chair, I take the triangular instrument on my lap and diffidently touch its strings. Bending over my shoulders, Walther places his hands over mine. His smooth cheek brushes against mine. I can feel the closeness of his mouth. I have but to turn my face.... Where will I find the words to describe such joy?

A joy that no longer feeds upon itself. A joy that demands more, and more. Forever more.

So sweet are the delights of the flesh that they are never enough. Our lips meet. Boldly. Rashly. Greedily. My whole body ablaze with desire, I abandon myself to this fire that consumes us both.

Our lip's part but our hands begin to play, together, caressing the strings, as if of their own volition. As if we were one already. We play such strange, enchanted, chords that even the drinking knights take notice and turn around to glance at us. But only briefly; they care not for our music and prefer their tales of war.

We play on. Sometimes our hands separate and seem to engage in a playful duet on the strings, then I place my hands over his or his cover mine, and we play as one musician. The music keeps us enthralled in the intricate unfolding of its magic sounds until, letting go of my hands, Walther moves swiftly to my side and kneels by my chair.

His sweet lips are so near I cannot resist another kiss; I feel his tongue probing my mouth and a surge of desire makes my body ache. I cannot tell how long that reckless kiss lasts, all I can say is that it feels like an eternity of bliss. Time has no boundaries for those who delight in each other as we do. "Alix!" Whispers Walther releasing my lips.

"My sweet lady! My life is yours, Alix, now that I have tasted the delight of your kiss. Grant me your mercy and allow me to give you better proof of my love!"

The intense and solemn cast of his face touches me even more than his smiles, innocent that I am, I do not yet know that mere desire can make a man turn somber.

"Do not reject me now for I would surely die!" He pleads.

"Friend," I whisper back, "God forbid I should ever reject you, but what you ask would surely taint my lord husband's honor and my own virtue!" I feel so weak it is a wonder these words pass my lips.

He swears that nothing will keep him from serving me faithfully for the rest of his life, but that by refusing to consummate our love I deny myself the only felicity this vale of tears has to offer us.

"Remorse is never as cruel as regret, Alix, and lost chances to enjoy the delights of love are never granted us again."

Thus, whispering to each other, we keep on exchanging endearments and furtive embraces while his hands guide mine over the strings of the psaltery. Seemingly forever.

Or at least until Elaine, bent over her embroidery in the far corner of the hall, starts fidgeting and moving about as if to remind us of the unseemly lateness of the hour. Should I feel remorse for the words I then utter in his ear?

"I shall send my maids to sleep in the children solar. No one guards the door to my chamber at night. It will not be closed."

CHAPTER 15

Some kind of animal cry in the woods brought me back to the present. I must have sat on that log contemplating the ruins of Comarque for the best part of three hours, wildly reminiscing about my life as Alix and the days that followed her surrender to her handsome rogue of a troubadour.

Dusk was seeping into the forest and for a second or so, I felt bewildered and afraid, even though there was really no cause for alarm; the path had been easy enough to follow, I wouldn't get lost. I stood up, and, with one last look at Comarque, now home to crows and vipers, and a promise to myself I would be back, turned and retraced my steps up the path.

I reached the road in growing darkness, numbly got into my car and drove off, the image of stark towers and crumbling battlements still in my eyes.

During the drive to Sarlat, more passionate recollections crowded my mind until, at one point, I became so agitated I had to stop the car and park by the side of the road. Closing my eyes, and taking deep breaths to quiet my beating heart, I leaned back against the headrest and waited for the present to overcome my invasive past so I could function in a more or less rational way.

Yet, I no longer resented Alix's interference in my present life. No longer felt estranged from her. I needed no Daphne to convince me I wasn't suffering from Multiple Personality Syndrome. Alix was me; I accepted her memories as mine, and found them just as precious as Sandra's, and what memories.

* * *

Our first night.

The wait in my darkened chamber where blazing logs in the hearth throw dancing shadows on the stone walls and the crimson silk hangings. I am sitting in my bed, holding up the sheet to my chin to cover my nakedness, nursing inchoate thoughts and yearnings. Through the half-drawn curtains, I can see the door, and the door opens, silently.

He is here, kneeling by my bed, embracing me with his strong arms. I let go of the sheet to return his embrace.

All my maidenly shames - if ever I had any soon evaporate under his skillful touch, coalesce into an aching need for his maleness.

The feel of Walther's powerful body against mine, the scent of his skin, the taste of his mouth... His hands! These inspired musician's hands that play my body like a precious instrument and coax from it a crescendo of exquisite pleasures until the fierce melding of our flesh makes my very soul sing like the psaltery.

Night after stealthy night of heedless passion and unbridled delights in Walther's arms.

Wild embraces which leave us both spent and hardly assuaged; regretting only the silence we have to keep as we take our pleasures, and the cruel dawn that puts an end to them.

For me the long daylight hours are spent waiting for night to come again; avoiding Walther's eyes when we meet for fear of betraying our secret - our fateful secret.

I cannot help being amazed by Walther's composure.

He spends most days hunting or tilting at the quintain with the men of our garrison; he is a great horseman. Whenever he enters my solar in the company of Sir Gilbert, he never fails to greet me with a great show of respect; azure eyes agleam with an impish light.

Whereas I tremble at the sight of him and can hardly swallow a mouthful during meals in the great hall, he appears quite at ease, eats, drinks and jests with our knights, while Bogo glares on, his face draped in disapproval.

* * *

At the wheel of the little Renault, on that twisting country road, these recollections pursued me and made me shiver, from apprehension even more than remembered desire.

I couldn't help dreading the outcome of our folly, sensed it to be bad, and fought the remembrance of it with all my will.

But sooner or later, I would recall what our fate had been. There was no turning back now, as there had been no turning back then. I drove on.

The road back to Sarlat was now nearly deserted and quite dark. Curiously, out of these vivid recollections emerged a clearer picture of my life as Sandra.

* * *

Ever since I could remember, I, born a Virgo as Sandra, had been on a quest for order and stability, peace and rationality. Suppressing in myself any rash impulse, I'd literally tamed my nature into a kind of dull conformity.

What kind of remembered fear had moved me to do so? Was I seeking in Sandra's life a haven from the turmoil of Alix's?

What had this sensible life gained me, anyway? Had my soul progressed? Had I been happier? Progress and happiness defy easy definition.

As Sandra, I wasn't a better person than Alix, that much was for sure. My interest in others' welfare was, in truth, far more superficial than hers. As for happiness... I had been happy enough with Michael, my husband, in a sedate and sheltered way.

Oh, there was nothing wrong with the sensual bond between us and we had indeed derived enjoyment from each other's bodies; but never at the expense of sanity. Still, I had loved Michael deeply and would gladly have given years of my life to find him back by my side. Even though I no longer felt the need to depend on him for happiness.

I wasn't prepared to dismiss Franco, either; my carnal affection for him had at least been untainted by dependency. Memories of my past and present lives seemed like the jumbled pieces of a difficult puzzle; so intricate in fact that there was little point in even trying to assemble it into a picture which made sense.

Well, fate, which had already wrought enough strange occurrence's, would no doubt lead me on to stranger ones....

* * *

Back in my Sarlat hotel room, needless to say, sleep eluded me for most of the night. Restlessly throwing off the covers, I crumpled the sheets, hugged the pillows, and behaved altogether like a lovesick dimwit listlessly yearning for a man's body. Incapable at first to put a face on the object of this vague desire, I couldn't even tell whose embrace I longed for.

It was only when dawn broke and I fell asleep, that the answer came to me in a dream. A man was lovingly and mutely stroking my hair; his face a kind of composite between Walther's lusty smile and Kurt Meissen strong and sad features.

* * *

I left Sarlat immediately after a copious petit déjeuner of croissants, butter, jam and caféau-lait, enjoyed nearly as much as if it was shared with a loved one.

It was hard to tell how long it would take me to drive the 100 miles or so to Bordeaux; I avoided autoroutes because their outrageous tolls were a rip-off, and secondary roads, though they afforded many picturesque sights, were unpredictable.

I had taken the precaution of leaving a message for Irene at the Ritz, with the date of my arrival in Bordeaux and the name and telephone number of the modest hotel where I had reserved a room. When I reached the small but quaint inn, in plenty of time for lunch, the desk clerk handed me Irene's reply. She wouldn't be in Bordeaux - with her "beau" - until Wednesday.

Muttering expletives in English under my breath, I grabbed my key from the startled concierge and, feeling thoroughly annoyed with Irene, followed the ancient porter bent in two over my small overnight bag.

I hadn't planned to stay on in Bordeaux after the musicians' departure. They were due to leave for Nantes on the Tuesday and it was my intention to follow them there. Which meant I would miss Irene and her nobleman when I had been looking forward to meeting them both in Bordeaux; but I could not afford to let La Fin'Amor depart once I had established contact with them, especially with Kurt Meissen. I had every intention of staying fairly close to him and pursue his acquaintance. If that proved possible.

* * *

The hotel room was charming. Handing the shaky old porter more than double the expected tip, I waved him out, sat on the bed and resolved to wait until after my musicians' first interview to decide on a course of action. It was time to treat myself to a proper gourmet lunch; just as properly washed down with a half-bottle of a respectable Chateau Latour perhaps.

* * *

La Fin'Amor's concert was a great success. The neo-baroque hall of the Bordeaux opera house was packed with a surprisingly eclectic audience of staid bourgeois in Sunday Mass attire and punky youths in Doc Marten's and green hair.

My third-row seat afforded a good view at the five remaining musicians; the three pretty girls in their sumptuous costumes, and the two men, the dark rebec player, and Kurt Meissen. I couldn't take my eyes off him.

His hair, now cut much shorter, must have been quite blond at one point but was now mostly white. His face intent rather than sad, seemed lost in a musical dream of his own. His eyes were indeed blue, like Walther's, but gentler, kind of misty, belying the austerity of his features.

He wore green and red again, but in inverse combination; a green tunic its hem richly embroidered, thick green hose on his long legs, and a red mantle over his shoulder. He looked closer to fifty than thirty and he still blinked on high notes.

The original group was unexpectedly seconded by eight dancers and singers - four graceful girls and four handsome young men, whom I took to be students - all richly dressed and suitably formal. They performed some of the steps I had enjoyed so much as Alix, estampies and caroles. The girls' gowns, brightly hued, with their long-rushed undersleeves, high waists and double low- slung belts looked to me quite accurate and made me wonder who had insisted on this painstaking recreation of medieval elegance.

The young performers also sang as a chorus in aubades, answering the rebec player solo part. These most beautiful medieval dawn songs that tell of the heart-rending parting of lovers at the break of day brought tears to my eyes as I searched the blank psaltery player's handsome face for an answer to the mystery of time.

I sat mesmerized through the whole performance. There was between the musicians that rare degree of synchrony; the kind of musical symbiosis found only in the best orchestras and which gives music its most meaningful voice. The extra dimension that makes the whole greater than the sum of its part.

Yet, one element of it bothered me; it felt as if the tone of it was not quite right. When it was over much against my wishes, I remained motionless in my seat, unwilling to break the charm of the performance, as the Bordeaux audience belied its reputation for prim formality by giving the performers a standing ovation, and clamoring for an encore.

The curtain finally went down. I gathered my purse and tape-recorder and made my way onto the stage, behind the curtain.

* * *

The first one to greet me is the young redhead who sings and plays the lute. She introduces herself in French as Cécile Dupont and shakes my hand with a smile. The others are expecting me, she says.

She takes me all around, introducing each of the young dancers in their own tongue; two of them are Irish, one Belgian, one German, two English and two French - they are indeed students.

The other two girl musicians in the group, who are British too, speak fluent French. The rebec player, a Welshman, nods rather curtly and goes on packing various instruments with great care; even though they are to perform again in the evening.

Kurt Meissen is standing aloof with his back to me. His size and his stance are so reminiscent of Walther that I feel a shiver run down my spine.

When Cecile approaches him and touches his arm lightly, he turns around and gives my face a long searching look.

Unabashedly curious. Our eyes meet briefly and I hold my breath.

Placing his psaltery down on a chair, he shakes my hand, a faint smile on his lips. His hand feels strong and smooth. As it touches mine, he flinches. Our eyes meet again. All my senses seem to meld into the look we exchange. No longer do I hear what Cécile Dupont is saying; in a trance, I take a step closer to Kurt.

Then, as he bends down to retrieve his instrument, I murmur in a voice that is no longer mine, "Pray, Fair Walther, do let me look at it!"

He must have understood my words; with a stiff bow, he hands me the psaltery. Our fingers touch briefly and his eyes widen in surprise. Taking the psaltery from his hands, I sit myself on his chair, and - literally against my will - place it in the right position on my lap and let my hands have their way.

Eyes closed; I play a few chords. Only a few, and the beginning of an old ballad of Richard the Lionheart, but it is enough for the other musicians to stop and stare. When I open my eyes, they have gathered around me, intrigued. As for Kurt, he is watching me, frozen on the spot; puzzlement slowly leaving way to alarm in his eyes.

I had never been near one of these instruments in my whole life. I stop playing long enough for my hands to re-tune the psaltery.

"You are not tuning it the way you used to, Walther. Why?" And I go on playing.

I have no control over my strange behavior; yet my heart hurts as I watch its effect on Kurt. He follows my fingers deft movements across the strings with a kind of consternation, and stares at me as if I was some demon sprung-up from hell. Does he recognize me? And himself?

I would give so much to share his thoughts! To comfort him and to make him understand that our meeting again - our destiny of love is but the wish of our own soul. But I can only go on playing and let him struggle alone against fears and doubts.

Perhaps seeking some means of escape, he looks right and left. He opens his mouth - as if forgetting he can't speak - swallows hard and, turning his back on me, leaves the stage with deliberately slow steps. Giving the impression that only through will power does he not give way to panic. I place my hands flat on the strings and the music dies.

As I watch his retreating back, I feel stupidly helpless. Torn between the urge to rush after this man and hug him, and a compulsion to stay put. I have a fair idea of what he is going through. Part of me wants to tell him it's all right and he is not going crazy; but something stronger holds me back. A kind of respect for his free will? He has to work through his emotions on his own.

The others form a circle around me. Somewhere in the darkened hall someone is clapping. Even the rebec player, Steve, looks at me wide-eyed.

"You play very well." He rather grudgingly concedes. "Where did you learn that piece?" I lie about some lessons taken many years ago in Canada; my eyes still seeking Kurt Meissen. He has disappeared.

"Well, you should keep it up." Cecile says, but without enthusiasm. "You're a natural."

They all join in kindly. Their approval makes my task easier; they answer my questions willingly and no one objects to my following them to Nantes - or wherever. They talk at length about their art, about medieval music and its growing public, about recording and records companies' greed. I merely read the questions I prepared in Montreal. My mind is elsewhere. Fear claws at my heart.

Have I alienated Kurt permanently by my weird behavior? I could kick myself. What good is it to gain the players' admiration if Kurt avoids me like a leper from now on?

I have botched it and I'm definitely off to a bad start. As they are all leaving one by one, I ask young Cécile to grant me a few more minutes.

"I'm afraid Herr Doctor Meissen did not appreciate my little performance. I was rather rude of me to borrow his psaltery in this way. If I write him a little note of apology, will you be kind enough to deliver it to him?"

She nods, avoiding my eyes. She is really quite pretty in spite of the freckles on her nose. And kind too; she touches my hand gently in a reassuring gesture.

"Oh, don't mind Kurt. He will be all right. I guess he was surprised to find his match; the psaltery is not an easy instrument to handle and play well. Such strange melodic lines you played! Anyway, don't worry, he is a kind man and not the type to bear a grudge." She pauses, darting me another wary look. "I really don't know what came over him. His reaction was a bit peculiar, wasn't it? But then he hasn't been himself since the accident." "The accident? Which accident?" My blood runs colder than the St-Lawrence in winter. "Oh, you didn't know. Well, he totaled his car two years ago. Went off the road in broad daylight and hit a tree; still doesn't know how it happened. His wife was in the death seat, she was killed instantly." Cecile's nervous mirth sounds ambiguous; is she in love with my handsome minnesinger? I refrain from interrupting. "He was in a coma for a week and when he came out of it, he couldn't talk. The doctors said he was suffering from paralysis of the vocal cords and that he might recover one day. Or he might not."

"How terribly sad!"

The others have already left, all except Steve who is still pottering around at the back of the stage and gathering music scores. And throwing curious glances in our direction. "Where did that happen?"

"Somewhere in Germany, I believe." She frowns. "In Bavaria, I think. He was researching some XIIIth. Century minnesinger he was writing a monograph about.

Anyway, I don't know the details. Perhaps you should ask Steve; he has known Kurt longer than any of us." Before I can stop her, she calls to the surly rebec player. "Eh, Steve, can you come here a minute? Mrs.

Pearson is asking me about Kurt."

He keeps on putting away his music sheets. Taking his time before closing his briefcase and coming over slowly without a smile on his long face.

"So? What d'you want to know about him? The man is a bloody wonder; best damn musician I ever met. It's in his blood, I say." After a short pause, he adds, reluctantly, "You're not too bad, yourself, lady."

"Thank you. Does Herr Meissen still teach medieval history at some German university as well? Tubingen, I believe?"

"Did." He shrugs. "After the accident, he stayed off work for a few months to recover. I mean, the man had a leg in a cast, broken ribs, a perforated lung and concussion, poor bloke!

After that, of course, what with having lost his voice, he couldn't lecture anymore, so for a while he prepared courses and had his assistant give them. Then his university sort of gave him a year sabbatical leave that was due to him, and he joined us on a permanent basis.

I don't know what he plans to do when his leave is over; as far as I am concerned, he is welcome to stay on." Young Cécile is nodding vigorously.

The man appears to be closer to Kurt than any of the others and I am determined to humor him. "So, it's sort of a... second career for him." I venture. "A profession he obviously enjoys to judge by his wonderful performance."

"Yep, I suppose he does like it." The rebec player agrees. "At times, though, he acts as if he resented music, well, some pieces at least, and even his own instrument; as if playing it wasn't what he was meant to do in life. Well, he must miss his work too, in a way."

"Does he have children?" I address my question to young Cécile.

"Two." She seems pleased to answer. As if talking about Kurt brought him closer?

"Already grown up. His son is a lawyer in Frankfurt and his daughter is studying languages somewhere in Switzerland."

Something in her tone confirms my first impression; this little girl is into Handsome Kurt in a big way. Is he under her charm? Isn't he a little old for her? Still, I like her; she is actually quite charming.

Steve is dancing on the spot and biting his lips; not hiding his impatience to be gone. It's getting late and I guess they want to go and join the others.

"Do you have any idea what caused this terrible accident?" I direct my last question at Steve.

"Nope. Well... it's...." He appears reluctant to say more. Perhaps out of loyalty to a man he seems to admire. As I wait silently, he frowns and finally adds, "I don't know for sure, but from what he wrote to me it had to do with his research at the time. He recalls that some kind of weird experience happened to him as he was driving and caused him to lose control of the car, but he can't remember what it was."

"But what makes you think that it had anything to do with his research?"

"I don't think anything, lady. That's what the man says. What he writes, I mean. He should know, shouldn't he? Hope he remembers what happened exactly, poor bugger. It won't bring back his wife, but it might make him feel better. Less guilty."

The man glares at me. But that's all right. He sounds genuinely sympathetic. I don't insist and thank him profusely. He grabs his briefcase and leaves in a hurry.

Scribbling a note of apology on the back of one of my cards, I hand it to Cécile who promises with a smile to deliver it to Kurt Meissen. I catch myself praying he will accept my apology.

CHAPTER 16

"Sandra, sweetie, don't be a drag!" Irene still sounded bigger than life; she always does on long distance calls, even if only from Paris. "Why can't you wait for us in Bordeaux? Olivier is so looking forward to meeting you! I told him all about your mute singer... And you must give me all the details. Have you been to bed with him yet?"

"Irene! Please!" I laughed. Pity I didn't feel like telling her about my nights with Walther; she would have enjoyed that. "Don't be crude! I just heard him play live, and it was wonderful. He has shorter hair now, but he is even better looking than on TV."

"Really? You make me regret we can't get to Bordeaux in time for their concert."

"I'll tell you what, Irene, why don't you drive to Nantes first. We can meet there and you can catch their show at the same time. I'll do my best to get you tickets.

I can't explain over the phone, but interviewing Herr Meissen is no picnic, especially...." I changed my mind about telling her of my strange new-found musical talent. There was no point; she wouldn't be listening, anyway. "I have to stay close to the group and there's no way I can wait here till Wednesday." I paused; she remained silent. "I have learned a lot since I last spoke to you, about the past and about myself. I'll tell you everything when we meet, OK?"

"Well, I should jolly well hope so, after all, if you're having major fun with all your past lives, it's thanks to me, isn't it? For recommending Daphne! How is she, by the way?" Her question took me by surprise.

How was Daphne? I hadn't called her nor had she called me. Truth of the matter was, no news of her was good news as far as I was concerned. Which, I admit, may sound pretty callous on my part, considering her support, the time she had spent helping me, and the friendship that had developed between us. The memory of our last encounter and her surprising change of personality left me with disturbing impressions. At times they came very close to premonitions of trouble.

"I haven't got a clue, Irene." I replied. "I might call her when I have had a chance to interview Kurt Meissen properly. So, are you going to join me in Nantes on Wednesday, or not?"

"Hum...." She was silent for so long I thought she had hung up. "Let me think... Why not? I don't know the place, even though some of my ancestors came from there. I'll have to let Olivier know of this change of plans; after all, he is the one doing the driving. He's pretty easy going, so I doubt he will raise any objections. He's taking a week off. Is there a decent hotel in Nantes? I mean a decent five star one?"

I stifled my laughter. "Of course, ask the concierge at the Ritz to look one up for you and have him book you the Bridal Suite." The quality of accommodation available in Nantes was a total unknown to me. And the least of my worries; whatever it might be like. Now that her curiosity was aroused, Irene would come anyway. Curiosity is one of her more endearing traits.

* * *

I had left the name of my hotel and my room number with nice Cécile Dupont; in case they changed their mind about answering some more questions after their evening show. She called around four, as I was lying in bed scribbling notes for my interview. Was she going to cancel? Had I scared off my Minnesinger before even getting to know him?

She apologized for disturbing me. She had a singer's voice; warm and melodious.

"You're not disturbing me. What can I do for you?"

"Well... It's not for me, actually. I gave your card to Kurt and he's wondering if you wouldn't mind meeting him before the concert. There is something he wants to ask you. I mean, he will hand you some written questions, I guess." She paused. "I hope you don't mind. It's not easy for him to communicate; he has to write down everything, you understand?"

"Oh, yes. No problem. It was very nice of you to give him my note. Now could you ask Herr Doktor Meissen if it would convenient for him to meet me in front of the opera house in one hour?"

She repeated my question. He must have been standing close by and must have nodded his answer, for she replied immediately.

"That will be fine. He'll be there. Our concert doesn't start until 8.30 p.m."

I replaced the hand-set with a trembling hand. At the thought of meeting Kurt face to face again, a myriad feeling soared through my mind like so many startled birds. I was both excited and apprehensive; impatient to meet him, yet wary of the impact this meeting would have on my life.

What was the meaning of it all, anyway? Why were my past life and love thus revealed to me? What was expected of me in return? I hadn't a clue.

Questions hounded me all the way to the opera, of the "Who are we? Where are we going?" kind. But I also wondered how I was going to find the right words to tell him the whole story? What if he thought me crazy and wanted nothing more to do with me?

I was so distracted I lost my way twice and had to ask for directions. With beating heart, and quickened step, I dismissed soul- searching in favor of a brief prayer to whoever was responsible for this bizarre situation, asking for help in making the best of it.

* * *

Kurt was already there when I reached the steps to the entrance of the opera house. Leaning against a stone pillar, clad - strangely enough - in tan slacks and a well-cut tweed jacket. His thick longish mane of pale hair brushed behind his ears.

He saw me at once and moved quickly to meet me half-way down the stairs. We shook hands. I felt slightly dizzy. Taking my elbow with a firm hand, he gestured with the other hand toward a café across the square. "You want us to go and sit at the terrace?"

He nodded and kept on propelling me in the direction of the tables. The feel of his hand on my arm sent a shiver down my spine. A rather unexpected reaction; so far, my physical response to the man had been a blank. He fascinated me, but in no way did he evoke the kind of passion that had devoured me as Alix. As yet.

I sighed. From relief or regret, it was hard to say. He heard my sigh and turning his head slightly, gave me a sidelong glance of concern.

When we reached the crowded terrace, he held my chair for me while I sat and pulled another one for himself. Very close to mine. He had come well prepared; fishing in both pockets of his Harris tweed coat, he brought out two neat little piles of scribbled notes and handed me the one on top of the first pile.

It said simply: "Who are you?"

I started telling him about Canada, Montreal, and the Travel Bug magazine; about my work there and the article I was writing on medieval music today. He listened for a few minutes and started shaking his head.

"Isn't that what you want to hear?" I inquired, with a strong inkling of what would come next.

Obviously, his notes didn't cover every eventuality, for taking a pricy fountain-pen from his breast pocket, he started scribbling furiously under the first question, turning the scrap of paper to finish the new one before handing it to me.

I read the predictable query. "No. That was not what I meant. Who are you really? Why did you call me Walther? How can you play the psaltery so well? How come you knew how to re-tune it in just intonation?"

"Phew! Hold it, please!" I protested. "You're not making this easy, you know!"

A smile hovered between his eyes and his lips. For a fraction of a moment, he did look like Walther and I felt the first stirring of sensual interest in the man. He sat very close to me, smelling fresh as lavender.

He must have shaved just before coming; a little nick on his right cheek was still oozing a drop of blood. The sight of it disturbed me greatly, stirring vague and deeply buried fears in me. Unable to understand why, I turned my head away.

He was waiting patiently enough for my reply. Could I tell him point blank he was - or at least had been - a great love of mine? There was no point in lying. Not at this stage of the game; but how much could be said without sounding utterly deranged? I decided to be as truthful as possible and to start from the beginning, making the tale as simple as I could.

"One day I saw you playing the psaltery on television...." The words came far more easily than expected; the warm light of his eyes like a beacon lighting my way through the whole incredible tale. He listened intently. Giving the impression he believed every word. When I reached Walther's gift of the psaltery to Alix, my voice must have betrayed my emotion; Kurt suddenly closed his eyes and placed his two hands over mine. I closed my eyes too.

I don't know how we must have appeared to the other patrons sipping their apéritifs at that café terrace, but it was a moment of grace.

His hands felt warm and comforting, untouched by the tremor that ran through mine.

When I opened my eyes, he was gazing at my face with a kind of awe. There was something so alien, yet so familiar about the touch of his strong hands that it moved me to bend down and rest my cheek on them for a few moments. He didn't appear surprised, just caressed me with his misty smile.

"Do you believe me, Kurt?" I asked.

He cleared his throat, as if to speak, frowned, and nodded without taking his hands off mine. I straightened up and looked deep into his troubled eyes.

"So, you are prepared to accept the idea that you were Walther von Altdorf in a previous life? That I was Alix and that we loved each other... rather unwisely?"

Letting go of my hands, he reached for his pen and quickly wrote a lengthy reply on the back of two of his prepared notes. So much for his careful preparation. I read it aloud.

"When my car accident occurred, I had gone to Bavaria to research the life of a little- known minnesinger by the name of Walther von Altdorf."

I interrupted my reading to look at him; he was no longer smiling. His nod was now a simple confirmation of his written word. I went on reading. "I had found a remarkable manuscript of his aubades and was planning to publish them with some biographical information.

Now you show up out of nowhere, bring up his name...and play the psaltery! Confronted with this kind of coincidence, one can either shrug the whole thing off or try to find out what the hell is going on. I choose the latter." "Thank you." I felt a great weight lift off my chest. "You're right, Walther was indeed from Bavaria and Queen Agnes was the one who introduced him at the court of King Philip Augustus, her husband. Walther was a relative of the German emperor."

Kurt Meissen's eyebrows rose. He wrote, "Where did you learn all that?"

I gave him details I had omitted in my first telling of Alix's life

He kept nodding approval while his expression grew more and more perplexed by the minute.

I felt the need for a break. "Your English is quite good, Herr Meissen."

He laughed outright - a strange but not unpleasant sound from deep within his chest and scribbled, "How do you know? You haven't heard me speak! Please call me Kurt." How could he laugh and not speak? I wondered. Our shared laughter felt good, anyway.

He was definitely a likeable man. More likeable than Walther?

Bold sparrows were picking forgotten crumbs on our table. The slanting rays of the setting sun extended shadows and bathed the square in mellow golden light. I let my eyes wander around the pleasant square and the handsome XVIIIth Century buildings that enclosed it, vaguely wondering if I had lived in other

times too. Would I recall another life one day? I looked again at the man by my side and caught myself wishing that, if it ever happened, he be part of it too.

"Thank you, Kurt." I smiled. "Call me Sandra, please, rather than Alix."

He wrote, "Why?" In large letters.

"Why?" I shrugged. "I don't really know why. It's just... Well, what would be the point of living several times if we always sought refuge in the past; felt such nostalgia about it that we forgot to live our present life to the full? Do you understand what I am trying to say?"

He didn't nod but took my hands in his. It was answer enough.

The waiter was hovering around our table. I asked Kurt, raising one finger, "Tea?" Raising two fingers, "Coffee?" And raising three fingers, "Apéritif?"

Kurt raised two fingers. I ordered two coffees and the waiter departed, shaking his head.

"I feel very fortunate to have been allowed back into my past." I went on. "But it scares me too. I mean, all the spiritual implications. I'm not...was not a religious person. Now I'm not so sure. Don't you feel some kind of apprehension about what you might learn of your previous life?"

Rummaging through his piles of notes, he extracted one, entirely covered with his neat handwriting and handed it to me.

"A strange experience happened to me at the wheel of my car and caused my accident two years ago. I don't recall the experience itself, but cannot shake the belief it was in some way connected with Walther von Altdorf."

"I see." It was my turn to nod. I went on reading. "I also think the loss of my voice is somehow caused not by the accident itself but by this strange "fit" that came over me as I was recapping what I had been able to learn of the man's life."

"You remember that much?"

He hesitated before writing his answer. His frustration with his mute state was palpable; with a stifled sigh, he took up the pen again. "Not so much remember as surmise. I would have been thinking of the man and the many pages of notes I had taken over the previous days. It would be logical to be planning my monograph."

"I see." What about his wife by his side? Didn't she rate a single thought? I dared not mention her for fear of inflicting pain. What kind of marriage had it been? Could the guilt and heartbreak of her death be the cause of his paralysis? Had he condemned himself to silence?

"Have you tried hypnosis?" I asked. He shook his head, the shadow of a smirk on his lips.

"Listen, you may be skeptical, but why not give it a try? What have you got to lose?" He jotted down an answer and handed it to me with an impish smile that Walther wouldn't have disowned. "The compassionate attention of beautiful women like you."

"That's a heavy price to pay." I remarked with a smile. "All the more so since you are not without other means of attracting their interest." The look we exchanged was both bold and intimate.

I fell silent too. The waiter brought our coffees. I bent down to get my purse, but Kurt held up his hand and handed him a crumpled note. When the man had gone, he selected a clean piece of paper and wrote in bold letters:

"Will you wait until after the show to have dinner with me? We don't have to talk, just look into each other's eyes and hold hands." The thrill I felt, Alix wouldn't have disowned either.

* * *

After that we were well-nigh inseparable. He held my hand walking me back to my hotel after our silent dinner that evening.

The next morning, when I came down, he was waiting for me in the small lobby of my hotel, a folded Le Monde in one hand, his pen in the other. Doing the crossword puzzle. We greeted each other with a nod and a smile, as if his presence was both natural and expected. As he was free until the evening performance, we spent the day together exploring Bordeaux; strolling along the wharfs and trying not to admire the mansions built with pelf from the slave trade.

We may not have talked, but there was between us an ease that made us relish each other's company. A fast-growing intimacy that didn't translate into overt sexual tension but rather into a subtle acceptance of each other's touch. A form of trust. I followed the group's van to Nantes in my car on the Tuesday.

I had already gathered ample material for my Travel Bug article and had taken numerous pictures of the group in their finery. My excuse for sticking around was wearing thin; but they didn't appear to mind. No one - not even Steve - gave any sign of resenting my presence; they seemed in fact to have adopted me. Cécile was even urging me to borrow Kurt's psaltery once more and play some pieces with them. Not on stage, of course, but just for the fun it.

I declined without giving any reason and she didn't insist. The psaltery was for Kurt and me. No one else.

Besides, there was this business of tuning the instrument which I still found puzzling. Before leaving the café, I had asked Kurt what he had meant by "just intonation," and he had taken the trouble to write what musicians now tune their instruments in accordance with the well-tempered scale introduced by Bach. Adding in a postscriptum that it had in fact been discovered by the Chinese. What did my hands know of all this? I personally was incapable of reading a single note of music. Yet, the way I had tuned the psaltery sounded better to my ears.

On the way to Nantes, we stopped for lunch in a Restaurant de Routiers, French equivalent of a truckers' greasy spoon - with a difference - Scrumptious and plentiful food and reasonable price. Kurt sat next to me, as if he didn't want to let me out of his sight.

While the musicians and dancers talked about the remaining towns on their French tour Rouen, Lille and Paris - we listened and exchanged prolonged looks and discreet smiles. I felt wonderfully alive and excited.

* * *

The musicians were booked for two concerts in Nantes, Tuesday and Wednesday nights, and had planned to allow themselves a few days rest before driving on to Rouen where they were due to perform on the Saturday. Kurt played so exceptionally well on the Tuesday night, bringing out such profoundly moving sounds and bell-like resonances from his instrument, that the show was - so to speak - a resounding success and the group got talked by the happy theatre director into staying on for another performance on the Friday night.

It was all right by me. I had found a decent and reasonable B.& B. and would have time to visit with Irene and her new love when they showed up. They arrived on Wednesday afternoon and left a message for me at the Grand Théâtre as if I was part of La Fin'Amor, instructing me to meet them in the lobby of the Hotel Mercure at 5 p.m. for drinks. To celebrate their engagement.

I was there promptly at five. By 5:30, I was dozing off in a club chair, marveling contentedly at the wonderful adventure my life had become, when they emerged from the lift holding hands.

The sight of them instantly brought me to my feet. A cry escaped me while I covered my mouth with my hand. "Sweet Mother of God!" For a fleeting instant, superimposed on Irene's elegant silhouette, my eyes - or my addle mind - had seen the plump and jolly image of Mother Clara.

By her side stood a tall distinguished-looking man who had, during the same instant borrowed the grizzled countenance of Sir Eudes de Beynac.

CHAPTER 17

Mother Clara reborn as Irene? Reunited at last with the only man she had ever loved, Eudes de Beynac? The evanescent vision left me utterly bewildered. What kind of a joke was this? Was I thus destined to meet every single person who had shared my life 800 years ago? Daphne had talked at length of what she called "Group Karma." It was a belief that people are often re-born in clusters in order to work out complex relationships. She was quite persuasive and while I had been willing to admit the possibility at the time, this was getting a bit much.

First Kurt - Thank God for that! Then Christine - which was quite sweet, actually - and now Irene and her man! What next? Black Foulk? Perhaps I was making it all up, after all. Where was Daphne to reassure me as to the state of my sanity. A small shiver ran down my spine....

Meanwhile Irene had spotted me and was making a beeline across the red-carpeted lobby with little cries of delight and out of control hand waving, while her white-haired companion smiled on indulgently. How could one entertain the thought that Irene had ever lived as a pious celibate nun? She was wearing a purple suit with a very short skirt unmistakably Ungaro - that would have looked over-the-top on anyone else. She looked stunning. I rose from my chair on shaky legs.

"Sandra! What's the matter with you, Sweetie? You look as if you've seen a ghost! Does purple make me look that bad?" Her throaty laughter drowned my denial.

"As for you, your cute mute is doing wonders for your complexion!" She exclaimed, turning heads within a range of sixty feet.

"You look positively radiant! God knows you needed that. And you smell lovely. I can't believe it, you're actually wearing scent, and a good one too! All right, where is he?"

I returned her two-cheek kiss, my eyes on the urbane man who waited to be introduced, vainly searching his face for a sign that he had ever been a fierce warrior of Eudes' ilk. Irene turned to him with a flourish and boomed, "Sandra, meet Olivier de Prézac, my lord and master! Olivier, this is Alexandra Pearson.

You already know enough about her to call her Sandra."

The man had enough poise not to look embarrassed. His keen brown eyes never left my face as he held my hand and brought it to within an inch of his lips. I didn't lower my own eyes and a spark of recognition seemed to fly between us. Sheer delusion on my part? Without giving us the opportunity to exchange any greeting, Irene inquired again, "Well, where is the famous troubadour?" "You will meet him later tonight, after the concert." I replied, still unsure it was such a great idea. "I managed to get you some tickets, thanks to him."

What made me want to bring Kurt and Irene face to face? For I was aware of a strong compulsion to do so. Had Walther ever met Mother Clara? Would meeting her again help to evoke memories of the distant past? How would Kurt react to Olivier, a man he had joyfully cuckolded in his previous life? These thoughts were making me dizzy. Covering my confusion with a smile, I added, "I hope you enjoy the performance."

"I'm sure we will." Olivier acknowledged with a nod. "Thank you for thinking of us.

Let's go and have that drink before the bar fills up. You will join us for dinner, won't you Mrs. Pearson?"

"Please, do call me Sandra. Yes, I'd love to join you for dinner, thank you."

So far, I had been sharing three late dinners with Kurt and was looking forward to sharing many more; but I couldn't very well refuse Olivier's invitation after asking them to change their travel plans and come all the way to Nantes.

Besides, I was glad to see Irene after all these months and spend some time with her. By the look of things, the man she had found looked worthy of her in every way. And I was glad of that too. All the more so if he was really Eudes reborn as a handsome and urbane companion.

* * *

Dinner was fun, but then everything seemed to be more fun since meeting Kurt in person. Kurt might well be Walther reborn, but he was real and attractive enough in his own right not to need reinforcements from his medieval past. The thought that he seemed to seek my company filled me with a bubbly feeling of elation.

Anyway, watching Irene and Olivier in the light of my "vision" of their common past was quite amusing. For as long as I had known Irene, she had always emoted around men. It was one of her techniques and it often worked; some men were actually flattered to see her exert herself so on their behalf and took her play-acting as a compliment.

During that dinner, she showed no sign of affectation. There was no gushing, no head tossing, no cooing; she was really herself. I mean, her very own deep-down self: charming, warm and attentive. She didn't even brush the subject of my regression and refrained from asking about Kurt. Olivier was bringing out the best in her, and the more closely I observed them, the more their eyes reminded me of the two lovers from the past. So, we mostly talked about them; Olivier's work for a European multilingual television channel, and their plans to settle in a larger apartment in Paris. They obviously relished each other on many planes. To me they appeared to have reached this rare state of indulgence for each other's faults that some couples achieve only after many years of turmoil. No extra-sensory perception was needed to feel the sensual undercurrent between them.

As dinner progressed from quenelles de brochet to mousse au chocolate, they relaxed enough to start asking about my strange experiences. I told them more or less the whole story, trying to remain truthful while glossing slightly over Alix's various appetites. When I mentioned Comarque, Olivier's eyebrows rose.

"Well, I'll be! I know that castle." He exclaimed. "It's about seven kilometers from my home. I used to go there with the Cubs as a kid. We had a lot of fun playing in the ruins and the caves underneath.

There was something about that place I always liked. Actually, I owe some of my best childhood memories to Comarque. I remember being quite happy exploring there, and very sad at the same time."

"Why, Dear?" Asked Irene, placing her manicured hand over his.

"Hard to say." His wry smile was full of warmth. "I would have preferred that castle to remain whole, I suppose. It's a fascinating sight, I'll take you there, Irene, it's really worth the walk."

When I brought up the names of Mother Clara and Sir Eudes, Irene began to nod and I felt my pulse racing, but she didn't interrupt. Olivier frowned. "This convent you mention, the old Prieuré in Espagnac, it's still there, you know. And so is Hautefort castle." He paused. "It's amazing that the life you are telling us about should be centered in a region that is so familiar to me! It makes me feel as if... I actually shared your past! How strange." Phew. How close was he going to get? Not close enough for me to tell them what I had seen of their past, anyway. These startling revelations would have to wait.

Though they gave no sign of being incredulous, they remained silent for what seemed a long time. So, I thought it best to conclude my medieval story as quickly and brightly as I could, to bring us back to the present, reminding them we should not be late for the concert.

As we walked the short distance from their hotel to the opera house, I half-listened to their impressions of Nantes while thinking of Kurt and the time we had already spent together. Beside the psaltery, we had at least something else in common: we both enjoyed good food. But, if I felt quite prepared to dine a second time tonight, it was not for the food but for his company.

* * *

Our tête-à-têtes over dinner had been the highlight of the three days I had known Kurt. Last night, we had actually "conversed" quite agreeably.

He had explained - in writing, of course - his knowledge of English by the fact his mother was English. A military nurse in Coventry during the Second World War, she had fallen in love with a German prisoner of war under her care. His father, a Luftwaffe pilot whose plane had been shot down over England during the Battle of Britain, had managed to bail out though grievously wounded, been taken and sent to a military hospital. As he returned the nurse's affection, he had sought her out after the war and married her. They had been happy, Kurt wrote, until his father's death, five years ago.

I thought it was a touching story, and told him so. He looked at me intently for a moment and wrote, "Come to England with me at the end of the tour."

A surge of joy made me want to laugh and cry at the same time. The grin on Kurt's handsome face made laughter more appropriate; I laughed and nodded vigorously. Yes!!!

For the first time in this life, I welcomed the unknown. Whatever had happened to us 800 years ago, I was willing once more to take a chance on life. And love.

Why do we find it so hard to change? To discard old habits and attitudes? Mistakenly assuming that they are us and that we cannot renounce them without renouncing our so- called personality? When they are, I believe, a mere security device against the world's perceived entropy. As Alix, I had not been scared of changes. Why should I be now?

Kurt had willingly agreed to meet Irene and Olivier after the Wednesday night performance. Which was nice of him. He was certainly easy going. Watching his infectious grin, I couldn't help wonder about his ability to laugh in spite of his handicap.

"You know, Kurt, your resilience is truly amazing." I remarked at some point. "Are you always in such high spirits, in spite of...everything?" My comment sounded like crass intrusion to my ears, and I regretted making it; but Kurt didn't appear to mind. Picking up his pen, he paused for a second before writing, and jotted down, "Give yourself some credit, Sandra. I enjoy your company. My life should have ended two years ago. It did not. Which taught me not to ask for anything more. When you don't, you get the best thrown in." With a sunny smile, he added, in large letters, "I met you, didn't I?" This kind of serenity came through in his playing.

* * *

The audience must have felt it during the Wednesday night concert; people seemed to hold their breath during his solo performances. I know I did, anyway.

Irene and Olivier were sitting five rows behind me.

I would have liked us to sit together, but I wasn't sorry to be spared her unavoidable nudging and whispered comments. I felt free to devote my entire attention to the music. And Kurt.

Was it the darkened room or my quasi- hypnotic concentration on him that made my lids so heavy that I had to close my eyes?

When I opened them, Kurt was still playing; only he was no longer Kurt but Walther playing the lute, and we were no longer in Nantes. We were back in the past and on our way to the Holy Land.

* * *

We are riding on a narrow dirt road along a swift and sparkling river between verdant hills. Green oaks grow on both side of the path and their branches shade us from the bright sun. What we see of the sky through their foliage is so intensely blue that it delights the eye as much as the myriad wild flowers in the fields along the way.

The April sun is so warm I feel my linen shift cling to my back. I let my blue velvet mantle slip from my shoulders onto the rump of my snorting grey mare and pull off my embroidered silk gloves to rub my sweaty palms on her silky mane. From the glass vial hanging from my belt, I shake a few drops of jasmine essence on my damp bliaud, in case Walther seek my company and ride up to the head of the column.

We have been travelling by land for thirty days in the company of three-score mounted knights I do not know and countless men-at arms I have no wish to know for they are dirty and foul-mouthed, and carry all kinds of nasty weapons the clanking of which is no more music to my ears than the persistent squeaking of their supply carts. These wagons appear to carry more whores than supplies The pace may be slow, but my saddle feels hard of a morning. Still, we have enjoyed many beautiful sights along the way. The city of Carcassonne, with its high walls and innumerable towers remains in my mind as the most impressive of them all; but this part of Provence we are crossing now is by far the most pleasing with its mild days and fragrant nights. Walther does not always understand the local language and rides up to my side often for counsel.

Eudes is irked by our slow pace; he is getting more and more impatient to reach Palestine and free our Saviors' tomb and His Holy City from the Infidels. As for me, I would thoroughly enjoy the journey if it were not for my longing for Walther and the fact that I miss little Robert and Eloise so much.

On the eve of our departure, Eudes informed me of his decision not to take the children along but to send them back to Hautefort with Helga for reasons of safety. I gave way to such a fit of temper that Eudes was left agape and speechless.

No doubt, my ill humor was in part attributable to enforced chastity since his return to Comarque a week before. But only in part. The thought of abandoning the children for months - years even - caused me great discontent, and still does.

With tears of frustration and anger, I reminded Eudes of his promise never to send the children away from us. It may be years before we come back from the Holy Land and I see them again!

In a meek voice, he finally replied that this rash promise had been made without taking proper account of the dangers that awaited pilgrims on the voyage. Remembering the hardships, he had endured during his first journey to the Holy Land with King Richard, he now thought better of it. The children would be safer in Hautefort.

"Surely, My Lady Wife, it is not your wish to expose the little ones to the perils of treacherous sea and Turk-ridden land?" He argued.

Unable to gainsay him, I gathered my skirts in a flurry and ran to lock myself in my chamber till well past bell ringing for complines. Only emerging from it when the sounds of Walther's lute playing reached my ears from the great hall.

Even though I agree with Eudes' decision not to endanger the children's lives, I am sorely grieved by it and have missed them all along the way. They are precious to me in many ways. Not the least of which is their innocence.

Sweet moments spent with Eloise during the past months have somehow preserved me from giving myself over entirely to sinful lust. Combing her golden hair, or guiding her small hand to form letters on parchment, I feel shriven from my nights with Walther.

For well do I know that my love for Walther is a sin in the eyes of God. Though I do not set store on the Church's dictates and have no wish to confess to any priest, there are times when betrayal of Eudes, who has been good to me, weighs heavily on my conscience.

It was tempting to follow the children to Hautefort rather than accompany my lord and my lover to Palestine; but I could not bear the thought of being parted from Walther. All the more so since my husband's return to Comarque had kept us apart for over a week before departure and deprived us of our nightly delights. Even though Walther was not scrupled about cuckolding Eudes in his absence, he deemed it unseemly to do so when he was back in Comarque under his own roof.

Which made me eager for us to be travelling; opportunities might arise on the way. So far, they have not.

As we round a bend on the road, the vista opens out; a wide valley extends as far as the shimmering sea. One of the young squires who ride by my side exclaims joyfully, "Look, My Lady! Villeneuve! T'is where we are to stay the night!"

He points out straight ahead at the wonderful sight of white towers rising from a green hill at the foot of which huddle many small houses with red clay-tile roofs. Under the cloudless blue sky, it is surely a delightful sight and it spurs the whole column to a brisker pace as weary men and beast look forward to their rest.

Most every night, we have enjoyed the hospitality of some lord or another, in large or small castle, keep or manor house. As yet, no chance of a nightly encounter with Walther has presented itself. We must be content to exchange burning looks at every opportunity and caress each other with our thoughts in others' presence. My longing for him knows no bounds and I fear my face will betray my lust whenever he rides by my side.

I am especially wary of Bogo, who always seems to press his mule forward and inflict his sour smell on us whenever he sees us riding together. Even though that sly cleric has been all smiles ever since I made him a present of a wrought silver cross with a large garnet, I do not trust his twisted and slimy nature. That Eudes would want to take him along for spiritual comfort and guidance is a source of puzzlement to me; the man is false and steeped in unspeakable sin. Surely the likes of him cannot have the Lord's ear? What gives him the right to grant anyone absolution?

To my relief, Eudes has made no attempt to claim his husbandly rights, and has yet to enter my bedchamber. Me thinks he will not do so before his year of penance is over. He is a man of his word and will abide by his vow.

The thought that he will discover then that I am no longer a maiden does not trouble as yet; I will think of something when the time comes. Unlike Queen Iseult, I will not ask my virgin maid to take my place in my husband's bed. This passage of my favorite story has always seemed hard to believe; can a man be so easily deceived?

* * *

For two days now, we have been staying here, in Villeneuve, the goodly chateau of Sir Romée. We are still on our way to Venice, to secure passage to the Holy Land; but that city is so many days away I have stopped counting and I am glad of a rest in such a splendid venue.

Sir Romée de Villeneuve has extended lavish welcome to us, with splendid feasts and richly appointed rooms in his beautiful residence. The whole stronghold is newly built on a rise of evenly matched white stone; larger than Comarque, though perhaps not as impregnable.

The walls of the great hall are painted in brightly hued design and the lord's residence is most pleasantly ornamented with tapestries and silk panels in the brightest colors imaginable on its white stone walls. Fragrant rushes are brought in every day and strewn on the smooth stone floors, and sweet scents pervade the rooms from strange herbs the servants throw on the fires.

Sir Romée is a fair enough knight, who might have stirred my interest had I not been so enamored of Walther. They say he has a jealous disposition and a fierce temper. Yet, his good sense appears to match his pride, for he will not join our pilgrimage, though he has granted leave to four of his knights to do so.

No argument from Eudes has so far persuaded him to travel to the confines of the known world in order to slay infidels for the greater glory of the Church. Last night he treated us to a feast the equal of which is not to be had, even at the court of King Philip, who tends to spare the expense whenever he can.

After partaking of much delicious fare, and watching tumblers and jugglers, Walther agreed to delight us with songs of his own composition. His voice holds such enchantment that it stilled the raucous knights into silence and Sir Romée who is a learned man compared him to the Orpheus of legend. Even the servants stopped and listened instead of pilfering food from the platters.

I watched my lord Eudes' face as he sat on Sir Romée' left, leaning against the high carved back of his chair and listening to the words of Walther's song. Walther sang of knights fighting in Palestine and praised the glory of suffering for Our Lord.

Eudes approved with the occasional nod, his chiseled featured suffused with unshakeable faith. I envy him his staunchness of purpose; passion has left me adrift in doubt, hardly willing even to seek Our Lady's succor for fear its price might be renouncing sinful dalliance.

* * *

I would have enjoyed our stay in Villeneuve exceedingly, if it were not for Douce d'Entrevènes.

I recognized her at once when we passed the postern gatehouse; she was standing by Sir Romée's side to welcome us, and the first sight of her made me tremble. For she is none other than the maiden who appeared so smitten with Walther at the court of King Philip; and who seemed to enjoy his attention at the time.

She is still affianced to Sir Romée de Villeneuve, lord of the castle, and they are to be wedded soon. Meanwhile, she is already in residence under the watchful eye of her betrotheds' mother. Whether she be a maiden still remains a matter of conjecture.

She appeared to have conquered her infatuation and greeted my lover with the graceful indifference of a seasoned chatelaine. I catch his glance on her whenever he thinks I am not looking, and though she keeps her eyes down, I do not trust her. The jealous demon who devours my heart gives me a taste of the torments of hell.

* * *

Still, I have to spend my days at Villeneuve in her company, and that of her future mother-in-law, Lady Astruge.

The arched windows of the ladies' solar offer a magnificent view of mountains and sea. I cannot stop gazing with wonder at this infinity of water wedded to the infinity of the sky. It speaks more eloquently of the grandeur of the Lord's creation than any priestly sermon.

Douce is standing by my side at the window. The sight of the sea is so familiar to her that she finds my reverence for it amusing; a smile briefly lights up her small sad face.

In other circumstances we could have been friends for Douce is not without grace, accomplishments and wit. Though her body is as a starved child's and she wears ill-fitting garment in dull hues, her eyes are large and bright and her hair is as spun gold. Something in her smile brings to mind Isabelle, my convent friend.

Does she still pine for Fair Walther? Does Walther still like to see his own image reflected in her luminous eyes?

I soon get weary of quietly talking in her goodly solar while munching on delicious sweetmeats made of almond paste. Lady Astruge, Sir Romée's mother, listens in silence; appears to devote all her attention to her intricate needlework, while darting suspicious glances in our direction.

Douce shows me some manuscripts illuminated by her with such skill that even Mother Clara would admire. She asks me if I like music, and picking up a lute begins to play a pleasant tune. Her singing voice is both surprisingly strong and melodious.

I decide to send Elaine to fetch my psaltery, and rejoice that Douce knows not how to play it. I also rejoice to see her blanch when I say, "'Tis a present from Sir Walther von Altdorf." Before leaving us in the solar, my lord Eudes has informed me with a courteous bow that he would be riding ahead with some of the knights as far as the castle of the Grimaldis, in a place called Monaco, where a council of pilgrims is to be held on the morrow. Sir Romée would accompany them and return on his own.

I am to join Eudes in two days with the rest of the knights and the smelly rabble of soldiers.

I wished my lord God speed, not daring to ask if Walther will be riding with him. Some instinct tells me Douce would like to know too. I thank the Lord God for Romée's mother vigilant presence. Tonight, I will send Elaine away from my bedchamber.

* * *

Not until matines, as I lay awake on my lonely bed, still unable to find sleep, does my door open silently to admit Walther. I am too overjoyed by his presence and too feverish from our long abstinence to inquire how he has spent the first half of the night.

CHAPTER 18

Thunderous applause jolted me back to the present. I was still in Nantes, ensconced in a red plush seat at the opera house, where the audience was giving La Fin'Amor's performance a standing ovation.

Still too bewildered to move, I stayed put while all around me people jumped to their feet and cried "Bravo!" The fat lady next to me remained seated too and fanned herself furiously with her program, sending waves of cloying scent in my direction.

The musicians soon attacked an Estampie Real as an encore, and spectators resumed their seats, satisfied to watch the dancers give the lilting music its sensual dimension.

* * *

Going in and out of the past on my own was in some ways more traumatic than being led there by Daphne's ministrations.

For one thing, it took me longer to gather my wits once back in the present. As if the past was clinging to me. Re-living Alix's passion for Walther was indeed marvelous, but rather overwhelming. Uncontrollable. The more I enjoyed its thrills, the more determined I was not to let it influence my budding relationship with Kurt. I was definitely attracted to the man, but something told me this attraction had to take its course without any interference from the past.

I think Kurt felt the same way. He seemed to accept the principle of reincarnation, and even the possibility of his having lived as Walther; but it was obvious that he was far from convinced though he made efforts to keep an open mind. He also appeared to like me in the present tense.

Last night, during dinner, I had summoned enough courage to ask him, "Why did you run away from me when I started playing the psaltery?"

Frowning, he had put down his knife and fork and reached for his fountain-pen. He held it over the paper for what seemed like a long time before starting to write. It seemed the answer to my question required some soul- searching and a more formal phrasing than his usual jotted replies.

"Because I was scared." He paused, and I remembered his tense back and measured steps. Controlled panic. He took a deep breath and went on writing. "Not only did you look oddly familiar even though I had never met you before, you were playing a piece by Walther von Altdorf!

A fragment of a song discovered only recently among the ruins of a monastery in Bavaria, and which I was including in my study of Walther! How could you know of it? Let alone play it so well? You even completed the missing melody line!

There was something eerie... supernatural... about your performance.

Part of me sensed that it was linked in some way with the strange - in truth, the horrifying - experience which had caused me to lose control of my car." So many exclamation marks! I thought, moving closer to him and craning my neck to read as he wrote. He glanced up from the paper, pain flickering in his eyes. Over his wife's death? But beside grief and guilt, his face betrayed a lingering fear. My heart went out to him. He may have sensed it because, he gave me a wry smile before writing the last sentence. "As far as I was concerned, you were bad news!"

I must have looked pretty upset reading it because he grabbed the paper back from my hand and added quickly, "So, I was wrong.

Nobody's perfect." With an impish grin, he scribbled some more.

"Did I ever tell you that you are the best thing to happen to me in a long time, well, two years to be exact? And that I would love to hear you play again. Soon. I'm not scared any more. Are you?"

I looked deep into his smiling eyes and shook my head.

I could well understand his cold shivers; I had experienced a few myself since the beginning of my strange adventure. Even though we crave the fantastic as entertainment, nothing in our modern upbringing prepares us for its intrusion in our own life.

From infancy, Reason is the only tenant foisted on our minds; supposedly to dwell there alone and unchallenged, occupying every room and banishing to the attic of childhood fantasies anything remotely irrational. In fact, or so it seems to me, few human beings live rational lives. Some follow the dictates of religions, while others know no other guide than their basest and usually inane impulses.

Yet they all seem agreed on one point; if some mysteries of life and death cannot be explained rationally or dogmatically, they are not to be taken seriously or allowed to interfere with the safe routine of everyday life.

Do we all, at some time in our life, get an "intimation of immortality" by feelings or visions? Or am I to be counted among the lucky few? Did Kurt get one at the wheel of his car with unhappy results? There was something else I had to ask him.

"Did doctors ever figure out what caused the...loss of your voice?"

He shook his head and frowned as if reluctant to put his answer on paper. Before writing, he pulled at his shirt collar to reveal a whitish scar snaking at the base of his neck. "They ruled out this as a cause, said it was paralysis of the vocal cords and that my voice might come back." He looked up with a half-smile. "I have forgotten what I sound like. Perhaps, I'll never find out."

* * *

By the time the two encores were over and the curtain came down, I was more or less functional and wondering what would happen when Kurt met Irene and Olivier back-stage. Would he turn away from them as he had turned away from me when I played the psaltery?

I stood up and followed the crowd down the aisle.

Irene and Olivier were still seated, waiting for me, and I had no need to ask for Irene's opinion on the concert.

"Wonderful, Darling!" She enthused. "The man is a musical genius! And you know what? I got this strange feeling I had met him before... Something like what I experienced with Olivier." Reaching for her companion's arm, she hastened to add, "Well, nothing as sensual, of course. You need not worry, my love."

Olivier, his face a blank, didn't reply and appeared in no hurry to leave the fast- emptying hall and make the acquaintance of the musicians.

By the time we reached the stage, the instruments were already packed and the musicians ready to leave. Instrumentalists and dancers greeted us with friendly smiles and briefly nodded thanks as Irene went from one to the next with enthusiastic comments on their playing and dancing. She was giving Kurt covert glances, touching her own cheek lightly with well-manicured fingers. A sure sign she found him attractive.

Kurt stood at the back of the stage, still wearing his medieval costume. I noticed that the bindings on his soft leather boots were tied the same way as Walther's, with a double intricate knot. He was watching Irene with amused curiosity and appeared to be waiting patiently for her little performance to end.

Then his eyes settled on Olivier, and his handsome face froze. It was a mild reaction compared to Olivier's.

His amiable features suddenly distorted by unmistakable hostility; Irene's friend was staring at Kurt with veiled malevolence. In a strange and abrupt gesture, his right hand flew to his left side, as if seeking the hilt of an absent dagger. He blinked twice and just stood there as rigid as a statue.

Holding my breath within the sudden hollow in my chest, I stepped over to Kurt's side and, with my back to Olivier, whispered, "The man you are about to meet was known to you in your previous life. You betrayed his friendship and he obviously bears you an unconscious grudge. Sorry, I should have warned you... I'll explain later."

Kurt put his hand in his pocket as if to retrieve his notebook and pen, then thought better of it and took a few steps in Olivier's direction with his right hand extended.

Olivier hesitated before stepping forward. His face still set in a sullen mask, he appeared to make an obvious effort to control a distaste he neither understood nor expected. His easy air of confidence had deserted him completely. The two men stood eye to eye, measuring each other for a second or so before Olivier finally shook Kurt's proffered hand. And stepped back without uttering a word. Kurt's shoulders stiffened under the red silk of his medieval finery. His face darkened as he watched Olivier in wordless puzzlement.

To me the scene felt like a slow-moving nightmare. Blithely unaware of the subtly hostile interaction between the two men, Irene was beaming. His face white and taut, Olivier turned to her and forced a smile on his lips.

"Well, Irene, I think we should let these people relax after their wonderful performance."

The higher pitch of his voice betrayed his emotions. He must have been aware of it for he cleared his throat with a discreet cough. "It's time to go back to our hotel, my dear. Don't forget we are leaving early tomorrow."

"What? So soon?" Irene's eyes widened; she looked thoroughly disconcerted. "But... I have so many questions for Herr Meissen about the music, and the songs, and the dances! And those bawdy verses I couldn't quite understand!"

Olivier laughed, self-control restored, his sense of humor obviously at odds with the puzzling animosity he felt against Kurt. "Yes, that's exactly what Herr Meissen must be afraid of. I think both he and Sandra deserve a rest tonight, don't you? You will see them tomorrow before we leave... We were all supposed to have breakfast together, weren't we?" The brittle tone of his question, betraying his expectation of a negative answer, wasn't lost on Kurt who frowned and showed signs of thorough aggravation with the man.

Olivier appeared not to notice and took Irene's arm with great gentleness.

"Come on, ma chère, let us say good-night."

And she did. Warmly and willingly. With none of the scathing ill-humor she would have inflicted on any other man impudent enough to tell her what to do. They were obviously looking forward to their night together.

As we bussed each other on both cheeks, she whispered. "Grab him! Take him to bed! Don't let him get away!"

Olivier held my hand for what seemed a long time while he renewed his kind invitation to spend some time with them at his family place in Périgord.

As I turned it down again, he murmured, "I will have to come and visit you in Montreal, then." Giving my hand a little squeeze.

In other circumstances, this could have been interpreted as a come-on and I would have dismissed him as a two-timer. He was looking at me with a kind of candid surprise as if he could not understand what made him take such an interest in me. All the same, it might perhaps be wiser to avoid Olivier's company in the future. I had no desire to muddy the waters where Irene swam so happily by raising the silt of their past-life tribulations.

Especially Eudes' somber attachment to Alix and the pain it might have caused him....

For there was no need to go back in time to surmise that Eudes had found out about Alix's and Walther's betrayal. Olivier's unconscious loathing of Kurt was proof enough. Or was it? Perhaps I was Just dreaming the whole thing and Olivier was simply jealous of Irene's overt interest for Kurt. Or else he didn't like Germans....

If this was not all delusions, how and when had Eudes discovered his marital misfortune? But more to the point, what had been the consequences of this discovery for the lovers?

* * *

Kurt and I left the theatre together. We made our way to the nearest brasserie through gusts of fierce rain and wind that threatened to carry my umbrella and me over the Nantes rooftops - Mary Poppins fashion - until Kurt took the umbrella from my hand, closed it, and removing his beige raincoat draped it over my head and shoulders. It smelled faintly of lavender and the feel of it sent a small shiver of pleasure down my spine. Holding on to my waist with one arm, he gestured toward the lighted windows of a café with the other, urging me on to a final sprint.

The old-fashioned brasserie was a brightly lit haven of warmth. Polished brass rails, red moleskin benches, starched white table-cloths and a haze of food aromas and cigarette smoke. Not a turn-off in my case; both my husband and Franco had been smokers and the smell of tobacco always evoked pleasant associations.

Not so for Kurt obviously, he wrinkled his fine nose and motioned with his chin to the farthest corner of the vast room where only an old man sat sipping a cognac and peering at a newspaper.

The old man lifted his head briefly from the racing form as we sat down in the next booth. Kurt immediately took out his pad and pen, his eyes formulating the question before he wrote it down.

"Why was this man so hostile to me? Does he hate Germans? You don't have to tell me I met him before, I KNOW I did. Now I understand what you meant when you spoke of certainty. Your friends are no strangers to me; I met them before, whether in this life which is very unlikely - or in another. So, tell me about them. Please."

"I have already told you about him. He was Eudes. My husband, the one you cuckolded so magnificently." I couldn't keep the laughter from my voice and the garçon who handed us the huge menus smiled in sympathy. Whether for the cuckold or for me, I couldn't say.

"Anyway, you betrayed his friendship, you rogue." The waiter was still hovering. "Let's order now, shall we?" I asked Kurt. "What would you like?"

He scanned the menu quickly and pointed to the plat-du-jour, Steak Diane. I ordered a buckwheat crêpe, a specialty from Britany, and for me a taste acquired solely to spite my mother who detested that part of France for obscure family reasons.

As soon as the waiter had departed, I added, still laughing, "Yes, you put a pair of horns on Eudes' forehead and it looks as if he still bears you a grudge, eight hundred years later. You were a real devil with the ladies, Walther! I wonder how many wronged husbands are out to get you in this life?"

His laughter was refreshingly earthy; a kind of lusty mirth that livened up his rather stern features until he did resemble his old self. Still grinning, he scribbled another question. "What about Irene?"

"I recognized her as Mother Clara... For what it's worth." I replied, allowing my right hand to seek his. "Remember? I told you about Clara. How she had been Eudes' mistress and how he kept marrying someone else every time." Kurt nodded. "Guess she finally got him this time."

He was shaking his head, not so much in disbelief as in surprise, as if he had just discovered there were indeed many more facts of life than he had taken for granted in his fifty-odd years on earth. He was not quite incredulous, but pretty close to it.

"What makes you so sure?" He wrote across the sheet, not bothering to straighten the paper.

"Well... It's so hard to explain... You have to experience it. And I am not 'so sure.' Far from it, in fact. I believe that what I experience is true but I might be hallucinating for all I know." I paused, feeling Kurt's eyes on my face like a caress.

"You told me just now that you knew Irene and Olivier were no strangers to you. Well, that's the way I feel. You don't need proof; you just know it is so. It may be disturbing at first, but after a while you get used to it. It's a very simple feeling, really. As long as you don't start questioning your sanity."

His eyes shone under the bright lights, widened by conflicting emotions. I felt more and more drawn to the man, and determined to help him untangle himself from his past. "Once you begin retrieving memories of a past life," I went on, "It becomes easier to access them even without the help of hypnosis." I was trying to explain the inexplicable, but a catch in my voice kept betraying the depth of my involvement in his own fate.

"I can only speak from my own experience, of course. I got to re-live some parts of my previous life; I had vivid dreams that had little to do with your ordinary garden-variety dreams; and I remembered past events as if they were part of my present life. I guess you can also have sudden, unexpected flash-backs and recognize people, as if their past images were superimposed on their present selves.

Which is what I experienced with Irene and Olivier. Either all this is true or I am certifiably insane. Take your pick."

Kurt must have sensed my bantering tone hid real fear; he placed his hands over mine in a gesture that had become familiar to us. I closed my eyes, letting this wordless comfort keep me safely anchored to the reality of the present.

I knew well enough what he meant by being scared; there were moments when the implications of my experiences swept me into a vortex of helpless confusion. Why was I granted these glimpses of the past? What was the meaning of it all?

I mean, ordinary life is puzzling enough as it is without having to wonder about multiple existences and their purpose. Only the most nagging question remained, was I helping Kurt or would my interference in his life compound his own problems?

I opened my eyes, feeling once more perfectly at ease, relishing this moment of companionable silence and his whimsical smile. Glad his touch was enough to induce a state of pleasurable anticipation; an intimation of great happiness.

I was getting hungry again; my dinner with Irene and Olivier all but forgotten. Though he had not eaten since lunch-time, Kurt gave no sign of impatience over the slow service. Yet, every time we had shared a meal, he had seemed to enjoy his food greatly.

Removing his hands from over mine, he took up his pen again and wrote, "I think I must have had such a flash-back at the wheel of my car. But I can't remember what it was about." "About yourself!" The words were out before I even thought them. "You must have realized Walther was in fact you!"

The thought seemed so overwhelmingly evident that I felt the need to repeat it, "You suddenly knew that you had lived 800 years ago as the knight troubadour whose life and work you were researching!"

With a dubious frown, he scrawled, "Why should it have scared me to the point of making me lose control of my car?"

Good question. However, startling such a discovery might have been, it should not have thrown him into a panic. Unless....

"You say you remember the fright just before the crash but... Can't you recall any of the thoughts and emotions that caused it?"

He nodded once, brushed back a strand of silvery hair from his forehead revealing small beads of perspiration, and stared straight ahead. I could sense the tension in his muscular body under the sedate tweed jacket.

I kept silent. The hum of voices and the clatter of cutlery a crude soundtrack to the drama that was taking place in this man's mind. I prayed no waiter would bring our food just yet. Kurt blinked once and closed his eyes. I held my breath. With a deep sigh, he took his pen and selecting a clean sheet of paper wrote slowly.

"Ever since the accident, I have tried to remember what happened just before the crash... I have tried to forget the fear. I couldn't recall anything but a nightmarish feeling of horror and helplessness. Now I'm not so sure... It seems to me I experienced this nightmare as Walther and actually re-lived it at the wheel of my car."

Turning his handsome face, he looked deep into my eyes, seeking reassurance - or denial before wording his last question.

"Do you think this is true remembrance or am I being influenced by everything you told me?

Am I making this up as an excuse for losing control of my car?" With an icy feeling of dread, I prayed he was indeed making this up.

CHAPTER 19

We ate in silence. I had lost my appetite and the buckwheat crêpes tasted like tissues. I kept glancing at Kurt. He winked at me in self-mockery a few times, but seemed to pay scant attention to the food he was pensively munching. Whatever efforts he was still making to remember his experience were obviously unsuccessful, and he seemed more and more frustrated.

He insisted on paying for that dismal meal as he had for the previous ones.

The rain had stopped and the wind brought us whiffs of low tide and seaweed. The moon, in and out of wispy clouds, splashed quicksilver on the wet pavement. Kurt walked me back to my hotel, holding my elbow to cross deserted streets. Declining a drink in the hotel bar, he took my hands in his and kissed them both lightly before turning on his heels and walking away.

I remained standing in front of the revolving doors, following the fast retreat of his tall silhouette with mixed feelings of yearning and apprehension. Just before rounding the corner, he turned and waved twice.

The small dimly lit lobby was silent too. As I retrieved my room key, the desk clerk informed me that Christine had called and wanted me to phone back. It was well past midnight, but I decided to return her call anyway; I might not get up early enough to catch her before she left in the morning. Lying down on the bed with pillows piled up behind my head, I dialed her number. She was still up and sounded pleased to hear my voice. "Hi, Mum! So how is it going with your German guy? Are you friends yet?"

"We are. We are. And whatever happens next, I am happy to have met him; he is a most attractive - and interesting - man."

"Good. I am glad. The reason I called is that your dear boss... You know, The Jerk, called and said there was no way you could take extra time off as you requested in the message you left on his voice mail. He wants you back in the office as soon as possible so he can take off."

Her voice held both amusement and indignation. "He was actually quite rude about it and said that if you didn't need the job any more, you should let him know so he could advertise for another editor."

"What a shithead!" I sat up abruptly, wishing the idiot was right there in front of me so I could slam the receiver on his fat head. He had no business upsetting Christine with his stupid remarks.

"Sorry, sweetheart. I should have spoken to him instead of leaving a message. The guy is thoroughly obnoxious. He's probably registered in some golf tournament in Outer Mongolia or Patagonia, all expenses paid by the magazine... Meanwhile he is messing up my plans in a big way.

I was thinking of following the musicians till the end of their tour." Not without a slight hesitation, I added, "And perhaps go to England with Kurt at the end of it. So much for that, now."

Christine allowed a small sympathetic silence to bring us closer before replying. "What can I say, Mum? I'm sorry, but he sounded as if he meant it. Pretty nasty, in fact; which surprised me as you always said he was the quiet type." "Well... Shy people can sometimes work themselves into a frenzy." Had I perhaps mistaken a soft spot for a soft heart?

I relaxed back onto the pillows. "Don't worry about it, sweetheart. I'll return to his bloody office and start looking for something else the moment I get back; time for me to move on, I guess, and maybe join a band... I'll explain when I get back. The girls in the office are very nice, but The Jerk is getting a little hard to take, anyway. Listen, what about you?

How did the exams go?"

"Fine, fine. I'm nearly through. As soon as you return to Nice, we'll celebrate."

We went on chatting for a while before hanging up, comforted by each other's concern. The message on my boss' voice-mail requesting more time off had been a spur of the moment impulse, triggered by Kurt's offer to accompany him to England.

I must have sensed it would be turned down because I had neglected to leave my hotel's telephone number. Without actually saying so, or making definite plans to follow him, both Kurt and I knew I wanted to. Now I would have to explain I had to make a living and must go back to Montreal without trying to help him find his past and regain his present.

How could I leave him thus? It felt like desertion. Besides the fact that I didn't look forward to finding myself alone once more after the brief taste of companionship he had given me? The whole crazy adventure could not end there.

Come on, Sandra, I berated myself, no whining. As the French say, night brings good counsel; so, sleep on it.

Instead of a solution, night brought many vivid dreams of the past. So graphic and colorful in fact that they felt more real than life itself.

* * *

Venice. Elbows resting on the stone balcony, I gaze at a vast expanse of water. Water as silvery as the morning clouds. Water lapping the front steps of our palatial abode. Water everywhere.

Though it is October a balmy breeze ruffles my hair. It carries the myriad smells of the sea and sweeps away the odors from the smaller canals. I breathe deeply, feeling a sudden unaccountable joy rush through my veins. I open my eyes wide to the shimmering light. Light in Venice endows everything with its own magic. At times is seems the whole silvery city is but a chimera born of the union of light and water.

Upon rising of a morning, I sit on this balcony overlooking the widest of the city's many canals. Galleys pass by swiftly propelled by their rowers. And many small wooden boats they call gondolas ferry merchants, nobles and ladies to and fro across the water.

Their black curved prows often adorned with bright ribbons, to match the gold, azure and vermillion of the passengers' attire. Courteous exchanges of greetings carry over the water, in counterpoint with the songs of the boatmen.

One or another of these gondoliers will lift his laughing eyes up to the balcony where we sit, and lean on his pole awhile the better to look at Elaine and me; singing with great boldness words that hold no meaning for me, and which I rejoice to hear.

When women are in the boat, they berate the boatman until, with one last "Ché Bella!" he pushes his merry craft away.

But men passengers, young and old, never fail to greet us most courteously as they glide by. Be they merchants or nobles, they are all splendidly arrayed in tunics and robes trimmed with precious pale furs even in the warmest weather. Some are fair to behold, and a blush comes to Elaine's cheeks as she throws them shy glances, her needlework forgotten in her lap.

Venetian men may be handsome enough but they are full of their own importance and talk more readily than they listen. They remind me of poor lady Adela's hapless lover. Lord God have mercy on their souls!

As for the women, they appear as inordinately proud of the peculiar reddish hue of their blond hair as of the shape of their bosoms, which they display in the most generous fashion. They wear an abundance of brilliant jewels to ornament their luxurious attire. Which I take no small pleasure in emulating. To do honor to my lord Eudes, of course. There is an air of ease and serenity among Venetians which gladdens the heart. Venice is a most exhilarating city, where beauty and pleasure thrive. I derive daily enjoyment from it, whether being ferried along its broad avenues of water bordered by arched stone palaces; or visiting its innumerable churches; or simply sitting here on my balcony playing the psaltery and looking across the shimmering waters, the rapture of Walther's rare embraces ever presence in my thoughts.

* * *

Eudes left Venice with the fleet four days ago, taking with him for spiritual solace ugly Bogo, the cleric, whose absence afford me much spiritual comfort.

Indeed, Bogo has proved most troublesome ever since our arrival in Venice; his distasteful countenance to be found behind every door I open, in every dark corner of every room of this labyrinthine palace. He never says a word, but his unblinking raven eyes and his thin scornful smile are enough to chill my bones, and spoil some of our trysts.

Why, one time Walther came to visit, I had to send him away with a mere kiss; Bogo having settled himself - whether by chance or by design - on a bench at the foot of the stairs to my chamber, thus barring the way to our delights.

On the eve of the host's departure, as my gondola was crossing one of the narrower canals, I espied Bogo in a dark lane talking to a man with his back to the water. The man, richly attired in a black velvet cloak bordered in silver, turned sideways. I gasped with fright; it was none other than Black Foulk. Raising the collar of my mantle with a trembling hand, I quickly hid my face lest they should catch sight of me, and observed them until they disappeared from view. What evil were they thus concocting in secret?

In spite of the joy Walther and this blessed city have brought to my heart, I cannot quite rid myself of disquiet; cannot help thinking that the coming together of those two villains bodes ill for us in some way. I fear for Walther.

Even though my lord Eudes is kind and gentle with me, his fierce temper has not deserted him. Wounded pride can still ignite his anger into violent flares, as I have witnessed more than once since we departed from Comarque.

Were the wretch Bogo to expose us, my lord would not take kindly to another betrayal especially from a friend - and his wounded dignity would goad him into exacting dire revenge on Walther, even if he were later to repent this rashness.

For the nonce, we are well rid of Bogo. And Eudes is gone as well.

Not that Eudes was ever in our way in Venice. Even before his departure, most of his waking hours were spent in the company of the pilgrims' leaders, trying to free them from the trap he helped - albeit unwittingly - set for them.

Old doge Dandolo - who is not as blind as he pretends to be, for he winked at me the first time I came into his presence - has proved himself far wilier than all these Frankish, Norman or Provençal barons whose only skill is charging on their war horses with lowered lance or raised up sword.

Doge Dandolo is a formidable old man; his advanced years - they are said to number 92 have not dulled his judgment. Methinks he could outwit the devil himself. He most certainly outwitted my lord Eudes and the other barons sent by the pilgrims to negotiate the price of transport to the Holy Land.

Even though thousands of knights and foot soldiers have made their way to Venice, their numbers are not as high as expected. Those who arrived have been herded on one of these small islands of which the Venetians have so many. Little better than a rock, it could hardly hold such a host, let alone feed it. Then, having at first supplied knights and men-at - arms with plentiful food and forage, Dandolo suddenly stopped; adamantly refusing either to furnish them with any more sustenance, or transporting them to the Holy Land. Unless they paid up all of the 85 000 silver marks, they had foolishly promised him. A vast fortune.

As many of the pilgrims had reneged on their promise to sail from Venice, the ones who had kept their word proved unable to raise the agreed price - even when the most zealous souls among them stripped themselves of all their valuables. Dandolo, the old fox, offered them a choice: starve on the lagoon islet or storm on his behalf the fractious citadel of Zara which had revolted against Venice and become a bothersome foe. I know not where Zara is, but that is where they have gone now.

I confess some admiration for old Dandolo's astuteness; he brings to mind the antics of Reynard the Fox which I found so amusing as jugglers told of them on village squares.

But my lord Eudes is not amused. As one of the parties who had negotiated the price of transport to the Holy Land, Eudes considered himself honor-bound to see this agreement respected; thus, reaping much ill-will from his fellow pilgrims.

I believe the other barons resent him not only for having contributed to their plight through his lack of acumen, but also for the fact that old Dandolo has lodged us in a fine palace instead of making us share the fate of the other barons on their accursed island.

Eudes has been away most days and oftentimes most nights; always sending word of his late return. Which I consider both considerate and fortunate under the circumstances. I made it my duty to wait for him and comfort him with mulled wine and soothing words. Among so many ruthless men seeking nothing but vainglory and riches, Eudes never loses sight of his holy purpose: to free Jerusalem from the Saracen bondage. Seeing him thus troubled, vilified by his peers, and betrayed by men and circumstances, I feel a growing compassion and a new respect for him, and not little guilt at bringing dishonor to his couch.

Can I help the love I bear Walther? To him only was my troth pledged the day I first laid eyes on him in my lady Adela's solar. Love is indeed akin to madness and no remedy was ever found for it. If I cannot be cured of this malady of love - which causes one much anguish through separations, obstacles, doubts and jealousy - am I not at least permitted to savior the joys it does bring now and again?

So, I also encouraged my lord husband to keep on pleading with the cunning old doge. A time-consuming endeavor which kept him safely away for hours on end.

Dandolo remained adamant and insisted on seeing Zara subdued before transporting the host to Palestine. This outrageous demand raised many a pilgrim's ire, and much dissension ensued among them. A fair number of knights - Walther among them declined to participate in the storming of a Christian town and refused to spill the blood of fellow Christians, however rebellious they might be. Or so they said. Some even left and made their way to Palestine by other means. Not Walther. May the Lord God be thanked for that.

* * *

In the end, the doge prevailed, and it is now four days since the host sailed off to take Zara; old Dandolo standing fully armed in the prow of his own galley at the head of the fleet. Farewelled by the clamors of the crowd.

It was a wondrous sight indeed. A sight such as few are fortunate enough to behold in a lifetime. Hundreds upon hundreds of richly ornamented ships and galleys sailing away, heavy with knights and foot soldiers, their war horse and siege machines.

Great drums pounding time for the galley oarsmen. Silver trumpets blaring. Crimson pennants and banners flapping in the wind; brightly painted shields and shiny coats of mail glittering in the sun. Noble ladies waiving from their balconies and shedding many a tear on the vermillion silk of their fluttering sleeves.

The festive occasion was made even more joyous for me by Walther's presence by my side.

As soon as unruly Zara falls - as it is bound to do under such an onslaught - I am to sail away from Venice to join Eudes in Corfu, an island somewhere in the middle of the sea. Not a thought to bring rejoicing to my heart. All the more so since Eudes' year of abstinence will be over by the time we reach Palestine.

Still, since my lord left, I go every day to St. Mark's cathedral - surely the most beautiful church that ever was - to pray for his safety and that of his little children I sorely miss. The least I can do to atone for my betrayal. Alas, I have no wish to leave this miraculous city for a Holy Land that seems to have little to offer save its Holiness. I cannot bear the thought of being parted from Walther.

* * *

The few hours of bliss we enjoy when he finds time to visit me have sustained my spirits during many a lonely hour.

After he is gone, I often fret lest his seed grow in me despite the potions I dutifully swallow after our encounters to keep myself sterile, for I do not like the use of wool plugs.

These "cups of roots" I have taken to drinking since we became lovers have not failed me as yet, and it is easier to secure their makings in Venice. I pound Alexandrian gum, alum and garden crocus together and mix it with ale.

Whenever I swallow the bitter mixture, I recall how Isabelle and I had once crept back to the copying hall in the dead of night to read by the light of a candle a tome Mother Clara had left on her lectern. It was a treatise by a certain Soranus on woman's health and body functions.

Mother Clara had read some passages to us but had declared the rest unsuitable for maidenly ears. Thus, pricking our maidenly curiosity. We had spent over an hour poring over the illustration and stifling each other's giggles. Among other fascinating items, I had taken careful note of Soranus' advice on the means of preventing conception. One had best be prepared.

Me thinks Mother Clara must have used some of Soranus' recipes herself during the years she was Eudes' beloved, for she had never borne him a child.

If truth be told, were I free to do so, I would gladly bear Walther's child. Though I no longer fear Eudes wrath, I have no wish to bring him grief and shame by giving him living proof of his misfortune. Even though my lord's prolonged absences have offered Walther and me countless opportunities to relish each other's embraces, my lover has not availed himself of many.

Walther's life in Venice is not one of seclusion. Welcomed in all the noble houses of Venice - by great ladies who have yet to bid me to one of their feasts - he appears to enjoy his fate and shows little concern for the plight of his fellow pilgrims. And it seems to me his scant knowledge of the local language includes an inordinate number of terms of endearment.

Yet, whenever I succumb to jealousy and despair of his fealty, he comes to me unbidden, bearing a token of his devotion and swearing his love anew. Once it was a fine gold pendant set with the clearest red garnet; another time a wondrous glass vial of the most exquisite scent to hang at my belt. My favorite remains the ballad he composed for me. Its hauntingly beautiful music will forever sing in my head, and its courtly words of eternal devotion fill my heart with the hope that - perhaps - Walther does love me as much as I love him. Our fates are forever linked.

Last night was proof enough his ardor, at least, has not abated.

We shared supper in my vast chamber, under clouds and angels depicted on the high ceiling, and it was indeed heavenly! Holding hands across the small round table Elaine had set up for us by the tall window. Feeding each other morsels of spiced meat or fowl in the most sensuous way. Sipping sweet wine from each other's cups, lifting these strange glass vessels to the light the better to admire their iridescent glow; the way Venetians do to enjoy the beauty of the wine as well as its taste and aroma.

Playing amorous duets of our own creation between courses. Walther on his lute and I on the psaltery. Letting our eyes meet or stray to the red-curtained bed that held promises of delights to come.... Postponing these delights until our frenzy knew no bounds. Yes. Last night was Paradise.

Cradled in his strong arms, I feared not the dawn. "Friend," I murmured in his ear when the first ray of light shone between the drapes of our bed. "Beloved friend, will you not sail on the ship that is to take me to Corfu, where I am, alas, to join my lord? I shall not endure a single day away from you and will surely succumb from grief on the voyage if you are not by my side!"

"Die? From such short parting?" Walther laughed. Throwing back the silk coverlet, he gazed at my bare form in the shaft of light.

"Me thinks you are strong and hale enough, and well able to survive without my care for a few weeks..." Caressing my contented body with his eyes and his soft fingers before adding, "Or even a few months.

I cannot follow you to Corfu, however much I so desire. I am pledged to await a party of Hospitalers and will depart with them on All Hallows. Do not grieve, my little dove. Our love can sustain such trial of fate and be but stronger for it."

I dared not say his fickleness had already imposed many more trials on my love for him than fate ever did.

Sitting up, he pulled apart the heavy drapes that enclosed us, flooding the wide bed with morning light. The sight of our bodies bathed in the golden glow of the rising sun rekindled our desires. We greeted the new day with many a moan and cry of ecstasy.

* * *

Walther left but a short while ago.

Magnificent in his new ermine-trimmed cloak in the Venetian style. I know not when I shall hold him in my arms again or lie in his. Having failed to persuade him to follow me to Corfu, I can but hope we will meet again in the Holy Land.

* * *

It is now twelve days since the host left and word has just reached us that Zara has fallen. My squires look all disheveled, running up and down the stone stairs, prodding porters laden with coffers and bales of all kinds to be taken to the ship. For we are soon to depart for Corfu.

Elaine packs my new silk bliauds, chemises, and cloaks in my chest with slow movements and sullen face. She would rather remain here and rues our leaving as I do. I stray to the balcony every little while, watching, in case Walther should appear. It is eight days since he was last here and he has sent me no word.

My heart leaps at the sight of a small boat approaching our entrance steps. One of the servants opens the door and the passenger of the boat stands up and steps on to our landing. It is not Walther, but a tallish man, richly attired in black velvet robes and wearing one of those soft bonnets in the Venetian fashion.

I know him not. Until he lifts his head and addresses me in respectful tones. Black Foulk.

"My Lady Alix," says he as I stand petrified with distaste and apprehension. "As we are to share passage to Corfu, I deemed it appropriate to come and pay my respects to you. I know you do not, alas, hold me in great esteem, but perchance, in the spirit of this pilgrimage, you will grant me your mercy and will now count me among your devoted servants."

CHAPTER 20

I woke up with a start, still shaking from the fear and loathing Black Foulk had inspired in me. Still bathed in cold sweat.

A dusty shaft of sunlight intruding into the drabness of the Nantes hotel room made me want to laugh with relief. I was safely back in the present. I stretched on my bed, elated to be alive and in love again.

Venice. The shimmering city. Sea, slime and spices. The smells of Venice still in my nostrils, I let myself re-live the night.

This had been no ordinary dream; I had just re-experienced every single thought, emotion and sensation of Alix, as intensely as if I was living them for the first time.

Is time a figment of our imagination? Are all our lives lived simultaneously? Multiple facets of a single soul the better to reflect the light of God?

Lying motionless and hardly awake still, I tried to concentrate on the pleasurable moments of my dream, but Black Foulk's image would not go away. I could still see him under my balcony, willing me to yield with his cold eyes while his lips uttered pleading words. His harsh face made even more frightening by the deceptive gentleness of his voice. I had hardly listened to his words, anyway, for while he spoke, I kept remembering the poor wretch who often handed me his bowl to fill at the convent's gate.

As Mother Clara noticed my revulsion for his hideous face - two ghastly red holes were all that was left of his nose - she had sighed, "Foulk de Sardac has no patience with thieving beggars. T'was but a half-loaf he stole, too."

I shivered anew, but still didn't feel like getting out of bed. Not until I had had a chance to recall more pleasant episodes. Like Walther's touch. Walther's strong body over mine on the soft Venetian feather couch....

I tarried a while on this satisfying recollection. Until my lover's features seemed to blur and I suddenly realized Walther had turned into Kurt.

I was making love to Kurt, and enjoying it with every fiber of my body; the last shred of cautious numbness swept away in thrilling surrender. I was fully alive. Alix-alive!

I sat up, dizzy with wonder and gratitude; fate had allowed me to find my love again. Whoever he was, I would not let him go. Walther and Kurt were one and the same, yet excitingly different. I knew that now, without the need for physical evidence of their common identity. I had, in fact, discovered plenty: The walk, both relaxed and purposeful; the wry irony of the smile; the slightly arch raising of the eyebrows; the whimsy. Most of all the eyes. Very blue, yet not cold. As warm, in fact, as a summer sky. Eyes alive with curiosity for the world and all who lived in it. Especially the female kind.

Was Kurt a womanizer still? The thought had stayed at the back of my mind since our first dinner together; the way he had of eyeing pretty women in the restaurant had not gone unnoticed. Well, who cared?

Men are different from us, and show a biological propensity for scattering their seed. A trait woman of our times, for some unknown reason, refuse to recognize for what it is: a part of their nature. Intellectually at least, I could live with the occasional straying of a man I loved. Or so I thought, until Franco had his fling with my so-called friend and literary agent. It turned out that I was far from immune to jealousy.

Neither was Alix. Yet, though quite aware of Walther's nature, she accepted it without bitterness. To her mind, the ideal of courtly love was just that, an ideal. Rarely attained, and suspect in many ways; she had met enough troubadours at Comarque to know that those who professed chaste love for the Lady of Their Thoughts were either hypocritical wretches, despisers of women, or, more likely, heretics.

Their extolling of Pure Love smacked of the Cathar heresy which was thriving in their own bailiwick, Aquitaine. The Cathars decried a flesh they believed to be the work of the devil, and their ideal was total abstinence. A rejection of life. Well, Alix was not inclined that way and did not consider chastity to be a blessed state.

As for Walther, he was obviously no Cathar and, though very talented, no troubadour either. He was a high-born knight who composed songs in praise of what he enjoyed most in life: battles and the love of women. His poems may have paid lip service to the courtly ideal and used lofty images, but he mostly sang of the carnal raptures of lovers. Even the mood of his music struck sensuous chords.

Could he be blamed for practicing what he preached? For living his art to the full, so to speak?

As Alix, I seemed to have made allowances for my lover's foibles, and I was still prepared to do so. Still thought there was something repellent - a kind of Hubris – about asceticism. How can denying our body, which is part of His creation, bring us closer to God? Being spiritually challenged hardly qualifies me for answering this kind of question, I suppose. If it was true enlightenment could flower only on the ashes of earthly desires, I guessed it would take me many a lifetime to get there. Ah, well... That didn't sound so bad at the moment, judging by this one.

Especially when the thought of meeting Kurt for breakfast sent a delightful surge of excitement coursing through my body.

I was still entertaining pleasant thoughts under the shower and humming the ballad Walther had composed for me when the phone rang.

"Hi, Mum! How are you? Are you up? Hope I didn't wake you?"

Christine seldom waits for answers to her questions, so I huh-huh'd amiably and let her go on.

"Listen, your friend Daphne whatever-her name-is, woke me up at five this morning and has since called back twice already. She wanted to know where you were staying and demanded the phone number of your hotel, but she sounded so agitated...I mean, weird...I didn't think I should give it to her. She said it was urgent and that she had to talk to you."

Drying my legs with one hand, I listened with growing annoyance. Why didn't I want to have anything to do with Daphne right now? Because I was having a hell of a good time and I didn't feel like letting the old crone interfere. That's why.

"When she called the second time, ten minutes later, she begged me to tell you to call her collect. As if I would wake you up at five in the morning. If you ask me, the woman is cracking...or has already cracked." A pause of hesitation, before blurting out. "Mum... Are you sure this woman is not putting bizarre ideas into your head? I mean, your story makes sense when you tell it, but...."

"No. No, I'm not crazy." I sat on the towel, letting the ray of sunshine caress my wet shoulders.

"I don't think Daphne is really nuts, either; perhaps a little stressed and confused. I'll call her. Don't worry. There are more things in this universe...."

"Oh, Mum, please!" She burst out laughing.

"You don't have to misquote Shakespeare to convince me, just keep her off my back! She gave me the creeps, to tell you frankly."

We went on chatting for ten minutes about nothing that mattered to either of us and I promised to enlighten her later about the cause of Daphne's agitation, if I ever found out what it was. I would call Dr. Blake later. Much later. The sudden resentment I felt for her was puzzling in a way, but there was too much to enjoy right now to dwell on that.

My watch said it was time to get dressed. The contents of my suitcase failed to live up to my flamboyant mood and revealed only one last clean blouse, a well-worn teal-blue silk whose only merit was to echo the color of my eyes.

Where was Alix's well-filled chest of priceless attire when I needed it? I stepped into my cream wool skirt; the small black smudge denying its pristine elegance would have to be bravely endured.

Perfunctory make-up, hairdressing limited to a tortoiseshell clip to hold my mane back, two squirts of scent behind my ears. Grabbing my overloaded and overworn Hermes purse, I rushed down the stairs.

I did not run directly into Kurt's embrace; he was standing in the middle of the small lobby and took three deliberate steps to take me into his arms. To be held against his chest for a brief moment and kissed casually on both cheeks, like an old friend, sent such a wave of pleasure coursing through my body that I felt myself grow faint.

He must have felt something too; the look of surprise on his face bordered on the comical. Dropping his arms abruptly, he gulped for air like a swimmer who breaks surface after a long dive. For a few never-ending instants, we stood there, facing each other like two young kids too shy to repeat a tentative embrace. Our eyes locked in thrilling discovery.

"Oh! How nice of you to call for me!" Words, any words were urgently needed to relieve our mutual embarrassment.

"You had not told me, I mean, you... I didn't know you were going to pick me up... It's awfully kind of you, Kurt. But... are you sure you still want to have breakfast with Irene and Olivier? I mean Olivier might be in the same mood as last night. I... really appreciate your company more than I can say, in fact - and I didn't mean to subject you to this kind of unpleasantness. I had no idea Olivier would take such a dislike to you...." With a sly smile, I added, "Though one must admit you had it coming to you in view of your past trespasses."

Brushing back a strand of silver hair from his brow, he retrieved his ubiquitous fountain-pen and pad from his pocket. Taking two steps to the front desk, he wrote a couple of lines under the curious glances of the concierge, and handed me the paper.

"Let him skewer me. It's a small price to pay to share your morning. There is something I want to tell you. Something to do with Walther and me."

My heart missed a beat, but there was no point in questioning him under the inquisitive eyes of the two men behind the desk.

"Can we go somewhere after breakfast?" I asked. "Are you free until tonight?"

He nodded, and with a grin extended his arms, flapping them like wings, and causing the concierge to shake his head and exchange a look with his clerk.

"Oh, I see, as free as a bird. Well, let's fly!" We left the hotel laughing. In the street, he pulled a folded page covered in writing from his pocket, showed it to me and put it back. He had written about whatever it was he wanted to show me, and I would have to wait until we were alone together to read it. Rats.

* * *

As we walked into the turn-of-the-century hotel dining room, Olivier immediately spotted us and rose with polite eagerness, pulling the chair next to him for me to sit down.

Irene threw us kisses without interrupting her one-way conversation with the waiter. She was apparently set on having Eggs Benedict for breakfast and was trying to explain to the bemused garçon how to prepare this most American of "French" delicacies; of which like Vichyssoise - the French know nothing. The young waiter, obviously relieved at my simple order of coffee and whole-wheat toast for Kurt and myself, retreated with a promise to repeat Madame's instructions to the chef word for word.

Olivier, heaping butter and strawberry jam on a piece of croissant, was already asking me about my plans. My attention had been focused on Kurt; I couldn't take my eyes off him, and Olivier's question startled me. As I opened my mouth to answer, Irene did so in my stead.

"If I may venture a guess, I think Sandra will follow the musicians till the end of their tour. She is now a full-fledged groupie! Don't blame her. Would do the same myself...in other circumstances, and...."

"Sorry to disappoint you, Irene," I intervened, a little put out. "But I'm not." Kurt turned his head sharply, seeking my eyes. "My boss won't allow it. He wants me back in Montreal in a week." I admit the stricken expression on Kurt's face caused me no small satisfaction. Olivier put down his cup of café-au-lait, turned to me and commiserated.

"What a shame, and how disappointing for you. A good thing we came then and had the chance to enjoy your company." And he went back to his croissant; his conviviality still not extending to Kurt.

Kurt dismissed the slight with a faint grin, as if to show he knew his disability to be a strong deterrent to dialogue; he was well aware that people, who tend to shy away from the handicapped anyway, were loath to address him knowing he couldn't reply.

All the same, my heart went out to him and I wished I could do something to help. I hated more than ever the thought of going back to Canada. There was no way I could leave this man now.

The question in his eyes - most certainly about my return to Montreal - would have to be answered in private. I still didn't know how.

"Well, I am very grateful to you both for coming." I said, addressing Irene. "Hope you enjoyed Nantes as much as I did."

Irene had gone back to perusing the menu, in case the chef's talents weren't up to her directives. She waved an indulgent hand in my direction.

"Great, sweetie. It was great. The concert was unforgettable. I'm glad we came.

I think it's a damn shame you have to go back to work, when your heart is...not in it."

Lowering her chin, she gave Kurt a pointed look over the top of her gold spectacles.

"Anyway. We certainly enjoyed ourselves, didn't we dear?" Her glance at Olivier held both gloating and wonder. He responded with a fond smile. "This hotel is not bad at all. Large room and a decent bed. We had a good night. Oh, talk about night, you'll never guess what I was in the dream I had last night...." The three of us looked at her with expectant half-smiles.

"A nun! I was a nun. And a fat one too! I kept stuffing my face with honey cakes. Horrors! Well, actually it was not such a bad life after all, except for the lack of... Well, anyway, let me tell you this was the most vivid dream I ever experienced in my whole life! It went on and on.

It must have been in the Middle Ages; the poor I was feeding were so ugly, and they wore such drab clothes, you wouldn't believe! Most depressing. And did they ever smell earthy! That's the weirdest part, I mean, I've never had a dream where I was able to smell and taste things...." Her voice trailed off. Olivier was looking at her with puzzled eyes.

"How come you didn't tell me about it?" "My dear sweet Olivier," She chided fondly. "

You want to know everything about me. What a bore I would become if you did."

"Not at all! Anything that concerns you is of interest to me. You should know that by now." Ignoring us, they went on exchanging endearments disguised as recriminations. Kurt scribbled a line on his pad and pushed the sheet across the table in my direction.

I glanced at it. "Why don't you tell them what you told me?"

Tell them about their past life together? Now? No way. Something told me they were far from ready. My eyes spoke my refusal. Kurt smiled and shrugged.

The arrival of the waiter, proudly carrying Irene's eggs Benedict and our coffee and toasts, granted me a reprieve. The eggs looked most appetizing under their smooth coating of Bearnaise sauce, and made my mouth water. Irene took a tentative bite and nodded approvingly to the nervous waiter still hovering by our table. When he left, she remarked indulgently, "Of course, you can't expect them to use real English muffins, but this will do. It beats the mush I ate as a nun in my dream... Except for those almond cakes dripping with honey!

Now, they were really something to dream about, let me tell you!"

Yes. A sweet tooth had been Mother Clara's little sin. Dear Mother Clara. Even though I found it absolutely fascinating to know who Irene and Olivier had been 800 years ago, I felt very reluctant to tell them so. How could these people be told about the cycle of births and deaths over a breakfast table? They would dismiss the whole thing as so much New Age drivel. California Consciousness! It's one thing to be entertained by others' bizarre and unexplained experiences; but when it comes to being involved personally, most people become surprisingly conservative and tend to reject the supernatural outright. Irene was munching contentedly and Olivier was sipping the last of his coffee, blissfully unaware of my quandary. I watched them both intently, wondering if I would ever summon the courage to tell them about our common past.

Another time, another place. Kurt must have sensed my qualms; with a reassuring smile, he placed his hand over mine and bent over to give my cheek a light kiss. Olivier happened to glance at us and caught the affectionate gesture.

The sudden change in his expression was truly astounding. His face turned ashen. Replacing his cup down on the saucer with a clatter, he ran a trembling hand over his forehead.

"Olivier?" Irene's voice held such genuine distress that it took me by surprise.

"What's wrong, dear? Are you unwell? Speak to me, darling!"

Olivier was shaking his head and attempting a smile. "It's nothing, Irene, I assure you. A small malaise. Please...." Addressing me, he added in a voice made hoarse by self-control, "If you will forgive me, Sandra, I think I will go up and lie down for a while. I am not myself today." Standing up and stepping briskly behind Irene's chair, he placed his hands gently on her shoulders to keep her from rising too.

"No, no. You stay here, ma chérie, and finish your breakfast. I'll be quite all right. I just need a little rest, that's all."

Bowing to me and ignoring Kurt, he turned and stiffly walked out of the dining-room. Irene was pushing back her plate and hastily gathering her jacket and purse.

"I can't leave him by himself!" She exclaimed. "I don't know what's wrong. You'll have to excuse me too. What can be the matter with him? I hope it's not his heart! I couldn't bear to lose him...like...like Harold!" Harold had been husband Number Two - or perhaps Number Three - and a massive heart attack had deprived her of his company, if not of his millions. Clutching her belongings, she gave my cheeks perfunctory kisses and accepted a long hug from Kurt who had sprung to his feet and was looking at her with obvious concern.

As he released her, she raised her hand to touch his head in a curious gesture reminiscent of Mother Clara's blessings.

* * *

"So? What now?" I asked Kurt, as if questions might help him recover the means to answer them.

Instead, he pulled out the folded sheet of paper he had showed me before and, pushing my plate out of the way, opened it on the table in front of me. His handwriting was steady and larger than on his scribbled notes; harmonious and easy to read. There was nothing flighty about it. A good sign.

"I had a vivid dream last night."

I stopped reading right there and then to exclaim, "You too! What is happening? Did we all have dreams last night? I did. And, was it ever realistic!"

The time was perhaps not opportune to dwell on that; just meeting his eyes made me re-live the excitement of it all. I went on reading aloud but very softly, "I was Walther and I was fighting under a hot sun amid many knights and foot soldiers; wielding my heavy sword with two hands, striking left and right,

251

peering through the slit of my helm; half-blinded by sweat, flashing swords and blazing shields; half-deafened by the clash of arms, the thud of maces against helms and flesh, the grunts and screams of men. A din I found both horrible and heady.

I was trying to save the life of a knight whose horse had been killed under him. He was bleeding from a leg wound. The device on his helm had been broken, his hauberk was torn. Fierce warriors wielding fearsome outlandish weapons surrounded us. Their blood-curdling yells swallowed by the clamor of battle.

When I succeeded in driving them away from the wounded knight and tried to help him get on my horse, he refused to take my hand, turned his back on me and ran back into the thick of battle. I knew who he was and why he hated me, but the strange part is that even though I called out his name several times, I cannot recall it now. Who was he? What is the meaning of this dream?" His brows knitted in frustration; he obviously could neither remember more nor make sense of what he was remembering.

"I don't know, Kurt. I honestly don't know." I sighed. "Things are getting a little too involved for me. I don't think one can ever get used to these psychic episodes. We just have to accept them and keep on living in the present as best we can."

Looking into his eyes, I added, "Only the present matters, Kurt. Even though I am glad I remembered Walther because...the memory has brought you back to me."

He grinned, but his eyes were full of concern, he lowered them to the paper between us and, using the margin, wrote quickly, "I am glad too. Why go back to Montreal? Stay with us and join the group. You can play the psaltery." "My playing the psaltery was perhaps a fluke, Kurt." Did I ever wish it was not! "I have no idea if I could do it again. It was really as if my hands were playing of their own accord; I had no control over them. It was...uncanny."

I paused and vaguely looked around the large elegant room, now emptying of its morning crowd. A waiter was hovering nearby probably psyching us to leave soon so he could deliver our messy table over to the busboys. Uneaten eggs Benedict and all. Kurt was looking at me with such unblinking concentration that I felt the need to break it with a small laugh.

"You must think I am a total weirdo..." His vigorous head shaking was reassuring.

"Anyway, I am both afraid and tempted to try playing the psaltery again. I will. Soon. As for going back to Canada, believe me, it's not by choice, but I need my salary." He frowned and dismissed the point with a wave of his hand.

"Besides," I added, "Dumping the magazine now would not be ethical; I mean, I have been with them for a number of years."

He seemed to understand, and wrote, "So when will I see you again?" He mouthed the words silently as he wrote them.

"Listen...." I took a deep breath. "I can't come with you to England, but...perhaps... you can join me in Montreal at the end of your tour? Have you ever been there?"

He shook his head, looking at me intently.

"It's a lively city, especially in the summer; it takes a harsh winter for people to really enjoy summer, the sheer physical joy of walking about in sundrenched streets. It's a fun place, you would enjoy it. There's always a festival of some kind going on: Jazz, fireworks, humor, films, you name it." I paused. Kurt was still looking at me. I met his eyes and added with a quiver in my voice. "We could have our very own festival...."

As his face remained a blank, I desperately looked for something else to say. "I... could...introduce you to Daphne. I am sure she would be thrilled to make your acquaintance after hearing so much about you. About Walther, I mean. And, who knows, something might come out of it."

I could see he was tempted. He certainly made no attempt to conceal his emotions; as if it would have been both futile and deceitful to hide what he thought or felt. Walther had been the same; his candor a large part of his charm.

Kurt might come to Canada, and something might indeed come of it. But meanwhile I would be back in my dismal routine, longing for him every moment of the day. And night. Waiting.

No. No more. I had been as patient in this life as I would ever be. Alix would not have waited. Waiting is hell, so to hell with waiting.

"Kurt, I have always loved you and always will." My throat was burning; in fact, my whole body seemed on fire. "I have waited so long for you. I want to make love to you again. Now."

For a few seconds, I felt such exhilaration, such a sense of coming into my own, that at first his startled look and raised eyebrows failed to dampen my joy.

Then I lowered my eyes and fell silent. Not looking at him hastily draining the last of his cold coffee. Not even daring to make a wish. Waiters and busboys busied themselves clearing the breakfast tables. A maid went by with a large basket of white carnations and lilies, the scent of which brought forth memories of incense in a golden chapel I had yet to visit.

CHAPTER 21

Kurt's abrupt rising from the table caught me by surprise.

Shoving pen and paper into his pocket without a smile, he extended a hand to me; whether as a good-bye or as an invitation to follow him wherever he was going, I couldn't tell. My heart sank, but I decided to follow. He didn't object; just walked towards the exit without turning around.

It was raining lightly outside. Under the hotel marquee, he paused as if venturing onto the shiny wet sidewalk demanded reflection; his face taut with obviously painful self- questioning. Ignoring me.

I could only stand there and look at him, wondering what had gone wrong. Until I realized that the wrenching ache that filled my chest felt somehow familiar beyond time and matter.

Well, just because I might have lived through this kind of rejection before was no reason to suffer it meekly!

Now or ever. Grabbing hold of Kurt's sleeve, I tugged on it until he turned to look at me.

There was no rejection in his eyes, just great sadness and perhaps even a little fear.

"Kurt, please." I could feel my voice breaking.

"Don't you remember how much you loved me? How much I loved you?"

He shook his head, but I sensed he was not saying 'no' to past or present love. In that very instant fear and pain disappeared as I realized we had no more need for words. Closing his eyes, he very gently enfolded me into his arms, hugging me like a child in pain.

Brushing my brow with soft lips, trusting them to express what he could not say. I had no need to hear him speak to know we had found each other again.

Our embrace cannot have lasted more than a minute or so, yet it felt as if time was abolished. Past and present had finally melded into a single reality. Something made me foolishly break the spell.

"Do you still love me as Alix?" He let go of me and shook his head.

"You mean you still don't remember?" He shrugged as if to say it didn't matter one way or another and his eyes kept on saying he loved me now, whoever I was, and that was all that mattered.

* * *

What more can I say?

We walked for hours. Silently. Hand in hand through the Nantes drizzle. Feeling flares of longing consume us whenever our bodies brushed against each other. Knowing full well where we were going, but tacitly postponing ultimate raptures as much as our desire for each other would allow.

Nantes became my favorite town that day, I liked everything about it: the pressure of Kurt's fingers on mine; our sudden fierce hugs; lingering looks of wonder; the taste of rain on his lips. Don't ask me what the city was really like; for me it will always be bathed in shimmering light. Like Venice.

* * *

Of our love-making I shall not say much either, for I feel unable to translate its magic into words.

In a symphony of pulsating notes, each one bringing us closer to an abyss of pleasure, our delights ignored past and present identities. My lover was both Walther and Kurt, I both Alix and Sandra. What flowed between us went far beyond the passion we had once shared; transcended the sensual thrill of skin against skin to bring us to the unfathomable joy of mutual fulfilment and completion.

The realm of time and matter dissolved into the nothingness of bliss, and from our embrace rose the subtle essence of an unearthly ecstasy.

Our "time to embrace" had come at last; our moans of rapture a most fitting hymn of gratitude to whoever had brought us together. The fire that kindled our flesh that day caused our souls to shine more brightly with the joy of life itself.

As dawn seeped into the hotel room and I listened to his even breathing, the wonderful peace of fulfilment was upon me. Whatever happened now, whether we remained together or parted, I knew our synchrony would endure beyond time and distance. Propped on one elbow, I watched as he slept through the truce of dreams, rapt in soothing visions that brought a smile to his lips.

I resisted the temptation to caress the smooth warm skin of his neck, and lay back on the pillow.

As I dozed off, I realized I was once more slipping back into the past.

* * *

We are sailing on a dark blue sea under an exceedingly hot sun. A lazy wind hardly moves the sail, and I pity the oarsmen below whose fate it is to propel such a large galley loaded with men-at-arms and their deadly accoutrements.

Elaine and I remained but a mere ten days in the verdant isle of Corfu, lodged in a handsome cloth pavilion amid the fragrances of unknown flowers and fruits, before Eudes came for us. He sailed in one morn, in this colorful Venetian galley round the deck of which knights had disposed their shields and planted their banners.

We are sailing away from Corfu - an earthly paradise where I would fain have tarried bound not for the Holy Land but for Constantinople, or Byzantium as some call it.

This strange turn of events sorely grieves my lord Eudes, for he is torn between his great desire to free Jerusalem from the Infidels and his fealty to Lord Montferrat.

At the behest of wily old Dandolo and a deposed Byzantine Emperor, called Alexius, Lord Montferrat has indeed ordered the pilgrim host to lay siege to Constantinople before they proceed to Palestine.

Eudes understands no better than I do why an army of Christian pilgrims has to storm this most magnificent Christian city for the sake of one Greek emperor or another. It is all the more confusing that these emperors - who, among other endearing traits, show a propensity for putting out one another's eyes with red-hot irons - all seem to bear the same name, Alexius.

One Alexius having usurped the throne, Lord Montferrat, his Frankish knights and their Venetian allies are thus to lay siege to Constantinople, remove this Bad Alexius, and replace him with his nephew, the "Good" Alexius, who promises to obey the Lord Pope. Eudes' conscience appears to trouble him greatly and he often talks to me about the Holy Land with sorrowful regret. He has such fond remembrance of that Outremer, as he calls it, the Land-beyond-the-seas, with its white cities, fragrant gardens and murmuring fountains, that I sometimes think his vow to return there owes a lot to these memories. He also spends a good part of the day kneeling on the galley deck in prayers, while I repair to the common room Elaine and I share with four other ladies and their companions. Among them - to my delighted surprise - the Lady Iselda, met at the court of King Philip. Her cheerful company gladdens our hearts and helps me surmount my longing for Walther.

Bar the knights in Eudes' mesnie, most of those on board are unknown to me and I care not to make their acquaintance. Yet am I glad to have met Conon de Béthune. I like Conon well enough; he may be a knight of mediocre countenance, sparse hair and mournful face, but he is a superb musician who composes albas, cansons, lays and virelays to rival Walther's in beauty. He entertains us ladies in the rough low-ceilinged quarters we call in jest our bower, sitting like us on pillows amid piles of chests and bundles, playing his lute for our delight. Bringing tears to my eyes at the thought of my beloved.

As for Black Foulk, he is not among us and I thank the Lord for his absence, even though he caused me little bother on the ship which took us from Venice to the isle of Corfu. Thanks to the heaving seas, I had been mercifully spared his unwelcome company; it seems the waves and winds I found so invigorating caused Foulk to suffer great discomfort.

For I do enjoy the sea, whether it be calm as a mirror or tossing our galley with angry waves. I relish the wide horizons and the fragrant isles where we drop anchor in search of fresh water and victuals. T's pity propriety prevents me from bathing in the turquoise waters of their white sandy shores. The incessant creaking noises of the ship or the whistling of the wind, even the beat of the oarsmen's drum, I no longer hear.

If it were not for the scant fare served to us, and the salt of sea water - nay, of sea air even - which coats our hair and stiffens our clothes, I would be thoroughly content with the voyage. If only I could be sure Walther would join us in Constantinople....

* * *

I lift the cloth panel at the entrance to our pavilion to peer outside. The wind has finally tired of raising billows of yellow dust over the encampment and merely tarries between the tents in playful eddies of fine sand. The four men-at-arms are already waiting with sullen faces and impatient feet to escort us safely through the maze of tents; Eudes deems it unwise for us to venture alone in the pilgrims' camp, where even knights are not always to be trusted.

Today, we shall walk as far as the Golden Horn, to stroll on the seashore to our hearts' content, admire the white walls of Constantinople across the water, and forget awhile the squalor of the pilgrims' camp, here in Galata.

Elaine and I wrap our cloaks tightly and draw our hoods over our heads before venturing out, to guard our faces from the dust and the leers of wanton soldiers. I have even taken to wearing a wimple - or a barbette, as Lady Iselda calls it - to protect my skin, so bothersome are wind, dust and hot sun.

Lady Iselda and her attendant, whose name is Marian, are to join us and we shall visit the stalls of the Armenian merchants at the edge of the camp, in search of fresh and dried fruit, silk cloth and silver trinkets.

I thank the Lord for Iselda's blithe and wise presence in this forsaken place where everything takes on the drab hue of the arid soil. Even the colorful pennants which made such a glorious display when the knights' pavilions were first erected, now flap in dull tatters in the wind.

It is now many weeks since Constantinople fell to the Frankish barons and the Venetians. The "Good" Alexius is now Emperor, and many pilgrims see no reason to remain here any longer. Yet, every day our departure is postponed.

As for Constantinople, I have yet to set foot inside its wondrous white ramparts and can only imagine the magnificence of the city they enclose. Eudes never fails to describe the marvels he sees most every day as he goes to the emperor's palace with the other barons.

He tells me I shall soon accompany him there to pay homage to Emperor Alexius, and he promises to take me to Hagia Sophia, the splendid church of Holy Wisdom. But whenever I inquire about our departure for the Holy Land, Eudes frowns and answers me not.

I espy Lady Iselda and Marian at the end of our alley, and we set out to join them, our morose escort close behind.

As we cross the immense encampment, avoiding the coarser parts where harlots have pitched their tents, we hold scented cloths to our noses against the stench of latrines. In muffled words we share our cares and our hopes. I cannot help voicing my impatience. "Why are we still here, Iselda, now that the legitimate Emperor is on the throne? Eudes resents the delay as much as I do, yet he appears not to know its cause. Or will not confide in me."

A mangy grey dog, his bony rump plagued with huge ticks, paws the dirt of the alley and growls at our approach. I tighten my cloak around my shoulders and pause while one of our guards chases it away.

Poor animals; they suffer greatly and bite readily from hunger or spite. Still, I fear them not as much as the vultures who hover above the tents and nearly attacked us one day, so bold have they become since the battles of the siege.

As we resume our walk, I add, "I loathe this camp and would gladly sail for Palestine. It could hardly be worse!" Iselda, daintily stepping over a dead rat, smiles wryly. "I am as anxious as you are to leave this foul place, Alix, I cannot eat another bite of horse flesh or taste that loathsome bread which surely is nothing but baked horse droppings!" With a brief stifled laugh, she adds in more serious tones, "My lord Nevers tells me Alexius is reneging on the promises made to our Frankish barons, and

Lord Montferrat will not leave until what is owed has been paid."

Surveying the dull sight of fetid rags hanging on lines between torn tents, blackened pots on smoldering fires and unkempt men sprawling in the dirt, she concludes with a sigh, "This is tedious." Tedious indeed.

But for one magical encounter with Walther a few hours of stolen bliss that entailed many secret messages and many risks - I have had to be content with glimpses of my beloved among many other knights in battle array. I saw him on his way to the siege, fully armed and lance in hand, his helm adorned with the German imperial falcon head. They say he was among the first to leap from a barge with water to his waist, and preceded all others to the onslaught. During the ten days the siege lasted, he was always to be found in the most perilous combats against the Varangian guards, those blood-thirsty Northmen whose cruelty strike fear in the stoutest heart. When the city was taken, Walther's shield was hung from the battlements in honor of his exploits on the walls.

Would I had been able to witness such feats; but ladies were confined to the camp, and all we knew of the battle was a distant clamor punctuated by clanging mangonels and other siege engines.

Conon de Béthune and others who were there - Eudes among them - are not stinting in their praises of Sir Walther's bravery. My heart is filled with pride as I listen to the retelling of his feats; but I would rather hear it from his own lips. Close to my ear. Resting peacefully in his arms after one of our celebrations of life.

* * *

Eudes is dead. Walther and I are to blame. And so is Bogo who betrayed us to my lord. The Frankish knights and the Venetians have stormed the city for the second time in less than a year, and

Eudes, who'd fought unscathed through the battles of the first siege, wasn't so fortunate in the second one. He now lies on his low narrow couch, bloodless fingers clutching the gold cross I brought to his lips as he breathed his last, but a few hours ago, his face made gentle by the peace of death.

The day is waning. I sit motionless by my lord's side, asking Sweet Jesus' forgiveness for the harm I have caused him and commending his soul to God's mercy. My psaltery lies silent at my feet, the only solace I could provide for him, for he seemed to relish my playing greatly, even Walther's ballads, and would urge me to play on when I stopped, thinking him asleep.

The cross in Eudes' hands is indeed beautiful; its rubies and sapphires softly glow in the glaucous light of the tent. I have long coveted it, the most precious jewel in my lord's treasure chest. I do not covet it now and will leave it in his hands when we lower him into his grave. As we must ere long for the heat of summer is already upon us in this benighted place.

Many months have now passed since we arrived here in Galata. which is nothing but a miserable camp crowded with thousands of nefarious knights and soldiers. Nothing but dusty trampled grass and filth. And heat such that the stench from Eudes' rotting leg causes me to retch. My mind wanders to this Holy Land Eudes has told me so much about and that we will never see.

For Eudes died here, in this accursed camp, across the Golden Horn from the gleaming white walls of Constantinople. These awesome ramparts and four hundred towers the Frankish knights and Venetians have again taken by storm. For the second time.

Instead of Jerusalem. To their everlasting shame, for Constantinople is a Christian city. If, after the first storming they had refrained from any looting, no such restraint was shown after the second one. Fire, bloodshed, rape and looting were the order of the day.

I bring to my face a cloth dipped in musk and cinnamon and breathe deeply, moving my shoulders in my linen shift to free them from its clammy embrace. Propriety does not permit me to discard my bliaud and heavy black velvet mantle.

I sigh and wish I could escape from the gloomy tent into the cooling evening air, like Elaine who was nigh fainting ere I sent her out. I feel so weary that it is a great effort for me to keep my eyes open, though I must for Elaine will soon be back with dear Lady Iselda, who has been a great comfort to me, and Lady Jehanne, and Lord Baldwin's wife, whose name I forget, and servants to help prepare my lord for his grave.

Alas, many more hours must pass before I can escape, and perchance find solace into my beloved's arms... I have not set eyes upon Walther since the day Eudes was brought back to me from the battlefield on a litter carried by four weeping squires, oozing his lifeblood from frightful wounds embedded with his fine chainmail from Turin. It is wonder he survived for so long; his body stronger than his will to live.

Now the news of his death seems to have reached every knight in his mesnie, for they all come, one after another, lower their heads to enter the pavilion, kneel at their lord's feet and murmur short prayers for the rest of his soul. I nod to every one of them. Some I hardly know. Each comes in, still wearing chainmail and carrying his battered helm in the crook of his arm; damp hair clinging to his sweaty scalp. Still pungent from the smell of battle. Yet, all wrinkle their nose as they kneel by my dead husband's couch.

Yes, they all come, his faithful lieges; even those who never paid us a visit during his long weeks of agony. And they all eye me in the most brazen fashion, for I am now a prize not unworthy of their attention. A comely widow who surely stands to inherit a part of her dead lord's vast estates.

I keep turning my head to watch the entrance to the tent. Each time the green silk panel is lifted by one of them, and a shaft of light illuminates the dust-speckled gloom, my heart stands still. But never do my eager eyes encounter the face of my beloved.

So, my mind returns unbidden to the agony of the past weeks.

Walther never came to visit the dying friend he had wronged; he sent Conon de Béthune in his stead. Conon is a kind-hearted man who brings me such solace as he can provide; why, without his help, I would have had to suffer Bogo to administer the last rites to my lord. I had forbidden the villain and his foul cohort's entry to the pavilion, but I could not allow Eudes to die unshriven.

When I confided my distaste for Bogo to Conon, he asked no questions and promptly came back with a kindly priest who heard Eudes' confession and blessed us both most gracefully.

As for Bogo, he dares not show his despised face around the tent. However, much I wish to please the Lord Jesus, I cannot bring myself to forgive that loathsome cleric who spied on Walther and me and betrayed us to Eudes. I know this for a fact from Eudes himself who confided in me during the long hours I spent by his side vainly trying to relieve his sufferings and playing my psaltery.

"Play a little more, Alix." I still hear him say. Eudes also warned me to beware of Black Foulk. Urging me to come closer as he was nearing his end and could only talk in whispers, he said, "Beloved Alix, I married you not only as a way to keep my promise to your dear father, but also to preserve you from Black Foulk's wrath. He feared me too much to dare take revenge, but be on your guard when I am gone, for the villain is vindictive."

I refrained from telling Eudes that the villain has been scaring Elaine by skulking around the ladies' pavilions - ours in particular whenever he is not slaughtering his fellow men. I will heed my lord's advice and guard myself from Foulk; but for the nonce, he is the least of my worries.

Eudes was a man of good counsel. 'Tis great pity his pride made him shun Walther's help during the battle. Had he set aside such conceit then as he did later when he felt himself dying, he might still be alive today. Vanity causes men to act in foolish ways. Conon it is who told me of Eudes' refusal of Walther's assistance. Conon marvels at such a feat of velour, for he knows not its cause, which was deadly pride. And perhaps also sinful despair.

Conon himself shows great reluctance to slay his fellow men; but - as all men of peace - he has been so often rebuked for his lack of boldness that he values bravery in battle, methinks, too highly. But who am I to judge? These matters are best left to men. Or so they tell us.

The last knight to leave the tent was weeping audibly and as I gaze at Eudes' ashen face I too feel tears running down my face for the pain I caused him. 'Tis true he need not have died for it; after all, I had been nearly faithful to him lately, having met Walther a mere three times since our arrival in Galata. For achingly short trysts, too, in smelly tents that made us long for the delights of Venice.

I sigh and lean forward to kiss my lord's bloodless brow, his flesh still warm to my lips, and I thank him silently for his forgiveness. Had I not pledged my troth to Walther, I could have learned to love this brave foolish man as he deserved to be.

As I sit by his lifeless body, I hear the comings and goings of the camp; men-at- arms exchanging swearwords and loud boasts as they drag heavy bags of booty in the dust; foot soldiers pulling heavy mangonels and other siege-engines no longer needed now that the siege is over; joyous squires leading snorting steeds to the troughs; psalm dying priests hurrying to the doomed with relics and Holy Chrism.

Yes, the siege is over. No clamor of battle drifts over the waters of the Golden Horn from Constantinople, only the cries of carrion birds fighting over the dead bodies washed ashore by the waves. And my lord Eudes will be buried in this Byzantine soil he had never meant to tread, for he had never ceased ruing his pledge of loyalty to Montferrat and his obligation to follow him in this wicked enterprise.

Yes, Constantinople has fallen to the pilgrims' host for the second time. The "Good" Alexius, who had promised to make obeisance to the Lord Pope - with little intention of keeping this promise - having run afoul of his fellow Greeks, was cast by them into prison, throttled, and replaced with yet another Alexius. Upon which the Frankish barons, after weeks of quarrelling among themselves, decided to storm the city again and put it to the sack. My heart goes out to the poor maidens of this town.

* * *

Someone is approaching the pavilion; I turn to watch and hold my breath.

I recognize the plumed falcon head on the helm he holds in his arm before my eyes reach his face.

He is here, looking magnificent in his long white tunic embroidered with a falcon head. I can scarce believe it. I rise from my stool and would have thrown myself onto his ironclad chest had I not caught sight of the squire who has followed him into the tent. Walther frowns, orders the man out with a wave of his mail-gloved hand, and smiles at me; in the falling light his eyes shine more brightly than the sapphires on Eudes' cross. He motions me back to my seat and lowers his knees onto the fine carpet covering the dust, kneeling more to me than to his dead friend. Wooing me all over again with eyes and voice.

"I did my best to save him from the emperor's guards" he says humbly, as if I was about to reproach him. "He refused my help."

"I know, beloved friend; Conon de Béthune told me. Do not blame yourself." I touch his bent shoulder, feeling the hard mesh of his hauberk through the cloth of his tunic. His recoil causes me to shudder. "Are you hurt, beloved friend?"

He dismisses my fears with a smile. "T'is but a flesh wound, my dove. I was wearing heavier mail; it deflected the blow and suffered more damage from it than my arm." Idly wondering how many priceless chainmail hauberks Walther owns - for they are worth a king's ransom - I inquire, "Who tended your wound?"

"My squire. He is well versed in the use of healing herbs." Turning thoughtful eyes to the face of my dead lord, he whispers, "T'is pity no herb could prevent Eudes from dying of his wound."

"Alas, Eudes was a proud man; but me thinks he forgave us in the end."

My words anger him. "What is there to forgive? Eudes was old enough to be your grand-sire and foolish enough not to bed you once you were wedded!"

"Walther! Do not speak thus in the presence of the dead! Eudes had made a vow to remain chaste for the first year of our marriage to atone for...to mourn Adela's death."

We had, in fact, been wedded much longer than a year, yet to my great relief Eudes had never attempted to avail himself of his husbandly rights, leading me to believe he was perchance unable to do so. Until he confided, but a few hours ago, that he had no intention of ever claiming them as he loved me for myself and not to satisfy his lust, and that if he resented being cuckolded, 'twas for the dishonor it might bring to his name.

"A foolish pledge indeed!" Walther shakes his head sadly. "It seems that, unlike me, Sir Eudes valued his own soul more than your body, fair sprite!"

His smile entices me to forgive the impropriety. I do not attempt to gainsay him; Eudes' delicacy had best remain a secret. "When will I see you again, beloved friend?"

I whisper, for devotion to my hapless lord and husband has not dampened, alas, the fires of my passion for fair Walther.

Instead of answering my question, he shrugs and abruptly rises to his feet. Bending over Eudes' body, he peers at his friend's ashen face, crosses himself and remains silent for a long while.

Still watching Eudes, he asks between clenched teeth, "How can you remain thus closeted with this putrid corpse? Bury him and go back to Comarque."

He turns around to face me, the thin scar on his left cheek tautened by anger.

"There is nothing for us here, Alix! There never was. Eudes hated himself for obeying Montferrat, and you had no choice but to follow your lord. As for me, I came for the love of you, my fair one. I wonder how many of us here among our vainglorious Franks had as little interest in the whole venture as we did. The result is the same."

His tone is low and angry as he voices thoughts that have been troubling me during Eudes' agony.

"We have succeeded in reducing the most beautiful city in the world to ashes and ruins. Greedy men who call themselves Soldiers of Christ have looted Christian churches, thrown Holy Relics into cesspools to steal the gold from their reliquaries! They have brought mules into Saint Sophia's great church to carry away their spoils and dismantled its

splendid altar into a thousand pieces!" He pauses, strangely shamefaced, before adding, "They dared to sit a harlot on the patriarch's chair, and now they will sit Baldwin of Flanders on the emperor's throne which is hardly less villainous - and who knows for how long he will remain there to make sure the Greeks bow to the Lord Pope in Rome.

Now that their palaces and churches are burnt to the ground or despoiled of their riches, the Greeks do not hold us dear to their hearts."

In the throes of his indignation, he glares at me as if I was part of the thieving hordes. "No longer can I can bear such wanton destruction! I may share the guilt of the other barons, but I want no part of that plunder they are still fighting over! I shall be leaving soon...."

He must sense I am near swooning for he pauses and looks at me with some compassion.

"Why look so stricken, my little dove? My domains cannot be left forever in the clutches of retainers. Besides, my cousin, the German emperor, requires my presence at court. I shall depart as soon as Eudes is in the ground." I feel myself losing my senses before I have time to tell him I am with child. His child.

CHAPTER 22

From the deck of the Venetian galley taking us back to Venice, I watch the lofty spires and domes of Constantinople disappear slowly from view. Already the mighty ramparts are but a greyer shadow in the mist. Every day from the camp at Galata, I used to gaze at them in awe, so mighty and forbidding were they across the blue waters of the Golden Horn.

My heart pounds with the drum down below as the long oars strike the water; each stroke taking us further away from the ruined city. From the ashes of my love. The sea breeze still carries whiffs of that incense the Greeks are so fond of. I breathe in deeply and pray it may sweep away the pain that fills my heart. Far better not to dwell on thoughts of Walther and a bliss best forgotten.

Yet, I want to recall our happiness, just as I wish to remember Constantinople in all its glory. Beauty and love kept alive in our mind and in our heart will endure for all eternity, for our soul is immortal.

* * *

I will never forget Constantinople as it was when I first set foot inside its awesome white walls that appeared to vie in height with the snow-capped Bithynian mountains in the distance, and entered the most magnificent city in Christendom. Everywhere the eye could see were rows upon rows of stone houses, ornate palaces, soaring bell towers and rich churches with gilded domes that rose even above the height of the ramparts T'was some months after the first siege; when Greeks still treated us courteously and did not spit upon us as they do now.

On that day, Eudes came to my pavilion shortly after dawn, sorely vexed to tell me of Lord Montferrat's decision; we were to winter in Constantinople instead of leaving at once for Palestine. Furthermore, we were summoned to the Imperial Court to pay homage to the new emperor, the "Good" Alexius.

To reach the imperial palace we crossed a fair part of the immense city and encountered so many wonders on the way that I can scarcely recall them all. Why, the size of the town was a wonder in itself and caused me to marvel greatly!

Riding along a wide avenue bordered with arcades, where I would fain have tarried as they sheltered silversmiths and goldsmiths, we had to hold our horses at a slow pace lest they slip on the smooth paving of the street, swept clean of any litter. Everywhere we looked were palaces, abbeys and splendid churches. All contended with one another in the richness of their materials and ornaments. Further along the way, we passed a magnificent edifice said to house a library; across from it, and hardly less splendid, was a vast silk emporium. Eudes would not allow me to dismount, thus sparing me the dilemma of choosing between books and adornment.

Though learning is very precious to me, I do not comprehend the Greek tongue and would surely have chosen to visit the silk emporium. For never have I seen brocades as sumptuous as the ones worn by the Greeks every day.

These strange people, whose faces are as blank as the exterior of their rich houses, have a great love for beauty; T'is pity their men wear long beards and their women cover their face with a surfeit of paint.

Eudes bade our party halt briefly at the great round church of Holy Wisdom, Hagia Sophia. Within its walls, soaring domes were borne by columns of jasper, porphyry and other rare stones adorned with silver, gold, mosaics and precious jewels, all aglitter in the light of a hundred chandeliers. These columns were said to cure any sickness when rubbed. I should perhaps have sought the one that could cure me of love....

In front of the church stood a wonderful statue of great size on top of a pillar so tall it hurt one's neck to gaze at it. It was a most clever representation of an emperor on his horse, all made of copper or some such metal. After crossing large squares adorned with a profusion of statues that brought a blush to my cheeks for, they were all of fair young men and maidens as naked as the day they were born, we passed by well-tended public gardens where even the poor can rejoice in the fragrance of roses and jasmine.

Reaching a vast place with fully forty rows of seats surrounding it, Eudes explained, "This is the Hippodrome, where the people of Constantinople and their emperor are wont to watch chariot races or wild beasts tearing at each other, and wager silver on them." Of the emperor's palace I recall a succession of halls - said to number five hundred - all resplendent with gold mosaics. Of the emperor, I remember only, at the end of the largest hall, a small man so encased in his heavy robes of woven gold and brocade and his bejeweled diadem that only his pale young face emerged to peer at us with wary eyes.

I do not think it possible that even in all the richest cities in the world there ever was so much wealth and beauty as in Constantinople.

* * *

Everything on this earth is transitory by nature. For, lo, what has befallen these riches! Will they profit those who destroyed them? It is said that every Frankish and Venetian knight will receive twenty marks of silver, while ten will be given to each man-at-arms, and archers will get five.

Would they put their new-found fortune to good use, and atone for the manner in which it was wrested from those they had come to help? Fellow Christians who now despise them with great passion.

Aye, most of the Greeks now lock themselves in what remains of their houses and spit on the Franks from their high windows - which I suppose is better than raining Greek Fire down on them. No one bothers with these malcontents, for the "pilgrims" prefer to bicker among themselves over the spoils.

* * *

Indeed, I was greatly afeared to go back to Constantinople after the looting of the town, and had no wish to do so. Eudes' funeral would be held at the camp in Galata, across the water from the walls.

But the Marquess of Montferrat deemed otherwise: Eudes de Beynac was to be given a proper funeral Mass in a consecrated church. My lord Montferrat took our party of knights in his own galley and had his own squires carry Eudes' coffin through the Golden Gate to a small chapel within the ramparts.

In the plundered white chapel, silver and gold still shone in marvelous scrolls on the high ceiling above the altar, out of the reach of looters. The priest droned on in the still hot air, his monotone reminiscent of our wedding Mass, bringing tears to my eyes. Where was Eudes, alas, to scowl at this cleric as he had done then to make him hasten through the service! The acrid smell of Greek incense made me so lightheaded that, had not Elaine urged a squire to bring me a stool to sit on, I would have toppled onto the white marble floor like one of the figures torn from their pedestals by the looters.

Ere even the priest pronounced the "Ite Missa est" I had risen from my stool and turned around. In the open doorway, bathed in a shaft of sunlight, Walther stood waiting.

My heart racing, I silently endured the maddening slowness of the squires who lifted the coffin, and followed it in measured steps along with my lord Montferrat. All his retinue and mine would follow us to Eudes' designated place of burial, outside the walls, for no one could be buried within the city who was not of imperial blood. Poor Eudes; he will not rest in this Périgord which was so dear to his heart.

As I passed by Walther, I kept my eyes lowered for fear they would betray me, straining to hear in case he said anything. "In your pavilion, after the burial."

His bow was so low and his words so hushed that I wondered if they came from his lips or my imagination, but he came to my pavilion. Alas.

* * *

I am still leaning over the wooden railing of the galley deck, the misty horizon now bereft of spires, and I shiver from the cold air that is blowing us away. The oarsmen are still following the beat of the drum, but the square sail has been raised, making their toil perhaps easier. The huge canvas fills with a wind that makes the taut ropes hum.

I am on my way back to Comarque. Many weeks will our journey last, but time is of no import to me. Elaine is watching me, deep concern writ on her sweet face. She need not fear, I will not attempt to drown myself from sorrow. Life is a gift from Our Lord God, not to be discarded when it no longer brings us joy.

Precious hope grows inside of me. Walther's child is mine; one more reason never to renounce my love for him. For I still love him and always will, though time and distance keep us apart.

* * *

He looked so splendid in his green tunic trimmed with grey fur when he entered my pavilion. It was perhaps unwise of me to ask, as soon as we were alone, "Fair Walther, will you take me as your wife? I am now free to be yours, and will not come to you a pauper for my lord Eudes has endowed me with a generous widow portion." Instead of answering, he takes my hands in his and brings them to his lips. Then he speaks in that low voice that never fails to send my heart aquiver as a psaltery under nimble fingers.

"I rejoice to see you stronger than when I left you in the care of Elaine and Lady Iselda, Beloved Alix. Your devotion to your lord was admirable and deserves much praise. You are as good as you are beautiful and would indeed be a worthy consort to the noblest of men."

Embracing my trembling body in his strong arms, he adds, his smooth tongue as deadly as the snake's, "Alas, Alix, I am not such a man... I am unworthy of your devotion and though you are dearest to my heart, I will not marry you."

"Why?" I feel panic rob me of my wits, and vainly try to repulse him.

"Why, Walther? Have we not known together delights such as only Heavens can provide? And did you not pledge your troth to me for all eternity?" Still holding me close to his heart, he nods.

"Aye. So, I did, and I will always serve you most devotedly, fair sweet friend. No one has delighted me as you have, Alix, and forever will I relish the joys to be known in your white arms! Every kiss from your honeyed lips makes my soul rejoice!"

With a heart grown cold and cheeks burning with anger and desire, I push him away and muster my pride to rebuke him.

"You are mocking me with empty words, Walther!" I cannot keep my voice from trembling.

"How dare you praise delights you have just spurned!"

He tries to embrace me again, but I find the strength to resist him.

He shrugs his shoulders and says, his voice earnest, "I do not spurn your love, fair Alix. I value it above life itself. You are, you always will be, the only woman I have ever loved." Caution urges me to judge him by his deeds rather than by his words; but I cannot help hoping against hope. "Why do you not wish to make me your wife, then?"

Bringing joined hands to his lips, he gazes at me with thoughtful eyes. On the ring finger of his right hand, a ruby glows dark as blood.

"Marriage, Sweet Alix, is the death of passion; love was never meant to flower between spouses."

I try to protest, remembering the bond of devotion between my father and mother; but Walther places a finger on my lips.

"Desire thrives on hurdles and soon turns to dull surfeit between husband and wife. Yet...." He pauses, the better to make me hang on to his every word.

"Were I to take a wife, you would be the choice of my reason, my heart, my loins! But it so happens that my freedom is dearer to me than life itself."

He places his hands on my shoulders in a gentle caress which I do not repulse. "Dearer even than you, little one...."

Anger and grief vie with each other to choke me. Walther caresses my neck, his eyes bathed in such sadness that I feel a great confusion take hold of me.

"Hear me, Alix, for I will not dissemble. You say you bear me great love, yet ask me to change my nature to prove my devotion to you. I have never asked you to renounce your own ways for my sake, and never will, for I worship you as you are!"

I open my mouth to protest that marriage to me would surely not require him to sacrifice his nature; but as if reading my thoughts, he shakes his head.

"Bear with me, Alix. Judge me harshly, if you must, but do not condemn me before you have heard what I have to say." Something in his tone compels me to silence.

"T'is indeed true that feats of arms, hunting and venery are what I live for. No. Don't protest! My music is but the essence of my life; a spirit I cannot distil without the must of potent emotions. The fever of battle... and amorous feats."

He shrugs and taking my inert hands in his, gently leads me to sit on a low stool. Without releasing my hands, he kneels in front of me, his eyes nearly level with mine.

"Bavaria, where I was born, is a magnificent but somber land of icy peaks and deep impenetrable forests; the ancient seat of my family an even more somber abode, where chatelaines soon etiolate. Why the very thought of taking you there sends shivers through my spine!" No jest is intended, if one is to believe the grave tone of his words.

"Ere I was fifteen I had won my spurs and the right to leave that bleak place as often as I pleased. It has been my want to roam many lands ever since. Some have held my fancy longer than others; but the ache to wander never leaves my bones, makes me yearn for newer skies, more perilous combats, and...." "More comely women!" I cry out, hooks of jealousy tearing at my insides. "Saying you were here because of me was a lie, then! One more lies from your lying lips!"

Lips whose kiss I would give my soul to relish in the certainty of requited love.

"No, Alix. By my troth, I spoke truly. I did vouchsafe my love to you and will never be false to my vow!" His voice falters, betraying a perplexing emotion which I can hardly reconcile with his rejection of my love.

"What is a vow without fealty?" I exclaim. "It binds you to nothing! Surely not to chastity, if I am to judge by your past behavior!"

His eyebrows rise in surprise and a smile hover on his lips, as he adds in the patient tones of a parent to a fractious child, "No other will ever take your place in my heart, little dove. You will always be The Lady of my Thoughts."

"I am honored, Good Sir" I rise abruptly from my seat and turn my back on him, unable to keep sarcasm from my voice. "What a solace it will be, while I pine alone in Comarque, to know I still reign supreme in your heart while strumpets of every kind enjoy your... ministrations!"

Walther's mirthless laughter cheers me not. "What would you have me do?" He inquires. "Stay forever by your side? Spin wool at your feet?" He grows impatient. "How do you propose to keep me from wandering, little one? Would you have me tied to the thread of your spindle, then?"

I repress a smile at the thought of Walther tangled in yarn at my feet, and let my pride speak for my anguish. Turning to face him, I cry out, "Then go now, Walther and roam to your heart's content! Spare my ears your meaningless words and savior your freedom, for never again will you know in my arms the joys you are now forsaking!"

Walther smiles, but I can sense his surprise. He has not known me other than docile and compliant.

"Anger brings fire to your cheeks, my dove... And inflames my desire!" His strong arms enfold me again. I close my eyes, praying for the strength to resist him. Something urges me not to forsake my pride. For my unborn child, I must not weaken.

Walther releases me, stunned by the coldness of my response.

He looks deep into my eyes, seeking perhaps the magic that used to bond us whenever our eyes met. The magic is spent and no more wish remains to be granted. Without a word of adieu, he leaves my pavilion never to return.

* * *

The galley makes her way alone through the immensity of the sea. Under a sky so blue that its beauty soothes despair. I follow the white wake of our ship far into the distance until my eyes tire of the glare.

Why did I keep the child a secret? Surely through pride; I will not have Walther wed me for other reasons than the love he professed to bear. Through spite also; he will never know of his child.

* * *

I like the bracing smell of sea air; I breathe in deeply and turn my back on the horizon.

Yes, Walther's child will be mine, and will be born a Beynac; for who is to know Eudes was not the sire? My child will grow up at Comarque with little Robert and sweet Eloise. And will never be told how much love his mother bore his father.

CHAPTER 23

Kisses on my neck increase in pressure, sending thrills of pleasure coursing through my body. I open my eyes. Propped on one elbow, Kurt is watching me with smiling eyes.

"You villain!" I cry, closing my eyes again more to savior the present than to recapture my dream. "You just abandoned me when I was with child! Your child, Walther, you rogue! It was all in my dream, as clear and vivid as if I was living it for the first time! I was so unhappy! How could you do that to me?"

Raising eyebrows in mock surprise, Kurt reaches for pad and trusty uncapped pen on the bedside table, impatiently tears off the first pages already covered in writing and sets them aside before scrawling new words on a blank sheet. Raising myself on the pillow and leaning against his bare back, I read as he writes; my senses fully awake to the feel of his naked skin against mine, to the male scent of his strong and lean body, to the curl of his silver hair on the smooth nape of his neck. "Never too late to apologize." He writes. "Let me make it up to you the best way I know how."

Replacing pen and paper, he turns around and with gentle hands on my shoulders, pushes me back on the pillows.

"Wait, Kurt, wait! First I want to read what's on those pages."

He shrugs, reaches back for the three sheets he must have written while I slept and hands them to me. I scan the pages while he watches; my concentration somewhat impaired by his patient exploration of as yet uncharted erogenous zones.

"You captivated me from the start." He writes, in his firm and angular hand, using a larger script than his usual scrawl. Not a bad start. "

I did get the impression I knew you from somewhere." He has underlined the sentence twice. "But there was also something disquieting about you; looking at you, I would get a physical impression of danger that I found rather unnerving.

Since my accident, I have been getting these flashes about places and people, and they usually turn out to be correct. So, I held back from letting you know at once how much you attracted me; I had to know more about you.

The more I did, the fainter my apprehension grew.

I don't think of myself as a coward, but when you spoke up and I realized I loved you too, for a fraction of a second, I literally froze with terror. I can neither explain this fear nor understand why it vanished the moment I decided to disregard it to tell you (well, you know...) I loved you."

"Whether I did love you in the past matters little; as you pointed out, there is only now. I'm glad the past sent you to me and I am glad it's now. I love you Alexandra, or should I say, Alix-Sandra?" I turn my head; our eyes meet and we exchange a smile of complicity. "Yes. Nothing like a new name to start a new life! But what am I supposed to call you? I like Kurt, it brings to mind 'courteous' and 'courting!' Besides, I would rather you did not resemble your Alter Ego in every fickle way. One is glad none of your amorous skills have been lost over the last 800 years, but one sort of hopes you do not practice them with as much abandon as you used to...."

Kurt laughs his strange laughter, so deep and infectious, as if his heart and lungs conspired to by-pass his damaged throat so as not to deprive him of this most human of traits. He obviously doesn't feel like writing any more. Why bother with words when kisses will do?

Anyway, by the time I remember I should have called Daphne yesterday, it's already noon and we are both very hungry. The call to Montreal will have to wait until after breakfast. Poor

Daphne. From the way Christine described her on the phone, she must be in hair-pulling mode by now. Ah, well....

I stretch across the bed, reveling in the feel of my body, listening to the reassuring sound of Kurt's shower and wondering if he would be singing under it if he could do so.

Out of the blue, I remember a waterfall as wispy as a veil over dark shiny rocks. There is also a pool of crystalline water where chirping birds come to drink and a clearing with very green grass and fragrant pink flowers - wild sweet peas, perhaps - which Elaine gathers with glee.

Yes, a beautiful place indeed, where my whole retinue of thirty knights and squires agreed to halt for a day on our way back from Venice to Comarque....

I seem to have reached the stage where evanescent memories of my life as Alix pop into my mind at odd moments and mingle with reminiscences of my own childhood, which, I suppose, they are in a way.

Kurt is still in the shower. I look around his room. Rather untidy, with jackets thrown about on furniture and dirty shirts in a heap on the floor. Good! Tidy men are usually nitpickers. Under his tweed jacket on the sofa, I spot the case where he packs his psaltery. Should I attempt to play it once more? Sheer indolence rather than diffidence prevents me from doing so.

Kurt emerges from the bathroom, a towel around his hips, wide shoulders still dewed with pearls of water, and my heart leaps. Do I deserve the love of such a man? I am no youthful Alix... But then Kurt is no teenager either. Yet, the joy of life courses through our veins. One can't help marveling at the wonderful versality of love; each facet of it as unique as the person who inspires it.

Room service is bringing us our third meal since yesterday afternoon. I raise the sheet around me to hide my nakedness, but

Kurt only lets the waiter in far enough to push the cart through the door, and wheels it himself close to the bed. The smell of hot croissants and freshly-brewed coffee is positively bracing.

While we munch on scrambled eggs and other goodies, and my sheet toga keeps slipping off my shoulders, I venture to ask about his plans.

"Will you be coming to Montreal?" I do not even pray for a positive answer. Nothing matters anymore; we will be together one way or another.

He nods several times between mouthfuls and my heart takes another leap. His smile says I need not worry, that he will always be there for me. I know.

"I forgot to call Daphne yesterday. Do you mind if I do it now, I'll use my calling-card." He shrugs and gestures towards the phone. It will be seven a.m. in Montreal. Daphne is an early riser from what she told me. Here goes.

Four rings before she answers in eager, expectant tones, "Sandra? Is that you?"

"How did you know it was me?" This woman has a knack for disconcerting me.

"You are a very reliable person, Sandra," Her brief chuckle makes it sound like an undesirable trait. "I knew you would call and actually waited by the phone all day yesterday. What kept you?"

"Well, I've been...rather busy. How are you? Why did you want me to call? Christine must have told you I would be back in Montreal next week...." Kurt throws me a soulful look that warms my heart. "Couldn't it wait until my return?"

She seems to hesitate and clears her throat noisily. "Listen to me, Sandra, do not, I repeat, do not attempt to reach more of your past! Do you hear me?" Her words curiously emphasized by the lowered tone of her throaty voice.

"I hear you quite clearly, Daphne, but it's a little late for that; my past is with me all the time without any effort on my part to recollect it. I dream about it; I re-live it... In more ways than one!"

"Oh, my God!" She sounds altogether crushed.

"There's nothing to worry about, Daphne! It's getting more and more riveting. Not always pleasant perhaps, but quite fascinating. So why shouldn't I try to learn more?"

"I can't tell you over the phone. Just take my word for it. I have had dreams... Many dreams. Of the past!"

"Great! Hope they were as interesting as mine. I'm getting quite used to my little forays in the past. You'll see, after a while you won't mind them at all. Just relax and enjoy!" This conversation is getting slightly ridiculous.

The tantalizing aroma of my second cup of coffee, still half-full, is beckoning to me, but Daphne is not amused.

"No! No! You mustn't laugh, Sandra! You don't understand, this is very serious!" She sounds more than a little unhinged. "What have you discovered of the past since you left Montreal?" She wants to know. "Please tell me!" First time I ever heard her whine. "Daphne, do be reasonable! It would take too long to tell you the whole story. I promise you a complete report when I get back."

"What about...Black Foulk?" She inquires, not without hesitation.

"What about him? I can assure you he is the least of my worries, past or present." Her sigh of relief is loud enough to cross the Atlantic on its own.

"All right. Now, at least tell me how well you have got to know your mute musician, Kurt Meissen?" She asks. What business is it of hers?

"Well... Pretty well, I would say." I look at Kurt slipping on a crisp white shirt and I grin. "Why?"

"Because. I can't explain until I see him. He has to come here. I must see him!" The urgency she tries to keep from her voice is both perceptible and strange. "It's extremely important, Sandra. For his sake...and mine." "Look, Daphne, I don't know what you want with him, but it so happens he might come to Montreal when he finishes his tour with the medieval group, and...."

"When will that be? I cannot wait months, Sandra! My health...is failing. Can't you prevail on the man to come now?" Kurt is buckling his belt and looking at me with questions in his eyes; I close mine briefly and nod to let him know I will satisfy his curiosity as soon as Daphne hangs up.

"What's wrong with you, Daphne?" My concern is sincere; Daphne might be a little weird and invasive at times, but one can't help feeling something for her, and being grateful for her help. I do owe her a lot. "Nothing serious, I hope."

"Oh, it would take too long to go into details, but yes, it is serious. Sandra, believe me, I would not ask such a favor from you...or your friend - for I have an inkling that you are friends by now - if it concerned only the state of my body, but... Oh, never mind. You say Walther, I mean, Herr Meissen, is prepared to come to Canada, so you just have to persuade him to come a little sooner, that's all."

"What do you mean, that's all! He isn't going to leave his friends high and dry just because you expressed the wish to see him! He doesn't know you from Adam. You're expecting rather a lot, aren't you? I would not even have the nerve to ask him, even though...."

Even though I wish nothing better than to be near him. Even though I think he would do it for me. Kurt is nodding. Our conversation is not hard to follow as our voices have reached the level of bridled irritation.

"Please, Sandra! I can't tell you how important this is for me...and Walther." Why does she keep calling him Walther? She makes me terribly uneasy. Torn between pity and a curious distaste, I answer, "All right, Daphne, I'll see what I can do; but I may not call you back before I return to Montreal, OK?" She reluctantly agrees, tells me to take care of myself and hangs up.

Kurt is already scribbling on his pad. He hands me the paper.

"You friend seems very anxious to meet me. Any idea why?"

"Not the least." I shake my head. "I gather it has to do with your past. Daphne is a curious woman who probably has psychic faculties. Now, I know you don't go for that kind of mumbo-jumbo, and I also know that charlatans are a dime a dozen; but Daphne is no charlatan, and..." I laugh, " For personal reasons I am now prepared to keep an open mind about psychic phenomena. Who knows what she has seen? She might be able to help you...with your...problem."

He makes a face and scribbles some more. "Do you want me to accompany you to Montreal?" I don't even have to reply, the answer is writ plainly on my face.

On the same paper, he adds, "I might get a student of mine to replace me in the group, and book a seat on your flight, Alix-Sandra. Or Alexandra, if you prefer." One thing is sure; it does not take long to get used to happiness.

* * *

Well, Kurt will join me in a week; my flight was full. Besides, the musician who is to replace him had to be located and given enough time to make his way to Rouen for the next concert. In

287

our last few hours together before I set off for Nice, I could feel Kurt's growing frustration with his infirmity.

He had to rely on the other musicians to get hold of the psaltery-playing student and make all the arrangements in his stead; in spite of the fact, they were none too happy to let their star performer go.

I am on my way back to Nice - the shortest way, no detour by Comarque this time. I drove until dusk, stopped in a small inn recommended by the guide and asked for a quiet room facing away from the road.

The night is clear and cool. Leaning out of my open window I watch the full moon silver the dark trees and folded umbrella of the silent hotel garden, and suddenly recall another moon-lit night long, long ago....

* * *

We have been travelling so long I lost count of the days. Sleep eludes me as I watch the silver glow of the full moon over the dark hills. Three times already has it waned and waxed since we departed from Venice. Comarque is nigh and I ought to rejoice; the long journey has wearied me and my cloak will not hide my girth much longer.

The night sky is so clear that stars shine more brightly, closer to us, as if the blessed who as some say - inhabit them took pity on our earthbound souls. From the dark woods a hooting owl makes itself heard. I shiver under my fur coverlet for nights are cool. It is not our want to sleep thus in the open air; but the day's march was arduous and no castle was in sight to offer hospitality when the sun went down. I listen to Lady Madeleine's raspy breathing by my side in the covered cart; at times her breath catches into a stifled sob.

Poor Lady Madeleine, she has grown so feeble in body that she is scarce able to ride. I'm glad she finds some solace in sleep, for her losses are grievous to bear. She sits in one of the carts drawn by oxen, and me thinks I may soon join her for the pace of my horse wearies me more every day.

Lady Madeleine has much to grieve for, having lost both her lord and her only son on the ramparts of Constantinople. Now, naught is left to her but her son's widow, Lady Rosamund, who is not even with child.

Lady Rosamund does behave in the strangest way; she has taken to wearing man's clothing, rides astride her horse, and favor's the company of foot soldiers and their harlots.

She is never without her gyrfalcon on her gloved right fist and goes hawking with the knights whenever they do.

There are only thirty knights, squires and men-at-arms left in our party to guard us three women and the six carts laden with spoils. That is without counting the servants who give attendance to the horses and oxen, and the loose women who follow the soldiers.

It is but two days since Lady Iselda of Nevers and her escort left our party to go north and I miss her gentle company. As she was most anxious to return to Nevers and her children, her lord had provided her with an escort so she might travel with us as far as the valley of the river Rhone. In my distress, I confided in her one day. She reproached me not but sadly shook her head.

"Hapless child! How could you hope to resist Sir Walther's blandishments when far wilier than you have succumbed! Count yourself fortunate that your lord, God rest his soul, is no longer here to deny paternity of your child!"

May Iselda find her children hale and full of cheer, as I hope to find Robert and Eloise. We are following the same route we took on our journey east, an old road the Romans built between hills and sea, plains and shore.

We meet all manner of travelers on the way; pilgrims, peasants and traders, on foot or on horseback.

Yesterday, we encountered a band of armed merchants surrounding three carts of goods. They drew their swords at the sight of our mailed knights, but sheaved them with smiling miens when they understood us to be returning pilgrims, and greeted us most warmly. Me thinks they came from Flanders by the way they spoke the Northern tongue. Our laden carts have slowed us so that we travelled in three months what we could have done in one on good horses. Everything bar my unborn child is a matter of indifference to me.

I caress my warm belly under my shift, its shape rounded as the moon's. The child is moving. Never will Walther know the joy of feeling the first stirrings of this new life he has created. I pity him.

The eagerness of discovery which moved me forward when we set out on this ill-fated pilgrimage has turned to quiet resignation. I ride among these men secluded by my melancholy from their joyous mood and prancing displays of satisfaction.

The weight of their spoils and the thought of the welcome that awaits them in the Périgord make them impatient to be home, and they resent the slow pace more than I do. Their fervent zeal to free the Holy Land long forgotten, they are well content to return to their domains with their lives and a fortune in silver. They are indeed a jolly lot, who would fain treat me with undue familiarity if my wintry reserve did not discourage all approach. All now avoid me as they would a leper.

All but Conon de Béthune. Has he perhaps surmised the cause of my sorrow? Oft will he play his lute for our enjoyment. He has composed for me a canson which he urges me to sing, and it be not one of these sorrowful ballads that bring tears to my eyes, but a joyful song which perhaps I may sing to my child one day, for it talks about the beauty of flowers, the freedom of birds and the sweetness of a spring morning, but never will I play my psaltery again.

CHAPTER 24

Spring is greening Montreal with bold new buds and timid grass. Hyacinths in bloom huddle against the sun-warmed red brick walls, their scent as welcome as the balmy breeze that carries it, bringing to mind the fragrance of Sister Anne's flower-beds in the convent garden, so long ago. People walk more briskly, smile more readily, revitalized by a yearly rebirth of their own. The long Montreal winter is over.

I look at my city with new eyes - Kurt's eyes trying to imagine what his response will be to the sights that have grown so familiar to me I no longer pay them any attention. As the plane on its approach to Dorval airport banked sharply over the wooded slopes of Mount Royal and the watery expanse of the Saint-Lawrence, I realized how much I had taken my beautiful city for granted.

My apartment feels a little strange, as if someone else lived there; someone I hardly knew. A self-centered someone, devoid of quirks and originality; intent on keeping her world neat and safe from the pains and joys of life.

Tidy piles of books on the coffee table still testify to the intensity of my obsession with Kurt; paperbacks on medieval music; art books on medieval instruments bought second-hand; library tomes on medieval history, long overdue... Shit. They don't waive fines for past-life regression at Westmount Library.

Well, at least the past comes back to me unbidden now, I don't have to pore over history books to find reference to places, people and events. So much has happened in the last two weeks!

I open all the windows and let the fresh breeze chase off the last hint of tobacco from the stuffy rooms, and brew myself some coffee, more to relish its aroma than to satisfy a need for caffeine. Sitting on the couch nursing my mug in the humming silence of the city, I wonder about the marvelous and exciting experience my life has become. I sit there in the peace of my shelter, not praying, or even meditating, just being grateful.

What have I ever done to deserve the chance to recapture my past life? Let alone my past love? And thus, live so much more intensely; for we are our past and the richer it is the more fully we live.

Kurt has made me appreciate the beauty of silence; my concern with his infirmity is strictly for his sake, as he seems to resent it more and more. I don't need him to articulate his emotions or mine; we are living them.

Men are not very good at expressing anything but abstract ideas, anyway.

I drain the last of my cold coffee and rise from the couch. I am about to retrieve the suitcase I dropped in the hall on my way in, and start unpacking, when something moves me to go straight to the office and give George, my shifty boss, a piece of my mind.

* * *

George does a double take as I walk into his office.

"Oh... Sandra. You're back already?"

"Yes. Thanks to you, George. Can you give me one good reason why you could not grant me a two-week leave of absence without pay?" I can't help raising my voice on the last words; Lynn and the others must be pricking up their ears in the next office. "What was so complex that you couldn't deal with it yourself?"

He fingers the side of his nose while casting around for a suitable lie.

"The July issue... You know... It's not quite... I mean, it still needs more than a bit of work, and deadlines have to be met." He looks around his office with great concentration. "Well, here you are, George." I literally throw my article on medieval music over the uppermost of the golf magazines that clutter his desk. "You can use this to fill in the blanks. I finished it during my vacation." I pause to emphasize the last word and give the others a chance to titter.

"And, George, next time your game is off and you have a bad day on the links, don't take it out on my daughter, O.K.? You were quite rude to her over the phone and I think she deserves an apology. And so do I. So, are you going to apologize?"

He finally looks up and stares at my face before a tentative smile vainly tries to liven up his bland features. "My! My! What's come over you, Sandra? I've never seen you in such a feisty mood, my dear. Must say, it suits you. You look great. Younger, too; d'you go to La Prairie in Switzerland for rejuvenation? Your hair looks...fluffy."

"Don't try to placate me, George. I'm really angry with you."

"I can see that." Instead of saying 'Sorry' he picks up the article finished on the flight from Nice - with such speed and ease I surprised myself - and leaves through it.

"What are all those sentences in Latin? Didn't know you could speak Latin." Neither did I, until Alix's memory became mine.

"I don't speak Latin, George, only priests do nowadays, just understand it. Anyway, it's part of the medieval music scene."

As I stand there without giving any sign of leaving, he finally mumbles, "Oh, all right, it's true I was in a bad mood that day. I should have been nicer to your daughter, but as far as you are concerned, you should know by now that this outfit cannot function without you." "Gee, thanks, George. So, I guess you wouldn't have fired me after all. I'll remember that in the future." Assuming that's all I will get by way of an apology, I grab my text back from his hands, turn my back on him and add over my shoulder, "Oh, and another thing, I'll work Monday, Tuesday, Wednesday and Thursday, but will be taking ten days off without pay, of course - from Friday onward." I walk out of his office; to be greeted by Lynn's silent clapping and the others' grins of support.

I include them all in a smile. "OK friends, let's get to work on that July issue." I end up working in the office till 9, fired by unusual - and contagious - energy. Join Lynn and Fred, the graphic artist, for a steak and a glass of red wine at a local pub. Get home to a hot bath. Sleep like a ground hog till 8 the next morning. No jet lag. No dream. Only the nagging thought of Daphne, who will have to be contacted eventually.

* * *

I have been back 24 hours and can't bring myself to call Daphne. Why? When I finally decide to dial her number, she answers immediately. Waiting by the phone again? "Oh, Sandra, I'm so glad you're back! Is Walther with you?"

"No, he is not. He'll be here next Friday. How are you, Daphne?"

"I'm fine." She sounds calmer than on our last telephone conversation. "Why couldn't Walther join you?"

"My flight was full, Daphne, and he had some arrangements to make." I can feel patience will be needed. "Why do you keep calling him Walther? His name is Kurt."

Her tongue clicks with annoyance. "No. He is back to being Walther, that's why he can't... Oh, never mind, I cannot explain over the phone. When will I see you?"

"Today, I guess. It's Saturday and I won't be going to the office. How about 5 p.m.? You can offer me a cup of tea."

"Can't you make it a little earlier? I'm so anxious to talk to you."

I glance at my watch and frown. "It's already 2 and I would like to finish unpacking and tidying up... Oh, all right. I'll be there as soon as possible."

She hangs up without another word. I vaguely pray that whatever she is about to reveal might help Kurt in his predicament. That's asking a lot, I suppose, but if you don't ask....

* * *

Daphne's hair is now cut quite short, brushed back and dyed jet black. Her elegant grey pant-suit hangs over her thin shoulders. The obvious weight-loss is not to her advantage, and new wrinkles crisscross her slackened cheeks. She looks calm enough, but the fixity of her eyes is disquieting.

I feel like hugging her, and yet the thought of doing so sends shivers through my spine. In fact, I am tempted to turn on my heels and run; truth is, the woman scares me. But I want to know what she does, and I won't if I take off. So, I stay.

I remain standing on the threshold while she steps back to let me in and patiently waits for me to enter the black and white entrance hall still redolent of white Hosta.

"Come in, Sandra. Don't be afraid, my sweet, especially not of me. Lord knows I don't wish you any harm. Never did. Oh, Lord! This is so difficult."

"Daphne, what's wrong with you? You look so... tired."

"No, my dear. I look ill." Her smile recaptures some of her former warmth. "Truth of the matter is I am a very sick woman."

While she takes my raincoat and hangs it in the closet, I observe her closely. The transformation, initiated before I left for France, is now complete; she is a totally different person. Outwardly, at least. She used to remind me of Colette, the French writer, in her old age, with her nondescript robes and capes, and her curly flame-red hair. Now she looks more like a decadent old aristocrat on his last leg. What can possibly have moved her to change her appearance so drastically? "What is... ailing you, Daphne?"

"Quaint expression. Must be Alix speaking. Well, it's quite simple, really. I had a cancerous tumor removed from my left breast six years ago, and I was sort of putting my faith in statistics, you know, if you survive five years, you are all right, kind of thing; but the cancer has returned with a vengeance."

Her bantering tone somehow far more moving than she realizes. Tears fill my eyes as I rest my hand on her arm.

"Oh, Daphne, I am so sorry! Is there anything I can do?"

She looks away and laughs. "Yes, you can tell me what naughty Alix has been up to since you left."

"Never mind Alix. Tell me more about you. Shouldn't you be in a hospital, receiving some kind of treatment? Who looks after you?"

She seems to appreciate my concern, takes my hands in hers and squeezes them. Her skin feels as dry as old leather.

"Do not worry about me, Alix. I am well looked after. A cousin of mine, who happens to be a nurse, is now living here with me. She will stay on...till the end."

I let the tears run down my cheeks without attempting to wipe them off. "You look so...different, Daphne. Do you mind telling me why?"

She laughs louder. "Yes, I do, don't I? The leopard has changed its spots, hasn't it? No, I don't mind telling you why.

Telling you why is in fact the reason that made me ask you here. I think you may understand... I hope you do. I am not going crazy, if that's what is bothering you."

She raises a bony hand to stop me from interrupting. "I have had my share of dreams and visions about the past - your past and Walther's - lately. I don't mind telling you they have been very disturbing. That's why I may have sounded a little...agitated over the phone."

I repress a smile but refrain from any comment.

"Now this kind of flashback is not new to me. If you recall, when we first met, I told you I had lived... and died at the time of the French Revolution. I've had intimations of other lives as well, but never this clear and... startling. I'll tell you more after I have heard what you have to say. Come on...."

She grabs my arm suddenly in a tight grip. My instinctive recoil takes us both by surprise.

"Sorry, Daphne" I mumble. "I'm a little nervous. Still jet-lagged, I guess."

She looks me up and down with puzzled brows.

"You don't look tired to me; you look ten years younger. And I like your scent, too. You never wore scent before. What is it?

"In Love Again." I confess with a grin. "Appropriate, it seems. Wipe those tears, Sandra. I've had an interesting life. No need for tears. Come on, let's go and have some tea."

Instead of leading me to the kitchen where we usually have our cuppa, she takes me to her Versailles drawing-room and motions for me to sit on the couch where it all began. Or rather where it all began to make sense. She pours the tea into Limoges cups from a silver teapot I have never seen before, and passes me a dainty cup with a trembling hand.

"First you tell me your story, then I will bring you gradually to a stage where my revelations will make sense and I can tell you mine."

"And how do you propose to do this, may I ask?"

She puts down the pot on the silver tray and looks at me with raised eyebrows. No longer hidden by a fringe of red hair. "Why, the usual way, Sandra.

I'll regress you to a time I deem appropriate." She sits down on her favorite chair and sighs. "Now, it is essential you to tell me everything that came back to you while you were in France, as well as what you have learned of Herr Meissen. I am all ears."

So, I do my best to relate what I have recalled through dreams, trances and visions, as well as recaptured memories of Alix's.

As surprised as Daphne at the extent of my recollections, I conclude, "What more do you want me to say? I can't give you every little detail. I could tell you, for instance, that it is far worse to see decaying corpses hanging from trees at crossroads than to watch them on the six o'clock news. For one thing, they stink, and believe me, their rotting faces pecked by crows stay with you late at night.

Oh, yes, and the stench, and the buzzing flies. I think it's a mistake to believe people then were more callous than we are. I would venture it's rather the other way round; we get our horrors pre-packaged and sanitized by the media. What else do you want to know? That Alix loves children for their innate truth and beauty? That she is a strong swimmer and does not fear the sea?

Which is not the case for many of her contemporaries, but I guess a knight in full armor had every reason not to relish travelling by boat.

Daphne is shaking her head. "This is amazing, Sandra!" Two red spots on her pale cheeks punctuate her excitement. "I have never encountered anyone capable of recalling a previous life, the way you do."

I now feel quite at ease on her familiar couch, kick off my shoes and stretch my legs.

"I have often wondered about that." I muse.

"How many of us out there are living the way I do, in two lives? Surely I can't be unique and other people must experience this kind of recollection."

I look at the bare wall in front of me. A few paintings, probably quite valuable, have been taken down from the walls, leaving rectangles of lighter grey on the beautiful painted wainscotting. Is Daphne short of money?

She opines eagerly. "Oh, but a lot of them do! But from my own experience at least, never as vividly as you do. You see, most people dismiss this kind of recollection as fantasy and do nothing about it; whereas you did everything in your power to search for the source of these visions. By doing so you made them even stronger."

"Yes, I suppose you are right. Now my medieval past is as much part of my memory as my childhood in this life. One thing is certain, pursuing the remembrance of Walther has certainly brought me closer to Kurt!"

"And vice-versa? Don't you know Walther better than you ever did?" Her Mona Lisa smile looks weird on her ravaged face. She lowers her eyes and stares at the clasped hands in her lap for a long while. "And in your opinion Kurt doesn't remember any of this?"

"As far as I know, he doesn't. As I mentioned, he had this one vivid dream of himself as Walther trying to help a wounded

Eudes during the siege of Constantinople...," I stop, suddenly jolted by the memory of Olivier leaving the breakfast table in Nantes.

"What is it?" Daphne looks up quickly. "Oh, nothing very important, really. I just remembered that when Olivier, Irene's boyfriend who is in fact Eudes...."

"I know. I know. You already told me. What about him?"

"Well, when he left the dining-room in a huff because Kurt kissed me, he was limping, sort of dragging his left leg like a wounded man. I didn't pay any attention to it at the time because I hadn't yet recalled the way Eudes died. Weird, isn't it?"

She shrugs. "When you come right down to it, everything is. Irene dreams she is a nun and Olivier remembers his wound... Shall we proceed?" She drains the last of her tea and motions for me to lie back on the pillows of the couch.

"We both know the routine by now." I have come here prepared to tell her off for expecting Kurt and me to do her bidding without asking questions. I no longer resent her manner, her change of appearance, or her strange behavior. My one feeling for her is now pity, and, at this stage of the game, one more regression matters little to me. It is the least I can do for her.

"Go ahead, Daphne, I am getting quite used to living in two worlds."

I close my eyes and let her take me back once more.

* * *

One of the knights in our party is a cousin of the Trencavels, who hold the walled city of Carcassonne, and he has prevailed upon us all to ride with him as far as the town and stay awhile as guests of his cousins.

The Trencavels are said to favor Catharism, which has many followers in their domains. I do not hold with the Cathars' belief that creation is the work of the devil, but the Trencavels are also known for their lavish hospitality. We still have some days of riding left before we reach Comarque, and the idea of a short rest in Carcassonne is welcomed by all our knights and men-at-arms, so I soon give my consent.

Lady Madeleine says she might even stay in Carcassonne and end her days there now that Lady Rosamund has absconded with one of the archers and more than her share of her dead husband's silver. Lady Madeleine and I puzzle over Lady Rosamund's heedless desertion with wonder and pity. How could lust make her thus forget who she is to consort with a lowly archer?

Could she perchance love him more than I ever loved Walther? This cannot be, for the love I bear my fickle lover will always endure in my heart, and I would have followed him to the end of the earth, had he ever asked me to do so....

We arrived within sight of Carcassonne yesterday. While they are nowhere near as awesome as Constantinople's, the turreted ramparts of the fortress strike an impressive sight indeed. They crown a hill, the green slopes of which are dotted with many fine houses and even churches surrounded by lower walls. Not without great hardship did our oxen pull the laden carts up the steep bank of the promontory to reach the château of the Trencavels inside the ramparts.

The sight of the castle itself proved worthy of such effort. Built over sixty years ago, it is very large and well appointed; its lofty towers rise as high as the steeples of the nearby basilica of Saint Nazaire and seem to watch over the flock of goodly houses clustering around it, like a benevolent shepherd.

The streets of the city appear as narrow and crowded as those of Paris, but many are paved and the people laugh more readily under its clement southern skies of blue.

Either this town numbers many knights or the Lord Trencavel is very lax and allows commoners to wear mantels of bright colors such as green and red, for the streets are crowded with brightly garbed men and ladies. It makes for a very colorful scene indeed. Young Raymond Trencavel welcomed us in a most courtly way and rose from his chair to give us all the kiss of peace, as he would to his brethren, the Cathars. He is but a youth,

long and slender still, but his eyes are bright and his manner gentle. In the great hall, adorned with many precious tapestries, he had trestles set last evening for a rich banquet, and sat Lady Madeleine on his right for she is old and deserves the honor, and me on his left, which he reminded me is the side of the heart. Though mine own heart is heavy with the thought of my lost love, I enjoyed Count Raymond's company all through dinner for he is wise beyond his years. I responded to his courtesy with smiles and laughter. And felt better for it.

We were served by young squires in clean liveries and even I, who has no desire for food save what is needed for my child to thrive, was tempted to partake of braised mussels, stuffed brown rolls and rosy almond cream. Talented minstrels entertained us through the long meal. I asked permission to retire when dance started and young Lord Trencavel escorted me himself to the door of the great hall.

We are to leave at dawn tomorrow and be on our way to Comarque. T'is pity for, as I sit on my enclosed bed in a spacious solar, I reflect that talking at length with young Raymond about his strange beliefs might have proved enlightening. If it can bring such compassion and wisdom to a young man's heart, Catharism may not be the hellish heresy that Bogo vilified so vehemently.

In truth Bogo's condemnation is in my eyes the most potent argument in favor of the Cathars.

* * *

We have crossed the River Beune on the stone bridge and a cry of satisfaction escapes us as we espy Camargue's tall keep above the trees. In spite of myself, I sigh with relief at the thought of the peace I will enjoy to prepare for the birth of my child, for I want no regrets to mar the joy of its coming. Soon will I embrace little Robert and sweet Elaine too, for I have sent word to Hautefort castle that we are back, so that Constantin de Born may bring the children back to Comarque.

We cross the first bailey and those of the villagers who are there at noon rush out of their wretched houses to greet us with unusual displays of devotion, touching our horses, our legs, the hem of our clothing as if we were really coming back from the Holy Land. I order my squires not to repulse them, and to throw some alms to the children.

The draw bridge is lowered at our approach and we cross the deep dark waters of the moat. Guards in strange liveries stand on both sides of the great gate.

Sir Gilbert, Eudes' faithful seneschal is waiting for us in the courtyard, looking wan and feeble. Ten paces behind him, among unknown knights in full armor, stands Black Foulk.

CHAPTER 25

Black Foulk steps forward and, motioning Sir Gilbert aside with an indifferent wave of his gloved hand, stands in front of my horse, his dark eyes agleam with triumph.

Before I can make a move, he takes hold of my reins and signals to one of his squires to help me dismount. The man obeys promptly, but I show no haste to leave my saddle lest my legs not support me. Swallowing my fear, I ask boldly, "What brings you here, Sir Foulk? Know you not that your presence is not welcomed in Sir Eudes' domains?"

Handing my horse's reins to the squire, he bows with affected civility before responding. "Comarque is no longer to be counted among Eudes' domains, my lady Alix." He pauses to glance at the massive keep with prideful eyes.

"I have claimed it for my own in fulfilment of a promise made by your departed lord many years ago; when you came to us as his ward."

Sir Gilbert attempts to speak; but Foulk turns his head and withers him with such a look that the poor old seneschal seems to shrivel in his fur-trimmed robes and lowers his head in shame. His raiment is soiled with mud and straw, as if he had lain on the ground. Or in some foul prison.

Anger lends me strength to confound the villain.

"That particular promise was voided when Sir Eudes endowed you with the rich fief of Rimeuil, Sir Foulk! Comarque belongs to Eudes' rightful heirs, of whom you are not one! Even if his oldest sons were slain, as I have been told, Robert and Eloise remain...as well as the child I am carrying now."

He takes a step back and shakes his head in disbelief. This revelation appears to cause him no small surprise. For once I am glad of my palfrey's great size, which affords me the satisfaction of looking down on the knave.

His brows knit in angry puzzlement as a cloud of pain seems to drift across his arrogant face.

I hasten to fill his silence. "You have no right to Comarque, Sir Foulk!" Raising my voice as much as my failing strength will allow, I speak to the crowd of men who fill the courtyard.

"Your unlawful presence in this castle will not be tolerated!" My haughty manner fails to impress; Foulk, his face a blank, stares on as I add, "You are despoiling Eudes' children of their rightful inheritance and the king's justice will ensure that you be punished for this treacherous deed!"

The felon now scoffs outright, "And which king might that be, my lady? Are you counting on rescue from King John of England or from King Philip of France? It is hard to tell which one of the two is more faint-hearted than the other." Foulk's men join in his laughter and their mirth grates in my ears. He looks up and, raising his voice so it may reach the farthest of the men-at-arm crowding the courtyard, he declares boldly, "Neither King John nor King Philip has any claim to these domains! We hold the place and let no man dispute our right to be here!" A murmur of approval sweeps through the assembly, as Sir Gilbert cringes and shakes his bent head.

I remain silent, searching my mind for the best course of action. I dare not urge my escort to resist; to judge by the size of Foulk's mesnie, my small retinue, hopelessly outnumbered, would be cut to pieces in no time. For many of Foulk's men are in full mail and lean on their tall swords.

I do not know by what means or when these men made themselves masters of the place, but their brutal miens and the foul smell which pervades Comarque from their presence bode ill for our fate. These men show no fear of God's wrath, let alone of my ineffectual anger.

With a sneer that could pass for a smile, Black Foulk addresses me again.

"Do not be afeared of me, my lady Alix! As long as I hold this castrum your place will be here. You will always be Comarque's chatelaine. Pray dismount now and do me the honor of accepting my hospitality, for this abode is but a bleak place without the radiance of your beauty."

Seething inside, I grant him a bow and respond with a straight face. "Why, Sir Foulk, it is most gracious of you in the circumstances, but Eudes' children require my care and I would as soon join them at Hautefort castle, together with the faithful knights and squires who have safeguarded our long journey. Pray do not think me ungrateful for declining your generous invitation," I tug on my reins, pulling them from the startled squire's hand and urges my lumbering horse to turn around.

For a too brief moment, Black Foulk remains motionless, startled by my sudden move, but he comes alive with a roar of anger, roughly tears the reins from my hands and grasps my right arm in a steely hand.

"Fie, woman! Would you have me play the fool for your amusement!"

My knights let out a collective groan and I hear the sound of swords unsheathed. I turn my head and raise my free hand to stay any rash move on their part. Flames of hellish anger still dancing in his eyes, Black Foulk sneers, "Allow you and your men to join my enemy in Hautefort? Do not dissemble with me, Lady Alix! I know you have already sent for the children!" He shrugs.

"Well, know that they will not come! Constantin de Born will never relinquish them now, for he knows that Comarque is in my hands and they are precious to him. He is no liege of mine and indeed I suspect he plans to lay claim to Comarque. Let him!"

His rage abating as quickly as it had soared, he bows again and his dark eyes seek mine.

"As for you, Fair Alix, you are a more precious prize to me than even these strong walls! A prize I would fain keep here safe from the roaming bands of lecherous soldiers that plague the land."

The felon's smile makes my blood run cold for it be even more wicked than his laughter. This man's changing moods are as unpredictable as the seas, and equally dangerous. I look around at the familiar stone walls, more forbidding than ever, and see nothing but a grim prison. Overhead the clear blue sky is suddenly host to a cloud of noisy blackbirds, and I catch myself thinking that serfs will be hard put to defend the ripened corn from their greed.

Still holding my arm, Foulk draws closer, so close that his hard chest presses against my legs. I feel myself grow faint and hardly hear the words he now utters in a low voice. "Sweet Alix! You are the reason I made great haste to leave Constantinople after Eudes' death to reach Comarque ahead of you; my true wish to welcome you as you deserve. To this day, never have you deigned to cast benevolent eyes on me, perhaps now will hear my plea!"

* * *

Elaine and I have been confined to my solar for close to a month now. But for foisting his unwelcome devotion on me daily, Black Foulk does not mistreat us in any way; we are provided with servants and food aplenty. But we cannot leave the castle and are allowed in the higher courtyard only under escort of his surly squires.

These brief outings cause us no pleasure. Foulk's men befoul the castle in the most loathsome way as if the use of privies was unknown to them. They have their sport of some toothless harlots in full view of all, drink much wine and quarrel among themselves whenever Black Foulk's is away. For he does leave Comarque on occasion; or so the few remaining servants tell us.

As if the conduct of his ruffians was not enough, Foulk had three of his archers hanged for some unknown offense four days ago. Their bodies dangle from the postern of the high courtyard, thus making our daily walk even more unpleasant.

I know not what fate has befallen my brave knights and men-at-arms, and this causes me great dismay.

I pray for them every day as well as for those of Eudes' men and retainers who were left behind; every one of them has vanished, and Black Foulk will not answer my questions. The servants who remain tell us little, so afeared are they.

Some of them pretend not to see Elaine and me when we call after them in the courtyard. One old swineherd I often gave wine to, whispered to me that Comarque has fallen into the hands of Foulk through treachery. Whose treachery? I have yet to discover.

Last night, we were awakened before matins by the most horrible cries of agony, all the more frightening to hear that, though muffled by walls, they seemed to arise from underneath the castle, from the depth of hell itself. We could not close our eyes again and huddled together till sunrise.

At first, the old woman who brought our food this morning would not answer our questions, hid her face fearfully in her sleeve and whimpered, "Pray, my lady, do not ask! They will beat me if I talk to you!"

As I persisted and gave her a silver coin for her trouble, she told us in a trembling voice that The Black Lord is using the caves under the castle as prisons, and sends there all those who oppose him. None of the servants are allowed near the narrow stairs that lead down there from the keep; and none have any wish to disobey.

I have never set foot in those cellars, where Eudes used to store supplies for the garrison, but I remember Adela - The Lord God have mercy on her soul - telling me about them.

She said they were vast and dank natural caves that had been there long before the castle was built and bore strange carvings of horses' heads on their rock walls. Eudes had taken her there once to show her where the wine and oil barrels were kept and she had never been tempted to go back, so eerie was the place.

When we dismissed the old woman, I resolved to find ways to seek help. Constantin de Born is Foulk's enemy, but perchance he thinks I remain here of my own accord. Perhaps he knows nothing of our plight and should be appraised of it. But how? In a letter? Pondering ways to send it, I remember the leather sling.

One of the possessions brought with me to Comarque 10 years ago, when I was but a girl, an orphan and Eudes' ward. Guilhem de Berguédan, my mother's lover - may the Lord God take pity on their hapless souls! - had taught me not only to play the lute but to swim in our pond and to ride a spirited horse as well.

One day, when I was about nine or so, he had made me a present of a soft leather sling of his own making, telling me that it was a shepherd's weapon, and showed me how to use it to hurl small stones or walnuts with great force at any kind of target. I soon became quite skilled at this game, derived much enjoyment from it and have treasured his gift to this day.

While Elaine looked on with questioning eyes, I retrieved it from the bottom of my chest. On a piece of white cloth torn from my shift, I wrote a brief letter addressed to Constantin de Born, and wrapped it around a small piece of stone brought back from Constantinople as a reminder of the frailty of human endeavor's.

I hurled the stone with all my strength and me thinks I can still use a sling to some effect for it flew in a wide arc, clear above the inner wall and moat - I heard no sound of splashing water - to fall outside amid the peasants' houses that cluster around the bailey.

I well know there is scant hope that it will ever reach Sir Constantin, but Elaine seems cheered by this futile attempt and I am glad for her sake. Even if the letter is found by one of the serfs, he will most likely hand it to one of Foulk's soldiers rather than to a monk or priest capable of reading it and taking it to Hautefort.

Would Sir Constantin ever attempt a siege to rescue us? It is doubtful for Comarque is well-nigh impregnable without mangonels and other siege engines.

At least, the children are safe as long as they remain in Hautefort. I miss them very much but pray for them every day. Pray that Sir Constantin keep them under his protection. I refuse to remain thus meek and helpless to await whatever fate Foulk has in store for us.

Without a brave knight to champion our cause, it rests upon us to find a way to escape the villain. Were you to hear of my plight, Fair Walther, I know in my heart you would not forsake me!

Alas, you are far away at the German emperor's court, and it is now my lot to endure the wearisome courtship of a man I despise.

To be fair, one is forced to admit that Foulk makes a great effort to behave with a modicum of courtesy. He raises not his voice to me, nor to Elaine, who is seldom required to leave the solar during his daily visits. She usually huddles in a far corner of the room like a mouse, making herself as inconspicuous as she can.

When addressing me, Foulk forces his voice into a gentle pitch, the better to keep repeating that he worships me now more than

311

ever. He waxes so lyrical that oftentimes I am hard put to keep a straight face. He has profited little from his friend Walther's example, for his attempts at seduction are as clumsy as a churl's and are more likely to evoke derision than desire.

On his first visit to the solar, he swore with a hand on his heart and his eyes on my bosom, that he lived only for the day I would grant him my love. And my hand in marriage as soon as my child is born.

"For you cannot hold Comarque alone, Sweet Alix, and have need of a strong man to defend your lands and protect you. A faithful knight who will revere you as no other ever did before. Forget the one whose lying tongue plied you with idle words only to abandon you!"

Which led to wonder if Walther had confided in him; or if Foulk had spied on us in Galata as Bogo had? Bogo himself, who made it his duty to know everything that happened in Comarque, was perchance aware of Foulk's secret fondness for me and, out of spite, appraised him of my illicit love for Walther. The next day, as Foulk strode into the solar, he brusquely ordered Elaine out of the room, causing me no small alarm for I do not trust his affectation of courtliness. He merely walked up to me, touched my arm with a gentle hand and, his dark eyes seeking mine, said with uncommonly soft voice, "Renounce the contempt you bear me long enough to hear my plea, Lady Alix.

You pledged your troth to a knight who proved unworthy of you. No, no, do not attempt to deny your love for Walther von Altdorf, a man I used to call my friend!

You were lovers. Bogo the Cleric appraised me of this in Venice!"

"A most trustworthy attestant indeed!" I sneered, turning my back on him to hide my dismay. By now he must surely suspect that the child I bear is not Eudes' but Walther's.

Were Foulk to reveal this to others, my child's legitimacy might be questioned and his inheritance denied. Either Foulk has no suspicion or he deems it wiser to bide his time so as to make better use of this knowledge. In his long address, he contents himself with extolling his own virtues once more, and concludes with a humble plea.

"I beseech you, Sweet Lady, grant me hope that my devotion will not go unrequited! I loved you long before you ever set eyes on that accursed German! Scorn not my love!"

Pity did enter my heart, but I could only sigh and turn away, thus igniting his anger anew.

He left the solar seething with rage for being thwarted again.

Be it as it may, Foulk's request for my hand came as no surprise to me, for I know well enough that affluent widows are a much sought-after commodity among ambitious knights and that we cannot hope to fend off suitors for ever. Unless we retire to a nunnery.

* * *

Foulk has just entered our solar.

Without asking my leave, he walks straight to my chair by the hearth, sits himself down and resting his fine cuffed leather boots on Elaine's empty stool, begins to observe me at his leisure.

He has taken to washing himself more often and wearing rich velvet tunics of red or green with inserts of gold embroidery; his pale face is clean-shaven every day and his black hair trimmed to cover his ears.

Hardly can I comprehend the sentiments this man inspires in me, for they ebb and flow between dread and scorn, derision and pity. When his eyes are on me thus, they at times seem to fill with compassion more than lust and pride. More often, alas, he seeks to impose his will and wrest admiration, for he knows not what love is. And it is reason enough to pity him.

During these past months I have come to understand that true love has no need of sustenance to endure, and that loving is a solace onto itself. Love is in the giving, not the taking; in the rejoicing over one's beloved existence, one's beloved happiness, even when one is no longer the cause of it. Love can flower brightest in renouncement.

I remain sitting by the arched window from where I have just thrown the letter wrapped around a stone. My sling is still under my needlework, where I hid it as he came in.

I watch Foulk's face in vain for signs of renouncement.

Seated in mine own chair, the villain is now waiting for me to address him.

His chin resting on his right hand, he observes me with a still benign smile, but three fingers of his left-hand drum impatiently on the arm of the chair. I remain silent.

Rising abruptly, he crosses the rush-strewn stone floor to stand over me. "You look ill, Sweet Alix. What is ailing you?"

Last night's fearful screams still echoing in my ears, I look deep into the darkness of his

eyes, hoping to find in them that fleeting gleam of compassion.

"Why are my faithful knights and squires kept away from me, Sir Foulk? And where is Good Sir Gilbert? Pray tell me where they have gone."

"Where have they gone?" His laughter is so hurtful I shield my growing belly with my arms for fear my child will suffer from such evil. "They have gone where they can best serve their master, my lady, to hell!"

Elaine cowering on a small stool whimper with anguish, for one of the squires, young Mark, had captured her heart.

Grief and indignation fill me with great wrath. I stand up to face him.

"You fiend! Do you not rejoice save when you kill and maim!" As I raise my arm as if to hit him, he grasps my wrists and brings his face close to mine. His breath is hot and smells of stale wine. His laughter has died and his eyes look sad.

"Do not pass judgement, fair and fiery friend, about matters of which you know little or nothing! These are harsh times and only might makes right. Is it not fair that I be allowed to kill mine own foes, when I can dispatch the Lord Pope's without sin? Aye, with his blessings even!"

Tears fill my eyes as I recall the noble knights and young squires who escorted us. I silently thank the Lord God for sending Conon de Béthune on his way before we reached Comarque. Conon had proposed to follow us here, but changed his mind and decided to go to Hautefort first.

"Are you then the devil incarnate?" I cry to his face. "These unfortunate knights had not borne arms against you! They were not your enemies! You are your own enemy!" He releases my hands and I turn my back on him. "Alix, turn not away from me! Your squires and knights are not dead, leastways not all of them. I have yet to decide on their fate. You could say their fate rests in your hands...." He leaves our solar without another word. The silence broken only by Elaine's quiet sobs and the song of a thrush on a tree far below.

CHAPTER 26

Daphne is telling me to wake up. I open my eyes, my mind still churning with the implications of Black Foulk's last words. I sit up on the couch, feeling dizzy.

"The bastard is blackmailing me, Daphne!" A brief smile brings out the creases in her tired old face.

"What would you have him do? You don't respond to his wooing...."

"Oh, great, you're taking his part again!" She shrugs. "No, I'm not, but tell me frankly: Have your feelings about the man changed in any way?"

Re-living Alix's captivity has left me feeling weak and perplexed. I force myself to take a few lungsful of air, expelling the last one rather rudely through my lips with such force that Daphne is startled by it.

"Oh, my! You must be tired of my prying, and I apologize for it. Just bear with me a little longer. I know you are doing your best to tell me everything; but you don't really do so. Sometimes, I have to be content with monosyllabic responses to my questions, and the picture I get is fragmentary at best."

"Of course, Daphne. Sorry." I reach for her hand and she squeezes mine with a nod.

"It's just that I have some questions too, and you are so...evasive about your own insights into my past. Besides, I already told you my feelings about Black Foulk; they are very confused. I have outgrown my dread of the man - up to a point - but not my distrust. For obvious reasons. He does inspire pity at times; he is trying so hard to force Alix's and even Elaine's - admiration. And not succeeding." I grin and shake my head at the memories.

"He keeps bragging about the number of Varangian Guards he slew at the siege of Constantinople. As if I cared. Now, in case you don't know, the Varangians were Northmen - mercenaries - and, to make himself sound more heroic, Foulk does not fail to insist upon their savage fearlessness. I think he is jealous of Walther's fame as a poet and warrior." Daphne nods and rubs her chin thoughtfully.

"Perhaps. What else?"

"He boasts of the spoils he brought back. After confiscating all that was won by my men, the rat."

Ignoring my disgust, Daphne inquires seriously, "So Foulk fails to impress?" "I'm afraid so. He's pathetic, really. One morning, he tells me I'm another reason for him to conquer a kingdom. As King Henry's son, he feels entitled to one, but he also deems me worthy of being his queen. Can you believe the arrogance of the man?"

Daphne nods absentmindedly, frowning, her eyes lost in the mist of faraway thoughts she obviously has no intention of sharing. She does look sick and I fear this session may have tired her even more.

"Daphne, I should let you have some rest. I'll come back tomorrow, if you wish. Is there something I can do for you?"

"Oh, but you already are, my dear." Her smile is actually quite sweet. "You are doing a lot for me. And yes, do come tomorrow around noon. We'll share lunch.

Now, what was it you wanted to ask me? You said you had questions too."

I swing my legs back onto her Aubusson rug and voice the question which had popped into my head when she had awakened me, just now.

"Why is it that I re-live events in linear sequence? Why can't I jump ahead and find out if this bastard got his deserts; skip directly to my old age, say, if I had one? I seem to relive the past only in chronological progression."

Daphne shrugs, but her hands are clenched so tightly on her lap that her fingers are turning white.

"Perhaps you are not ready for it, Sandra. This is not a computer game to be played any way you like. Why it is so, I can't tell you."

"You can't tell me because you don't know or because you don't want to?"

"Well... You have to understand I'm not a seer, Sandra, in fact I've never been so confused in my whole life.

Things are happening to me that I don't understand; I'm bound to a past that is terribly alien to me but which I have to confront and cannot disavow."

I feel like saying "Enough already. Tell me what you have seen, for God's sake." But her deep sigh makes me feel ashamed. I stand up and rest a hand on her thin shoulder. She looks up at me and smiles. I can't believe how much weight she has lost in such a short time.

"Please be patient, my dear, I think it will all become clear soon."

"You mean when Kurt gets here?" She nods. "Yes. Trust me. Please." I guess I have little choice.

* * *

I get home to find a message on my answering machine. From Cécile Dupont. The name doesn't immediately ring a bell, but the tenor of the message brings her clearly to mind: The attractive young redhead, the lute player.

She is calling on his behalf, informing me that he has managed to get a seat on an earlier flight to Montreal, by way of Amsterdam, and will be arriving on Wednesday instead of Friday. She gives me the flight number and time of arrival; her frosty tone leaving no doubt as to her feelings about Kurt's unexpected trip to Montreal.

This piece of news sends me into a spirited little estampie around my coffee table. There had been no need for good-byes in Nantes; just a long kiss which had left its lasting imprint on our lips. Our lives seem to be so amazingly bound together that a few days - or even a few weeks - apart hardly matter. Kurt is close to me at all times. Only problem is, far from dampening desire this closeness makes it even more acute.

The rest of the day is spent cleaning up my small apartment with buoyant enthusiasm until everything shines; biting a pencil while writing up a list of delicacies to fill the fridge; feverishly looking up recipes, especially the one for that chocolate-orange cake with Grand-Marnier sauce; and emptying all the closets of vases. Flowers will fill this place with beauty and fragrance. Music. There must be music, too.

Not medieval songs from a rival group, surely; I have no recording of La Fin'Amor. Mozart, then. Kurt is sure to appreciate him, who doesn't? They say that the loss of one sense makes the other four far more acute.

But voice is not considered a sense, so I guess it wouldn't apply to Kurt. I can vouch for the delicacy of his sense of touch, though.

His flight will touch down at 6.30 p.m. which will allow me to put in a full day's work at the office. That should placate George and soften the blow of my taking off Wednesday instead of Friday.

I can't wait to meet Kurt at the airport. We have so much time to make up for.

* * *

I wake up at six on Sunday, deciding life is too beautiful to sleep it away.

I dial Christine's number in France. She tells me she was just about to pour beaten eggs into a pan to make herself an omelet aux fines herbs for lunch. It's noon in Nice.

"Mum, it's 6 a.m. in Montreal, what are you doing up so early on a Sunday?"

"Kurt is coming."

"Yes, I know, you already told me. About 12 times."

"Yes, but he is coming on Wednesday, instead of Friday; he went to the trouble of looking for an earlier flight, from Amsterdam."

"You don't say." I picture her teasing grin as clearly as if I had a videophone. "He sounds pretty keen. No wonder you sound so overjoyed. Well, you'll be pleased to know I met a really cool guy yesterday..."

We go on exchanging little tid-bits of endearments for a few minutes, rejoicing in each other's merry voices. I hang up with a smile, shower, dress, and set off for a long hike through the greening paths of Mount Royal.

I don't think I have ever enjoyed the Mountain so much. Young ferns are uncurling in the underbrush; trilliums - red and white peek out from the dark green moss and lacy lycopods. People walking or jogging on the paths greet me with friendly "Bonjour!" or "Hello!" and seem to relish life as much as I do.

Back home I turn on my computer and retrieve the novel started and abandoned months ago. Writing is a game, and right now my mood is joyful enough to start playing again. I read through a few chapters; they stink. Have I changed that much? Well, as far as my prose is concerned, any change can only be an improvement.

* * *

Daphne looks better than yesterday. A dark red wool sweater lends a glow of color to her wan face, still bare of make-up. Her hair is still combed back and she smells faintly of lavender.

"Come in, my dear." She takes the proffered flowers with a smile and closes her eyes to inhale their scent.

"Thank you, Sandra. There is something both sensual and virginal about the fragrance of white lilies. The latter just religious conditioning, I suppose. You know, the Virgin Mary's flowers and all that. Did you know that, in the original text, she was said to be 'well-behaved' and that she became a 'virgin' through a mistranslation?"

"Very handy. Couldn't someone correct the mistake eventually?" I laugh. "Why? It made her story more interesting. Have you heard that song 'We all need a little magic in our hearts and in our lives...' I think it's true."

"Oh, here! I forgot to give you this yesterday." I hand her a very small package wrapped in gold foil. "A little souvenir fromFrance."

With a faint idea of what she would like, I had gone to an antique gallery in Nice, found this exquisite Sèvres pill box and bought it for an outrageous price.

Hanging up my coat without her help, I let her examine the package curiously and continue with her train of thoughts,

"Well, we seem to get more than our share of magic, you and I, Sandra, and some of it is rather unpleasant."

"Tell me about it. I had trouble enough trusting my own eyes when they showed me Irene as Mother Clara and her friend Olivier as Eudes, believe me. I still can't help wondering if it was sheer delusion on my part. Wishful thinking, perhaps?"

"That's not something you would wish for." She points out sensibly enough.

"I don't see what is so difficult to accept about Group Karma. Our character is shaped through interactions with others, and it makes sense that some relationships may take several lifetimes to be resolved. When you first met Irene, did you ever feel you'd known her before."

"Not really, I just took an instant liking to her. She did, though. I remember her mentioning it at a later date. But then she was 'into' New Age philosophies at the time we met; I don't think she would take me seriously if I told her about Mother Clara now."

"She doesn't exactly take life or herself seriously; that's what we like about her." Daphne concludes with a grin.

She precedes me through the drawing-room to a double door and opens it to reveal a paneled dining-room with a long Sheraton table set with two place mats side by side at one end, Precious China and crystal glasses.

"My cousin Wilma will not be joining us. She is off to Ottawa today." As I look at her questioningly, wondering if I should offer to stay with her tonight, she quickly adds, "She'll be back this evening, don't worry." She motions me to a chair. "Please sit down, Sandra. I'll just put these flowers in water and join you presently."

"Daphne! You shouldn't have gone to this kind of trouble! A sandwich in the kitchen would have been fine. Can I do anything?" "No, thank you, my dear. I didn't do a thing and we'll be served... As we deserve to be."

I am still pondering what she means by that when she comes back carrying the lilies in a Baccarat vase which she sets on a coaster at the other end of the long glossy mahogany table.

"There. Now we can feast our eyes on their beauty without their scent interfering with our food. Right. Let me open my present... How lovely! A perfect little masterpiece!"

She holds the tiny marvel in her withered fingers and contemplates every angle of it, nodding all the while.

"Beauty does elevate the soul, I think. Provided it is not worshipped for its own sake but as an intimation of something greater.

That was our problem in the XVIIIth Century, we made too many sacrifices to the cult of beauty. Well, I learned my lesson on that score." With a fond smile, she adds, "Thank you, Sandra."

She is about to cover my hand with hers but seems to think better of it and rings a small China bell by her plate instead. It brings forth a young waiter in black tie carrying a platter of salmon mousse he presents for our approval before serving us with a flourish.

"Daphne, I'm really overwhelmed. What can I say?"

"Nothing. Eat and enjoy. We have never shared a proper meal before."

The mousse is delicious. And so is the Guinea fowl which follows, as well as the Vacherin with raspberry sauce. The waiter announces the vintage of each notable wine before filling our glasses. Her eyes shining, Daphne asks me all kinds of questions about Périgord in general and Comarque in particular.

"So, you did not actually go inside the castle, did you?"

"No. I was on the wrong side of the river Beune and didn't know it could be crossed on a small stone bridge, about 300 yards from where I sat."

"Oh... The bridge still stands then...." She frowns, a forkful of fowl half-way to her mouth. Before I can ask her how she knows about it, she adds quickly.

"Now tell me about the town of Sarlat." Over dessert, when the aroma of freshly brewed coffee reaches us from the pantry, she asks lightly, her eyes on my face.

"So when will I see Kurt?"

I bite my lip. No point in trying to hide the fact he will be arriving sooner than anticipated.

"Thursday morning, if that's convenient. He'll be here Wednesday evening."

"Good." She nods, obviously relieved. "You know, I have been thinking about the laws of physics and came to the conclusion they might very well apply to love." Her chuckle turns into a fit of coughing she drowns in a glass of water. "Sorry, Sandra... Where was I? Oh, yes, the Law of the Conservation of Love decrees that no love is ever lost." "What about hatred?" I feel a chill between my shoulder blades.

She shrugs and clears her throat. "Hatred is self-destructive. At the end of times only love will remain."

We lapse into silence until, putting down her empty coffee cup on the saucer, and wiping her pale lips on her damask napkin, she looks up and says, "Whenever you are ready, my dear, we can go exploring some more. I think we are getting somewhere."

* * *

Foulk brought me a casket full of jewels this morning. He placed it at my feet with a bow and said, "I know humble adornments, such as I can provide, will never be worthy of your beauty, Sweet Alix. Accept them nonetheless as a token of my fealty."

I waited until he had gone to look at the contents of the chest, stolen from Greek ladies no doubt.

Some of jewels are of the finest workmanship in enamel, silver and gold; crosses, clasps, buckles and rings adorned with green jasper, turquoise and even precious rubies, coral, pearls and sapphires. Some of the stones are engraved with signs to enhance their virtues, for many ailments are cured by wearing them. Alas no gem has been found that will rid me of Foulk!

The jewels are beautiful and costly. Had they been offered to me by Walther, I would have delighted in them. But those times are long gone, and never more will the charm of gems captivate my vanity.

I merely admire them now and vaguely try to picture these Greek ladies who were despoiled of them, constrained in their hieratic garments like bishops in their robes, their faces painted masks of sadness. Gems are but stones, and as such useful to me now to weigh the letters I intend to keep hurling through the window of my solar.

Elaine looks on in horror as I select a heavy turquoise and silver clasp around which to wrap the letter, I have just written to Mother Clara, informing her of my captivity and Foulk's threats over the lives of my knights and squires. For Foulk is adamant, they will all die most cruel deaths if I refuse to marry him the day after my child is born.

I will, of course, submit to his will and become his lady. And I shall not even curse him, for his black deeds will one day cause his fall, without any need for me to poison my soul with hatred.

Today, I made him swear on the small cross Mother Clara gave me that he would free all the men in my service on the day we were wed. Will he keep his vow? I have no way to fathom his true nature and can only pray that he be not bereft of all mercy.

Is Bogo appraised of Foulk's intentions? For Bogo is in Comarque, or so the old woman who brings our food tells us. The Judas takes great care not to show his unsightly mien in the courtyard when we are there. We prodded so much, Elaine and I, plying the old crone all the while with the wine saved from our meals, that she told us that Bogo was the one who tricked Sir Gilbert into letting Black Foulk and his knights into the castle. This fails to surprise me.

Before hurling the letter beyond the moat, I draw a large cross on the cloth in the hope it will be given to a priest. Let it not be Bogo!

* * *

As I open the one book left to me, Sir Chrestien de Troyes' Yvain, and prepare to reread the story of this brave and fickle knight, a great uproar erupts in the courtyard. Shouts and clamors are heard; sounds of running and clash of arms. A veritable commotion. My heart leaps with hope. Elaine and I look at each other. Is Comarque under siege?

But, alas, the tumult soon dies down. Familiar noises of the castle are heard again; a knell tolling for my hope. Peire, the old smith, resumes hammering at his anvil, and the fat cellarer yells anew at the men rolling heavy wine barrels on the stone courtyard. Yet, something is not as it was. Foulk's men-at arms are silent; their loud querulous calls no longer echo against the stone ramparts. Instead, angry voices are heard, shuffling feet and the clangor of chains.

I rise from my chair. As I am about to pound on the door and ask our guards to let us out, it opens on Black Foulk. He boldly enters the solar, a dark gleam in his eyes, and motions to others to follow, for he is not alone.

Four of his most repulsive men-at-arms surround a tall man, his blond hair crimson with blood, his neck encased in an iron collar from which hang heavy chains.

"Walther! Oh, my beloved! What have they done to you?"

Hardly have I time to extend my arms to him before Black Foulk pushes me back roughly and taunts, "Rejoice, Lady Alix, in the sight of your fair friend! He has travelled many days to bring you his homage, and it would be contrary to the laws of hospitality to prevent him from doing so!"

CHAPTER 27

With a grating laugh, Black Foulk steps aside only so far as to allow me a full view of my wounded lover.

Walther hurls himself forward to reach me, tautening the heavy chains they have shackled him with like a wild bear; so much does he strain on them that his brutal captors can hardly hold him.

"Precious Alix! Thus, I come to you begging forgiveness!" My lover's voice is sweeter to my ears than the honeyed sound of the psaltery.

One of the coarse soldiers raises his gloved fist as if to smite him, but Foulk barks, "Let the minstrel have his say. It is not often we are entertained by the likes of him!" Walther sears him with the cold fire of his eyes before beseeching me anew.

"Ever since we parted, Beloved Friend, not one hour has passed that I not rue the senseless pride and delusions of freedom that made me forsake you! If you have nothing left for me but scorn and cannot find it in your heart to absolve me, know that I have already suffered dire punishment for my wanton conceit. Naught have you ever asked of me but my love, and I refused you. The shame is mine, and it is perchance just punishment that I should come to you in chains!"

Bright sunshine fills the solar, enfolding him in golden light as he speaks with firm and tender voice. "Be it as it may, Sweet Alix, I so rejoice to see you that no torment our friend here can devise will ever make me regret coming to you! "

His words fall on my parched heart as the dew of angels; a balm to cure all ills. Tears of joy wash my pain away. "Oh, Good Sir, you are indeed forgiven!" I take a step forward, but Foulk bars my way while his laughter drowns my words of forgiveness in its bile.

"A most fitting repentance, my lord Walther! And a very foolish one! Doubly foolish, I say, for one should never repent, all the more so when it is too late!"

Walther turns to him sharply. "What says you, dog?"

Foulk's hand flies to the dagger at his belt and rests on its hilt for ominous moments, but he pulls it not out of its sheath.

With a shiver of revulsion, I recognize this silver sheath encrusted with garnets; the dagger belonged to Jehan, my youngest squire.

Once more I attempt to reach my beloved, but Foulk grasps my arm and pulls me back, glaring at Walther all the while. Finally, he smiles; a smile more chilling than his scowl.

"You will repent these ill-advised words at your leisure, Friend! Yes, you are too late! The Lady Alix has already pledged her troth to me, and we shall be married as soon as she is delivered of Sir Eudes' child."

"No! No!" I cry. "Hear him not, Walther! As the Lord God is my witness, I am but a captive forced to surrender to this villain to save my knights and squires from cruel death! Look how he has greeted you whom he used to call friend!"

Walther looks from Foulk to me, his face troubled more by doubt than by the blood snaking from his forehead to his cheek. Foulk's lips curl in arrogant derision under that searching gaze.

My hands join of their own volition, and I give a silent prayer to the Sweet Virgin mother of Our Lord; may she guide my beloved's judgement and protect him from Foulk's wrath. In the hushed solar, only Elaine's quiet weeping is heard.

Walther's eyes settle on mine. "I know you speak the truth, Fair and Brave Alix." He nods once as if to salute me, in spite of the hurt the cruel iron collar must inflict on his neck. "May the Lord God's mercy rest upon you and your unborn child."

Such love flows from his eyes to mine that I feel myself consumed by it until nothing remains but an unearthly delight! Heavenly joy enfolds us in its mercy and we are granted instants of such rapture as surely only the blessed must know. No one, not even Foulk, can take from us the bliss that we share!

The wretch must sense this; with a roar of fury, he steps between my longed-for lover and me and grasps both my arms until I cry out in pain.

With inordinate strength, I wrench myself free and address him with great anger and contempt.

"Fie on you, Sir Foulk! A brave knight it is who mistreats a widow with child and puts a friend in chains! Sir Walther von Altdorf has never done you any harm! Were you not brothers in arms on the ramparts of Constantinople? Hide your face in shame from the eyes of the Lord lest he dispatch you this instant to Satan's hell where you belong!" Seeing the villain flinch causes me no small gladness. Forgive me Lord Jesus "Are you cursing me, woman? Know that if I go to hell, I will take you with me for company." There is madness in his bitter laughter as he points to Walther. "But he will precede us, for he has indeed caused me great harm by stealing your love from me."

"My love was never yours nor will it ever be, Sir Foulk! I despise you most heartily and will only submit to your will under duress! You...."

Such profound and sudden grief distorts Foulk's harsh features and dims his dark eyes that my words die on my lips, cut short by a wondrous pity I do not comprehend. With a wild gesture of dismissal to the four soldiers, he shouts, "Take him away!" A horrible fear chills my blood.

"No! Wait! Do not avenge yourself on him who was your friend for the words I uttered in anger. Do with me what you will, but in the name of Our Lord let him go!"

Foulk looks at me, his face hardened again into arrogant mockery. "I cannot do so, My Lady. Bands of murdering brigands make our roads unsafe for travelers without a strong escort. Unfortunately for our noble friend, he left his escort at Hautefort and came to Comarque with only four ill-fated squires.

Now, the five of them put up such a fight against my men that...." He pauses, as if to emphasize his next words. "Had I not shown mercy, Sir Walther himself would have been slain like his squires."

With a wave of his hand Foulk dismisses the soldiers and their prisoner before adding in a bantering tone, "Better our guest remains here awhile...to enjoy our hospitality." He laughs.

"And perhaps witness our wedding!"

With the howl of a stricken wolf, Walther throws his chains around the necks of his two nearest guards and proceeds to throttle them before the other two start raining a hail of blows onto his head and back, and drag him out of the solar still fighting, leaving only their own sour smell behind. Cringing with horror at the sight of their brutality, I hurl myself forward in a futile attempt to follow, but Foulk prevents me once more.

The ominous sound of the oaken door closing on the last man-at-arms is an intimation of my lover's fate.

Throwing myself on my knees at Foulk's feet, I take hold of his sleeve and beg, "Have mercy on him, Sir Foulk, I beseech you! For my sake!"

"For your sake? Indeed, there is no need for me to do anything for your sake! What you have to give, woman, I can take without your leave." And he departs without another look.

* * *

I remain kneeling on the hard stone slabs, stricken with grief, until Elaine rushes to my side to help me rise. I would rather tarry thus, as if the hurt in my knees made me share in some small way my beloved's torments. Elaine's distress denies me this futile solace and I let her help me to my feet.

"Oh, my lady! Being so overwrought will do naught to help Sir Walther but much to harm your precious child!" She berates me gently as she half-carries me, small as she is, to my bed, and urges me to lie down. "Rest yourself awhile, and summon back your senses for I fear they have taken leave of you!" "Dear sweet Elaine." I smile.

"You are wise beyond your years. How will I ever repay your kind and gentle concern. I know your soul is beset with sorrow on account of young Mark. Take heart, dear one, Mark may still live, as Walther does. We must keep our hope, for despair is a grievous sin."

She goes to one of the carved chests, retrieves the bottle of a soothing draught given me long ago by Sister Anna when I left the convent. Pouring some in a silver cup, she brings it to my couch and helps me sit up, urging me to take it.

"Drink, my lady. This will soothe your grief and bring calming sleep." I decline to swallow the mixture and lie back wearily on the pillows, heart pounding and head a spin with dark thoughts.

"I seek not the oblivion of sleep, dear Elaine. On the contrary, I wish what little wits I possess be alert enough to find a way of delivering my beloved!"

Resignedly she looks around for somewhere to set down the cup in case I change my mind, and taking one step toward the nearest window-sill, she trips on the casket of Foulk's jewels, spilling the draught all over her dress.

I sit up suddenly. Elaine, her cheeks red with confusion looks at me with a small shamefaced smile. "Pray forgive my clumsiness, my lady."

"A most fortunate one, dear friend, for an idea has occurred to me... Foul Foulk himself has given us the means to thwart him!" Still uncomprehending, she looks from the casket to me.

"Don't you see? We hold a fortune here, in this casket! And what better use for it than to bribe his villeins to our advantage?"

A smile lights up her delicate face, only to be replaced by sad discouragement. "They are so many. We cannot bribe them all!"

Leaving my bed I walk to the largest window, the arches of which offer between their four stone columns the best view of the Beune River valley and surrounding forested hills, as if this peaceful vista could provide inspiration. A kite soars above the trees, swoops down and soars again; how I envy it its wings and freedom! The sky is as blue as Byzantine turquoise but the sun bestows no more magic on this room. Golden light may linger in my heart with my lover's image, but in my solar only shadows remain.

Should I attempt to throw another letter on the chance some serf may find it and take it to a friar? But the clasp or ring necessary to weigh it might be put to better use buying the loyalty of Foulk's covetous helpers....

Yet, Walther von Altdorf has many friends and relatives who surely would take up arms and lay siege to Comarque were I to send word and appraise them of his predicament.

Will Foulk ever dare harm the German emperor's cousin? Is his intention to ask a ransom for Walther's release? For greed feeds upon itself and the gold and booty from Constantinople may have given him a taste for more.

Sarigny

Foulk's covetousness and ambition are indeed notorious, but me thinks envy and spite now hold even stronger sway over him. Verily it does not bode well for my hapless lover.

* * *

The stone steps are narrow and slippery, plunged in darkness between the few rushlights held in metal loops on the curving wall; they go on winding down and down, seemingly forever, to the depths of hell itself. I lift my skirts with one hand and grope my way down along the stone wall with the other, clenching my teeth in revulsion at the feel of slime on my fingers. Elaine precedes me, lest I falter on the stairs. She follows the guard who took the ruby cross but a short while ago, and silently hid it away under his foul jerkin without even a nod of acknowledgement.

Still, I am grateful to him. He is the old servant's husband, bent and grizzled, and risks cruel death for taking us down to the cellars. He carries a torch which gives out more smoke than flickering light, raised high above his head in the dark sections of the stairs. Its strong smell of resin lessens the musty odor of decay that pervades the place.

In spite of myself, I am reminded of our ill- fated escape from Dame Mathilde's house, the day Lady Adela was drowned. May the Lord preserve us all from Foulk's evil ways!

The dank stillness is made up of a myriad of muffled sounds; the shuffling of our feet, dripping water, gnawing rats and the echoes from the keep above, where the guard's dwell and the ale-wife has been given room to brew her hops and barley into the ale they drink by the hogshead.

I start counting the steps to keep my mind from dwelling on the fate Foulk may have in store for whoever he detains in such a horrifying place. I cling to the strong and tender image of Walther, defying his captors to convey his love to me. Oh, my beloved, whatever fate decrees for us, nevermore can our souls be parted!

Our guide turns around, raises his torch, signals for us to halt and places a dirty finger to his lips. From the basket of food she carries, Elaine takes two servant mantles of coarse wool which we throw over our shoulders, closing them to hide our clothes; we raise the hoods over our heads, plunging our faces in shadows.

With his stubbly chin, the man indicates a narrow-arched passage at the foot of the stairs. It is lit by rushlights, but a pale glow of greyish light is visible at the end of it. We follow the man through the narrow passage, at the end of which a soldier guards a small cave, one wall of which is pierced by a window-like opening barred with thick iron.

These caves do indeed riddle the cliff onto which Comarque is built like holes in a cheese, and some of them open onto the outside through apertures in the cliff wall. "Food for the prisoner." The old man says gruffly.

"Which one?" The guard asks, laughing senselessly "There be a host of them down here, but they be mostly in the big cave." "For the one they bring in but two days past. The chained one."

The guard points to another dark passage on his left and, frowning at the sight of Elaine and me, reluctantly lets us through. The narrow tunnel veers sharply to the right to open into a vast chamber.

By the spluttering flames of large tallow candles stuck on tall iron spikes, the room is revealed as another cave. Natural stone pillars of varying sizes appear to support a roof plunged in shadows. To the largest of these pillars a solitary man is chained upright, his arms pulled to the sides by heavy chains fastened to rings in the stone. "Walther!"

He lifts his weary head from his shoulder as I rush past the old man and Elaine to throw my arms around his waist and embrace him. "Alix! My sweet love! This foul hole is no place for thee! Go back to your solar, my dove, lest you cease loving me; so unworthy of your sight is my boorish attire!"

His loving grin is meant to reassure, but anguish tears at my heart with sharp claws. His naked arms and chest bear many traces of his unequal fight against his captors, and congealed blood blackens his golden hair and brow.

I reach for his face and gently caress his cheeks, now rough with unshaven hair. Our eyes meet again, transporting us for brief instants into a realm of bliss.

"Oh, dearest Walther, never has my heart ceased to be yours! The lovers' joys we knew together have never left my memory. Would I could take your place and suffer your torments!"

"Would I could hold you in my arms, Fair Alix! But grieve not for me, my gentle dove, I am the most fortunate of mortals for being granted your forgiveness and your love." Elaine and the old man have left us alone to find their way into the larger cave where those of my knights and squires who survive are imprisoned. May she find young Mark still alive. I fear Walther for all his strength and courage, will not long withstand the torture of his chains nor the cruel position in which they hold him.

"Alas, beloved friend, I cannot bear to see you thus! I must try to relieve your sufferings by any means, fair or foul! I will entreat that fiend Foulk! I would lose my very soul to save you...."

Not even the iron collar prevents him from shaking his head. The finger I place on his bruised lips silences not his protests. "

"No! Alix, No! Do not abase yourself on my behalf! You excel in all virtues and must save yourself and the child! I count for naught, but you and... our child must survive!" He kisses my fingers most devotedly.

"The moment I was brought to your solar, I knew it was our child you carried, and my heart leapt for joy!"

With closed lips he begins to hum the melody he had composed for me in Venice, then attempts to mouth its words of love we had sung so many times together; but his parched throat betrays him.

Bracing myself against the onslaught of my tears, I look around for water and espy a jug and a cup at his feet albeit out of his reach. I fill the cup, bring it to his lips and let him drink his content, wondering at the joy that fill his azure eyes with light.

I refill the cup and offer it to him again, but he declines with a smile. Pouring its content over a small piece of linen I keep in my sleeve, I gently wash his beloved face of the dried blood, hardly daring to touch the wound on his head lest I hurt him. But he winces not from the pain and encourages me with his eyes. Then very softly, he says, "Listen to me, dear heart. You must be prepared to lose me again, and not through any whim of mine this time."

I search his face for the meaning of his words, until comprehension halts my hand and causes my heart to cease beating.

"No! Oh, Dear Lord, no! I will not let Foulk hurt you!"

He sighs. "Hark, beloved child, Foulk can no more let me live than I can stop loving you. He knows I left a strong escort in Hautefort and that, if he let me go, I would surely be back with Sir Constantin to lay siege to Comarque and deliver you."

"No! Do not speak thus! Foulk is full of greed, he may ask the emperor your cousin for a ransom! He may keep you here in chains, but he will not dare...." Even as I say the words, I know them to be wishful and without substance. I desperately try to find a reason for hope.

"Will not Sir Constantin come to your rescue if you fail to return to Hautefort?"

I throw my arms around Walther's body and rest my head against his strong chest.

"Oh, my beloved, surely we cannot be parted now that we have found each other again!" "Do not deceive yourself with false hopes, my dove. You must be braver than you have ever been for our child's sake."

I hold back my sobs and let his gentle voice sing in my heart a while longer.

"Life was pleasing to me, and generous in its bounties, yet, Beloved Alix, know that no joy ever compared to the delights I knew in your arms. Verily, I have never thus spoken to anyone...."

His voice betrays surprise as he adds, "I will mourn my own death for taking me away from you! But remember that the sorrow of leaving you will be lightened if I know you will not give way to despair. Remember also that the love I bear you will endure beyond death. Nothing can ever part us again, Alix, for our souls are now bound together for eternity."

I let the tears flow unchecked. Lowering his head as much as the cruel ring of iron will allow, he begins to sing again very softly. "The sweet cooing of a dove will ever remind me...." His song grows louder while I remain so close to his heart that it seems to beat in my own breast, and that, as I mouth every word of the song, we sing with but one voice. All sense of cruel time is lost, replaced by sweet rapture.

* * *

Loud steps and curses interrupt our desperate embrace.

Black Foulk enters the cave, followed by a whole troop of his men. With brutal wrath, he wrenches me away from Walther and, facing my lover with seething malevolence, says, "I know a way to silence you, my friend!" Grasping Foulk's sleeve I attempt to pull him aside, but indifferent to my screams he pushes me away and orders two soldiers to hold me.

Demented with horror, I watch four other men surround my lover.

One of them grabs his hair and brutally pulls his head back while the other pries his teeth open with a blade. Black Foulk unsheathe his dagger.

A horrible strangled cry....

CHAPTER 28

"You will now calm down, Sandra, calm down! Stop screaming. There, there, my dear, you're back in the present. Everything is all right, there's nothing to fear. Open your eyes now and look at me. Wide awake now." "Jesus, Daphne! Walther! Foulk cut off his tongue! He cut out Walther's tongue and threw it at me!" I keep my eyes tightly closed. "Yes. I heard you."

Heart hammering in my chest, unable to stop myself from trembling from head to foot, I finally open my eyes and stare at Daphne. She is bending over me, eyes bright with compassion in a face of shadows. Gargoyle's face.

Her hand, cool and soothing on my brow, helps me breathe better.

My mind becomes a total blank and I lose all notion of time and place, huddled in a fragile twilight between the brightness of today and the darkness of the past.

After a while, I become aware that Daphne is back in her place and I turn to look at her. Her head is resting against the back of her chair, her face deathly pale, her eyes closed. She looks more dead than alive.

I sit up and a wave of nausea washes over me. Breathing deeply, I keep my eyes on Daphne. She is obviously on the edge of total collapse.

"Daphne, you look so weak! Let me help you up to your room. When is your cousin due back?"

Still motionless, she opens her eyes and attempts a smile.

"You don't look too great yourself. Wilma will be here soon, don't fret. I'm all right, and we have to talk. I have been going through this for a while, you know. Not that one ever gets used to this kind of...." She lets the words trail off into silence.

"Can I bring you something?" "Yes. A glass of water, please."

Still in a daze, I get up and go to the kitchen, pour myself a glassful of water and bring one back for Daphne.

When I hand it to her, she swallows two pills, one after the other and leans back in her chair. "Look, why don't I make us a cup of tea?" I offer, feeling my strength coming back. "Excellent idea. You know where to find everything, don't you?"

When I return pushing her tea-trolley with the squeaky wheel, Daphne is looking a little more alive.

"There is obviously some connection between this...atrocity and Kurt losing his voice, isn't there?" I ask. She drains her hot tea before answering.

"Most probably."

I was expecting more from her, but she keeps staring at her empty cup as if she was about to read the tea leaves.

"But what kind of connection?" I insist.

"I'm no seer, Sandra, but from what you told me, I would guess Kurt re-lived that experience while at the wheel of his car. You say he had been doing extensive research on Walther von Altdorf, so the man was obviously on his mind."

She sits up in her chair, her face suffused with some of her old fire. "Supposing a sudden flash-back makes him realize that he was - he is - Walther, and re-live this...mutilation. Wouldn't that be enough to make him lose control of his car?"

"I'll say!" I take a deep breath to forestall the shivers. "But what could possibly trigger the remembrance?"

Daphne shrugs. "Anything can trigger this type of spontaneous recollection. The stimulus may be either physical or psychological. A sight, a thought...." "But... What about the loss of his voice?"

"In the throes of his vision, he loses control of his car, slams into a tree, sustains serious injuries, and, upon coming out of a coma, finds himself unable to speak.

I would say, he has carried the trauma from his earlier life into this one."

"Does this mean that if he re-lived this...nightmare again, he might recover his voice?"

"Yes, it's a possibility. If he could be taken back through the trauma and then made to understand it has no bearing on his present life. Provided his vocal cords are not damaged, of course."

"My God, Daphne, this is horrible! How can I bring him here knowing what you plan to put him through? Assuming he lets you hypnotize him, which is not a given."

She shrugs resignedly, but the sparkle in her brown eyes belies the weariness of her face.

"There is so little we understand about the whole process of reincarnation, my dear. Even when we accept the concept, its laws remain a mystery. We can only assume we come back to learn new lessons and are gradually transmigrated to more advanced states."

Catching her labored breath, she raises a hand to forestall interruptions.

"Many people in every culture have attempted to understand and explain these laws over the centuries, but who is to say they were successful?"

She pauses and her hands reach out to her shoulders in search of an absent shawl.

"Are you cold, Daphne? Would you like me to get you a sweater of something?" She nods.

"On the shelf in the hall closet. A green shawl. Thank you, dear."

As I drape it around her thin shoulders and settle back on the couch, she continues with her train of thought.

"Most believers who studied the question tend to agree that we, our souls that is, evolve through successive reincarnations until perfection is attained. This spiritual evolution requires both love and knowledge."

She holds her cup out for a refill. "Knowledge of what?" I ask as I pour.

"Of oneself, mainly, and the law of cause and effect.

Know Thyself, Socrates and all that, you know." She drinks quickly and replaces cup and saucer on the trolley.

"That's all very well, but how can we help Kurt recover his voice?"

She seems reluctant to answer and pulls the shawl across her chest in a familiar gesture. The fragrance of freesias and lily-of-the valley in the vase behind me fills the silence with its own form of beauty.

"Your first concern is for Walther, or Kurt if you prefer, because you love him. Which is good. But what about yourself, my dear? Don't you want to understand your own destiny better? All along our sessions, I have tried to keep my own perceptions from influencing you unduly. The validity of what you experienced has always been yours to decide, because it's first and foremost a matter of personal faith; but perhaps the time has come to ask yourself some questions about your own life."

"Daphne! I haven't lived through all this without asking myself lots of questions. Not that I found many answers, but still... The fact that my life as Alix was full of emotional turmoil seems to explain why I shun them in this one."

Daphne nods. "Yes, Alix did suffer many losses, didn't she? Her parents, her husband, her...." She stops abruptly to let me go on. "As Sandra, I have always tried to keep my life simple, predictable, secure; and totally devoid of extremes - either pain or joy. Rather dull, really. Well, you'll be glad to know that I've had it with bland caution, and am now fully prepared to take chances! I want to live!"

"Good. But that latent vitality was there all the time, my dear, carried over from one life to the next, like your ability to play the psaltery. You will rediscover other latent traits in yourself as you remember more of Alix's life. And that's why, while I'm still around... No, no, dear, don't look so stricken. Death is not sad when the purpose of life has been accomplished."

She leans over to pats my hand like a kindly grandmother, bringing tears to my eyes.

"Anyway, all this to say that I think you should go back once more to face your past and its many trials."

The twinkle in her eyes discourages pathos, but her request takes me by surprise.

"You mean now? After what I've just been through?" With a shiver of revulsion, I try to stop the terrible images from invading my mind again. "But why?"

"Because you don't know everything there is to know about Alix and you might not recover all these missing memories on your own; or it might take years to do so, whereas I can help you access them immediately. Besides, some insight useful to Walther might come out of it. Trust me. Do it now."

Even though the prospect of experiencing more medieval brutality makes ignorance of the past sound like a good idea, I am prepared to face whatever Alix's fate holds in store for me. And Walther.

"All right. I'll do it, if you think it might help Kurt."

"Your fates are closely intertwined, my dear; your souls greatly affect each other. Let me take you back once more."

* * *

I open my eyes to the dancing flame of a candle. Outside the circle of flickering light everything is darkness. I remember and shudder.

"Walther!" The word is not even a whisper, a breath of anguish, which yet brings Elaine to the side of my bed.

"Oh, my lady! I was so frightened! I thought you would never come to your senses." I keep looking at the flame, fascinated by the life that makes it dance in the wind, change color from red to yellow, to blue....

"Pray speak to me, my lady! I beg of you! You have lain thus, so pale and lifeless for many hours."

What a strange noise she makes swallowing her tears. I look at her curiously.

"Who brought me back up here, Elaine?" Back in my own solar and my bed. She turns her head away. "T'was Sir Foulk himself carried you, my lady." She bites her lip and with a timid smile, adds quickly,

"Mark is still alive!"

Fear constricting my throat, I murmur again, "Walther?" In such a low voice it is wonder Elaine hears me.

"He...lives, my lady."

I try to raise myself from the pillows but the black despair that weighs on my chest prevents me from moving, nay, from breathing even. Elaine bends over me and slides her arm behind my shoulders to help me sit up.

"In the Sacred Name of Our Lord Jesus, do not give way to despair, my lady! Think of your unborn child! Sir Walther is... still alive."

"Still? But not for long; the monster will not allow it!"

I close my eyes, and when Elaine comes back bearing a cup of Sister Anna's draught, I drink it, fall back on the pillows, and abandon myself to the black vortex of nightmares.

* * *

Through the half-closed curtains of my bed a shaft of candle light wakes me again.

The sound of voices raised in anger. Black Foulk? Revulsion sends more shivers coursing through my aching limbs than the fever which makes me tremble and wander in my mind.

Am I awake or dreaming? There seems to be no purpose in keeping my eyes open. Heavy steps and the noise of a closing door precede whispered words I fail to comprehend, and a silence hardly broken by the crackling of a fire in the hearth. Someone approaches my bed, stands in front of the light and bends over me. A cool hand on my fevered brow makes me open my eyes wide, and look. "Mother Clara? Is it really you?"

"Yes, child." "Walther?"

She brings a finger to her lips. "Hush, Alix, speak no more. Fever has weakened you and you must conserve your strength."

"But I must see him! Oh, dear Mother Clara! Foulk... You must implore Sir Foulk for Walther's life before it is too late!"

Her face in shadows looks so much older than I remember. I feel a tear fall on the hand I extend to her.

"I beseech you, child! Think only of yourself and your child! Sir Walther is no more. I am here at Sir Foulk's behest, so concerned is he with the state of your health. He wishes me to care for you and has given me permission to take you back with me to the convent." I turn my head away from her kindly concern.

"If Sir Walther is no more, I have no wish to live. If you harbor any pity, let me die with the child I carry."

My words so appall Mother Clara that she grasps my shoulders with strong hands and shakes me vehemently.

"Never utter such wicked words in the sight of the Lord, willful child! Think you He has given us life merely for our enjoyment of carnal pleasures? Fie! T'is time to renounce them and think of your soul's salvation!"

Her face betrays such emotions that I wonder briefly if the reproof be not directed as much to herself as to me. A great weariness throws a veil of indifference over everything, even Mother Clara's presence, even the forthcoming birth of my child. I surrender myself to fever and despair, seeking only the mercy of oblivion.

I know not how long I remain thus, but fierce pains bring me back to my senses. Terrible pangs, as if demons lurking in the darkness of my room had leapt onto my body to tear at my insides with their claws.

My moans bring Mother Clara and Elaine to my side, greatly distressed. Mother Clara raises her eyes to Heavens and murmurs angrily, not so low that I cannot hear,

"Oh Lord, will you show no mercy to this mother and child? It is too early for the infant to be born!"

* * *

As I raise my eyes to the crucifix on my wall, the flickering light of the candle throws moving shadows on Christ's naked body may He forgive me for the thoughts of Walther that cross my mind.

It is now seven years since I was brought here on a litter, hardly breathing, after losing my still-born infant and most of my life-blood. Following her example is the only way I know of repaying Mother Clara for the care and affection she has bestowed on me through these years. As well as the protection she has extended to me against that devil Foulk who has never dared to defy her and reclaim me. Though I dutifully observe the rules of our Priory, I am, alas, far from saintly by nature, and oft feel great shame for the false image of chaste piety I present to others. For, verily, no day - or night - passes that I pine not for Walther' embrace. I may have renounced the ardors of lust but the memory of their delights, I fear, will hound me and make me long for him to my dying day. And evermore. There are times, in the dead of night when sleeps elude me, that I could vouch a loving presence lingers by my narrow couch, urging me to be serene. The rising sun melts these illusions like April snow on green grass. Once, wondering if Mother Clara was ever besieged by such longings for Sir Eudes, I made bold to confide in her. She did not remonstrate with me, merely shook her head and said mildly, "Patience, Sister Alix. Patience is perhaps the lesson you have to learn in this life. Time is of no account to the Lord, so wait and pray. The spark of divine love will one day ignite your soul and make it burn with an even brighter flame than your devotion for Sir Walther."

Poor Mother Clara. Me thinks she is still waiting for this heavenly fire to happen to her. Me thinks the news of Eudes' death seven years ago dealt her a heavy blow from which she never quite recovered. She now allows herself so little sustenance that she is but a shadow of her jocund self, though her eyes still betray a great love for all creatures that dwell in the Lord God's Creation.

It is understood I will become prioress in her stead when He calls her to His side. Not through any wish of mine but through hers and the good sisters; with one or two exceptions, they will cast their votes in my favor. Even Sister Anna. Through prayer I shall seek to be a worthy successor to this saintly woman I admire and love most devotedly.

Be it as it may, a kind of peace has been granted me in this holy abode, where we have been spared the wickedness abroad in the land.

For the Lord Pope's host and its leaders Simon de Montfort and Arnaud-Amaury have wreaked great evil on the hapless Cathars to the south of us. Intent on crushing the 'Heresy' of the Albigensian and their ilk, these holy warriors have spilled their blood by the thousands, sparing neither women nor children, and butchering or burning at the stake those who escaped the sword.

Though it be the Lord Pope's will, Mother Clara avers the massacre to be inspired by Satan, and says so to the face of the Prior himself, who scowls but dares not remonstrate with her, for his tongue is no match for our dear prioress'.

With scant surprise, we heard that Black Foulk had joined Simon de Montfort and outdoes him in deeds of pillage and destruction.

But a wandering friar we sheltered and fed one day told us that Foulk also harbors rich Cathars at Comarque. For gold.

One day the Lord Jesus will give me the strength to forgive him. I rise from my knees and prepare to make my way to the chapel, with fond gratitude for the gladness of these past days.

Indeed, these were most fortunate hours. First a messenger arrived but two days ago bearing news of Elaine; she has been delivered of a healthy boy to the great cheer of her dear lord, Marc d'Aunoy. Later that day, Sir Constantin de Born arrived at the convent with a large retinue, informing us he had brought Young Robert and Sweet Eloise to greet me! They were on their way to the castle of Salignac where Eloise is to marry young Renaud, the count's eldest son.

I could scarce believe my eyes at the sight of Eloise. Though but fifteen, she is tall, fair, courtly, and far livelier than her mother, hapless Adela - may the Lord show mercy on her soul. Eloise appears to be endowed with great assurance for one so young, and it gave me much satisfaction to note that her bright eyes betray a great thirst for learning.

We embraced and mingled our tears with much joy in remembrance of the gentle hours of our common past. She promised to name her first daughter after me, and I gave her a necklace of gold and amethyst purchased in Venice and worn with pride in the days I still valued adornment.

As for young Robert, who is to be knighted soon, he has grown into a most handsome young squire. He is now betrothed to Sir Constantin's daughter, but methinks his laughing eyes and curly black hair must already have caused many a maiden to blush and sigh.

He greeted me with a most courteous bow, but insisted on addressing me as 'My Lady' instead of 'Sister Alix'. When came - too soon - the time for them to depart, young Robert, with one knee on the courtyard stones, seized the hem of my habit and, bringing to his lips, proceeded to kiss it with great devotion. Then raising his merry brown eyes to my face, he whispered these strange words, "Lady Alix, your image will dwell in my thoughts forever as one most worthy of my fealty. Would that I could pledge my troth to you, who has given hers to the Lord Jesus! Know that my sword and my heart will always be there to serve you. In life or in death."

With a chaste kiss on his brow rather than a blessing I feel unworthy to bestow, I took his hands in mine and helped him rise, unable to utter a single word.

The memory of the good news about my dear Elaine and the few hours spent in the company of these two handsome children causes my heart to rejoice still. May their good natures endure through life's many trials and may they never lose their hope, faith and charity.

* * *

The candle by my couch is almost burnt out. I keep my eyes on its sputtering flames, wondering how long it will endure. Yet my cell is bathed in light from many more candles held by misty forms who must be my dear sisters. They surround my bed with the hum of their prayers, while a novice bathes my forehead with a scented cloth.

Oh, the fragrance of lilac in a spring garden.... Why is such reverence shown to me, unworthy as I am? Oh, yes. I am - I was their reverend mother and love them all dearly as the daughters I never had. As I feel life gently flowing away from me like receding sea on the shore, I know that, on my soul as on the sands of time, is still graven one name. That of my beloved Walther.

* * *

I wake up on my own. Daphne is observing me, elbows on her knees, chin in her cupped hands. She straightens up, her face peaceful, her eyes dreamy.

"So, my dear, you seemed content enough at the priory. I would say the religious element in your life is a little more ritual than spiritual, but who am I to judge? Pascal may have been right and prayer may be the best way to induce faith." Her flippant tone both reassures and irritates me.

"Her options were rather limited, wouldn't you agree? I think I would do the same now given the circumstances. Although there is one thing I wouldn't sacrifice again." "What?" She looks genuinely intrigued.

"My psaltery. Alix swore never to play her psaltery again, and to make sure she kept her vow, threw it into the fire.

CHAPTER 29

On Wednesday I rush out of the office and drive too fast to Dorval Airport. I park the car, forget to lock it, and reach the Arrival section with pounding heart and trembling hands as Kurt's plane is touching down. I wait twenty minutes for the travelers to deplane.

The passengers' door swings open and he is here, looking around at the people who wait behind the rail. I wave and our eyes meet. With a grin, he waves back and looks for the shortest way to reach me through the clumps of traveler's and welcoming parties. "Welcome to Montreal, Kurt."

He drops the leather bag he carries and takes me in his arms. His lips are on mine and it's Nantes all over again. I feel so dizzy I cling to him as much for support as to convince myself I am not dreaming. His heart is racing mine. Underneath his calm exterior, I sense great tension.

I'm so glad today was bright and sunny. The sky at dusk is still luminous as I drive home along the meandering lakeshore road rather than the more direct but sterile highway. I keep glancing at Kurt, happy he seems to relax and appreciate the scenery.

The vividly green grass and vernal trees; daffodils and tulips abloom alongside the silver expanse of water gilt by the setting sun; the cool lake breeze redolent of lilac ruffling our hair through the lowered windows.

Upon entering the apartment, he appears just as satisfied with the humble elegance I've strived to create, and looks around my living room with approving nods, stopping in front of each picture; my antique Chinese prints and the Dutch still-life badly in need of reframing that Michael had bought on a whim in Amsterdam.

Jacqueline de Sarigny

By-passing my mother's Louis XVI chairs, he chooses to sit on my cream leather sofa. A wink and a naughty smile bring me to sit on his lap before I even think of taking off my jacket.

In his arms, the clouds of apprehension that have darkened my mind since that awful Sunday session dissolve into euphoria.

He is here; everything will be all right. As I caress his handsome face, his lips, his closed eyelids with a myriad of light kisses, I cannot help marvel at the number of physical traits carried over from his former life. His face, though older is as lean and strong as Walther's. His hair must have been as blond at some point.

Every fiber in my body recognizes him and my heart is filled with gratitude. Fate has made us closer in age this time around. Walther was fourteen years older than Alix, while Kurt is only seven years older than I am. I do wonder at this, but only very briefly, for my attention is soon captivated by more interesting activities. It's almost two hours later that we see the need for a verbal - or otherwise - exchange of ideas.

"Are you hungry?"

He nods, eyebrows raised in anticipation. The table is already set with two place mats, Limoges plates, Baccarat glasses and a bowl of red roses; a pen and pad by Kurt's plate.

The platter of spiced partridges en gelée on their bed of rice salad awaits our appetites in the fridge. I hand Kurt a bottle of Pouilly to uncork and he looks at the label with an appreciative nod.

After the first bite, he closes his eyes and breathes in deeply, in a fair rendition of a mystic in ecstasy.

"Oh, come on! Don't make me blush. Walther was a voluptuary, and, thank God, you haven't lost your touch; but you were never much of a gourmet as far as I remember."

With a wink, he writes quickly. "I'm compensating. I no longer chase women." "Well, this is good news and bad news. Does this mean I'll spend the duration of this relationship - hopefully the rest of my life - in the kitchen?"

"He shakes his head and scribbles. "I'm a good cook."

"Halleluiah. Thank Heaven for small mercies. We lapse into silent enjoyment of the entree, the assortment of French cheeses and the meringue cake with orange sauce. Over black coffee, I finally ask him point blank, "Do you now believe, I mean really believe, without a shadow of a doubt, that you have lived before as Walther von Altdorf?" He nods several times and quickly writes on the pad, "Yes. As weird as it may seem, I do. Since you left, I have been having more vivid dreams, even fleeting visions during waking hours. One of them was very...

" Lifting his pen for a second until the right word is found. "Very disturbing. I was in a dark place and I was trying to take you in my arms, but I couldn't and it made me both unhappy and enraged."

"You were chained to the rock wall, beloved. Don't you remember?"

He rubs his chin and shakes his head, deep in thought, before adding on the page. "At times, I think I do, or I'm about to, and then everything goes blank again. Yesterday, I woke up full of hatred for a man whose face stayed in my mind all morning. Someone I don't remember ever meeting. In this life, at least."

Letting go of the pen and resting his elbows on the table, he wearily lowers his forehead on the palms of his hands. I understand his confusion only too well, and curse my helplessness; but he has to come to term with his own past and, perhaps, the less I interfere, the better it will be.

"Look, I know how disturbing these recollections can be. They seem to intrude on reality and make you doubt your own sanity;

but only if you don't accept them for what they are, memories of a past life. Once you recover more of them, they begin to make sense."

I take a deep breath before adding, "And that's where Daphne can help. It's not easy to probe on your own, but she is so experienced in past-life regression that she can probably lead you back until you get a clearer picture. And not from my point of view, this time, but from your own."

He raises his head and takes up the pen again. "I never said I wasn't prepared to meet her. I owe her thanks for contributing to our...reunion." He looks up on the last word and smiles.

* * *

The ringing phone does not wake Kurt, but rouses me from a deep and restful sleep strangely devoid of dreams.

"Hello? Mrs. Pearson? Wilma Blake speaking, Dr. Daphne Blake's cousin. Sorry to call so late but Daphne insisted I contact you immediately."

"What happened?" A chill wind of apprehension cuts through my drowsiness. "She is not...well?"

"No. She is not. She is back in the Royal Victoria Hospital. She has a room in their palliative care section."

I had heard of it, and it was bad news; it meant terminal patient. The realization Daphne was dying hit me with as much force as if I had not known she was doomed ever since my return from France.

"Are visitors allowed?"

"Of course, that why I called. Daphne is expecting you and your friend tomorrow morning as early as you can come. I tried to talk her out of it, but she wouldn't listen." Wilma pauses long enough to sigh.

"Such a shame, really. Daphne is such a brilliant mind and a generous person; she has been so good to me through the years, and helped so many people!"

"Indeed! Tell her we'll be there, if you speak to her before I do." Kurt is now awake and listening to my end of the conversation.

"Oh, I'll see her; I'm calling from the hospital. I'll stay with her to-night. She's not in pain, they have her on the pump, you know, but her mind is as clear as ever. I'm glad you can come. I'll see you in the morning."

"Yes, good-bye, Mrs. Blake, and give my love to Daphne."

"Will do." And she hangs up. Replacing the handset, I tell Kurt.

"Daphne is very ill, she wants to see us early in the morning." Perhaps I should tell him how sad this news makes me, but there is no need; slipping his arm under my shoulders he draws me into his warm embrace and start kissing my eyelids while I add, "I guess your jetlag will come in handy. You'll probably be up around five a.m. So, shake me awake, will you?"

Meanwhile I snuggle against his strong body, delightfully prepared for the inevitable outcome of such a move.

* * *

The second phone call wakes us both. It's five a.m. and Irene got mixed up again in her time zones.

"Am I waking you up, sweetie? Oh, I'm sooo sorry! One of these days, I'll learn to work it out. Listen, we are getting married on June

12, at Olivier's place, and you're invited, of course. I'll send you an invitation and a map.

"When will you see your mute singer again?" Her voice carries well past Kurt who pretends to be still asleep, a grin on his lips, his pillow pressed to his ears with both hands. Without waiting for an answer to her question, Irene continues, "I have to tell you that Olivier is terribly upset with himself for what happened in Nantes!

I mean, he says he was very rude to your friend. I didn't notice anything, did you? Anyway, Olivier says that, thinking back over it, he can't understand what came over him.

He told me he liked your friend, but that he felt this strange compulsion to hate him. Thank God, his malaise wasn't serious and he's over it now, that's why I'm calling.

You must bring Kurt too; I promise you Olivier will behave. So will you invite him?" "Oh, yes. I'm sure he'll be delighted. Thank you for thinking of us, Irene. I'm very touched and I wouldn't miss this for the world." The emotion in my voice doesn't go unnoticed; she asks, "Sandra? Are you all, right? You sound all gushy."

"I'm fine, Irene. It's just that...I think you are a wonderful person who deserves to be happy with Olivier. And, Irene...I love you very much."

I hang up before she can add another word, and take the phone off the hook, smiling to myself about the justice of it all. She who gave is now getting. Her good nature has endured in this life through all those marriages and relationships. She had fun in the process, made quite a few men happy, and found her lost love in the end.

Even though Mother Clara's selfless life may appear to some far more meritorious than Irene's, who is to say God shares this point of view?

* * *

On the way to the hospital, I finally summoned the courage to tell Kurt that the loss of his voice might be linked to a traumatic experience undergone by Walther. Without mentioning what I had witnessed, choosing my words carefully, I explained that for a chance to recover his ability to speak, he should perhaps be prepared to re-live this very dramatic episode of his past life. He threw me a curious glance and frowned, as if to say, 'Why didn't you say so before?' Perhaps I should have, but I knew he would want to know more and I was reluctant to give him the time to write too many questions.

As we now go up to Daphne's room in the elevator at seven a.m., my qualms return. I take Kurt's hand and seek his eyes.

"Listen to me, beloved. If Daphne still has enough strength left to hypnotize you, you may have to re-live something terrible. Do you still want to go through with it?"

He squeezes my hand and bends down to kiss my brow lightly. I'm glad he cannot ask me if I know what it is all about.

The elevator stops and we both make our silent way to Daphne's room.

When we go in, she is sitting up in bed, propped up by pillows, her left hand hooked up to a small IV. machine on a stand. She looks at us with bright, surprisingly cheerful eyes. I step forward to kiss her and hear the door slam violently behind me. Surprised, I turn around.

Kurt is leaning against it, deathly white and trembling from head to foot.

"Kurt? What's wrong?"

He doesn't answer but strange noises issue from his lips. Taking three steps in slow motion, he stops at the foot of Daphne's bed, extends his right arm, and points with a shaking hand at Daphne. His mouth opens and close, like a fish in an aquarium, tempting one to laugh. I don't.

Everything seems to slow down and freeze, as in those nightmares where one is unable to move. Kurt keeps staring at Daphne and shaking his head very slowly. I look from one to the other, so stunned that I do not immediately react when he utters in a strangled voice, "You!"

He is still staring at Daphne with absolute puzzlement. And raw fury.

"Will... you... leave... me... no... peace!" His words as labored and toneless as an automaton's.

Daphne remains stock still, her eyes shiny with a kind of triumphant compassion. "Kurt! Your voice! You're speaking!"

I murmur, hardly able to do so myself. He appears not to hear my muffled words and looks around the hospital room with baffled eyes, as if it's reassuring chintz, fruitwood furniture and flowers could restore his sanity. Taking another step closer to the bed, he mutters in low, angry tones, "Félon du diable! I should make you suffer for letting me die of thirst in that hellish hole!"

Daphne mutely puts her frail hand to her heart and nods.

He stops, shakes his head as if to clear it, and wipes his forehead with a trembling hand, "Mein Gott, what am I doing?" Looking from me to Daphne in utter confusion, he rubs his mouth before addressing Daphne, "Madam, please forgive me for saying such terrible things to you. I don't know what made me..." His eyes focus on her and he frowns.

"Who are you?"

"I am, I was, indeed Foulk de Sardac, better known as Black Foulk, my dear Walther. And I did leave you to die from loss of blood and thirst in that cellar."

It is my turn to stare at Daphne with open mouth, too horrified to make a move, as I suddenly recognize in her face the shadow of Foulk's hated features.

She goes on speaking in soothing tones, "You will eventually remember everything, Walther. Do not fight the memories, let them come to you, good or bad. Come here, closer to me, without fear or hatred. As you see I am now but a harmless old woman at the end of my day. I cannot hurt you any more, nor do I want too." She pats the side of her bed gently. "The time has come to forgive, more for your sake than mine, my children, for hate hinders the progress of one's soul needlessly. Resentment makes one weary."

Kurt swallows hard and licks his dry lips as if still in the throes of lethal thirst, but his fists unclench and his whole body seems to relax as the mesmerizing effect of Daphne's voice is felt by both of us. As we listen spellbound to her words, we are drawn to this bed-ridden old woman and move slowly nearer as if caught in the slow unfolding of a dream.

"The temptation to make me pay may be quite strong in both of you, my dears. A perfectly natural reaction; but rest assured that the law of cause and effect has already avenged you better than you ever could. I have suffered as much as you did, if not more, in many different ways through many different lives. Yet I lament the harm I caused you both to this day and wish to atone for it in any way possible."

Her eyes unfathomable pools of empathy, she addresses Walther, "Come closer, Walther, my friend." His eyes on her face, he obeys and sits on the edge of the bed without a word, while I stand on the other side.

"Yes, I murdered you and many others, Walther, but even in that lifetime, I paid for those deaths a hundredfold. You see, even though you were out of the way, I had to renounce Alix's love, which she would never have given freely, anyway."

Her bright eyes settle on me, dimmed for a mere instant by a mist of regret. "Alix was near death, and I allowed preachy Clara to carry her back to her priory, going so far as to release those of her squires and knights who were still alive. Which was pretty generous of me in the circumstances?

Alix recovered eventually, but by that time I was so embroiled in shifting allegiances that I could not afford to reclaim her. You see, Walther, I did fear retaliation, more from your local friends than from your German relatives who probably knew nothing of your demise and were too busy fighting the Pope.

I had to reckon with Sir de Born and others among your brothers-in-arms, who waited for any opportunity to avenge your death with much profit to themselves. So, I decided to find myself a strong ally, the strongest, namely Simon de Montfort. I joined the Pope's army, and had myself a jolly good time of it, burning, killing, raping and looting." Daphne's harsh laughter startles us both; it sounds uncannily like Foulk's. She raises a placating hand and grins impishly. "Sorry about that. One finds it hard to shed old habits. Being a warrior marks your soul for many a lifetime. Something always remains of the exhilaration of battle, of the smell of blood." She sighs. "I had to unlearn my cruel ways during several dreary lifetimes as a woman. Not that woman cannot be vicious too, but on the whole, they relish killing far less than men do. Anyway, to come back to Foulk's story, my ally proved to be my Nemesis in the end.

Bogo denounced me for harboring Cathars, a trumped-up charge as he knew I didn't hold with their ridiculous beliefs and had only sheltered some of them in order to relieve them of their riches. Because he bore false witness against me, those two worthies, Simon and Arnaud Amory had me burned at the stake as a heretic."

She pauses and shakes her head. "Even the executioner betrayed me. I had paid him to strangle me, and he didn't, the son of a rat! Now, burning alive is a very painful death, my dears, when dry wood is used for the pyre; there is little smoke and one dies very slowly. So did Bogo, incidentally, die in the flames, accused - not by me - of being a sodomite and a devil worshipper."

She pauses with a mirthless chuckle, but neither of us is able to utter a sound as we wait in thrall of her voice for her to continue. "We have evolved, I suppose. We no longer burn people at the stake for their beliefs, we bomb them, of smother them with ridicule if their creed contradicts the new scientific orthodoxy. I guess it's not as painful. Still... Now, as I just said, if I wish for forgiveness from both of you, know that it is not only for my sake, but for yours, my dear children. Walther has recovered his voice, and fate has allowed me to help you find each other again, so, I implore you, let no more resentment and thoughts of revenge burden your souls!"

With a start, Kurt straightens up, looks from Daphne to me and clears his throat.

"How could I start speaking again, just like that?" His voice is wonderfully modulated, warm and deep. Such a sexy accent. I love it. Daphne shrugs. "A kind of abreaction. The release of pent-up emotions." She rubs her chin thoughtfully, with preternatural calm. "You re-lived your...mutilation a few moments ago, didn't you? Just as you had at the wheel of your car?"

He nods. His shiver brings me to his side and when I rest my hand on his shoulders, he slips one arm behind my waist and draws me closer. Daphne's smile erases from her face the last trace of Foulk's hated mask superimposed on her features a while earlier. "Yes, your voice is back, and your whole life as Walther will probably be restored to you piecemeal. I am sorry in a way that my time is too limited for me to be of further assistance; but living with Alix will help. Can you remember what caused your car accident?" "Yes. The sight of a castle that had belonged to the Hohenstaufen's, emperor Frederic's family. Walther had spent part of his childhood there. As the towers appeared, rising on a hill in the distance, all of a sudden, I found myself in a kind of black void filled with images of Walther's life. As the scenes unfolded in front of my eyes, I knew I was Walther. I tried to keep control of my car until... the nightmare in the cave, when I passed out."

"I see. Do you remember anything else now?" He raises loving eyes to my face before answering. "Yes. Alix, and the great love I felt for her, and still do. Music, and battles. What you said just now about the exhilaration of combat is true. In my dreams, it seems to me now, I have often longed for the tumult of the fight, the clamors and yells, the clash of swords against helms or shield...."

The look of comprehension they exchange doesn't stop Daphne from shrugging.

"Bah. So much mayhem for a rush of adrenaline. Go skydiving." A knock on the door precedes a nurse in pale blue uniform and a smile who comes in briskly carrying a tray.

"Perhaps we can talk about this some more, later today. Or tomorrow." Daphne concludes letting her head fall back on the mound of pillows.

When the nurse leaves, I ask Daphne, "You found out you were Foulk before I left for France, didn't you?"

She nods. "Yes, it all came back to me in a terrible vision.

I had had intimations of it before, but dismissed them, thinking I was being influenced by your own recollections. You can imagine how I felt."

"So, that explains your changed appearance? But why?" She purses her lips and shrugs.

"Who knows why? I just felt a compulsion to look different. Part of my act of contrition? I felt terrible about you two."

Kurt rises to his feet, still holding on to my waist. Without looking at each other, we each extend a hand and take one of Daphne's, holding it for a few seconds before retreating to the door. Her eyes are closed, but when I turn back to wave, tears are running freely along the deep lines of her cheeks.

* * *

After a long silent walk along the Mountain's green paths - so silent, in fact, that I wonder at one point if Kurt hasn't lost his voice again - we sit on a bench under a maple tree and start talking quietly about the subject which is foremost on our minds.

The implications of this strange reunion after so many centuries are so spiritually momentous that it will no doubt affect our conversations - and our lives - for the rest of our days. The whole thing is too wondrous to do more than circle around it with cautious questions and answers. There will be lots of time to try and understand its meaning.

Meanwhile I just enjoy the pleasure of talking to Kurt, more than I ever thought possible. I think he is thrilled to have recovered his voice. At one point, he even starts singing a few bars of Walther's ballad his ballad - then breaks into a little yodel, just for the fun of it, before laughing out loud like a happy child.

After a hasty lunch in the hospital cafeteria in which we hold hands rather than talk, we return to Daphne's room and find her sleeping peacefully. Of a common accord, we sit down and prepare to wait.

Jacqueline de Sarigny

Perhaps sensing our presence, she soon opens her eyes, spots us and smiles.

"I knew you would forgive. Well, I hoped you would, anyway."

Rising from my chair I move to her side and bend down to kiss her cheek.

"Yes, Daphne. Oh, incidentally, I have decided to write our story, and dedicate it to you."

She nods and bites her lip. "As we are staying in Montreal for a while, we'll come to visit every day. If it's all right with you, that is." "Of course, I want you to. It won't be for long anyway." As I hold her hand, I hear myself murmuring, "Custodi Nos, Domine, et sub umbra alarum protege nos." As if Latin prayers were the most normal thing to say in the circumstances.

Daphne inquires casually, "Wilma was not waiting for you in the hallway, by any chance?"

"We saw no one in the hallway. Why?"

"Oh, never mind, I wanted you to meet her, but that's all right, you can make her acquaintance tomorrow. She is such a dear and so faithful. She brought something back from Ottawa. Alix dear, open that closet over there. There's a black leather case on the lower shelf. Take it, and bring it here, please.

Good. Now, bring that chair closer, sit down and open the case."

I do as she says and open the black leather case. Nestled in a red velvet is a magnificent inlaid psaltery. Speechless, I look from Daphne to Kurt now standing by my side. Daphne is beaming. "It's a present from me to you and Walther. I meant for you to get it after I'm gone, but why not now? This way I can enjoy it too. You always refused to play for me in Comarque castle, but I think you like me better now, so you will, won't you, dear?"

She sighs and looks away before adding in a firmer tone of voice, "The luthier who procured it for me was recommended by Sotheby, and he had it shipped from England, while you were in France. This is an XVIIIth. Century instrument, alas, and not a medieval one, but the man said it was in excellent shape and played very well, with fine tone and volume. Besides, I think we've all had enough of medieval things."

As I hold the precious instrument on my lap, I caress the smooth marquetry, and the gleaming brass guide pins, murmuring, "Daphne, how can we thank you?" "By playing it, my dears."

I dare to let my fingers skim over the strings. The psaltery resonates with the most subtle harmonics. Kurt bends down over my shoulders. Our hands touch and fly over the strings. We start playing chords so softly, so lightly, that at first it seems the sounds of the melody can be heard only with our hearts. But the music must be beautiful because Daphne is smiling through her tears.

THE END

www.ingramcontent.com/pod-product-compliance
Lightning Source LLC
Chambersburg PA
CBHW071507260626
47170CB00002B/286